YINNI

Love By Design

Copyright © 2024 by Yinnie Lin

All rights reserved. No part of this publication may be reproduced, stored or transmitted in any form or by any means, electronic, mechanical, photocopying, recording, scanning, or otherwise without written permission from the publisher. It is illegal to copy this book, post it to a website, or distribute it by any other means without permission.

This novel is entirely a work of fiction. The names, characters and incidents portrayed in it are the work of the author's imagination. Any resemblance to actual persons, living or dead, events or localities is entirely coincidental.

Yinnie Lin asserts the moral right to be identified as the author of this work.

Yinnie Lin has no responsibility for the persistence or accuracy of URLs for external or third-party Internet Websites referred to in this publication and does not guarantee that any content on such Websites is, or will remain, accurate or appropriate.

Designations used by companies to distinguish their products are often claimed as trademarks. All brand names and product names used in this book and on its cover are trade names, service marks, trademarks and registered trademarks of their respective owners. The publishers and the book are not associated with any product or vendor mentioned in this book. None of the companies referenced within the book have endorsed the book.

First edition

This book was professionally typeset on Reedsy.
Find out more at reedsy.com

To Mama Nene and Papa Jose

"Fashion is the armour to survive the reality of everyday life."

— Bill Cunningham

Contents

I   Part One

Chapter 1	3
Chapter 2	14
Chapter 3	19
Chapter 4	31
Chapter 5	43
Chapter 6	54
Chapter 7	63
Chapter 8	75
Chapter 9	86
Chapter 10	93
Chapter 11	100
Chapter 12	108
Chapter 13	113
Chapter 14	123
Chapter 15	132
Chapter 16	142
Chapter 17	152
Chapter 18	158
Chapter 19	165
Chapter 20	177
Chapter 21	188
Chapter 22	195
Chapter 23	206

Chapter 24   214
Chapter 25   221

II Part Two

Chapter 26   227
Chapter 27   232
Chapter 28   241
Chapter 29   251
Chapter 30   257
Chapter 31   263
Chapter 32   268
Chapter 33   276
Chapter 34   285
Chapter 35   298
Chapter 36   305
Chapter 37   313
Chapter 38   322
Chapter 39   327
Chapter 40   338
Chapter 41   351
Chapter 42   356

III Part Three

Chapter 43   363
Chapter 44   368
Chapter 45   372
Chapter 46   378
Chapter 47   384
Chapter 48   390
Chapter 49   395
Chapter 50   401

Chapter 51	409
Chapter 52	416
Chapter 53	426
Chapter 54	431
Chapter 55	438
Chapter 56	443

IV   Epilogue

MAHALIA	451
About the Author	460

I

Part One

"Clothes mean nothing until someone lives in them."

— *Marc Jacobs*

Chapter 1

> Dear Mahalia,

I take a deep breath.

> We regret to inform you–

And there it is.
　Yet another rejection.
　I don't need to read beyond those five words to know what follows is more than likely a copy-and-paste response of a dismissal to a job I applied for.

> – that your application for the Studio Assistant position at DEMZARA Designs has been unsuccessful.

But, of course, I read the rest anyway.
　Receiving emails of rejections is routine for me at this point but it's always so jarring to actually go through it. Reasons for 'not moving forward' with my applications are often vague and cryptically constructed, the concluding paragraph always alluding to suggestions of applying again and 'paths realigning in the future'. As if this isn't the *third time* I've applied to the same company in the last 12 months.

Still, I appreciate the email.

Most of the time, I exist in a state of limbo where I don't hear back from companies and I wallow in the dreadful abyss of uncertainty for weeks—if not *months*.

The email is short, a whiplash of a job rejection, but the sting always lingers much longer. Regardless of the countless times I've been dismissed and ghosted from the endless list of jobs I've applied to in the past, I always feel the aftermath of the dismissal clinging on to me like velcro.

Releasing the breath I'm holding, I straighten myself up.

Note to self. Don't read emails at work.

I typically avoid going on my phone when I'm working but my shift is due to end soon and the restaurant is quiet. It's the slow interval in the afternoon, just after lunch and before the transition to dinner when service picks up again.

My hands, restless as ever, were twitching to do something. And, as a result, I found myself browsing through my phone.

Sighing, I close the Mail app and slip my phone back into my pocket.

"Okay," I mutter to myself. "Time to clock out."

Intent on not letting the rejection from yet another fashion company get to me, I make a mental note to work on more applications tonight as I head towards the back of the restaurant.

Waitressing at Tito Boy's, a Filipino restaurant in Kensington, was a part-time job I had when I was studying at the London Institute of Fashion and Textiles. I'm a fashion designer, or aspiring to be one, depending on how you look at it. I graduated from LIFT last July and I've been floating around the fashion job market since.

Hence, going full-time at Tito Boy's.

I'm in the middle of untying the apron around my waist when Alana, one of the waitresses I'm currently working a shift with, walks in through the back doors leading towards the kitchen.

"Table 10 is being difficult." She rushes in. "And someone at the corner booths just sat himself down *without* reservation."

"We take walk-ins, Alana." I remind her gently, taking note of her frazzled

CHAPTER 1

state.

Alana is half-Italian and half-Chinese, a second-year student studying Business at Goldsmiths and she started working at Tito Boy's last December when we needed extra staff over the Christmas holidays.

"I know but it's one of the reserved booths." Her lips begin to quiver as she continues, "He just strolled in, no greeting, not even a glance my way. Literally walked right in, wearing some stupid sunglasses on his face, as if he owned the place. And those guys in Table 10 won't *quit*."

"Still?" I turn towards her as she brings her hands to her face, pressing her palms against her eyes. "What happened?"

"They're just being..." Alana bites her lip. *"Loud."*

My eyebrows furrow. Loud is usually our code for microaggressions.

Alana and I have a system when it comes to the customers dining here at Tito Boy's. Being a waitress at the restaurant, part-time for three years and full-time for just over 6 months, I've come across a lot of individuals who seem to consider themselves above service workers and I've been subjected to derogatory remarks and borderline racist insults from less-than-pleasant patrons in the past.

"Hey, don't worry." I try to reassure Alana whose eyes are beginning to gloss over. "They look like they'll be leaving soon. Take a 10-minute break, I'll get the bill for them."

Grabbing my apron from the table, I begin retying it around my waist, peering over through the glass divide.

"Aren't you clocking out soon?" She bites her lip, glancing at the clock on the wall.

"It's only 10 minutes, Al." I turn towards her. "Don't worry, okay? I'll take care of your other tables as well."

I offer her an encouraging smile, reaching out to give her a comforting pat on the shoulder.

"Thanks Hallie," She whispers. "Sorry, I'm just so overwhelmed with uni and deadlines and those assholes outside are being such dickheads."

"No need to apologise, I've been there," I assure her. "Take 10 and I'll see you when you're ready."

Alana nods, composing herself before heading towards the back office.

Grabbing the plates of food ready to be served from the kitchen window, I step back out on the restaurant floor. I mentally note the empty tables that need cleaning as I serve the plates of food to the rest of the customers, my eyes catching the booth in the corner.

The person currently in the reserved seating is on their phone, messaging someone by the speed their thumbs are tapping across the screen. Oddly enough, they're still wearing their sunglasses indoors, black aviators glinting under the light as it covers their eyes.

Cautiously, I approach the individual sitting there.

Clearing my throat to make my presence known, the person glances up momentarily before diverting their attention back to their phone.

Please don't let them be one of those customers.

"Glass of water. With lemon. No ice." He instructs. "Filtered would be ideal but bottled is fine."

I blink at him.

Wonderful.

I didn't even get the chance to deliver my customary greeting. Based solely on that interaction, I can predict the kind of customer this person is going to be.

"Sorry for the inconvenience," I quickly adopt my Customer Service voice. "But this booth is reserved only."

I assess the stranger wearing the black aviator sunglasses, indoors of all places. He's dressed head to toe in athleisure; a white t-shirt peeking out of the bottom of an oversized grey hoodie with matching grey sweatpants and white high-top trainers.

A white baseball cap sits on top of their head, a monogrammed emblem 'AV' embroidered in tiny, barely noticeable letters on the visor, blending with the white monochrome panels of the fabric.

It wouldn't be the first time the restaurant is visited by celebrities or influencers who want to be inconspicuous. Famous people often dined at Tito Boy's and we even have a handful of stars who are regulars. Partly due to the Head Chef's reputation in the culinary world but I digress.

CHAPTER 1

"Did you make a reservation with us?" I ask.

He looks up but doesn't say anything and it's hard to discern his facial features underneath the aviators.

"Can I get your name?" I request instead. "If it's your table, I'm more than happy to accommodate."

He pauses before shaking his head.

"No," He says, bluntly. "Thanks."

My eyebrows knit together and I squint my eyes in an attempt to see a semblance of emotion under his sunglasses. A longer silence follows as he leans forward and continues to type on his phone, ignoring me completely.

"Well, these booths are for customers who booked in advance." I motion towards the table with the small metal plaque labelled 'RESERVED', trying my hardest not to show the irritation I'm beginning to feel.

"Understood." The stranger nods.

I stare at him, sharpening imaginary daggers in my head as he continues to disregard me.

Being exposed to customers with an inflated sense of entitlement is a regular occurrence in the restaurant so this is no surprise. Dealing with them, however, is an entirely different challenge.

"I can gladly seat you at a free table in the restaurant, there's a table by the window—"

"No, thank you." He interjects. "The lighting bothers my eyes."

I tilt my head to the side.

The sunglasses make sense. The attitude, however, doesn't.

"I see." I nod, forcing my Customer Service voice to stay neutral but I can hear it curling around the edges with agitation. "But, once again, this is a *reserved* booth—"

"How much do I need to pay to sit at this table?" He interrupts once more and I can't help but visibly bristle this time.

"You don't *pay* to *sit* at a specific table," I answer with a slight frown. "But it's a requirement to call in advance if you want to reserve one, like other customers who—"

"The restaurant is practically empty." His tone is sharp and I can sense a hint of annoyance in his voice. "What's the issue with me sitting here?"

My hand twitches against my side.

"The issue is we have a system in place," I begin. "Yes, the restaurant isn't busy at the moment but there are customers who reserved the table and if they show up then—"

"Can I speak to the chef?" He cuts me off for the fourth time.

"Pardon?"

"The *chef.*" He says it in a slow, almost mocking tone and I feel my tolerance for bad behaviour reach maximum capacity, hospitality be damned.

Breathe, Hallie.

Requesting to speak with the *manager* is one thing, but asking for the chef before even ordering? That's certainly a new one.

"He's on a *break.*" I mirror his tone.

My eyes focus on counting the embroidered monogrammed letters on his cap to subdue my rising frustration.

And not having to deal with difficult customers like you.

The customer turns his head towards me slowly.

"That's rude."

Oh shit.

Did I say that out loud?

"Yes, you did."

He carelessly tosses his phone on the table and it clatters across the granite countertop.

"Sorry," I blurt out instantly. "I didn't mean that."

He crosses his arms to show his displeasure.

"You mean, you didn't mean to say it out loud?"

I curse inwardly, resenting how the job rejection is causing me to behave completely unlike myself right now.

Underneath the baseball cap, I see a knot form in between his eyebrows and I let out a quiet exhale, opting for honesty.

"I'm really sorry," I sigh dejectedly. "I'm not having the best of days today. But that's not an excuse to take it out on you, I apologise."

CHAPTER 1

He doesn't say anything but I can feel his eyes assessing me behind his sunglasses.

"I'll leave when they make an appearance," He states after a long pause. "Whoever reserved this booth."

He says it as if he's doing me a favour and I'm running out of energy to deal with him so I just nod.

"Lemon water, did you say?" I ask.

"Filtered," He clarifies, then as if suddenly remembering his manners adds, "Please."

Forcing a smile, I ring out my best Customer Service voice.

"Coming right up."

Heading back towards the kitchen, the phone at the front desk starts ringing and I quickly divert to answer it.

"Tito Boy's Restaurant, how can I help?" I pick up on the third ring.

"Hallie?" Questions the voice on the other end and my eyebrows draw together in confusion.

"Marc?" The receiver crackles with static that makes me cringe as it rings in my ears.

"I tried calling the kitchen but no one was answering."

Marc is a second-year architecture student at Imperial College. Like Alana, he also works part-time at Tito Boy's. But unlike Alana, he doesn't take his job as… *seriously*.

I glance at the digital clock at the front desk.

"Rowan's still out and Alana's taking a break. Hero and a couple of people called in sick this morning so we might be short-staffed for dinner."

A pause settles on the other end of the line and I can sense Marc's hesitation over the phone. There's only one plausible reason he'd call the kitchen line before the number at the front desk.

"Please don't tell me you're calling because of why I think you're calling," I say.

Another long pause.

"Can you please cover my shift tonight?" He pleads. "It's deadline season, you know how it is. Uni's been beating my ass and I'm stressed as shit with my coursework."

I release a heavy sigh. "Aren't you *closing* tonight?"

"Yes, exactly why I'm calling."

"Marcus," I let out another, overly dramatic sigh over the phone. "If you spent more of your time in the library rather than the club, you might actually get your coursework done."

"I know," He groans. "My mum already gave me a bollocking about it."

"Then listen to your mother."

"Please, *Ate*."

He uses the Filipino honorific for an older sister and I roll my eyes, although he couldn't see me.

"You genuinely better be doing your coursework," I warn him. "If you end up clubbing tonight, I'm putting you on closing shifts for the next two weeks."

"It's a Wednesday," He comments. "Who goes on a night out in the middle of the week?"

"Students," I reply, flatly.

"Okay, fair enough." He chuckles. "But I swear I'm doing assignments for once. Can you cover?"

"Fine."

"Thanks Hallie," He chirps. "You're a lifesaver!"

"Alright, bye."

Checking the clock displayed on top of the monitor by the front desk, I hang up the phone and sigh at the time.

5:15 PM.

There goes working on my portfolio and applying for more jobs after work. I note down the shift swap, crossing out Marc's name and writing my own.

"I think someone tried calling the back office." Alana approaches the front desk. "I didn't get to it in time."

"It was probably Marc. He needed his shift covering tonight." I reply, processing a bill for another table. "How are you feeling?"

Alana gives me a faint thumbs-up, hovering next to me.

CHAPTER 1

"I'm better," She replies, peering over at the table plan on the monitor. "Are they still here?"

"For now but don't worry, I'll cover that table."

"What about Sunnies?"

I glance over at the reserved booth. "Leave him to me."

Alana nods, relieved. She sends me a small smile of gratitude before greeting a couple entering the restaurant. Outside, a wave of new customers surge, lining up by the door and waiting to be seated.

Grabbing the electronic tablet on the front desk, I begin walking to the kitchen. I'm re-configuring the menu settings for the evening shift when I accidentally bump into someone.

"Sorry!" I gasp.

A low grunt. "Christ."

"Are you okay?" I ask, turning towards the customer.

"You're one hell of a force for someone so slight," He grunts, a hand instinctively pressing behind my back to steady me.

Blinking at the fabric of grey cotton, I didn't realise how tall the sunglasses-wearing stranger is until I'm staring at the aglets of his hoodie.

"Sorry." I tilt my head up and awkwardly step away from him. "I'll get your drink from the kitchen."

"No need." He shakes his head. "I'm leaving now."

"Is someone at the booth?" I attempt to look over him, checking if new customers claimed the table he was previously occupying. "I can find you another table—"

"Hey, can we get the bill!" A voice echoes in the restaurant.

I jerk towards the noise, a lot louder than the indoor voices of patrons, and my eyes narrow at the rowdy table of four.

"Just a moment!" I call out in reply before turning back to the tall customer, still sporting his sunglasses inside. "I can seat you closer to the kitchen for better lighting, or *less* in your case, just—"

"Can you hurry it up?" One of them shouts.

The irritation of being interrupted resurfaces and I resist the urge to stitch their mouths shut with an imaginary sewing needle.

"I'll be with you in a second!" I declare promptly before turning to Sunnies. "Sorry, if you just bear with me, I can—"

"What's taking so long?" Another voice from the same table exclaims. "The waiting staff here are a joke."

Loud snickering erupts within the group sitting at the table as someone deliberately knocks over a glass of water, causing it to spill.

I blink in disbelief.

"Was that really necessary?" I question.

"That got her attention." Another jeer.

I turn to them angrily. "Don't you have better things to do than be menaces in public spaces?"

The entire table frowns, narrowing their eyes at me as my own reply catches me off guard. I'm about to go into full apologetic mode, *again*, when a voice calls from the kitchen.

"Is there a problem here?"

The familiar voice belonging to Rowan Ramos, the Head Chef at Tito Boy's, echoes in the restaurant as he emerges from the kitchen.

"That waitress is getting mouthy." One of them gestures towards me, their 'customer is always right' attitude apparent.

"Hallie?" Rowan frowns, turning to me.

I try not to shrink under his gaze. "It's not—"

"She's fine," Sunnies cuts in and then adds, loudly. "That table over there is a clusterfuck of loud-mouthed idiots."

From the corner of my eye, I see Alana's mouth drop as Rowan blinks in surprise.

"Man, what the hell is your problem?" The group bristles.

"My problem?" He directs his attention to the table. "This is a restaurant. If you're going to behave like clowns, join a circus. I'm sure there's an act vacant for a group of idiots with god-awful dining etiquette sharing the same half a brain cell between them."

The air prickles as the 6-foot-something-sunglasses-wearing stranger starts a verbal altercation with the other customers in the middle of a restaurant. There's something in the way he presents himself, almost

CHAPTER 1

intimidating in the way he commands a room with his presence.

Rowan, ever the mediator, steps up.

"This restaurant does not condone harassment of any kind," He says, directing his attention to the table of four. "Towards staff and customers alike. So I would appreciate it if everyone kindly pay their bill and leave."

The group rolls their eyes before making a disrespectful show to drop money on the table.

"Keep the change." They scoff.

Assholes.

"Thanks for dining at Tito Boy's." I plaster on a polite smile, strain seeping into my Customer Service voice.

Sunnies doesn't say anything else, just gives a small nod towards Rowan's direction before leaving the restaurant shortly after.

"Could someone clean up that table please?" Rowan asks.

Wordlessly, I nod and begin making my way to the back kitchen.

Chapter 2

The rest of my shift went by quickly. Time flies when you're having the most fun wallowing in a pit of rejections and feeling sorry about yourself, after all.

With cashing up done and Alana already gone home, the only job left to do is one final clean of the restaurant floor before it was time to close. Mop in hand, I wipe the floor lazily, my mind flashing back to the email I received earlier in the day and falling back into the well of my self-pity.

The transitory period of life after university is a disorienting one. 'Graduate Blues', they call it. But I don't think it's very accurate. Though definitely *melancholic* in tone, blue is not quite the right colour I would describe it.

It's a lot of *grey areas*.

Black and white anxieties blending into varying shades of uncertainties.

I can create an entire swatchbook of the drab and muted and dull and murky areas of my life since leaving uni and going into the overcasting world of work.

The sound of clattering in the kitchen, followed by an even louder curse stops my train of thought.

"*Shit!*"

My heart jumps to my throat and I instinctively tighten my grip on the mop handle, watching as jet black hair and dark brown eyes come into view.

"Rowan," I sigh in relief as he emerges from the kitchen, stacks of plastic food containers in his hands. "God, you scared me!"

CHAPTER 2

"Sorry!" He laughs sheepishly, eyes forming into crescent moons. "I dropped a pan. Or four."

Rowan Ramos, unrelated to Alberto "Boy" Ramos despite sharing the same last name, is the unofficial-official Head Chef at Tito Boy's. Unofficial since Rowan and Tito Boy both disliked the notion of a rigid kitchen hierarchy and much prefer to treat everyone equally, if not like family. But also kind of official since he's the person in charge of overseeing everything in the restaurant, second only to Tito Boy himself.

"I swear you're clumsier than I am," I mutter. "How are you allowed in the kitchen?"

"Talent," He retorts with playful arrogance. "What are you still doing here? I thought Marc and Alana were closing."

"I sent Alana home already. And Marc asked me to cover his shift," I reply. "Deadline season."

"Yikes," He comments. "That's one aspect of uni I'll never miss."

"You went to culinary school," I snort, levelling a pointed look at him. "Was one of your assignments handing in cottage pie at midnight?"

Rowan attended the Royal School of Culinary Arts, or The Scullery as it's well-known here in London, and started working at Tito Boy's shortly after graduating. He had a reputation of being a virtuoso of sorts in the culinary industry, having won a multitude of competitions and earned an abundance of awards in his career.

"*Deconstructed* cottage pie, actually." He nods.

I blink, imagining the ingredients of the classic meat and potato savoury dish in all its individually assembled glory.

"Somehow, I believe you," I reply with a laugh, entirely aware of the culinary school's eccentric reputation.

"How's your portfolio coming along?" He inquires and I lift my shoulders in a nonchalant shrug.

It's not news to Rowan I'm searching for jobs in fashion. Everyone at Tito Boy's pretty much knows of my harrowing hunt for employment since finishing uni. More than anything, they're constantly encouraging me here, being a pseudo-family and all.

"It's coming along," I answer. "Received another rejection earlier in the afternoon."

"Oi," He raises an eyebrow at me. "What are the rules about phone use at work?"

I mirror him in reply, "We have *none*."

"Well, maybe we should implement it." He muses, ruffling my hair in that annoying way that a big brother would to their younger sibling. "Is that why you were moping around all day?"

"I wasn't moping," I interject, swatting his hand.

"You received your very first customer complaint," He says pointedly. "Remarkably out of character for you, Hals."

Frowning, I continue mopping the floor, a little forcefully this time. "Table 10 were being assholes."

"I'm referring to the guy in the corner booth," He tsks.

I blink. "What?"

"Sunnies," Rowan needles lightly. "Your knight in cosy athleisure."

My frown knots deeper.

"Yes, well, he was kind of being an asshole too," I mumble. "Sat himself down in a reserved booth, refused to acknowledge my presence, consistently interrupted me whenever he could *and* acted like he owned the place so excuse me if I wasn't going to tolerate his behaviour initially."

Rowan lets out a low whistle. "That rejection really got under your skin, huh?"

Gloomily, I watch as he reaches under the front desk and begins to pack the containers into a brown paper bag.

"You'd think I'd be used to it by now," I mutter to myself, miserably. "But it's still so jarring."

It could be worse, I suppose. I could have gone through an entire interview process only to be rejected in the end. But at least I would have gotten an interview. I'm perpetually stuck at the stage of automated rejection emails with rarely any progression on how to improve and it's incredibly dispiriting.

"I'll lock up," Rowan announces. "It's getting late."

CHAPTER 2

"Sorry," I mumble, feeling myself wither at my own self-pity session.

"It's fine." A look of understanding flash across his face. "I've been there too, you know."

"Now *that*, I find hard to believe."

Rowan sighs in jest, shaking his head.

"Contrary to popular belief, opportunities were *not* handed to me on a silver platter." He remarks. "You're forgetting I'm from a family of migrant workers. Food was served on a *banana leaf*."

Similarly to me, Rowan is also half-Filipino. He comes from a family of foodies, the eldest and only male amongst four siblings, his younger sisters following his footsteps and embracing the passion for culinary arts. He's become somewhat of an older brother figure to me too which, as an only child, I'm grateful for.

"Since you're done mopping and moping," Rowan begins. "Go home. It's nearly half 11. It takes you nearly an hour to get back to your flat."

He adopts the authoritative voice he uses when he's barking out orders in the kitchen.

"Don't be out any later than you need to be." He adds.

I sulk sportively. "We don't all conveniently live a 15-minute walk away in the posh streets of Kensington, chef."

"Head home, Hals." Rowan chuckles. "And here."

He slides the brown paper bag over to me and I blink questioningly before peeking inside, the aroma of Filipino food making my mouth water.

"Rowan, there are at least four *large containers worth* of dishes here," I gasp. "And dessert, oh my god. *Taho*."

I eye the tub of soft tofu with sago pearls and arnibal sauce and I almost want to cry.

"You're welcome." He nods. "Now go, it's getting late. Eat your rejection away with some homemade *sopas*."

My lip quivers as I stare at the plastic container containing creamy chicken macaroni soup.

"Rowan." I turn to him.

The kind gesture tugs on my chest and I feel my eyes begin to water.

"God, Hallie, don't cry." Rowan flusters. "It's just food. We're in a restaurant, we have plenty."

He awkwardly nudges my arm in an attempt to console me and I let out a warbled laugh.

"I really appreciate it, thank you."

While it might not carry much significance for Rowan, it really means a lot to me.

"Taunts, aside." He says. "Don't let rejections get to you, okay? When one closet door shuts, another set of wardrobe doors open."

I blink blearily at the fashion reference, wrinkling my nose in gratitude.

"Or something like that, I don't know." He shrugs. "I read it in that damn magazine you keep hoarding at the restaurant."

"Yes, *Kuya*." I sniffle, teasing him with the Filipino honorific for an older brother.

"Alright." He responds with a playful eye roll. "Get out of my kitchen, Hartt."

Chapter 3

After grabbing my belongings from the staff cloakroom and clocking out, I say goodbye to Rowan and leave the restaurant.

Clutching the brown paper bag to my chest, I stroll out into the cobblestone streets and tree-lined avenues of Kensington. It's approaching midnight so it's already dark out but, thankfully, the underground is only a ten-minute leisurely walk from the restaurant.

(Fourteen minutes strutting in high heels, seven minutes fast-walking in platforms and three and a half minutes sprinting in plimsolls.)

Kensington is one of London's more upscale neighbourhoods so I felt relatively safe walking at night after work. The journey home after a closing shift tends to be quieter which is something I've grown to appreciate over the years of living in the city. Rush hour in London, particularly on the tube, always makes me feel a little claustrophobic so I try to avoid travelling during peak hours as much as possible.

Just finished work! On my way to the flat!!

I quickly text Gigi, my best friend and flatmate, as I reach High Street Kensington station. Tapping my Oyster card on the reader and walking through the barrier, I'm grateful for the calm commute. The journey from the restaurant to my flat near Southwark takes just under an hour, even accounting for the tube transfers.

Both Gigi and I had the most insanely fortunate blessing of securing a reasonably well-priced flat at Leathermarket Court, a residential building within walking distance to The Shard and London Bridge station. Hunting for flats in London is not for the faint of heart and we scoured the property market, fighting tooth and nail with estate agents who were hellbent on renting flats with way above market value prices and extortionate additional fees.

Thanks to Rowan and his connections, we were introduced to Mrs Webb, an eccentric woman in her seventies who owns multiple residential and commercial properties across London. Married four times but now widowed, she spends a lot of her time cruising the Mediterranean with much younger beaus.

It's way past midnight when I arrive at the iron-wrought gates of the building complex, the courtyard gardens quiet. Entering the code to the gate, I walk to the entrance and towards the communal postal area. Bills, letters, stacks of MODUE magazines addressed to Gigi, and a few packages in my name for my online clothing commissions-based business have accumulated throughout the week. I collect them from our mailing slot before heading towards the lift.

One of the perks of renting our two-bedroom flat is the lift that opens directly into our apartment. Gigi and I are situated on the building's highest floor so having a lift conveniently accessible by the hallway saves us from trekking seven flights of stairs. While our flat isn't the most spacious, it's an open-plan layout with expansive windows that take in a lot of natural light. It accommodates Gigi and I, all at a more affordable price than the standard rate everyone else is paying in such an expensive city.

Considering the lateness of the hour, I'm expecting Gigi to already be fast asleep so it takes me by surprise when the lift doors open and the hallway is lit by a light coming from the living room. Usually, the flat would be engulfed in complete darkness by the time I arrive after a closing shift.

"You're still up?" I call out as I make my way towards the light source, already aware of her whereabouts.

"Hey doll," Gigi acknowledges me with a small wave. "How was work?"

Sitting at her usual spot by the dining table, Gigi is poised elegantly in

CHAPTER 3

front of her neatly arranged workstation of magazines and journals, her eyes fixed on the screen of her laptop. She's wearing her matching satin pink pyjamas, her hair up in rollers and her cat-eye glasses over a mud mask covering her entire face.

"Eventful. Dealt with top-tier customers today." I reply.

A soft meowing catches my attention and I turn to find Calix, Gigi and I's informally rescued stray, stretching languidly on top of the already done-up sleeper sofa.

I redirect my gaze towards Gigi. "You set up my bed?"

A proper bedroom was one of the small sacrifices I had to make to accommodate the ever-demanding lifestyle of an aspiring fashion designer. Gigi had been a saint, letting me have the bigger room in the flat so I could turn it into a design studio. With space for sewing machines, cutting tables, mannequins and pattern-making tools as well as a built-in wardrobe to store textile materials, the make-shift workshop allowed me to facilitate the commissions for Mahalia Made and other personal projects.

But that ultimately meant slumbering my nights on a pull-out couch in the living room.

"I refuse to see you sprawled out on the floor of your studio for the nth time this week," Gigi answers, sending me a knowing look.

"Commissions have been chaotic recently," I comment as I walk over to the sofa bed and give Calix a belly rub.

"I'm aware," She nods in understanding. "But that's no excuse to be breaking your back, Mahalia Hartt."

The lens of her glasses illuminate with a blue tint as she turns to me pointedly and I pout at her silent reprehension, holding up Calix next to my face for double effect.

Gigi rolls her eyes at me playfully.

"Thank you." I send her a small smile, grateful nonetheless.

I met Gigi when I studied at LIFT. We were both in the same year but in different courses, Gigi having taken Business whilst I took Design. Our paths crossed during the second semester of first year when Gigi, as part of the editorial society at LIFT, interviewed design students to feature in the university-based fashion magazine, Elevate.

It was a student-led initiative but Gigi's supervision as co-editor made Elevate flourish over the three years she ran it. The magazine even gained accolades at the end-of-year Graduate Showcase within her collegiate cluster. Gigi is a go-getter and when she goes, she gets. So it's no surprise that she's now an editorial assistant, and working her way to becoming a junior editor, at one of the leading fashion magazines in London—MODUE.

"I come bearing sustenance," I announce, lifting the paper bag as I set it on the kitchen counter. "Courtesy of Rowan Ramos himself."

"Oh my god," She pauses her aggressive typing before leaping from her chair and rushing towards me. "I want his hand in marriage."

Gigi peers over my shoulder as I begin unpacking each plastic container with a different dish. Tinola (green papaya ginger garlic soup), adobo (marinated chicken in soy sauce and vinegar), afritada (braised chicken in tomato sauce with vegetables)— *heaven*.

"I'm pretty sure he won't be opposed to it," I snicker. "Just don't turn me into a child of divorce and deprive me of food from my home country. Rowan's the only chef that makes extra food."

"Better start cosying up to the other chefs then," She quips, rising from her seat to fetch a bowl and spoon from the kitchen cupboard. "Oooh, *sopas*."

Crossing the living room to retrieve my laptop from the media unit under the TV, I place it on the dining table before I start plating my own food, opting for a bowlful of taho.

"Why are you still up?" I ask, curiously.

Gigi sighs loudly. "I'm putting together a presentation for the upcoming print issue."

"They moved you to print?" I gasp in excitement, sitting down opposite her. "Gigi, that's huge!"

Gigi initially worked as an intern at the magazine, doing written coverage for shows during Fashion Week but she worked mainly on the digital side of the publication, not print.

CHAPTER 3

"One of the junior editors in Entertainment eloped with some European man she met on Babble," She reveals. "So I'm stuck with covering her work."

My mouth twists. "The dating app?"

"She was supposed to do a piece on it but she's up and left the magazine. We've heard nothing from her to confirm whether or not she's coming back but she's posting her new and lavish lifestyle everywhere on social media." She adjusts the rollers on her head before refocusing her attention on the screen. "I don't mind the work but managing digital and print assignments of two different sectors was not on the agenda nor the pay grade."

"Anything I can help you with?"

Gigi shakes her head. "Not unless you happen to be well-versed in the world of billionaire bachelors on a bloody matchmaking platform."

"Wow," I release a breath. "That's what you're covering? Sounds like something *Faux* would churn out."

As soon as I mention the tacky celebrity tabloid, Gigi's expression sours.

"I know," She frowns prettily. "I honestly don't understand why they gave it the green light. It's practically a gossip-fuelled op-ed on the dubious ethics and ambiguous moral compass of plutocrats but whatever. It is what it is. That's Entertainment's concern, I won't question it."

"At least the assignment will help you eventually write your own cover story, right?" I offer, trying to reassure her. "How's the 10-page spread feature on Fashion Royals going?"

"Ever the optimist," Gigi lets out a small smile. "And it's good, I've done all the research for Europe so now I'm moving to the monarchs in the Mediterranean. Thanks for lending me some of your old research notes, by the way."

"You know me and my love for princes," I giggle. "Fashionable ones, at that."

"Me too, I can't wait to write it." She nods determinedly. "By the way, Lola rang the landline."

At the mention of my grandma, I turn towards Gigi.

"She did?"

"I told her you were working overtime at the restaurant," Gigi replies. "She'd like you to give her a ring when you can, she isn't too sure whether or not you've been receiving her messages."

I soundlessly shift on the chair, restless.

Ever since leaving uni, my workload has been nonstop. Attempting to balance waitressing at the restaurant, doing commissions, portfolio work and job applications left very little room for communication outside of a 'working' environment. I rarely find a moment for myself, let alone other people, especially with such a packed schedule.

"How long was she on the phone for?" I ask.

"Around an hour," Gigi replies. "I think she was waiting for you to get back from work so she could speak to you."

I nod again, feeling threads of guilt knot itself around my chest.

My grandparents had been the ones to look after me ever since my parents passed away in a car crash over two decades ago. It happened during a snowstorm in Switzerland and I had been a baby at the time so I had very little memory of the event.

My childhood was spent living with them in Switzerland until I was old enough to attend St. Faustina's, an all-girls boarding school that my mum also went to. Her side of the family wasn't particularly interested in my well-being so it became the responsibility of my dad's side to look after me. Whilst I enjoyed living with my Mama and Papa in Interlaken, my uncles felt it wasn't ideal for them to raise another child at their age so the only option was to send me to boarding school.

Regardless of being shipped off to England, my grandparents still looked after me and became my surrogate parents in every sense. I would visit them during every school holiday and they made consistent efforts to see me during term time, even though all of my uncles were resistant to the idea.

"I think they're just really missing you," Gigi comments. "Lola says it's been a while since you visited them."

My mind flashes to my first Christmas back in Switzerland during my

CHAPTER 3

first year of uni.

... wasting her time ...

... won't get anywhere ...

... such a disappointment ...

Reflexively, my hand twitches as fragmented memories of harsh criticisms from members of my family resurface. I shake my head to prevent the thoughts from fully manifesting.

"I'll give them a call tomorrow," I say quietly.

Gigi gives me a small smile of reassurance before turning her attention back to her laptop. A comfortable silence settles between us as I check my emails and do the usual backend work to make sure that everything is operating smoothly with my small business.

Mahalia Made is an online store that I launched during my second year of uni to leverage my design portfolio. I sell digital downloads of patterns I created thanks to the Pattern Cutting semester I took at LIFT as well as commissions for glitter garments that I make, a surprisingly well-to-do niche in the market. The store is also a source of additional income. As someone who lives in an extremely expensive city, it's next to impossible to get by paycheck-to-paycheck with waitressing alone.

I'm scrolling through my personal email when a particular subject line reading 'Application Status' catches my attention.

My eyes widen at the sender.

> **HOLMES London**

Sitting up and scrambling to open the email, I drag my finger across the trackpad of my laptop and tap twice.

> Dear Mahalia Hartt,

> Thank you for submitting your application for the Design Intern position at HOLMES London.

My heart is pounding in my chest and I can hear it echoing in my ears. This is usually the part where I read the copy-and-pasted paragraph of a rejection response.

Twice in a week is manageable but two in one day?

This is going to be tough.

I brace myself, expecting to receive yet another dismissal for a position I applied for when my eyes widen at the next sentence that followed.

> Upon reviewing your portfolio, we would like to invite you for a formal interview to further discuss your application at our London Studio.

I let out a loud gasp, "Gigi."

"What is it?"

"Oh my god."

"What?"

"Oh my god!" I turn the screen towards her.

Gigi scans the email, her eyes quickly darting across the screen and soundlessly mouthing the content of it.

"Holy shit, Hallie!"

"Oh my god…"

Her expression is a mix of bewilderment and confusion as she turns to me. "When did you apply for Holmes?"

I try to recall the timeline, my mind jumbled as the email sinks in. I've applied to so many jobs over the past few months that it was hard to keep up with them all.

"About two months ago?"

She reads the email a few more times, probably to double-check it wasn't a skilled attempt at a phishing scam.

CHAPTER 3

"Sorry, let me rephrase that, *why* did you apply for Holmes?"

My mind draws a blank. Riding the endless rollercoaster of job searches has been so stomach-turning, I've resorted to submitting applications for any available positions out of desperation. To be quite honest, I don't even remember applying to the studio, let alone anticipating an actual reply.

"I've heard horror stories there, Hallie." Gigi continues, an apprehensive look on her face. "Unfair dismissals, workplace harassment. Interns were getting sacked on the spot and executives were being reduced to tears. More than half of their workforce left, just *last year*. It's dire."

I visibly wince.

Holmes' reputation at the moment is less than stellar. The company had been subjected to tons of controversies over the years and the media reported on every little *faux pas* that they could, fashion or otherwise. Things became a lot worse after the death of Sterling Holmes, the CEO of the British fashion house, and the company frayed at every overlocked seam.

"You don't think I can do it?"

Gigi dismisses my doubt immediately.

"You're capable of anything," She affirms. "But it's *Holmes*. They're well-known for employees being torn to threadbare tatters in the tight-fitting depths of the brand's own Herringbone hell."

I blink.

"Words of a fashion critic, not mine," Gigi states. "And it's not the case of whether you can, Hallie. It's whether you should."

Threads of insecurity sew themselves into my chest.

"You're right," I wrinkle my nose despondently. "It's too ambitious."

"No," She shakes her head, then fixes me a determined look. "You're not being ambitious *enough*. You can do so much better than Holmes."

I sigh quietly.

"I've been applying to every design position out there," I say. "But all I've gotten so far are rejections after rejections— if I'm lucky to even receive one."

Whilst the concept of Holmes is less than ideal, it's better than nothing.

Gigi pauses, contemplating. She eyes my laptop screen before typing on her own laptop, long nails clicking rhythmically on the keyboard.

"Okay, let's see what we're getting ourselves into."

The collective 'we' warms my heart and I turn to Gigi, flashing her a grateful smile. Regardless of circumstance, Gigi has always been a constant in my life, supporting me through thick and thin. The thread to my needle, as cliche as it sounds.

"So, the latest news on Holmes." She clears her throat, eyes flickering across the screen of her laptop as she reads. "Their acting CEO was taken to court for embezzlement, their Head of Communications is still on probation after a case of sexual harassment and, of course, their Creative Director and Senior Designer is still off the grid."

I grimace. "God, that *is* dire."

"Their actual work isn't faring any better." Gigi winces.

Neither of us needs to read any articles about it because it's common knowledge with everyone in the industry at this point. After the death of Sterling Holmes, the brand was never the same. The British fashion magnate had reputable shoes that nobody could fill, not even his own children. And it showed with every collection that fared poorly under his son's creative direction.

"Conflicts, controversies and traumatic tales aside," I attempt lamely. "They were acquired by Vante last month, so."

I click the link of the latest article showing up online and show Gigi my screen, the French atelier logo displayed alongside the emblem of the British label.

"Now, *that* is a fashion brand." Gigi taps her perfectly manicured nail on the screen. "My dream man's entire closet is filled with Vante."

"I think every person's dream man wears Vante."

"True," Gigi laughs in agreement before her expression shifts, an idea forming. "Why not give Vante a try?"

I meet her gaze directly. "And move to Paris?"

"Lola and Lolo live in Switzerland." She mentions my grandparents, studying my reaction. "You'll be closer to home."

CHAPTER 3

"I barely speak the language." I shake my head. "I'm a seven-year-old conversationalist at best."

If Holmes is barely within arm's length for me, Vante is completely out of my reach.

"Why don't you apply?" Gigi persists. "Are they hiring?"

"I can barely get hired here in England. What makes being hired in France, the literal home of Parisian Haute Couture, any easier?"

Gigi studies me before shrugging nonchalantly. "You're Mahalia Hartt."

"That name doesn't mean anything to anyone, Gigi." I let out a sigh.

"What are you talking about?"

"At least, not in the industry."

"Not yet," She counters. "Don't even think about hosting yourself a pity party right now. I will gatecrash it."

"I wasn't planning on throwing a pity party," I mumble, already anticipating her argument. "It's actually called a 'sorrow soirée'."

"Sad siesta, forlorn function, etcetera etcetera." She dismisses me with a knowing gaze. "None of that."

I roll my eyes, unable to suppress a laugh at how well Gigi understands me.

"I wonder what made them choose to interview me." I ponder out loud.

"Besides your insanely stacked CV and extensive portfolio?" Gigi muses, raising an eyebrow. "Probably your viral Disney Prince collection."

I think back on the blood, sweat and tears that was my Graduate Collection.

My final major project for uni was a collection of suits that were Disney-inspired. It featured a total of thirty designs, half of which I made into fully-fledged garments. Since I specialised in Menswear, it involved a gender-swap concept where I took the colour palette of each Disney Princess' outfit and turned it into different suits fit for their Disney Prince counterpart with details and embellishments on the pieces that reference their story.

It was well-received by the public too, becoming moderately popular and accidentally trending on social media.

"Virality does have some influence nowadays." I nod.

I try not to think about the amount of sleep I lost during the entirety of my third year and, worse, leading up to the showcase. Staying up for nearly 72 hours straight and relying mainly on liquids for sustenance, wasn't the most ideal of practices but it had to be done.

"Even though I'm not completely sold on the idea of Holmes," Gigi begins. "It's still an opportunity to get into the industry."

I turn towards Gigi, beaming.

Holmes isn't the goal, but it's definitely a significant milestone. Getting my platform Mary Janes in the door is difficult enough as it is. Especially when there are plenty of other Hauretto high heel-wearing hopefuls simply strutting their way in.

"I feel like I'm sending my child to the fashion frontlines." Gigi remarks.

"I'm not in the trenches just yet," I remind her with a laugh. "I have to pass the interview first."

"Which you will," She reassures me. "You're Mahalia Hartt, after all."

Chapter 4

In the week that followed, I focused on organising my portfolio and preparing for the interview at Holmes.

The studio headquarters of the British brand is located at Westminster, an ornate-looking building on the outside but modernly refurbished on the inside. With marbled beige floors and warm lighting, the entrance of the studio resembles the lobby of an upscale hotel rather than a typical office space with fluorescent lighting. The ambience differed from what I initially anticipated and I find myself surprisingly at ease, rather than feeling nervous.

"Good morning," I greet the woman sitting behind the reception counter. "I have an interview today for the Design Intern position?"

"Of course," She offers me a small smile. "Last name?"

"Hartt," I reply. "Two 'T's and without the 'E'."

My feet shuffle, tapping restlessly against the floor as the receptionist types away on her computer. Staying still isn't exactly my strongest suit, and I find myself drumming my fingers on my portfolio to alleviate my anxiety.

"Ah yes, right here. Half 10, Mahalia Hartt." She confirms, nodding. "You're early."

She glances at the wall clock behind her, which is showing 9:30 on the dot.

"I didn't want to risk being late," I explain, gesturing to my A1 folder and the luggage I wheeled in next to me. "I took the tube."

The receptionist's gaze briefly flickers to the sizable, vintage-styled suitcase and nods.

"Feel free to sit and wait in the lobby until then," She signals toward the plush velvet lounge chairs by the entrance. "Our exhibition showroom is also open if you'd like to pass the time."

I perk up at the mention of the gallery, a recent addition to the London headquarters following Vante's acquisition of the brand. Newly integrated into the studio, it's a semi-permanent exhibition set up to showcase the history of Holmes, providing insight into the British fashion house's past and present as well as the future envisioned by the Parisian atelier since its acquisition.

I nod enthusiastically as she gestures down the hall.

"Thank you." I beam.

Walking towards the gallery, I step into the showroom, taking in the spacious and elegantly decorated setup. I'm a huge fan of exhibitions and learning about things in fashion, from its inception to completion, is something I enjoy. My eyes scan the space, widening in excitement as I spot a back wall adorned with rows and rows of magazines being displayed behind a glass casing. I guide my suitcase towards the opposite end of the room and gaze in awe at the various publications. The entire back wall is lined with at least 50 or so magazine titles from all over the world.

Certain magazines appear more than once but they all have a common theme– a Holmes garment featured on the model gracing the cover.

I blink at the copy of Elevate, LIFT's editorial publication.

My jaw nearly drops as I realise it's the first issue Gigi co-edited and featured interviews with my design cohort.

I pull my phone out of my pocket, quickly snapping a picture to send to Gigi. I'm about to take another picture when a voice, deep and resonant, sounds throughout the room.

"Photos aren't allowed here."

Alarmed, I turn around, shoving my phone back into the pocket of my blazer. An apology is ready to leave my mouth but I pause as I take in the sight of the stranger, standing a few meters away from me.

He's tall, a lot taller than I am. He didn't need to be standing next to me

CHAPTER 4

for me to know that. Well-dressed in a tailored navy suit, a black turtleneck underneath and black oxfords to match.

"Oh, I'm— I'm sorry. I didn't realise."

Silence hangs between us, draping somewhat thickly as he lingers by the entryway of the exhibition space. His expression is nonchalant, almost edged with boredom.

"The gallery isn't open to the public." A frown lines his face. "Who let you in here?"

He does very little to mask the contempt in his voice and I try not to look affected by the rudeness of his tone.

"I have an interview today," I reply politely. "At 10:30."

He extends his arm to check his watch and I squint my eyes. Of course, his watch is a *Windsor*, his wrist alone could probably pay for my accumulating six-figure student debt at uni.

"It's 9:35." He remarks.

His gaze shifts as he looks me up and down. His eyes, shockingly light, sweep over me and the colour is hard to discern in the lighting of the gallery. I want to say blue but they look almost grey, the blatant staring that he's currently doing causing a nervous fluttering in my stomach.

"I wanted to be early," I explain. "I had to bring my portfolio and haul around a huge suitcase in the tube so I didn't want to be late. Getting a taxi would have been an option but it's also expensive. Not to mention, rush hour."

Despite my tendency to overshare when I'm anxious, my voice is surprisingly steady. His eyebrows draw together as he takes in my vintage suitcase and A1 portfolio case I'm carrying.

"Very punctual of you."

His words are clipped, an iciness around the edges. The stranger continues to study me without another word and I can feel my nerves escalating. Not the most ideal state to be in before an interview.

"I'm Hallie." I extend an arm. "Mahalia Hartt. I'm here for the Design Intern interview."

"Mahalia." He repeats my name slowly, as he begins walking in my direction.

I tilt my head, intrigued.

The drawl in his speech, though very faint, is instantly recognisable to me.

"Just Hallie is fine," I offer, noting the small folder in his hand as he walks towards me. "Are you here for an interview as well?"

He tilts his head to the side as he reaches me and I squint slightly.

Grey.

His eyes are genuinely grey. The lightest shade, if possible. They're so desaturated, it's almost void of colour.

Closer, his features are more distinguishable. Blond hair, so light it's almost white, frames his symmetrically angled and proportionate face. If a room's distance makes a person do a double take, an arm's length away will make them never look away.

"You can say that." He shrugs.

"Don't tell me you're an interviewer," I say jokingly.

The stranger responds with a look, silent and serious.

"You're an interviewer?"

My eyes widen as I take a step back, half contemplating to retreat to the lobby. The display behind me shakes as my portfolio hits the glass mirror and bounces against my suitcase. I wince as it reverberates against the glass, quickly checking for any damage and sighing in relief when everything seems to be intact.

"Relax," The stranger comments, his velvety reply echoing in the empty gallery. "I don't work for Holmes."

"Oh." I blink.

"Yet." He adds.

"Oh?" My brows knit in confusion. "So you *are* here for an interview?"

"Sure." He replies nonchalantly.

How cryptic.

The trepidation I feel neither increases nor decreases at his ambiguous responses.

"What position?" I attempt to make conversation.

CHAPTER 4

His eyebrows furrow, grey eyes flickering up and down, before answering with a wan lilt, "Design Intern."

I stare at his deadpan expression.

Is he serious?

A long pause settles between us, the corner of his mouth twitching slightly before he clears his throat.

"I'm kidding."

A hint of amusement flashes in his eyes before he masks it again with his usual stoicism. He lifts a folder in his hand and swings forward the camera previously out of my eye line.

"Photographer?" I raise an eyebrow. "I didn't realise Holmes did photography in-house, I thought they outsourced."

He hums, lifting his shoulders nonchalantly. "They do both."

"Were you recommended?" I ask curiously.

Whilst I'm still piecing together the inner workings of the industry, I'm not completely clueless about how it operates. I've somewhat grasped the surface-level dynamics: it's 25% what you know, 50% how you know it and 100% who you know in the industry.

The numbers don't add up, of course.

But then again, nothing in fashion adds up, it flows in the opposite direction— hence, *The Trickle-Down Effect*.

I wait for the photographer-hopeful to answer but he doesn't respond to my question, instead opting to dismiss the topic altogether as he motions towards my outfit.

"Is that an original?"

Nervously, I tug on the skirt of the co-ord I'm wearing.

"Yes, but also no," I respond. "It's a *Holmes Original*, one of their blazers from their 1998 Spring/Summer Collection. But I jazzed it up a bit."

Originally a large, longline double-breasted tweed blazer with contrasted trim lapels, I transformed the item of clothing into a two-piece co-ord in the style of, well, my designs. If I were to create my own line, that is. I figured it would be an ideal talking point during my interview, something to flaunt since every applicant probably has an ace or two up their sleeves.

Mine happens to have heart-stitched patches.

Literally.

He's eyeing the structurally inaccurate hearts embroidered on the arms of the blazer when he turns to me.

"Do you make a habit of desecrating originals?" He deadpans. "With your little… heart patches."

I blink at his dismissal. "It's called *upcycling*."

"Right. The current fad."

"Sustainability isn't a trend." I frown, crossing my arms. "It should be common practice."

"You do realise the field you're going into is fashion?" He retorts.

I repress the urge to strangle him with the strap of his camera for his obvious mansplaining, feeling my inner environmentalist being summoned.

"Well, I sleep better at night knowing I'm doing my part," I assert. "Everyone should at least try to make their own conscious choices when it comes to their clothing consumption. Fast fashion's consumer footprint contributes to so many environmental issues—carbon emissions, deforestation, textile waste, chemical and microplastic pollution. Don't even get me started on labour exploitation. I think we all need to be a little more mindful and adopt a more sustainable and ethical approach to fashion, designer and wearer alike."

He blinks.

"Plus, "throwaway" culture is *not* a cute trend." I gesture towards the suit he's wearing.

Fast fashion is a crime.

"Are you insinuating my clothes are cheap?" He questions.

"What?" I tilt my head to the side. "No, I was just generalising—"

"This is a Vante Original from 05."

Narrowing my eyes, I shuffle closer to him to assess his blazer, blinking at the stitches and inspecting the tiny subtle details of the lapels and the cuffs.

"Oh my god," I gasp quietly.

"It's from their—"

CHAPTER 4

"Autumn Solstice Limited Collection," I gape. "That's not just an original, that's an archive piece from the Vante Vault. They've only made six others from the original design, one of them belonging to a European *royal*. One suit is worth tens of thousands of euros."

I feel a little lightheaded at being a literal arm's distance from an iconic piece of clothing.

"It's, uh, not mine..." He reveals, a little apprehensive. "Technically, it belongs to my dad."

I look up at him, tilting my head to the side. "Using second-hand clothes is sustainable enough."

He blinks and it's mesmerising how his grey eyes look, almost changing in shade depending on the light.

"Either way, that's definitely going to earn you points if you mention it in your interview," I nod. "Vante recently acquired Holmes, in case you didn't know."

He clears his throat, bringing his arms forward to almost shy away from my analysing gaze and my attention shifts to the folder in his hands.

"Is that your portfolio?"

It's A4-sized, tiny in comparison to my A1 portfolio case strapped across my body.

He stares at me for a moment and I'm expecting him to ignore my question when he unzips the folder and it flicks open to a random page. I catch a glimpse of several portraits and some landscape shots before it settles on a greyscale skyline.

"New York City?" I ask.

Attempting to peer over, I'm even more surprised when he hands his folder over to me. The immovably stoic expression stays on his impossibly handsome face as I flip through the black and white cityscapes, identifying shots of the Rockefeller Center, Times Square and Central Park.

"I studied at MIDAS." He comments.

Manhattan Institute of Design and Art Studies.

Of course, he would have studied in one of the most prestigious creative arts schools in New York.

No one in this industry is just *anybody*.

Looking through his photography work, I can genuinely say it's impressive.

His portfolio is strong— a range of landscapes, portraits and fashion editorials. I marvel at the bold uses of colour, dramatic lighting and meticulously composed scenes, gasping in surprise when I spot a familiar face in a black and white photo.

"Oh my god! That's Valentina de Hauretto!"

He doesn't seem the slightest bit phased. "Yes."

"You've photographed New York City's It Girl?" I gape at the model known for her heterochromia eyes and perfectly balanced facial features.

"I guess?" He responds nonchalantly.

"You guess?" My eyes widen at his blasé attitude. "It's *Valentina de Hauretto*. She's Vincent de Hauretto's daughter. Not to mention, absolutely *gorgeous*."

I blink, awestruck at the black-and-white portrait of the iconic shoe designer's eldest child.

He pauses for a moment. "Not my type."

"Beautiful women, who are literal models, aren't your type?" I ask, unconvinced.

The irony of the statement isn't lost on me, considering the model-like aura he exudes and the fact that he himself looks like he stepped out of a fashion editorial.

"And models are *your* type, are they?" His scrutiny carries a note of judgement.

"Everyone's my type, technically." I shrug sheepishly. "I don't discriminate, love is love at the end of the day."

He tilts his head to the side before narrowing his eyes sportively.

"Are you coming on to me?"

I blink, letting out a small snort.

"Just because everyone's my type, doesn't mean not just *anyone's* my type…" I trail off, realising I don't actually know the stranger's name.

My eyes catch the small logo printed on the corner of his folder: 'Jean-

CHAPTER 4

Luc Photography'.

"Jean-Luc," I nod, looking up to study his face. "French. That makes sense."

"Half-French," He supplies.

"That explains a lot, actually."

He narrows his eyes at me. "I'll try not to take offence at that."

"I'm not trying to offend you." I let out a short laugh. "It's just an observation. You do have a very Parisian aura about you."

He maintains his stoic expression. "Do elaborate."

I look up at him before leaning back slightly to fully assess him.

He is *beautiful*. Intimidatingly, so. Very much giving off the vibe that he knows it too with the way he carries himself, almost commanding the room with his presence.

"I think it's the turtleneck," I muse. "Or maybe it's the arrogance, you wear it well."

He lets out a short exhale, amused.

"Are you always this talkative before interviews?"

"Honestly? Not really. Or, at least, I don't know." I shrug, laughing out of nervousness. "This is my first interview for a job in fashion. So it's a new experience for me."

"You don't apply much?"

"Oh, I apply *plenty*. Most are rejections, the rest is radio silence."

His eyes meet mine and at least he has the decency to look somewhat empathetic. "Sorry to hear that."

"Rejection is redirection." I shrug, pursing my lips.

When one boutique door closes, another atelier door opens.

"I've been hunting for jobs in the industry since finishing uni last year," I disclose. "Holmes is the first fashion house to actually offer me an interview so I'm grateful."

"Do you keep up with the news? You do know Holmes is in hot water at the moment?"

"Desperate times call for desperate measures," I shrug, then catch myself. "Please don't tell them I said that."

He lets out an amused huff, akin to a short chuckle. "I'm here too, aren't I?"

"True," I blink up at him. "You know, if you don't get the job, you should consider modelling agencies."

The corner of his lips quirks slightly. "For my looks?"

"No," I roll my eyes. "For your photography work."

I rifle through my bag, bringing out the stacks of different business cards I keep in my purse.

He reads the card. "SELDOM Agency."

"Anagram for MODELS, cool right?" I gush, tapping on the logo. "I have a friend who works as a talent scout there. They're a smaller agency than your average, but they've cast for fashion publications and they've done ads for high-end fashion brands."

"So you think I won't get the job." He looks at me, a teasing lilt to his voice.

"That's not why I'm offering," I quickly backtrack. "Sorry, I didn't mean to be presumptuous. I'm sure you'll get the job, your editorial work is fantastic. I'm just giving options, sorry."

He flips the card between his fingers, eyeing the information on the back.

"It's good you're well connected." He states.

"I try," I respond with a shrug. "I mean, we kind of have to be in this industry."

Networking isn't my strongest suit when it comes to navigating the world of fashion. As a designer, I spend more time in the studio than out of it so gaining contacts and connecting with people in the industry is an overhaul effort on my part.

"You should definitely try SELDOM though, if it doesn't work out with Holmes," I say. "Give me your socials and I'll send it over to them."

He looks a little skeptical as he replies, "I'm not on social media."

"Not even your photography work?" I question.

He pauses, grey eyes debating.

"It's @jnlc.vnt." He eventually reveals.

CHAPTER 4

"VNT?"

"Like dot jpg and dot png."

"Oh cool," I turn to him quizzically. "I didn't realise they had a new file format for images."

The corner of his mouth twitches up but he doesn't say anything, schooling his expression back to an easygoing nonchalance instead.

"I have a small business for fashion commissions," I say. "I'll follow you on there."

Opening up my socials, I search for his photography account and follow him. I watch as he takes his phone out of the inner pockets of his blazer, the notification of a new follow popping up and he begins to scroll through my account.

"Small businesses have a few thousand followers," He starts. "You have nearly 50k followers on…"

He blinks at his phone screen, narrowing his eyes to read my handle.

"Mahalia Made," I reply. "One of my posts went semi-viral a couple of months ago, so I got a sudden influx of followers. Actual conversions from followers to customers and sales are probably 10%, so not really a lot."

"Still," he continues scrolling through my account. "That's impressive."

We spend the next half an hour or so in conversation about photography and design which was unexpected considering his initially standoffish behaviour. He's surprisingly knowledgeable about Holmes and fashion in general, something that I also didn't expect from someone coming from a photography background.

He asked questions about operating a small business, curious about my involvement, and I gave my input on the very little marketing experience I have running Mahalia Made. It was encouraging to talk to someone who was genuinely curious about my work since I can usually tell when people start losing interest when I'm in conversation with them.

I didn't even realise how quickly time had flown by until he speaks up.

"You should probably head to reception and sign in for your interview." He says, nodding back towards the entrance. "It's almost 10:30."

I quickly check my phone for the time and gasp. "You're right, thank you so much."

Handing him back his portfolio, he wheels my suitcase towards me and I smile at him in thanks.

"Good luck." He nods. "You'll do well."

"Thank you, you too."

I offer him another grateful smile, not feeling as nervous as I thought I would be.

"I'll see you around, Mahalia." He calls out to me as I head towards the exit.

"Bye, Jean-Luc." I wave. "Good luck with your interview!"

Chapter 5

After my interview, I didn't hear back from Holmes until an email came in detailing extra forms I had to complete as well as non-disclosure agreements to sign as the next steps of the application process. This was followed by a rigorous month-long process of extensive back-and-forth emails, short turnaround times for multiple design tasks and even shorter interviews with members of the Design Team.

It seems promising, sunk cost fallacy taken into consideration, with how long it's taking for the entire job process to roll out.

But I know better than to put all of my embroidery threads in one sewing box.

While Holmes would be an ideal opportunity, I've learned to manage my expectations. And so to avoid the excessive anticipation of the results of my interview, I distracted myself by working on other job applications and revising my portfolio in the meantime.

This is how I found myself perched in a booth at Tito Boy's restaurant, design portfolio all over the table, brain frazzled at 8 o'clock on a Monday morning. I needed a change in scenery since I spent the entire weekend cooped up at the flat applying for more jobs but overworking is catching up to me and I'm struggling to stay focused.

"Let me guess, doing portfolio work in restaurants is sustainable practice too?"

A voice brings me out of my already dwindling concentration and I glance up to find a familiar face on a somewhat stranger.

Light grey eyes, platinum blond hair.

"Jean-Luc?"

Staring at patterned fabric swatches all morning is clearly making me hallucinate. I blink repeatedly to confirm he's actually in front of me and not just a figment of my imagination. He's angles and edges, standing before me with sharp eyes and an even sharper jawline.

"Morning." He nods towards me.

He's inspecting my design portfolio, a scattered mess on the table as I stare at him, still confused.

"Customers aren't allowed in," I say, checking the time to make sure I haven't been completely engrossed in my work. "At least, not yet. The restaurant opens at 11."

"Hinode let me in."

I blink. "You know Hero?"

"Unfortunately." He replies, deadpan.

Just as he mentions the Sous Chef, I hear his loud voice calling out from the back.

"Snaps, did you lock the front door?"

The Sous Chef in question emerges from the kitchen, dressed casually in denim-washed jeans and a white v-neck t-shirt underneath an apron.

"Oh, hey Hallie. I forgot you were here."

"I literally came in with you and Rowan an hour ago."

Or really, pestered the Head Chef to let me do work as he opened the restaurant.

Rowan, ever the diligent culinary artist, likes to come in early and do admin work in the office. Hero and I had a habit of taking advantage of that whenever we could. He uses the facilities in the kitchen, and I use the space in the dining area. It's a nice change of environment from my make-shift studio at the flat and I genuinely like being at the restaurant.

"Does Tito Boy know you're turning his restaurant into a design studio?" Hero looks at me, mock disapproval in his voice.

"Rowan gave me permission," I retort. "Does Tito Boy know you're using his kitchen as a food lab?"

"Rowan gave me permission," He mirrors my response. "Hals, you do realise this is a *restaurant*. It makes more sense for food to be here than *fabric*."

I cross my arms. "Yes, well, Rowan *and* Tito Boy both gave me permission."

"Of course, ever the *favourite child*." Hero snorts, flicking my forehead.

I glare at him. "You're annoying."

While Rowan plays the role of a supportive older brother, always looking out for me, Hero is the opposite. He's like the annoying younger brother, despite him being a couple of years older than me, and we had a habit of bickering from time to time.

"Don't be rude, we have a guest." Hero looks at me pointedly before gesturing towards the stranger. "Anyways, this is–"

"We've already met." Jean-Luc interrupts him.

Hero looks between us, intrigued. "Oh?"

"At Holmes," I explain. "Jean-Luc and I were interviewing for jobs at the studio."

"Jean-Luc?" Hero blinks, his brows furrowing.

Turning towards the head of platinum blond hair, Hero looks him up and down before Jean-Luc narrows his eyes glaringly.

"Ah, yes. That's right. My man, *Jean-Luc*." He nods, a little too playfully. "Haven't heard that name in a while. Since, you know, I haven't seen the face that goes with it for some time."

I blink at Hero's suspicious drivelling as Jean-Luc responds with a passive-aggressive glare.

"How do you know each other?" I ask.

"We were roommates at MIDAS," Jean-Luc answers, a little terse.

"Imagine that," Hero muses. "Four whole years of rooming with this guy and I just now find out that *Jean-Luc* is *interviewing* at *Holmes*."

"Yes." Jean-Luc ends the conversation.

My eyes dart between them, curious as to how their friendship formed. I've known Hero since working at the restaurant and he's recognised for his loud and chatty personality. I've only met Jean-Luc but he doesn't strike me as someone who would tolerate, let alone entertain, the company of hyper-energetic individuals like Hero.

"Anyways!" Hero continues. "Nice of you to finally show up in my ends, Snaps. How's life treating you since your semi-permanent move to London?"

"You recently moved here?" I turn to him, inquisitively.

Jean-Luc nods.

"All the way from Paris." Hero lets out a whistle. "What happened to New York?"

There's a pause between the two as Jean-Luc stares at the table, gaze suddenly fixated on my portfolio.

"Mon père," He finally responds. My ears perk up, vaguely registering the French. *"But I'd like to avoid talking about my personal life at the moment."*

The entire statement that followed is in French, my brain working subconsciously to translate it and I didn't even realise he was speaking it until Hero is responding in the same language.

"You're making me speak French? Really?" Hero replies, switching like clockwork. "Tout de suite?"

"Would you rather I speak Japanese?" Jean-Luc retorts, still in French.

Hero answers a lengthy response, in Japanese this time, which completely goes over my head. Realising I'm no longer privy to the conversation, I focus on organising the images of my portfolio instead.

"Merde," Jean-Luc clears his throat. "You speak French?"

He pauses, fixing his attention to me and I look up sheepishly.

"I understand it a little bit," I reply. "Not Japanese though so, don't worry."

Next to us, Hero chuckles.

"Don't mind him," He turns towards me. "Snaps here is just a little Polaroid picture of paranoia."

Hero playfully grabs hold of his cheek and gives it an affectionate squeeze. Jean-Luc stares at him, face completely expressionless, save for the glare in his eyes.

I bite my lip to stop myself from giggling, amused by their exchange.

"Finished?" Jean-Luc questions, tone flat.

Hero shakes his head.

CHAPTER 5

"I'm about to slave away in the kitchen to make your favourite Full English breakfast, as a welcome to London, and this is how you treat me?" He gasps, dramatically. "This friendship is wounding to my soul."

Hero makes an elaborate show to pierce an invisible knife through his chest and I shake my head at his theatrics.

"Get back in the kitchen, Hinode." Jean-Luc remarks.

"The disrespect." Hero lets out another melodramatic gasp before nodding towards me. "What about you Hals? Eggs?"

I brighten at the mention of my favourite breakfast food.

"Yes, please."

"Benedict or Florentine?"

"Surprise me," I comment excitedly.

Free food is free food and, despite his tendency to be positively aggravating, Hero is a fantastic cook— almost as good as Rowan.

"Alright," He adjusts the apron around his waist and nods towards Jean-Luc. "Sit down, Snaps. Make yourself comfortable."

Jean-Luc hovers awkwardly by the table and I gesture towards the empty side of the booth.

"You're more than welcome." I nod.

"Thanks."

"Don't worry, our little Hallie is harmless." Hero winks at me and I shoot him a knowing glare. "Just be careful of the glitter."

I can't help but sulk. "They were *sequins* and that was one time."

"Sure thing, *Sequins*." He snorts. "Play nice, children."

Hero pats our heads condescendingly and I swat his arm in annoyance. Jean-Luc remains impassive the entire time as Hero heads towards the kitchen, whistling the tune to *'How Do You Like Your Eggs'* before completely disappearing to the back of the restaurant.

"I can't believe you know Hero," I turn towards Jean-Luc.

"Small world." He acknowledges with a nod.

"So, *Snaps?*"

"My nickname at MIDAS," He explains with a shrug as he also adds, "Everyone had one."

47

"What was Hero's?"

"Wasabi," He answers, prompting a quiet laugh from me.

"That's definitely one way to describe him."

"Fitting though."

"Very." I nod in agreement.

Hero is British-Japanese and works part-time as the unofficial Sous-Chef at Tito Boy's. He studied an undergrad culinary course at MIDAS, which explains Jean-Luc's familiarity with him, and he's currently doing his master's degree at The Scullery. Under Rowan's guidance, he's also working on a cookbook so he likes to come in early to work on recipes he wants to perfect.

"Sequins?" Jean-Luc queries after some time.

I groan. "As you know, I have a small business. And, in my business, I take commissions. The glitter garments I make are my most requested work."

He stays quiet, listening attentively as I continue.

"On days when glitter is involved, I'm usually covered in it. I had an order for a dozen matching sparkly corsets for a bridal party…"

"Covered the entire restaurant in glitter for months." Hero's voice chimes from the kitchen, head peeking out of the partition window. "It nearly turned into a food safety violation."

"He's exaggerating," I pull a face. "It wasn't that bad at all. But I kind of have to carry this everywhere now."

Reaching into my tote bag under the table, I retrieve a vintage, brass-plated lint roller.

"Pretty." He nods.

"It was a graduation gift from my grandpa," I disclose. "He made it himself."

Jean-Luc reaches for the hand-crafted vintage roller, seemingly impressed by the craftsmanship as he admires the engraved patterns of floral motifs and gemstone embellishments. He lightly scratches on the adhesive, rubbing the specks of glitter between his thumb and index finger.

"That explains the glitter I found in my photography folder," He

CHAPTER 5

comments.

I stare at him. "Are you serious? I made sure to be glitter-free during that interview, I used an *entire* roll of lint remover!"

The familiar glimmer of amusement dances in his eyes.

"Oh," I blink. "Ha ha, very funny."

He regards me for a moment. "Any word from Holmes?"

"I'm still back and forth with them," I answer. "But nothing official yet."

"Sounds promising," He remarks, nodding. "They're investing their time in you."

"Maybe." I shrug, uncertain, but I'm grateful for the small spark of reassurance. "I'm really hoping so but I'm also applying for other jobs in the meantime. What about you?"

He's about to respond when Hero's voice echoes from the kitchen.

"Ma-ha-lia!" I flinch at the loud noise, my waitressing instincts momentarily triggered. "Order's up!"

"You don't need to be so loud, *baka*," I complain as I approach the kitchen partition. "We're the only people in the restaurant."

At the sight of Jean Luc and I's breakfast plates, an Eggs Benedict and a Full English, my mouth waters.

"I've been calling your name for 10 minutes, *tanga*," Hero smirks, teasingly. "But you both seem to be very deep in conversation."

I feel a warmth creeping up my neck.

"What, pray tell, could you be talking about that you're both intensely gazing into each other's eyes?" He questions cheekily.

"You're annoying," I retort.

Hero only chuckles. "Please handle model boy with care alright? He's a little fragile."

"Model boy?" I blink, tilting my head to where Jean-Luc is sitting.

He's casually dressed in athleisurewear, a matching dark grey hoodie and gym shorts. He looks like he'd been to the gym, or possibly going to one, if it wasn't for the white high-top trainers that are most definitely not meant for exercising.

"I fear I've revealed too much." Hero glances over at me. "Don't mention anything to Snaps."

Retreating to the booth, I watch as Jean-Luc quietly examines the designs in my sketchbook.

"You can move my things out of the way," I tell him, setting down his plate of Full English and cutlery in front of him.

"Are these for Mahalia Made?" He gestures towards the different drawings of long dresses and elaborate notes on each design. "They're not Menswear."

"Personal sketches," I confirm. "When I get bored, I like to doodle. Ideas of outfits, garments, imaginary collections. It gives me a break from commissions and portfolio work."

He lifts a piece of paper with one of my sketches and holds it up in the light, eyes squinting.

"They're just random doodles so it's not very good." I reach out for the single sheet of paper, embarrassed at the rushed and unfinished nature of some of them.

"Just random doodles?" His eyes dart between the different sketches, lining them up. "They're impressive. I see the vision here, great job."

A fluttering spreads across my chest at the praise.

"Oh, thank you."

Falling into conversation with Jean-Luc was relatively easy. We talked about design and photography, our discussions picking up from where we left off back at Holmes, as we begin eating. Since I'm not the most well-versed in the art of conversation, I expected an awkwardness to settle between us on more than one occasion but he's a surprisingly good conversationalist. He's pleasant and polite, offering his opinions and leading them into new discussions, very unlike the standoffish stranger I met on the day of my interview.

"Hartt, did you say?" He inquires about my surname, folding his hands together as he finishes his plate.

"Not *that* heart." I point to his chest. "As in stag, hart. But with two Ts instead of one."

"German?" He asks.

CHAPTER 5

I shake my head, wiping my mouth with a napkin once I'm also done eating.

"Swiss. My grandpa was born in Romandy."

"Explains you understanding French." He nods.

Just as I'm about to ask him for his last name, the sound of my phone ringing echoes throughout the restaurant floor. I blink at the 'No Caller ID' displayed on the screen before picking my phone up from the table.

"Hello?" I answer.

Jean-Luc rises to take his empty plate, extending his hand to collect mine and carrying both to the kitchen before I can protest.

"Hi, is this Mahalia Hartt?"

My eyebrows knot in confusion at the unfamiliar voice on the line. "Yes, speaking."

"Hi Mahalia, it's Lois from Holmes London." The voice on the other end replies and my breath catches in my throat. *"We're calling in regards to your job application for the Design Intern position at our studio."*

For a moment, I freeze, my heart rate increasing as I listen to the peppy-sounding voice of the woman on the phone.

"Yes. I– Yes."

Jean-Luc looks at me curiously as he sits back down on the table, placing a glass of water in front of me.

"As you know, it's been an intense couple of months with the design tasks and the team interviews. We've been incredibly impressed with how well you've managed the workload as well as your performance in the task themselves."

I bite my lip.

Leading with something positive is often a prelude to less favourable news. My fingers drum nervously on the table as I wait with bated breath for the impending verdict.

"After discussing your application with the team at the studio, we're thrilled to offer you the position of Design Intern at Holmes."

Extend my gratitude and inquire about feedback for future improvement. That's usually how it goes with rejections after an interview, right? Or maybe, they're not the type of company to provide feedback–

Wait.

I blink.

Hold on.

My mouth hangs open, the words not fully registering yet.

What.

Thrilled to offer me the posi–

"Mahalia." Jean-Luc's voice jolts me from my inner monologue.

"Yes!" I squeak, choking on my response. "Sorry, I'm here!"

Across the table, Jean-Luc is looking at me curiously.

"Thank you. This is wonderful news to hear." I manage to say, a slight tremble in my voice. "Thank you so, so much."

Frazzled, I barely register Lois' voice as she continues speaking over the phone.

"Now, I've been informed that your notice period is two weeks..."

My hands begin to shake and I nervously drum my fingers on the table to distract myself. Opposite me, Jean-Luc continues to watch me closely, eyes flitting to my restless fidgeting. His own hands skim along the granite counter top but they pause before reaching mine.

"We'll be sending you all the details via email."

The rest of Lois' words fade into the background as the reality of the situation slowly sinks in.

"Of course," I respond, feeling a little overwhelmed.

"We're delighted to have you on board, Mahalia."

A warmth bursts in my chest.

"Thank you," I reply. "Truly, I'm so grateful."

The call ends and I find myself gazing at my phone in disbelief. I don't even know how long I zone out, my eyes fixed on the wallpaper display of Calix on my home screen.

"Everything okay?" Jean-Luc asks.

My heart is still racing in my chest, a sudden wave of lightheadedness washing over me. The past few months have been a cloudy film of uncertainties played on a loop but now, the prospect of finally making progress is a wide, open clearing in my head.

CHAPTER 5

There are no longer grey areas.

For the first time in what feels like the longest time— *colour*.

"I got the job," I announce, looking up in awe.

Jean-Luc's eyes widen before the corner of his mouth twitches into a small smile. "At Holmes?"

"At Holmes," I repeat with a nod, the words feeling foreign yet so real. "I got the job."

Chapter 6

Starting my job at the studio was a maelstrom of introductions, interactions and integration— the three 'I's of being an intern, I suppose.

The first week at Holmes consisted of meeting the team, familiarising myself with the responsibilities of the Design Intern role as well as assimilating with various sectors of the company.

I'd spoken to the other members of Design during the application process and it was a relief to find that they are as pleasant in person as they were in my interviews. Pollux, a mid-level designer, has been part of the Holmes team for almost half a decade whilst Estelle has been transferred temporarily from her senior role at Vante to oversee much-needed work until they've found someone permanent for the British brand.

With horror stories of working at the company lingering in the back of my mind, I adopted the mindset of expecting the best whilst preparing for the worst.

It's a Saturday afternoon and, feeling drained after my first week at Holmes, I've spent the majority of the day recuperating.

Curling under the duvet, I sink further into the sofa bed comfortably.

The idea of procrastinating the day away sounds tempting but the work I need to do for Mahalia Made has been piling up ever since I started working at Holmes.

"No rest for the wicked," I let out a loud sigh before getting up.

I'm halfway through reassembling the sleeper sofa in the living room when my phone rings on the coffee table.

"You're alive."

CHAPTER 6

The voice of my grandma sighs in relief as I answer the call.

"Hi, Ma." I respond.

"Ayy, nako." She clicks her tongue. *"Is it really that troublesome to call or send a message to your Papa and I, Lia?"*

Swiping through my phone, I tap the video call button and I'm quickly greeted by my grandma's face on video. Her dark brown eyes blink at the screen, eyebrows furrowed slightly before she sees me and they instantly soften.

"You really should pick up your phone," I hear my grandpa in the background. *"Your Mama has been fussing about you non-stop."*

"Sorry *po*," I reply, hoping to mitigate my awful habit of failing to keep in contact with the Tagalog honorific. "I've been so busy with work."

Bright hazel eyes and a beaming smile greet me this time as my grandpa appears on the screen.

"How was your first week at your new job, Lili?" He asks.

My heart warms at the nickname he's used for me since I was a baby.

"It's going well, Papa." I mirror his smile. "Quite hectic though since I'm still in the process of getting used to everything."

Phone in hand, I walk to my bedroom-turned-design-studio.

"Are they treating you nicely there?" He asks.

"As well as they can," I reply.

Grabbing a pen and paper to do an inventory check, I make a note of fabrics, threads, zippers, buttons, fasteners and other textile supplies I would need to restock for my commissioned work.

"All the people I've met are lovely, so far," I add.

"Good good." He nods.

Despite quickly adjusting to new environments, it's always taken me a bit more time to feel comfortable around new people. Not that I'm shy or hesitant in social situations, I actually like meeting new people and talking to them. I'm just a little clueless when it comes to interpreting social cues and engaging in awkward small talk.

"Make sure you're eating properly," My grandma chimes in. *"Your Papa and I will send you another care package soon, okay? Berries are back in season so*

the market will be selling the chocolate-covered cherries you love so much."

Warmth blooms in my chest.

Even though we're living in different countries, my grandma is always doing what she can to make sure that she's taking care of me.

"You don't have to do that, Ma." I say, watching as she gives the phone to my grandpa and goes off-camera. "I know the post office is far."

"Don't be silly," I can almost picture my grandma's dismissive headshake. *"Tell her to not be silly, Josef."*

"Don't be silly, Lili." My grandpa repeats then adds in a hushed tone. *"You know there's no swaying your Mama."*

"My eyesight might be getting worse but my hearing is still sharp," She calls out and I couldn't help but laugh.

On the screen, I watch as my grandpa shakes his head at me before his gaze shifts behind the phone. A soft expression graces his face and it doesn't take me long to realise that he's watching my grandma, as he often does, with his kind eyes.

"It would be ideal to see my granddaughter in person before my vision worsens," My grandma says as she reappears back on the screen. *"Your Papa and I miss you."*

I stop my scribbling on the notepad, biting my lip as I stare at the pattern paper on top of the cutting table.

The topic of visiting is something I've always distanced myself from. I'm aware that I should make the effort sooner rather than later since I haven't seen either of my grandparents in person for a really long time but the implications of visiting are always a little more complicated.

Fragmented recollections of Christmas from four years ago re-emerge in my mind.

… wasting her time …

… won't get anywhere …

… such a disappointment …

My chest tightens as my hand twitches out of anxiousness.

"I miss you both so much," I reply, quietly. "Once I'm fully settled in my job, I promise to come visit."

CHAPTER 6

"*Good good.*" My grandpa returns, joining my grandma on the screen.

The call continues, different conversations going back and forth between us— from my recent endeavours at Holmes and updates about Tito Boy's to sharing snippets of life in London and my commissioned work at Mahalia Made. Even though my grandparents have very limited knowledge of certain aspects of my life, their willingness to engage in conversation is something that I deeply appreciate.

For the next couple of hours, I found myself speaking to them over the phone and watching as the familiar rooms of the house in Interlaken come into focus. Memories of my childhood spent in the very same spaces tug at my heart and the familiar feeling of homesickness settles in my stomach.

"*We're going to make dinner now, hija.*" My grandma smiles warmly at me. "*You take care, okay?*"

"Of course, Mama." I return her smile.

"*Love you, Lili.*"

"Love you both."

Ending the call, I feel a considerable weight lift from my shoulders. Catching up with my grandparents is always a highlight of my day, especially when it's been a while since I last spoke to them.

"Hallie!"

The mechanical hum of the lift signals Gigi's arrival at the flat, her sing-song voice echoing down the hallway.

"In the studio!"

Gigi enters the room, dressed in her usual all-black attire whenever she's doing 'off-duty, extra-overtime' work at MODUE during weekends.

"I feel like I haven't seen you at all this week," She states. "How was your first week?"

"I'm settling in well, surprisingly," I reply. "No unwarranted aggression on the frontlines yet."

Gigi laughs. "Glad to hear that, sartorial soldier."

She gives me a mock salute before drooping tiredly over the fluffy bean bag next to my dressmaker dummies.

"I can't believe they made you work 12-plus hours on a Saturday," I comment. "With a *5 AM* start too."

"Fashion knows no boundaries," She sighs. "This weekend was the only time they could schedule the celebrity shoot with Audrey Darlington. The magazine's been back and forth with her team for months."

"You're still covering for Entertainment?"

"Unfortunately," She nods. "The workload eased up a bit though. Our Editor-at-Large is hybrid working again instead of strictly working from home but staffing is still such an issue."

"It's the same problem at Holmes," I comment. "Design has *one* member left from its previous team of *five*. They've had to assign a senior designer from Vante to help cover the work for Holmes."

"How is everyone?"

"All really lovely, actually," I answer. "Considering there are only three of us at the moment, Pollux and Estelle were both really welcoming. No red flags so far."

"They're buttering you up," Gigi comments teasingly. "But I'm happy your first week went smoothly. I was rushing around London doing coffee runs and delivering magazines to newsstands for my first week at MODUE."

"I'm anticipating the chaos," I laugh. "It feels too good to be true right now."

Gigi rises from the cushioned beanie to head to her room and I follow her out as I walk back to the living room.

"And your photographer paramour?" She calls out from her bedroom. "How is he?"

Plopping down on the armchair, I open up my laptop and go through emails for commission requests.

"I don't know why you insist on calling him that," I snort in reply.

Gigi emerges from her bedroom after changing out of her outdoor clothes, settling in her usual workstation by the dining table.

"You won't stop talking about him," She laughs, dark brown eyes twinkling. "This is the first time you've ever had an inkling of an interest in someone."

CHAPTER 6

"You're exaggerating." I roll my eyes. "I like people. I like everyone."

"Okay, yes." Gigi waves a hand, opening her laptop. "Your pan-lover preferences aside, you don't *like*-like anyone."

"Are we suddenly five years old?"

"I'm unquestionably correct and you know it," She muses. "In the years I've known you, you've expressed *one, singular, solitary*—"

"Okay, I get it–"

"—*individual* instance where you've shown the faintest interest beyond platonic attraction in someone. And that was Barista Boy."

Recalling my mortifyingly helpless infatuation with the full-time barista during during my first year of uni, I cringe.

"He remembered my drink," I say. "Every single time."

"As complicated as your venti soy matcha latte with whipped cream, caramel drizzle and all those different syrups is–"

"Every single time," I interject. "And he asked how I was doing every day."

"A bare minimum for someone who works in the establishment."

"He never forgot how to spell my name," I add.

"The bar is really on the floor, Hals." Gigi snickers with a knowing look. "You pined over him for months."

I blush in embarrassment. "I did not pine."

"You visited the same coffee shop every single day."

"It was literally opposite our uni building!"

"Not to mention, you wouldn't even step foot in another café." She laughs good-naturedly.

"Sue me for being loyal," I pout. "They don't make that kind of matcha latte anywhere else."

"Ah yes, those consumable glittery flakes are truly one of a kind."

"You liked the edible rose petals in yours!" I huff.

Gigi grins at me teasingly.

"I'm just saying, Hals." She sing-songs. "I can tell when you're beginning to like someone."

A text message coming through lights up my phone and I glance down at the notification curiously.

> *How was your first week at Holmes?*

After breakfast at Tito Boy's, Jean-Luc and I exchanged numbers.
 I didn't really expect anything to come out of it, thinking he only asked out of politeness, but he's been messaging me every day since.
 Our conversations revolved mainly around our professional lives rather than our personal ones which I'm glad for since I actually have more to talk about the former than the latter. He inquires about my design projects and I reciprocate by asking about his photography and his freelance work.
 Good! I type. *Everyone's friendly and surprisingly easy to work with so far. I don't feel uncomfortable or anything, overall it just feels–*
 I pause, realising that I'm probably sharing more information than necessary and I promptly delete the entire message.

> *Good!*

I send instead, then cringe at the ridiculously dry reply before attempting to salvage it.

> *Very productive!*
> *Enjoying it so far!*
> *How's freelancing?*

I cringe even more at my quadruple texting.

> *When life gives you scraps, make a quilt.*

I snort out loud at his reply, his message reminding me of the project I need to finish for my grandma's birthday as I begin typing a response.
 "Oh honey, you're down bad," Gigi smirks.
 I blink. "I'm just replying to his messages."

CHAPTER 6

"Exactly," She teases. "You never read messages let alone reply to them, you leave me on delivered *all the time.*"

"I do not," I protest.

Gigi eyes me curiously. "What's he like?"

"Tall," I answer, remembering how he towered over me during our first meeting at Holmes' exhibition space.

Gigi laughs.

"You have to give me something to work with here, Hallie." She rolls her eyes playfully. "What does he *look* like?"

I pause for a moment, reflecting.

"He's *pretty*," I say. "But in a sort of masculine way?"

Jean-Luc wasn't your typical blond-hair, blue-eyed Parisian Adonis. Certain things about him made him a little more… *distinguished.* Like his light grey eyes and wavy, blond hair that looks white, almost.

"Like *platinum* blond?" Gigi scrunches her nose.

"I think it's natural," I comment. "His hair looked far too healthy for it to be bleached that light."

She snorts. "And *grey* eyes?"

"A10, I swear." I nod. "The lack of pigment was shocking to the system."

I contemplate his eyes. The most striking feature about him. So piercing that you can physically feel it when he's looking at you. I remember the intensity of his gaze whenever he peered over in my direction, both at the studio and the restaurant.

His grey eyes were so focused and intentional, it was almost difficult to maintain eye contact.

Add his sharp nose, defined jawline and high cheekbones into the mix and he's quite possibly the most intimidatingly beautiful man I've ever met in my life.

"Mahalia Hartt!"

"Yes?" I blink.

Gigi's tone is teasing as her face breaks out into a grin. "Were you daydreaming about your shutterbug sweetheart?"

I roll my eyes, grabbing one of my thimble plushies from the couch and throwing it in her direction. "Absolutely not."

She catches it, laughing lightly, and I'm about to further retort when my phone dings with a barrage of texts– all from the same person in question.

Gigi eyes my phone knowingly.

"*You* might not claim to be daydreaming about him," She grins, throwing the plushie back to me. "But *he* is definitely thinking about you."

Chapter 7

The following week at Holmes is a little more chaotic. Workload began to pick up and I've started taking on more tasks required in the studio. Due to the transition of Vante's acquisition, additional staff are being transferred over from the European studios to leverage and distribute the workload across sectors, resulting in a mild frenzy within the office.

The past week has been a flurry of activity. Construction workers have been in and out all week, fixing new lighting and remodelling the fourth floor, as per the very specific request of a new member of the board who wanted his own dedicated office space.

By the time Friday morning came around, the office was in high tension as we anticipate the appearance of our interim Director of Communications.

To prepare for the arrival of the most recent addition to the Holmes studio, the Design team had been requested to come into work an hour early for a briefing.

Don't tell me you skipped breakfast again?

I can almost envision Jean-Luc's headshake of disapproval.

This week has been chaos :(

My reply is delivered as soon as I step out of the tube station and I begin making my way to the studio.

So that's a yes.

A lengthy sigh is the next thing I imagine him to be doing.

There's so much happening at Holmes
It's only my second week but
I'm ready to commit
DESIGN DESERTION IN THE FASHION FRONTLINES
Kidding!
I need this job haha

Scanning my employee card to enter the Holmes building, I nod towards security greeting me at the entrance as I hear someone calling out in my direction.

"Hallie!"

I turn towards the voice to find Pollux hovering by reception, the body of a dressmaker dummy under his arm. He waves me over and I begin walking towards him.

"How is everyone holding up?" I ask.

"By the most delicate of threads," He snorts as we head towards the lift. "Ymir and Saoirse are ready to abandon ship since they'll be working under the new DOC. Estelle's been trying to reassure them for the past half an hour."

"She's worked with him before?"

He nods, adding dramatically, "He's the sole fashion scion of Vante Atelier."

"What?" I gape.

"Uh-huh." Pollux nods. "Holmes' interim Director of Communications is none other than the son of the Parisian Atelier's Chief Executive Officer. Estelle told me when I clocked in this morning. She broke the news to Ymir and Saoirse, hence why they're ready to hand their notices in. They're worried he's going to be Sebastian 2.0."

"I didn't even know Cedric Vante had a son."

CHAPTER 7

Pollux blinks. "How can you call yourself a designer if you don't know the *Peroxide Prince of Paris*."

The title sounds vaguely familiar. But then again, I'm not well-versed when it comes to the *tittle-tattle* of the industry on an international scale. Keeping up with the fashion fads and fodder in London was complicated enough, media coverage concerning Holmes was relentless and almost impossible to keep up with.

"I stay informed with fashion *trends*, not fashion *tabloids*," I comment. "Mostly."

I've always prioritised focusing on the actual craftsmanship of creating clothes in fashion rather than the curated lifestyles of celebrities that exist within the industry. It was only by studying at LIFT and pursuing the trade on a professional level that I realised the significance of social standings.

The importance of names, most especially.

"You have a lot to learn, young designer." He states. "Reputation, good and bad, is one of the most important factors in the industry. Particularly that of fashion progenies."

My mind drifts to the former Creative Director and senior designer gone MIA at the very studio I'm working at.

All the controversies concerning Sebastian Holmes were so convoluted, it's a challenge to stay in the loop. I should probably cover my bases and do more research on the enigma that is Cedric Vante's son to avoid any complications.

"Want to sneak a peek at our temporary DOC's office?" Pollux asks me.

I contemplate for a moment before nodding enthusiastically, feeling my phone buzzing repeatedly with new messages.

Lunch today then?
I'm back in London.
Tell me all about it.

A flutter of excitement erupts in my stomach. Over the past couple of weeks, it's become something of a routine to message Jean-Luc every day.

I don't have expectations from him or anything but it's nice to talk to someone who seems genuinely interested and willing to engage in what I have to say, not just for the sake of making conversation.

The lift chimes to signal our arrival on the fourth floor, Pollux and I stepping out to look around the floor space designated for the new Director of Communications.

"This is insane," I remark, marvelling at the surroundings. "I can't believe they renovated a completely new office for someone who's *temporarily* working here."

Pollux shrugs, seemingly unfazed. "Progeny privilege."

The usual floor-to-ceiling glass walls overlooking the view of the River Thames are covered with black-out curtains. Temporary walls have been put up to enclose smaller rooms and new lighting fixtures have been added.

Even though the actual Communications team is based on the first floor, the entire space of the fourth floor now belongs to Holmes' provisional DOC. It seems silly, if I'm being honest. The rationale behind the decision remains a mystery, but no one dares to question it.

"The secondary studio is also up here but it hasn't been used since Design downsized," Pollux adds before gesturing towards the room furthest away from the lift. "That's his office down there."

On the opposite end of the floor is his work suite, separated from the rest of the space with tempered glass. The black-out curtains hanging from the glass walls are drawn open this time but the room is in complete darkness. I notice a cluster of cardboard boxes just outside, spotting labels for office equipment such as a printer and a water cooler. Alongside the workplace supplies are more flat-packs with labels indicating enlarger baseboards and diffuser heads.

"There's a darkroom up here?" I question.

Pollux studies the boxes for a moment. "Darkroom?"

"A studio that develops film photography."

"I have no idea," He replies with a shake of his head. "I'm not up here often."

I'm about to further comment when his phone dings to signal a new

CHAPTER 7

message.

"We're being summoned," Pollux chimes.

He hands me his phone and I read the text he received from Saoirse, one of our colleagues working in Communications.

> *Pre-boardroom meeting running late. Please make sure all the humidifiers are on all four levels and the sanitation machine is in the conference suite. Thank you so much!!! S x*

"God, the ridiculous demands of a germaphobe," Pollux comments before turning to me. "Do you want to do the humidifiers or should I?"

"I'm curious to see the metal machine," I admit with a laugh as we head back down the hallway.

"Alright, you handle the chunky death trap." Pollux nods as we step into the lift. "Then meet back at the main studio."

As soon as the lift reached the first floor, I quickly head to the huge conference suite where the studio meeting to welcome the new Director of Communications is going to be held.

Entering the boardroom, I locate the sanitation machine, a hefty block of aluminium in the back of the room. Following Pollux's instructions on how to operate the contraption, it doesn't take long before the slab of metal begins humming. I exit the boardroom, promptly closing the door behind me as I send Pollux a quick text to let him know the job is done.

Heading towards the lift, I'm turning the corner when I unexpectedly collide with someone.

"Christ."

A sense of déjà vu washes over me as I look up to find a familiar-looking navy suit and, now, an even more familiar face.

"Jean-Luc?"

The not-so-stranger blinks at me in confusion before his expression morphs into recognition.

"Mahalia."

"Oh my god!" I grin with excitement. "You got the job too!!"

My body reacts intuitively, and before I can fully process it, I'm propelling myself forward to hug him— the joy of seeing him in person again overtaking me.

His entire form stiffens and I quickly step back, offering an apologetic smile.

"Sorry."

"It's fine."

I take in his appearance.

He's wearing a navy suit with trousers to match. A pair of sunglasses sits on the pocket square of his single-breasted blazer and, under the tailored jacket, he's wearing a black turtleneck. As usual, he looks sharp and flawlessly composed, exuding the same air of cool confidence as the first time I met him on the day of my interview.

"Congratulations!" I beam. "You never mentioned hearing back from Holmes, is it your first day?"

"Yes," he nods, clearing his throat. "First meeting."

A warmth spreads across my chest at seeing him again in person.

"I'm so happy you got the job," I say excitedly. "I still sent your socials to SELDOM, by the way. Just in case you thought I didn't. They love your work."

"Ah, yes. They, uh, got in contact actually." He admits, glancing at me briefly before shifting his gaze away.

"It makes sense that you didn't need to take them up on the offer though," I say, cheerily. "You're here!"

There's a hint of apprehension in his gaze as he scans our surroundings, eyes darting towards the boardroom door behind me before checking his watch.

"Aren't you a little early to the meeting?" He asks me.

"Oh no," I shake my head. "I needed to press a button on a metal machine."

His eyebrows knot in confusion. "Metal machine?"

"This monstrous sanitising death trap," I explain with a laugh. "The boardroom needs to be disinfected before our new DOC arrives for the studio meeting. Such were the crucial demands from our darling nepo

CHAPTER 7

baby germaphobe."

Jean-Luc blinks. "Nepo baby... what?"

"You know, *nepotism* baby." I give him a pointed look. "I heard he only got the job because he's the son of the CEO."

He narrows his eyes, looking somewhat offended.

"Comms are in a bit of a panic because Cedric Vante's son is temporarily overseeing their department," I continue, lowering my voice to a whisper. "He doesn't even have the proper qualifications, supposedly. People are saying he's overly critical and difficult to work with."

"Difficult," He repeats, gaze stoic.

"If his demands are anything to go by," I shrug. "Apparently, he's also really fussy and disproportionately hygienic."

"Seems like he's already made a reputation for himself," He observes, monotoned.

"Not a very positive one," I remark, scrunching my nose.

"I take it you're not a fan of him." He states.

There's an aloofness to his voice as his entire demeanour seems to shift.

"I don't know him personally so I can't really judge," I reply. "And he can't help the family that he's born into, obviously. But don't you think it's a little disheartening, not to mention completely biased, that someone with actual qualifications might have lost the job to someone else because of their last name?"

He stays quiet, the dip between his eyebrows creasing even further.

"If we were to put it this way," I begin, wistfully. "A Hartt, me, is a nobody compared to a Vante."

His expression hardens. "That's not true."

"It's not an opinion to be argued against," I shrug. "It's fact. I mean, imagine if both of us applied for the Photographer role and I got the job because I was Cedric Vante's daughter-in-law or something."

Something flickers in his grey eyes.

"Or if we applied to the role of the Design Intern and you secured the position just because you're Sterling Holmes' son. As is the case with our current senior designer that has seemingly disappeared from the face of the Earth."

Jean-Luc pauses, lost in thought.

"Never took you as one to participate in office gossip."

"I don't," I clarify, shaking my head. "But it's hard to ignore when those assertions are the only talk of the studio."

My phone pings, a notification popping up with a message from Pollux informing me that he's on his way to the main studio. The previous message from Jean-Luc this morning catches my eye.

"I'm needed downstairs in Design before we meet with the DOC," I state, offering him a smile. "Lunch today still?"

He meets my gaze, eyes softening. "Sure."

It's half an hour later when familiar faces from every department at the studio start filing into the conference suite. Scanning the room for a certain head of platinum blond hair, my brows furrow when I struggle to spot Jean-Luc.

There's tension in the air as everyone chatters amongst themselves quietly and my attention is drawn to the sterilising contraption in the corner, quietly humming.

"Morning all." A voice, smooth and deep and undeniably familiar rings out in the boardroom.

All eyes turn to a man dressed in a navy suit, black turtleneck peeking out as he strides confidently towards the front of the room.

I blink, tilting my head as platinum blond hair comes into view, stepping up to the elevated stage.

"I appreciate you all being here." His hardened gaze sweeps over each face in the room. "I won't take up too much of your time as this introduction is largely a formality."

The majority of eyes in the room are staring at him in awe, some in trepidation, whilst I'm furrowing my brow in confusion. Collective breaths are held in anticipation as he scans the room.

"I've had the pleasure of meeting some of you already." He says.

Steely grey eyes melt into molten silver as they finally land on mine, his

CHAPTER 7

gaze softening for the briefest moments.

"But for those who are new," He continues. "Allow me to formally introduce myself."

His gaze lingers on me, far too long than necessary, and a shiver runs down my spine.

"My name is August Jean-Luc Vante."

He punctuates every title, liquid silver turning back to gunmetal grey as he averts his gaze.

"Newly appointed interim Director of Communications here at Holmes London, Senior Executive at Vante Atelier and apparently..." There's a comical lilt to his voice but his facial expression is unsmiling. "Nepo Baby Germaphobe."

My jaw drops, confusion morphing into shock as I realise.

A pause hangs in the air before the tension breaks as Jean-Luc— no, *August?*— candidly evaluates the room.

There's a flurry of quiet snickers and animated chatter at the self-deprecating comments he makes for himself. Next to me, Pollux joins in the conversations, chuckling.

My mind spins as I grapple with the revelation that should have been blatantly obvious, had I delved beyond Vante's history as a fashion empire and looked further into the background of each, individual Vante.

"I'm sure all the sudden changes are less than conducive to everyone here at the studio," The lone successor to the Parisian fashion house continues. "But I will certainly do my best to ensure the transition is as smooth as possible. Any concerns about my 'lack of experience' and 'proper qualifications' as I've heard, I'm more than willing to address them. However, I'm hoping that the results and outcomes achieved at Holmes will serve as sufficient proof that I'm more than qualified for the role."

There's an underlying tension amongst the crowd as he talks about the elephant in the room.

Better to acknowledge the privilege now than to ignore it entirely, I suppose.

He determinedly makes eye contact with each person present, the tension in the room lifting somewhat. His pointed gaze returns to me and I feel a prickling across my skin at the incisive nature of it.

"As Director of Communications…"

His words fade into a murmur, the humming of the sanitation machine like static white noise playing in the background as I begin to zone out. I can't fathom the oversight on my part as my thoughts begin to spiral.

I look across the boardroom as the meeting continues. A mix of amused and confused expressions etched on everyone's faces. The atmosphere around me is a lot more energetic, a lively attentiveness focused on the new member of the studio as people hang on to every word he says.

"Thank you all for your time," He concludes, his gaze flitting over to me once more. "This *nepo baby germaphobe* kindly appreciates it."

The deadpan expression on his face causes the uneasiness I feel to double as I recall the things I was casually sharing with him outside of the boardroom.

"Talk about an introduction," Pollux whispers. "It seems like Baby Vante has eyes and ears everywhere."

A flash of platinum hair crosses the conference suite, wasting no time to mingle or make small talk as he heads straight for the door. The clash and clamour of my anxious thoughts intensifies and I watch as he swiftly exits the room.

Around me, the buzzing voices persist.

"— his bone structure —"

"— those eyes —"

"— natural hair colour—"

Amidst the comments from everyone else around me, my statements about him are the loudest.

Excruciatingly demanding.

Disproportionately hygienic.

Nepo baby germaphobe.

My entire body is on auto-pilot as I immediately rush out of the boardroom to catch up to the temporary DOC. He's at the other end of the hallway and I'm expecting him to take the lift but he surprises me by walking towards the door leading to the emergency exit stairs.

CHAPTER 7

Jean-Luc?

August?

What do I even call him at this point?

"Mr. Vante!" I call out.

Mr. Vante?

Internally, I cringe at the formality of my address.

He pauses by the door, broad shoulders stiffening, before disappearing through it.

"Wait!"

I follow him, relieved that we won't be addressing the issue out in the corridor. The last thing I want is to create a scene and embarrass myself further with people around as witnesses.

"Jean-Luc—"

He turns towards me sharply.

"August." His voice snaps.

I nod, my own voice wavering. "A-August."

He's halfway up a flight of stairs, a flash of irritation emerging on his features. The usual, cool stoicism on his face is nonexistent as his grey eyes squint at me almost accusingly. He ascends halfway up the flight of stairs, looking even more intimidating, looming over me from his angle.

"I am so—"

He cuts me off instantly.

"I have meetings to attend for the rest of the morning."

I blink, an odd sense of déjà vu washing over me at his interruption.

"I didn't—"

"I'm an incredibly busy person, *Miss Hartt*." His voice is noticeably different—cold, clipped, *cutting*. "If it's an urgent matter, send an email or schedule a meeting."

He leaves no time for me to reply, ending the conversation as he walks away.

My mind is in tatters, wearing thin as I piece together new information that would have been glaringly obvious, should I have done prior research.

Jean-Luc, the Parisian photographer I've become acquainted with over the past month or so, is none other than the heir to the most prominent fashion powerhouse in the industry— *August Vante*.

Chapter 8

"You did what!?"

The shrill voice on the other end of the line belongs to none other than Gigi who I ended up calling to prevent my thoughts from spiralling catastrophically.

"I know, I know," I reply.

"You didn't."

"It's bad," My inclination to repeat myself when I get overly anxious resurfaces. "So bad."

"Tell me you're joking."

The anxiety I feel fills me to the brim, spilling at the edges. With everyone talking about the 'surprisingly charismatic' and 'otherworldly gorgeous' Director of Communications, I couldn't bring myself to join Pollux and the others during lunch, hurriedly leaving the studio instead to try and clear my head.

"I wish I was." I bite my lip. "I really wish I was."

"You called him a nepo baby germaphobe behind his back?" Her shrieks turn into raucous laughter, each high-pitched snicker adding to my anxiety. *"And he found out?"*

"Technically, I said it to his face."

Out from the suffocating atmosphere of the studio, I find myself aimlessly roaming the streets of Westminster.

"That's gutsy."

"I feel like throwing up my guts," I heave quietly. "He looked ready to slice me open with rotary cutters."

My hunger is practically nonexistent at this point but I still found myself wandering into a quaint neighbourhood filled with coffee lounges, tea rooms and bistro bars near the studio.

"*Ouch.*"

"It was an *accident*," I bite my lip, walking mindlessly into a random café. "I didn't mean anything by it and I thought he was *Jean-Luc*— I didn't know he was *the son of my boss!*"

"Wait, *Jean-Luc?* Your *Jean-Luc?*" Her confusion is evident, even through the phone. "*Good lord, Sterling Holmes has a secret son?*"

"Not Holmes, *Vante.*" I shake my head violently, although she can't see me. "The new Director of Communications is Cedric Vante's son and he's— oh god."

I look outside, gasping aloud as I spot the recognisably tall and fair-haired figure heading towards the same café I'm currently in.

"*What?*"

"He's here."

"*Who?*"

"Jean-Lu– *August.*" I whisper urgently, wincing as he enters the establishment. "*He's here.*"

I turn around frantically, ducking my head down to prevent him from seeing me.

"*Hold on, you're telling me.*" Gigi begins. "*That the only offspring of fashion mogul Cedric Vante, also happens to be your* photographer paramour? *The literal* Peroxide Prince?"

"Genevieve, focus!" I urge.

My anxiety is a thread unwinding from its spool as I fidget nervously inside the café.

"*Yes, I'm trying!*" She exclaims. "*Small world, huh?*"

"Two sizes far too small," I complain. "I'm going to end up blacklisted in fashion."

Approaching the counter, I can hardly focus as I stare up at the drinks menu, quickly saying a random order instead.

"*Okay first of all,*" Gigi begins. "*Stop catastrophic thinking. All you need to*

CHAPTER 8

do is apologise, say it was a misunderstanding and maybe kiss ass for a bit."

I wince.

"He might find it funny," She quips.

I object instantly. "He looked far from amused."

"Then you might want to reassess getting back to the good side of your dashing camera enthusiast."

"I'm going to lose my job," I groan.

"You are not going to lose your job," Gigi argues. *"They can't fire you over this, honestly. Granted that you shouldn't have been talking shit about him to begin with. But it'll be fine. Just talk to him, clear the air. You already know him, after all. The worst-case scenario is a disciplinary action and a talking-to from HR."*

The thought of immediately losing my job, two weeks in sends me into a tie-dye spiral.

"But I doubt he would be an asshole and do that," She continues. *"Since, you know, he's practically head over heels in love with you."*

"Gigi," I groan.

As it stands, her statement could not be further from the truth.

"You'll be fine, okay?" She reassures me.

I take a deep breath. "Okay."

There's audible commotion over on Gigi's end as I hear the rustling of different voices over the phone.

"Hallie, I'm going to love you and leave you. The shoot is running late and it's eating into my lunch time."

We exchange goodbyes and I hang up, attempting to blend into the surroundings as inconspicuously as possible. With my head down and eyes trained on my black chunky Mary Jane shoes, I hover nervously around the serving station as I wait for my drink.

"Soy Matcha Latte for Hallie?"

The barista's call makes me look up, only to jump back in surprise when I find piercing grey eyes staring in my direction. August is standing just a few meters from me as I stare up at him, startled.

I open my mouth, an apology on the tip of my tongue, when he suddenly narrows his eyes at me.

His expression hardens and my words die in my throat.

"Matcha for Hallie?" The barista calls out one more time.

Molten silver turns into steely grey, glancing at my drink before reaching towards it.

"Yes, thank you!"

Lunging forward, I rush to grab the cup, offering the barista a quick smile and nodding towards the head of platinum blond hair in awkward acknowledgement before rushing towards the exit. I push the door open and finally step out into the street, feeling a sense of relief.

Said relief is short-lived when a stranger, hurrying into the café, bumps into me. The force of the collision sends the lid of my drink flying and the hot liquid spills all over the front of my yellow co-ord outfit. It takes a solid five seconds for the incident to register in my mind as I stand outside of the coffee shop, the hot drink burning my skin.

Not the bouclé fabric.

I wince, feeling the scalding liquid seep through the material of my oversized cardigan as well as the white blouse I'm wearing underneath.

Glancing downward, I take a moment to examine my clothes, now adorned with streaks of vibrant green from the spilt matcha.

Inside the coffee shop, I catch a glimpse of August with his back turned, pulling on handfuls of serviettes on the counter. I waste no time as I'm out of his peripheral vision, seizing the opportunity to rush back to the studio.

I spend the rest of my lunch break trying to remove the stain from my clothes and failing.

Vinegar. Baking Soda. Lemons.

As it turns out, removing a distinctly green stain from a thick and incredibly dense fabric is a lot harder to do with the ingredients readily available in the staff kitchen.

In fact, I've somehow made it worse.

Observing the unfortunate state of my entire outfit, I wince. My yellow bouclé cardigan *and* matching mini skirt are now marred with green

CHAPTER 8

splotches.

I trudge back towards the main studio defeatedly, Pollux greeting me as I enter.

"That is an astonishingly bright shade of green."

Standing by the table with a measuring tape around his neck, he scans my appearance.

"Ceremonial grade matcha," I mumble.

"It's like Monet's water lily paintings," He comments as I frown in confusion. "Inverted colours."

Resignedly, I groan as I remove my cardigan, noticing my white blouse underneath isn't faring any better.

In hindsight, lemon juice was probably not the best choice to remove the stain. I don't know why I thought colour-matching the discolouration would be a good idea.

"By the way, our design meeting got rescheduled for later this afternoon," Pollux informs me. "Baby Vante dropped by and Estelle went with him for a conference call with HR in Paris."

The thought of attending the meeting later with streaks and splatters of green matcha all over my white blouse and yellow skirt makes me recoil miserably.

Walking over to the main worktable, I decide to distract myself with the piles of deliveries addressed to the Design team.

"Did these just arrive?" I ask.

"Fabric swatches. Our courier dropped them off during lunch." He replies. "We're working on rebuilding material inventory. We've had no luck accessing any information regarding future collections since Sebastian's account was locked."

I blink. "You shut down his account?"

"Nope," Pollux shakes his head. "*He* did."

"He's allowed to do that?" I gape.

"Sebastian *is* Holmes." He replies, by way of explanation. "He's allowed to do as he so pleases."

It's no secret at the studio that Sebastian operates without consequence but hearing about it is still a little troubling. The fact that Sebastian is able to do anything and get away it really highlights the power imbalance at play in the industry. It's absolutely derailing but it's the unfortunate reality that people with less influence are often subjected to the problematic actions of those in positions of power and prominence.

Most notably, name.

Subsequently, reputation.

"Estelle and I are working backwards," Pollux continues. "Hence gathering material inventory with past manufacturers and suppliers."

"Isn't that how fabrics are usually sourced?"

"Usually, yes." Pollux nods. "But Sebastian is very… selective. He likes manufacturers to create specific fabrics *exclusively* for Holmes which means materials being produced from scratch. So he switches between suppliers depending on who's able to meet the turnaround time for every collection."

My eyes grow in astonishment. "Doesn't that add weeks to the production process if he's requesting for fabrics to be created from scratch *every time?*"

"We don't question it." Pollux shrugs.

"Is that even sustainable?" I frown, more so to myself.

"Nope," He answers. "But like I said, we don't question it."

The articles about Sebastian's unsettling and questionable work protocols are apparent and the studio's tendency to conform to it, even more so.

Focusing on my tasks at hand, I retrieve the cutter from the worktable and start opening up the parcels for the inventory.

The signature prints of Holmes; tweed and flannel with different variations of plaid and pinstripe dominate the majority of the fabric swatches with handfuls of silk, viscose, nylon and fabrics for the lining of the garments mixed in.

Organising the fabric swatches is a relatively simple task. Normally, I would categorise them by material and colour. The textile weight (lightweight, medium-weight, heavyweight) and texture (smooth, textured,

CHAPTER 8

knitted) as well as coordinating them by colour spectrum is a system I had in place for Mahalia Made.

However, it felt more intuitive to organise the textile samples based on seasonal themes and specific design collections for Holmes. Folding the fabrics neatly on the grainline, I arrange the swatches according to the swatch book guidelines created for past and future collections.

I've just about finished unboxing all of the parcels on the table when I notice the last package, a designer paper bag with the distinct monogrammed logo of Vante, two angular lines meeting at the apex to form a serif 'V'.

"What's this for?" I ask, eyeing the tissue paper peeking out at the top.

Pollux glances up from his desk. "No idea, it was already there when I got here."

Lifting the bag, the substantial quality of the card stock is weighty—*expensive*. I blink at the tag attached and tilt my head at the sight of my last name written on the label.

"Hartt?"

The letters are written neatly in cursive, the penmanship unfamiliar to me.

Rifling through the tissue paper, my hand suddenly touches something soft and delicate, woollen fibres tickling my skin.

Definitely cashmere.

Lifting the cloth out of the bag, my eyes widen at the oversized, cream-coloured jumper. Measuring it against my frame, the proportions are closer to a dress for me more than anything, the length falling just above my knee.

It covers my outfit entirely and I blink in realisation.

Sending Gigi a text, I express my gratitude via an onslaught of texts and a bunch of crying emojis.

OH MY GOODNESS
THANK YOU
YOU'RE A GODSEND
ILYSM

Slipping the sweater over my head, the fluffy fabric droops over my frame, concealing the matcha stains on my clothes.

The oversized nature of the jumper meant the sleeves were longer, my hand disappearing under it. As someone who's surrounded herself with fabrics for more than half of her life, I've become particular when it comes to texture. The fabric is soft to the touch, providing me with a sense of comfort.

"At least that's your wardrobe dilemma sorted," Pollux remarks as he glances over in my direction.

I nod, feeling a lot better about attending the meeting later.

Being a recent addition to the team, I only had to be present and take notes while Estelle and Pollux delivered a presentation to August. They provided updates on the forthcoming collections for Holmes as well as delving into the current status of the department as I sat in and logged important information.

August is attentive, eyes sharp and focused as he listens.

The look of concentration on his face as he asked questions about design and commented on the logistics of the department only highlighted the sharpness of his facial features. The slant of his brows, the angle of his nose, the definition of his jawline. Under the fluorescent lighting of the main studio, the wisps of his platinum blond hair look even whiter as it curls against his high-set cheekbones, his light grey eyes even more hypnotic.

It's unfair how devastatingly handsome he is.

"Is this meeting not holding your interest, Mahalia?" August's voice snaps me back into focus, his piercing gaze fixed on me. "You've been zoning out for the past 10 minutes."

My eyes widen, caught off guard.

"N-No, sir— *August*," I apologise quickly. "It's my thinking face."

He blinks languidly at me.

"And what are you thinking about?" He asks.

I rack my brain for an appropriate reply, my earlier conversation with Pollux coming to mind.

CHAPTER 8

"It's nothing Comms related," I bite my lip. "Just passing thoughts about, um, textile production and consumption."

August is looking at me expectantly, as if waiting for me to continue.

Nervously, I glance over at Estelle and Pollux who are staring at me with slightly alarmed expressions on their faces.

"Like ways in which we can be more efficient when it comes to sourcing fabrics and minimising the waste that comes with it," I swallow. "I was made aware of the current systems in place for Holmes. I, um, didn't realise that we request fabric to be made from scratch for every collection. I'm just— thinking about the aftermath of that, I guess. Like reusing or re-purposing or donating or selling excess material…"

I fade off, uncertain about the complete scope of the post-production process at Holmes and whether they've implemented sustainability measures within it.

August hums.

"Noted," He nods. "I appreciate your input."

He doesn't say anything else as he turns his attention back to the presentation being delivered. The meeting concludes shortly after, August barely paying attention to me as I finish jotting down the minutes of the session.

"Mahalia," August finally acknowledges me.

I offer a strained smile, feeling like a child being scolded by an adult as he assesses my outfit. His stare lingers a beat too long and I wonder if I've violated a dress code of some sort.

"Thank you all for your time." He nods before leaving.

The room feels less stuffy now that August left and I let out a small sigh of relief.

"Good Lord, Baby Vante is beautiful but he is *brutal*," Pollux whispers. "I'd hate to get on his bad side."

I can only nod in agreement.

"Don't take it personally," Estelle assures us with a thin smile. "August is *impossible* to impress."

My fingers twitch inside the sleeves of the jumper as I simultaneously play with the garment hem. The softness of the fabric calms me and I'm thankful it's able to relieve the disquiet I'm feeling. I can only imagine the stress levels in the Communications team, the sector August is directly overseeing.

The workday finishes, my journey back to the flat brief as my thoughts gravitate towards the temporary DOC. My mind was so occupied by the troubling turn of events of the last 12 hours, I didn't even realise Gigi finished work early and arrived at the flat before me until I found her in the living room.

"Nice sweater paws," She comments in greeting, sitting in her usual spot at the dining table.

"I really appreciate you sending over the jumper," I say. "I hope it wasn't too much trouble."

Her eyebrows knot in confusion. "What are you talking about?"

"The jumper you let me borrow?"

"What jumper?" She turns to me, quizzically.

"This one I'm wearing right now?"

She pauses before narrowing her eyes. "Hallie, I have never seen that jumper in my life."

"You didn't send it to me?"

"I was assisting with a photo shoot all day."

I blink, glancing down at the cashmere jumper. "I thought this was a freebie?"

"It wasn't a product-focused shoot," She asserts, shaking her head. "It was a celebrity shoot for Entertainment."

"Then who—"

My mind flashes to the café earlier.

Matcha.

August.

There's absolutely no way. I think. *But then again, who else?*

Gigi tilts her head in confusion, inspecting the oversized woollen knit. "Plus, this looks fancy. We never keep expensive products unless they're gifted, we always send them back."

CHAPTER 8

I quickly pull the jumper over my head, fingers skimming over the garment to locate the tag. My eyes bulge out of their sockets when I see the price printed on the label.

€2,200.

Our jaws drop at the numbers.

Gigi blinks as she checks something on the sleeves, her eyes widening. She holds it up for me to see and I squint at the initials embroidered on the cuff of the jumper.

AJLV.

Chapter 9

The following week at Holmes went by relatively quickly and I found myself completing my third week at the studio without any notable hiccups.

Part of the smooth sailing nature of said third week is largely due to my efforts to sidestep any potential conflicts.

Read: Avoiding the Nepo Baby himself.

It was easy to do since August and I worked in different departments. Our work never crossed and on the odd occasions that he did drop by the main studio to speak to Estelle, I ended up conveniently running errands to the fabric storage area or doing tasks in the sewing rooms. I've taken to using the stairs, limiting bathroom breaks and steering clear of the fourth floor entirely to avoid him.

The employee cafeteria seemed like the only secure haven since he rarely made an appearance in a room full of people.

It sounds ridiculous, I know.

In hindsight, skirting around the issue is probably not the wisest approach but I'm still trying to figure out the best course of action regarding the turn of events.

Glancing at the familiar jumper neatly folded on top of the worktable in my studio, I inwardly wince.

The cost of the garment still makes me a little lightheaded.

A quick online search confirmed that the jumper is indeed a Vante Original, and from their most recent collection too. The search also confirmed that the item of clothing is expensive. A monthly salary's worth

CHAPTER 9

and that's *excluding* the customisation of all four of his initials.

Tearing my eyes away from the neatly folded jumper, I groan.

Despite my early uncertainty about who the sender could be, the customised initials embroidered onto the sleeves are enough confirmation.

AJLV.

August Jean-Luc Vante.

He doesn't strike me as the type of person to gift someone he barely knows with a cardigan worth nearly their entire month's salary, especially not with a personalisation of his name. But then again, he's practically drowning in so much money it wouldn't even break the bank for him.

Posting on Mahalia Made's socials, I share some stories of commissioned work I've done lately. My eyes blink at a recent story from August's photography account— @jnlc.vnt.

My left hand twitches and, not so gently, I smack my palm against my forehead.

It couldn't have been any more obvious.

I didn't realise they had a new file format for images.

The off-handed comment I made about his username handle plays back in my head.

God, I truly must have looked like an idiot to him.

Recalling the interactions I've had with him, I sigh. Technically, August never actively lied about anything. He was just really good at *avoiding* certain truths and I was just really bad at *assuming* them.

The latest story on his account showcased the familiar neighbourhood of Kensington, the same area near Tito Boy's. I would normally engage with his content, even write comments and send messages, but now, I just feel removed from him.

For the past week, communication between us has been nonexistent. It's the longest we've gone without speaking since we met and I try not to dwell on the fact that I do miss talking to him.

Or, at least, Jean-Luc.

Grabbing my laptop, I decide to finally do a deep dive research into August Vante.

Vante's Vision: A New Horizon at Holmes London

Presently, there isn't a lot of news about him which I found odd. Seeing as he was recently appointed the Director of Communications role at Holmes, you'd think every media outlet would be writing about him.

I open the most recent article available which details August's achievements in the most recent years.

His tenure as an Executive at Vante Atelier is four years, starting as a Junior when he graduated MIDAS at 22 and advancing to Senior at 24. Achieving a director role in any fashion company at 26 years old is far and few between. Especially with a degree in Photography and a minor in Business. However, anything is possible when you're the sole progeny of Parisian fashion czar Cedric Vante and former supermodel turned philanthropist Adeline Vante née Terre.

Nepotism truly does wonders.

Diving further into his background, it comes as no surprise that August's entire life is fashion.

"The Peroxide Prince of Paris," I read one of the articles out loud. "Now that's a mouthful of a title."

August started his career as a literal *baby* model, appearing in numerous commercials and catalogue shoots. His surprisingly *natural* head of platinum blond hair and boyish looks earned him the moniker in his prepubescent years. At fourteen years old, he became Paris' fashion 'It Boy' and was anticipated to be actively involved and continue his parents' legacy in the industry.

The expectations for him were high and the tabloids wrote about him constantly.

But certain media coverage of him back in the day wasn't the most positive. His teenage years were marred with a reputation that tarnished his prospects. He was labelled as a wild partygoer and a notorious playboy. Underage drinking, driving under the influence, amplifying his penchant for drugs, alcohol and wayward rebellion tenfold.

The playboy has a plaything in every city he poses in.

CHAPTER 9

An article writes, the story over half a decade old.

Who Is The Peroxide Prince?
Meet Haute Couture's Heartbreak Casanova
An Extensive Guide to the Parisian Playboy's Fashion Flings
Runway Romances and Confessions at the Catwalk
The Fashion Feud Between Style Scions
Top 10 Trends: Intimate Affairs and Illicit After-Parties

I frown at the list of endless headlines, falling down a rabbit hole of hyperbolic accounts and tabloid narratives regarding August's intimate involvement with women in the industry.

Sensationalised stories of different affairs with models and reports of non-monogamous links with multiple actresses, all happening simultaneously. Articles detailing his clandestine relationships with women in high places who were years, some *decades* older than him.

It's like opening Pandora's box.

Images of August in and out of different fancy hotels every season were plastered all over the media. One particular article even chronicled his amorous endeavours nearly *every single night* when he attended shows at all the fashion meccas.

At 19 years old, August was expected to dominate the runway scene, walking at every prominent brand in every single fashion capital.

But he didn't walk a single show.

In fact, he refused to.

And he stopped modelling altogether.

Even caused pandemonium in the media when he eventually enrolled to study photography at one of the creative arts universities in New York City.

His hiatus made headlines.

A particular article catches my attention involving NYC's It Girl, Valentina de Hauretto. They ran the same social circles, interlocked in the same fashion milieu and it makes sense. All the landscape of New York, him photographing Valentina.

Nothing was ever explicitly confirmed regarding their relationship but tabloids still rinse and recycled the story, regardless. They were close, tightly knit, as some publications wrote.

The more I read about the gossip written about August, the more my head spun.

The Peroxide Prince's reputation is terrifying, to say the very least.

I stare at the handsome and flawlessly proportioned face on my screen in his younger years, the age I am now. There's only a few years between us, his 26 to my 22 but he feels much older and more experienced, far too accomplished to be involving himself with just anyone in the industry, let alone a nobody like me.

"Knock knock," A lilting voice brings me out of my thoughts. "How's the stalking going?"

I look up as Gigi enters the studio and I turn my laptop towards her direction. Her gaze lands on the screen, a collection of tabs with pictures and articles written about August opened.

"Is that the Peroxide Prince?"

"Yep," I nod. "Back in his heydays. Well, the age we are now, technically."

"Model, notorious playboy and heir to the Parisian atelier." Gigi cites a clip from one of the articles out loud. "He's your photographer paramour confirmed?"

"Without a doubt," I sigh.

"And the jumper culprit?"

"Well, if the initials AJLV are any indication..."

My mind recalls back to when I met him at Holmes' studio under the guise of Jean-Luc. Of course, I was the person that made the assumption based on the name of his portfolio but he didn't correct me. Even at the restaurant with Hero, he still chose to keep up the pretence.

There was a reason he didn't want me to know who he was and that logical reasoning is staring at me right in the face.

"But at least you've sorted things out between you, right?" Gigi spoke aloud, breaking my reverie.

CHAPTER 9

"Not necessarily," I shake my head. "I've kind of been avoiding him."

Jean-Luc the Parisian photographer is an entirely separate entity from August the Director of Communications at Holmes. I don't think I have the capacity to deal with either of them right now. Maybe, not ever.

"I'm kind of hoping to avoid him until Holmes finds a new DOC," I say. "He's only temporary so he'll be leaving in a few months, I overheard Estelle talking to Pollux about it."

"So you're just never speaking to him again?"

I nod. "It saves me from complicating things and further embarrassing myself. He must think I'm an idiot."

"You're not an idiot, Hallie." Gigi shakes her head. "Just the tiniest bit oblivious."

I wrinkle my nose dejectedly.

"At least he hasn't given you any grief about what happened," She says, in an attempt to cheer me up.

"I guess."

Gigi watches me for a moment before grabbing my hands.

"Take a break from the wallowing and eat," She begins, tugging me out of the studio and dragging me to the living room. "I brought us food from Tito Boy's."

I sit myself down at the dining table, watching as Gigi goes to the kitchen.

"You dropped by the restaurant?" I ask, noticing the familiar brown paper bag on the countertop.

"I'm surprised *you* didn't," she answers. "There was an event going on, like a gastronomy masterclass or something."

"Oh no," I wince, slapping a hand on my forehead. "I completely forgot."

Rowan had been planning the culinary workshops at Tito Boy's for months, even extending an invitation for me to attend the launch of his 'cooking symposiums'. I accepted without hesitation but with starting my new job at Holmes, it slipped my mind completely.

"Was it really busy?" I ask.

"Insanely," She nods. "They had photographers, reporters and everything. Your beau was in attendance."

I blink. "He was?"

"MODUE Digital were there covering for Arts & Culture," Gigi replies. "I saw one of my colleagues from work and they told me about it. Everyone was surprised to see him."

Ever the extroverted enigma, I think.

"August doesn't do appearances, apparently." Gigi discloses. "He hasn't turned up in a function that isn't fashion in years. And if it is, it's strictly under Vante."

A part of me understood why. If the media incessantly wrote about my every involvement with people and places in the most negative way, I wouldn't step foot out of my house.

I glance at the designer carrier bag with Vante's logo on top of the dining room table. Returning the jumper to August and apologising would be the ideal thing. But then again, I don't want to add fuel to the fashion fire.

As long as I steer clear of any clashes and confrontations then I shouldn't have any problems.

Read: Continue to avoid the Nepo Baby himself.

Chapter 10

> From: august.vante@holmes.co.uk
> To: mahalia.hartt@holmes.co.uk
>
> Subject: HR Meeting
>
> Mahalia,
>
> Please report to the Human Resources office this morning.
>
> - AV

I stare at the email I receive first thing on a Monday morning. No warm greetings, no pleasantries, no casual inquiries about my weekend.

Just a directive.

My mind instantly conjures up the worst-case scenario: possible termination of employment. A meeting with HR first thing at the start of the week boded ill for various reasons.

The incident from last Friday being one of them.

I trudge over to the office, fighting to keep down the feeling of projectile vomiting because I genuinely feel sick to my stomach.

Knocking on the door, I wait for someone to call me in before entering. Inside the room are two sets of cubicles each equipped with computers in the far back corner of the room. In the middle was a marble coffee table with soft soft-looking chairs as well as a little kitchenette.

"Hi! Mahalia, come in!"

A brunette woman with green eyes flashes me a welcoming smile. I recognise her as Lois, the person who handled the admin paperwork and correspondence related to my Design Intern position at Holmes.

"Hi, Lois." I wring my hands together. "Just Hallie is fine."

"Of course, Hallie." She nods. "Don't be nervous! I can imagine how it might seem, to be called into HR first thing on a Monday. But it's nothing to fret about, how is your first couple of weeks at Holmes going?"

Her comment does nothing to alleviate my anxiety and I smile tightly.

"It's going well," I reply. "A lot to learn but I'm excited to get my hands stuck in."

"That's the attitude! We love that here." She beams, her attitude peppy. "We just need to inform you of a temporary revision in your contract due to certain changes here at Holmes."

I blink in confusion. "Revision in my contract?"

"It's nothing to worry about," She comments in reassurance but I feel my stomach churn with unease. "I've been informed that your new managing director will personally provide you with the full details."

My head spins, the words coming out of her mouth stretching thinly and tangling themselves in my brain.

"But to give you a quick rundown on the changes regarding your original contract," Lois begins. "We're temporarily transferring you from Design to Communications."

The spinning stops before a pin suddenly drops, my silence prompting Lois to continue the conversation.

"We're still in the process of recruiting, but it's taking a bit longer than usual," Lois shares. "And with Men's Fashion Week coming up in June, we're prioritising the workload surrounding the event. So, we're shifting resources around to make sure everything runs smoothly in the meantime."

My thoughts are suddenly spools of thread vigorously unwinding.

"Estelle's reviewed the workload in the Design department and con-

CHAPTER 10

firmed that it's manageable for now," She continues. "That's why we're moving you to the Comms team in the meantime for additional support."

"Right..." I nod along, trying to process the information as she delivers it.

"Your probation period is on timeline with the new changes. You'll just be working in a different department temporarily and reporting to a new manager."

I blink at that. "And, um, who will that be?"

"For this particular change and focus on workload," Lois begins but I can already sense where this is going. "You'll be working under Mr. Vante's son— August."

"August?" I repeat, feeling anxiety forming in the pit of my stomach.

"Yes," Lois nods. "Our new Director of Communications. Platinum blond hair, blue-grey eyes. Impossible to miss. He introduced himself at the meeting last Friday."

"Of course, yes." I nod robotically. "I met him already."

"Fantastic! August also requested that you visit his office for a detailed discussion about your new role and its responsibilities."

Suddenly, I feel winded. "Now?"

"Right after our meeting, yes. HR will handle the necessary paperwork, we just needed to inform you about the changes beforehand. The revised contract will be sent to your email so all you need to do is sign and send it back to us before the end of the day."

The meeting with Lois is on a constant anxiety-ridden loop in my mind as I pace back and forth outside the Director of Communications office.

Contract adjustments are manageable and I'd like to think of myself as adaptable enough that I'd be able to manage the shift in my role. However, the prospect of working under August poses an entirely different challenge.

Holding the paper bag with his jumper in one hand, I knock on the door with the other.

"Come in."

Taking a deep breath, I slide the door open and enter his office.

"Good morning," I greet quietly, my hands wringing the ribbon handles of the gift bag.

August's office is dimmer in comparison, almost in complete darkness, and my eyes take a while to adjust. The ambience is almost sinister and I imagine him turning around in a swivel chair, cat on his lap, ready to disclose his diabolical mastermind strategies to divide and conquer the industry.

Fortunately, he's only standing by his desk, leaning casually against the polished mahogany wood and there isn't a cat in sight.

"You certainly took your time." His tone carries a hint of reprimand as he acknowledges my presence.

August is wearing a forest green, almost black, suit with a dark grey turtleneck underneath. His hands are tucked into the pockets of his dark green trousers as he peers over me, almost lazily.

My eyebrows knot in confusion.

"I've been watching you restlessly pace back and forth outside for nearly 20 minutes." He deadpans.

I blink. "You could see me?"

"The wall is glass." He gestures towards the front of his office where the blinds are partially drawn on either side.

Mentally, I wince.

From the outside, his office looked empty but from the inside looking out, the view of the corridor is clear as crystal.

God, I must have looked like an absolute idiot.

"Sorry," I mumble, feeling heat creeping up my neck.

"I assume the meeting with HR went well?" He inquires.

"Yes," I nod, watching as he pushes himself away from the desk. "I'm just a little... confused."

"As to?"

His grey eyes are assessing me in a way that makes me nervous.

"The role," I say, then add, "My background is in Design. I have no experience in Press or Marketing or... anything Communications-related."

His movements are fluid, assured, as he turns to sit behind his desk. He

CHAPTER 10

signals to the seat opposite him, my own movements feel rigid as I sit myself down.

"Doesn't your CV include you running an online business?"

At the mention of Mahalia Made, I bite my lip.

"Yes but— not to a professional extent, s-sir," I admit as his eyes narrow at the formal address. "I-I mean, August."

I inwardly grimace at my nervousness.

"Holmes initially intended to hire an intern specifically for the Press Team. However, the selection process has been slow," He sighs. "Staffing issues have persisted for months and while the new HR team are diligently working on it, we're in need of all available help for the upcoming Men's Fashion Week."

August reaches out towards a small lamp on his desk, readjusting the brightness and I'm momentarily distracted by the action.

Against the light, his features are even sharper. Chiaroscuro taking effect as the warm glow casts a shadow on one side of his face. He looked every bit of the Peroxide Prince in the tabloids, if not more mature. And still intimidatingly beautiful.

"I understand your hesitation," He continues, snapping me back to attention. "But please recognise that we also need your cooperation. I'm going to be honest with you, Mahalia. Holmes is in the trenches. You have an acting CEO on bail, the previous Director of Communications under legal probation and a Senior Designer still absent without leave."

His gaze doesn't waver as he locks eyes with me and I do my best not to shrink under it.

"I've consulted the board in both Holmes and Vante about the situation," He declares with an air of finality. "Your position as Design Intern is still secured."

Shuffling my feet nervously, I glance around the dimly lit yet spacious room of his office. Unpacked boxes are scattered in one corner, yet despite the apparent disarray, the room is still well-organised. My eyes narrow in the dark, recalling the cardboard boxes that had been outside of his office last week.

"I have something that belongs to you," I clear my throat. "Your jumper?"

Presenting him with the same Vante carrier it came with, I slide it over to his desk.

"I had it dry-cleaned," I quickly add, remembering his supposed hygienic tendencies.

He barely glances at the designer paper bag.

"Did they use hypoallergenic laundry detergent?" His tone carries a hint of mockery and I blink.

"I'm not sure—"

"Then I have no use for that."

His indifference shouldn't affect me, yet it does.

"August, about the things I said last Friday—"

"Is this really the appropriate time to have this discussion?" He questions, tone bored.

"Umm, n-no, but—"

"Mahalia," He interrupts me, raising a hand. "I was born into this industry. I've had articles written about me about worse things. I hardly think much of idle office gossip and hearsay opinions belonging to an intern."

His grey eyes are like daggers, sharp steely gaze cutting through me.

"Oh," I nod, his reply stinging a lot more than I anticipated.

"I understand that you're new to the industry but I expect a level of professionalism on your end," He asserts, his direct criticism hitting home.

I can only nod, swallowing the prickle of hurt that settles in my chest.

"Ymir and Saoirse are both aware that you'll be joining them in Comms," He continues. "Ymir deals with PR and Saoirse manages Marketing. Your role will involve assisting them with all comms-related tasks and obligations for Men's Fashion Week. As you know, this will be Holmes' first show since Vante's acquisition. I need a daily overview sent to me at the beginning of each day along with end-of-day updates. These updates should encompass all aspects of Communications– Public Relations, Marketing, Press, Buyers. Ymir and Sasha will guide you on the tasks at hand."

Already, I feel overwhelmed, but I try to suppress the rising sense of

CHAPTER 10

anxiety within me.

"Any questions?"

Who are you, really?

"No," I shake my head. "None at the moment."

Chapter 11

The next day, I found myself being uprooted from Design to Communications.

Per August's request, I was required to come into the studio an hour earlier than the usual starting time to speak to Ymir and Saoirse, the people I'll be closely working within the Comms team for Men's Fashion Week.

"I'm new to everything," I confess as I follow them inside the office.

Being abruptly shifted from varied sectors has left me feeling on edge and the change has been a source of anxiety for me. I've barely fully adjusted to the dynamics of the Design team and my role as a Design Intern so finding myself taking on another role in an entirely new department with a completely different team is a little unnerving, to say the very least.

"We know," Saoirse says. "Don't worry."

"It's a little chaotic at the minute with all the changes." Ymir nods. "But it's nothing we can't manage."

Assuming her role as the Senior PR Officer, Ymir is the person responsible for the public-oriented affairs at Holmes whilst Saoirse, as the Senior Marketing Executive, works in developing marketing-related campaigns for the brand.

They collaborate closely with each other and have both been working mid-level positions in the company for a few years, only just recently taking on more senior roles since Vante's acquisition.

"We're currently having to double up on roles until HR hires new team members," Saoirse reveals. "The senior staff in the department left quite recently so you can imagine the chaos we've had to deal with and adapt

CHAPTER 11

to."

"August mentioned it to me," I confirm.

"He's a little intimidating," Saoirse comments. "But at least he gets the job done."

She glances over my shoulder at the door, almost as if speaking about the infamous nepo baby will conjure him into existence.

"Surprisingly," Ymir adds.

They lead me to my desk in the middle room and I feel oddly disquiet at being surrounded by a dozen or so computers with no one sitting by them.

Whilst the Design team were located on the second floor, the workspace for the Communications team is a wide open-plan area located on the floor below. The setup made sense, considering the Comms team had multiple sub-sectors consisting of public relations, marketing and social media. But the bustling hub that normally housed around a team of twelve was reduced to four, with August and I added to the team to make six.

More than half of the workforce quit, just last year.

Gigi's voice echoes in my head.

"The girls in Social Media are Eden and Lara," Ymir includes. "But they work from home these days. They come into the office usually twice a week, but more during busy periods like fashion month and brand functions."

"It's a bit chaotic right now but we're managing," Saoirse reassures me.

"Your job as Comms assistant is to help Saoirse and I manage the workload for Men's Fashion Week by providing additional support where we need it," Ymir explains.

"Usually, mid-level employees handle the tasks related to fashion week events," Saoirse adds. "Which did use to be Ymir and I. But since the PR and Marketing senior operatives left Holmes and we took on their roles, we're still in the process of hiring mid-levellers."

"Hence taking on multiple responsibilities." Ymir nods.

"I have very little experience in Communications," I respond, honestly. "My background is in Design."

The last thing I want is to be considered a deadweight, especially since I'm just starting out.

"Don't worry too much." Ymir turns to me, shaking her head. "I mean, it's not like our new DOC fits the job criteria too."

I blink at that.

"We were quite skeptical about him initially," Saoirse chimes in. "I'm sure you're aware of the Peroxide Prince's reputation."

"But who better than to run damage control for a fashion brand than someone who's had their fair share of negative publicity throughout their career?" Ymir comments.

"Weathering all the bad press and negative scrutiny makes him a pro, at this point," Saoirse adds.

I think of the very far and few between articles currently written about August.

The media wrote very little about him being a Senior Executive at Vante, never even mentioned his photography as Jean-Luc. But the gossip around him as the Peroxide Prince and his playboy tendencies had been a constant throughout the years. Granted that it eased up after graduating from MIDAS but still.

His personal life had been tabloid fodder and the media ate it up every time.

"Jokes aside, he does seem to be taking the work seriously," Ymir adds. "So far, so good."

Saoirse nods in agreement. "Despite his reluctance to work at Holmes in the first place."

"Oh?" I inquire, curiosity piqued.

"We heard he originally wanted to work in one of the New York City studios under Vante," Saoirse answers. "The vintage turned contemporary brand."

"Grayson?"

Created in the 90s, Grayson was funded by Vante through a fashion programme when the Parisian conglomerate was reaching towards new consumer market. The NYC-based brand was widely known for its

CHAPTER 11

vintagewear and was driven by the surge of the subculture styles of New Yorkers from decades past, an eclectic blend of the Beat Generation, Punk Rock and the Downtown Art Scene. With DIY aesthetics as well as bohemian influences, it drew inspiration from the nonconformist styles and hipster culture of the city and the brand itself became iconically *New York*.

So the rebrand from vintagewear to contemporary came as a surprise to a lot of people. It started catering to an entirely different aesthetic and design philosophy but still tried to keep the same target audience and market segment. The label became the main reference of every LIFT student's case study when it came to the pros and cons of rebranding in fashion.

"Typical, isn't it?" Saoirse laughs lightheartedly. "Things get handed to him on a silver platter but he demands it in gold."

The sound of the door sliding open cuts our conversation short and we all turn our heads to find August, dressed in a dark maroon suit, entering the Comms room.

"Ymir, Saoirse." He acknowledges them with a nod.

"Boss," They chorus.

"I appreciate you both coming in early today. I'll make sure the extra hour is added as overtime," He says before turning his attention towards me. "Mahalia."

I straighten up in my seat, finding it a little unsettling being referred to by my full name.

"Good morning," I greet him, albeit a little awkwardly. "Just Hallie is fine."

Piercing grey eyes assess me and he blinks almost lazily.

"Have you been relayed the information on your responsibilities as well as expectations as the Comms assistant?"

"Yes," I respond.

"Good." He adds, voice monotoned.

There's a pause before a loud thud on my desk startles me. I glance up to find August towering over me, tall and imposing, as he stands with a stoic expression on his face.

Another resounding smack on the table makes me visibly recoil.

"I need these delivered to the flagship store."

My eyes flicker down to the stacks of folders on my desk.

"The flagship store," I repeat, meeting his gaze again with a questioning look. "In Regent Street?"

"No, in Champs-Élysées," He replies sarcastically before continuing. "Yes, in Regent Street. Deliver them *directly* to Isla Moorhouse, the senior manager of the store."

I blink at his tone. "Directly as in—"

"In person," He cuts me off, making his additional instructions clear. "She needs to receive them herself. No one else."

August leaves the room without another word and I begin filtering through the many folders as Ymir and Saoirse exchange confused glances.

"What did you do?" They ask, simultaneously.

"I didn't–" I begin to respond but my words are interrupted by August's voice echoing from outside of the corridor.

"*Now, Mahalia.*"

I scramble to my feet, quickly shoving the folders into my tote bags and slinging them over my shoulder.

The journey to Regent Street should have taken 30 minutes on the tube. It's only three stops from Pimlico to Oxford Circus but the tube strikes as well as maintenance delays on the Victoria line, *today of all days*, made the journey almost impossible and I ended up taking over an hour to reach the strip of high-end retail shops.

Walking from the office to the store would have reduced my travel time by half but carrying two bulky totes of catalogues in platform shoes would have ruined me.

Similar to the exterior architecture of the Holmes' headquarters, the flagship store is an ornate building with warm lighting, marbled flooring and polished brass accented countertops. It had tall, expansive windows and sophisticated lighting fixtures to showcase the garments from the

CHAPTER 11

latest collections but I barely had any time to appreciate the meticulously organised displays as I rush over to the girl behind the register.

"Hi! I'm Hallie, an intern over at the Holmes office," I greet her, out of breath. "I'm here to drop off the catalogues from the previous collections?"

Mia, her name tag indicates, nods with a friendly smile. "Sure."

I set down the heavy tote bags full of archived Holmes directory on the counter, causing it to shake with the weight before sliding the two I'm holding on top.

"I was told to give them to Isla?"

Mia tilts her head to the side as she responds, "Isla isn't working today."

I blink. "What?"

"She's on annual leave at the moment," She elaborates. "She won't be back until next week."

"Really?"

"If you leave them with me, I can put them in the office for when she gets back," She offers, reaching out for the tote bags on the counter.

August's earlier instructions replay in my head.

"No!" I stop her, bring the tote bags closer to my chest then wince out an apology. "It's okay. I, uhh, was told to personally hand it to Isla."

"Usually, it's fine." Mia frowns.

"Not that I don't trust you!" I hurriedly express another apology. "It's just our new DOC's orders."

An image of August's stern expression flashes in my mind and I shake my head trying to clear the image.

"Oh," Mia nods knowingly. "Okay."

"I'll bring the catalogues over when Isla's back from holiday."

She nods again. "She'll be back on Monday."

"Perfect, thank you."

Grabbing the tote bags from the counter, I flash a strained smile before heading back out.

The trip back to the studio ended up eating into my lunch. Avoiding the tube this time, I decided to walk the 36-minute journey from the store, a journey that I deeply regret as I struggled to carry the tote bags.

"Please keep the doors open!" I exclaim breathlessly as I rush towards the lift about to close.

Powerwalking the journey should have taken me less time but the heavy tote bags and my platform shoes made the journey difficult. I'm about to thank the person in the lift when I come face to face with the last person I want to see.

"You've overrun your lunch break," August comments.

"I just got back from the store," I explain, my voice strained. "I had to walk to the studio."

August blinks.

"You didn't take a taxi?" He questions.

I heave quietly, "I wasn't aware that was an option."

A hush descends in the lift.

"Was no one at the store?" August's gaze drops down to the tote bags I'm still carrying. "Why do you still have the catalogues?"

"You specifically instructed to hand them over to Isla," I cough out, lungs burning. "She's currently on holiday."

"Oh." August's response is nonchalant. "Ringing the store beforehand would have been useful."

"Yes," I reply, trying not to sound painfully out of breath. "I'll keep that in mind for next time, thank you."

I say nothing else as I stare at the buttons of the lift.

"Is there a reason why you're heading to the fourth floor?" He asks.

I blink.

"I'm not heading to the—"

The sound of the lift opening, as it dings, prompts me to reassess my surroundings.

I curse, having forgotten to press the button to the first floor.

"Since you're here," August begins. "I need the cardboard boxes outside of my office flattened and taken to the recycling bin downstairs."

I blink at his request but he doesn't give me time to reply as he takes both tote bags from me, pushing me out of the lift with him. He slings the bags effortlessly on his shoulders before sweeping the catalogues from my

CHAPTER 11

arms.

"I'll be going for lunch," He calls out, walking down the corridor. "I'd like them gone by the time I'm back."

Sighing quietly to myself, I say nothing else as I begin walking towards the haphazardly stacked piles of cardboard boxes outside of his office door.

Chapter 12

An entire week of assisting Ymir and Saoirse with preparation for Men's Fashion Week whilst simultaneously running around doing the most ridiculous and random tasks for August was chaos.

I'm on my third trip of picking up complimentary outfits from the store to be sent off as PR packages for celebrities and influencers when I hear August's voice echo in the Comms room.

"Where is all this glitter coming from?"

I look down at the garment bags in my arms and my eyes trail to my hands, sporting specks of tiny, shimmery particles.

Cursing, I immediately rush to the door.

The entire Comms team is present today with Eden and Lara, the girls from Social Media working in the studio instead of working from home. Everyone glances in my direction, tight expressions on their faces.

"Sorry, that's me." I wince, remembering the commissioned piece I was working on last night that incorporated a lot of glitter.

"I wasn't aware Holmes had any *glittery* garments being sent out." August's voice held no amusement.

"We don't," I shake my head. "This is, um, from me. I dropped a package off at the post office on the way to the store. It had a bit of glitter."

A bit is an understatement.

The commissioned corset I had been working on is covered entirely in different shades of pink glitter.

August observes me, stoic and nonchalant.

"Mahalia, the clothes being sent out are going to be endorsed by big

CHAPTER 12

names on both social media and public appearances for the Holmes catwalk show," He begins, unimpressed. "Quality checks over at the store have been performed on these garments and they have to be maintained in top condition."

There's a tense silence as everyone looks at me.

"I know," I inhale. "I'm sorry, I'll clean it up."

I head to the table in the corner where I've been asked to assemble and package up the PR parcels for the high-profile guests attending the show.

Quickly grabbing the lint roller from my bag, I begin clearing out the glitter around my workstation.

Since I've been tasked to organise the PR bundles for Holmes' brand ambassadors and celebrities for the day, I didn't need to be fully present at the huddle. I still listened to what the meeting is about regardless but kept quiet, lest I end up triggering August again in some shape or form.

The anxiety I've been feeling hasn't lessened since working under him and I've been doing my best to keep focused and level-headed. I didn't realise the tense silence extended far beyond what I was feeling until August wraps up the mini-meeting and leaves the Comms room.

"God, he's terrifying in person," Eden comments as soon as the door slides shut.

"I think I much prefer working from home and seeing his face on a virtual call," Lara adds.

I refrain from contributing to the conversation, especially since what happened with August still makes me all too anxious.

"How are you getting on over there, Hallie?" Saoirse calls out towards me.

"Good," I reply. "Have we received all RSVPs from the celebrities attending the show?"

"The majority of it, yes." Ymir answers. "I'm still waiting for confirmation from a few guests but the list of names I forwarded to you with the outfits they've chosen for the event are the people to prioritise at the minute."

I nod, looking down at the list of names attending the Holmes catwalk show.

NYC's It Girl, Valentina de Hauretto.
Romeo and Mateo Conti of Casa de Conti.
London's rising model and presenter, Henry Atkinson.
Actress Audrey Darlington and her co-star Zander O'Hara.

"We still can't believe they said yes," Eden gushes. "It's been impossible to get one of them to show up in events, let alone both of them."

"Isn't Audrey with River Williams?"

"Isn't Zander?"

A chorus of giggles echoes in the Comms suite and I feel my anxiety ease up a little.

"I'm in the middle of sorting out the travel, accommodations and a style team for all of them." Ymir discloses.

"We've already brainstormed the content we'll be filming for the celebrity endorsements," Lara says.

"If you need an extra pair of hands," Saoirse gestures towards my direction. "Hallie can help."

I give them a nod of agreement.

"We're going to need all of the positive reinforcements we can get for Holmes," Eden sighs.

It's just after 5 PM when I finally finished writing the last handwritten note for the PR packages and everyone at Comms left the studio earlier. I'm tidying up my desk, using the lint roller to clean up any glitter I might have missed when a voice stops me in my tracks.

"Where are today's updates, Mahalia?"

I startle at the voice and whirl around to find August hovering by the desk full of elegantly wrapped gift boxes.

"The updates?"

I pause before slapping a hand over my forehead.

"Shoot, I completely forgot," I say quickly. "I've been working on the PR packages all day, I'll do them now—"

"It's the end of the work day."

"I know, I'm sorry. It won't take long."

CHAPTER 12

I hurriedly grab my notepad and scan the bullet-point list of the notes I made for the day.

"I've been doing brand ambassador and celebrity sponsorship-related tasks all day," I begin. "This morning, I picked up the physical invites from the calligraphist and I was back and forth between the office and the store collecting the outfits that Ymir sent over to Isla."

I glance over at the Holmes designers' bags in the corner and hurriedly grab a pen.

"Um, I have to return those at the store, let me just make a quick reminder, sorry."

I grab a sticky note, quickly scribbling on it before turning back to August who's watching me intently.

Awkwardly, I smile before continuing.

"I spent the afternoon writing out personalised messages for our brand ambassadors," I clear my throat. "And the rest of the working day was dedicated to packaging up the PR bundles for the celebrities attending the catwalk show. Ymir said we're still waiting to hear back from a couple more ambassadors but otherwise, I've done all the PR packages."

I gesture towards the desk animatedly and August looks over at the parcels all wrapped in bows.

"Is gift-wrapping on the long list of your tinkering talents?"

I wrinkle my nose at the word.

He makes it sound like a useless skill to have. Which, fair enough, I probably shouldn't have spent nearly two minutes tying up a perfect bow that will end up being undone within two seconds but still.

My hands like making the effort, no matter how much other people think trivial of it.

"Yup," I nod, holding up my hands and moving my fingers back and forth in tiny wiggles.

His gaze flickers to my left hand, grey eyes squinting and I reflexively ball my fingers into a fist.

"I'll send you an email on today's update in more detail," I say, rushed.

"No need." August shakes his head. "Though, I'm not in favour of a repeat performance of today."

"It won't happen again," I reassure him.

"It won't," August echoes. "Seeing as I'll be expecting to see you in person for your updates from now on."

"In person..." I parrot him, confused.

"Half an hour. In my office. End of every day." He says.

Wide-eyed, I turn to him.

"Is that a problem?" He looks at me pointedly.

I close my mouth, shaking my head.

Something shimmery catches my eye as he turns to leave.

"Um, August?" I call out.

He directs his attention back to me expectantly.

"You have glitter," I gesture towards the cuffs of his blazer. "On your sleeve."

Reaching for my lint roller, I hand it over to August.

Stoically, he examines me, eyes narrowing before letting out a non-committal noise. He doesn't say anything else as he takes the roller from me and exits the room, leaving me standing by my desk to second-guess my entire working existence at Holmes.

Chapter 13

"He *despises* me."

I'm not usually one to rant or complain. I'm a generally passive person with a tolerance for people and their less favourable habits. However, facing hostile behaviour on a daily basis is physically and mentally draining.

And August Vante has me venting and vexing nonstop.

Gigi, for the most part, finds it amusing.

"Not possible," She chimes, linking arms with me as we walk out of High Street Kensington tube station. "You're Mahalia Hartt."

Today is one of the rare days that Gigi and I are free to meet up and do something outside of the flat. We're both so busy with work that it's been almost impossible to spend time as flatmates, let alone friends, and we live under the same roof.

Our footsteps echo on the pavement as we make our way to Tito Boy's, our chosen spot for the evening.

"You don't understand, Gigi." I continue, exasperated. "He's always scowling at me."

Recalling the perpetual frown on his stupidly handsome face, I sigh. Ever since discovering that August is Cedric Vante's son and that I'd be working under him indefinitely, I've been in a constant state of anxiety.

"Plus, he's so… petty." I scrunch my nose in displeasure. "I swear he sends me off to do errands knowing they're unreasonable. Last week, he tasked me to buy this particular type of *pomegranate wine*. Not for a gift bundle or PR package or anything like that. Just for his own indulgement."

I recall his ridiculous request when I met him by the lift after my lunch break.

"It took me the entire afternoon to find the wine, Gigi." I say. "No one sells it in London. It's made on some tiny island in the Mediterranean."

I huff, flailing my arms as Gigi laughs.

"I'm not his personal assistant." I purse my lips. "I'm interning for design. I should be looking at sample silhouettes, not sample *spreadsheets*. My time should be dedicated to making patterns and sourcing fabrics and creating prototypes, not tracking down outlandishly expensive pomegranate wine from the Mediterranean!"

Gigi blinks at me with an amused expression on her face.

"I feel like there's a disconnect in my brain," She muses. "Is this not the same person you were cosying up to and having breakfast together with at Tito Boy's just a couple of months ago?"

"That was Hero's doing, not mine." I shake my head. "And that's when he was *Jean-Luc*."

"Ah yes, your shutterbug sweetheart." She nods knowingly. "Maybe he's just trying to spend time with you. *Maybe he likes you*."

I blink at her, incredulous. "Oh, sure. The son of *the* Cedric Vante is utterly in love with me. So much so that he always looks at me like he wants to gut me with a seam ripper."

Gigi snorts. "I mean, if I happened to meet an incredibly talented designer who ended up gossiping about me and calling me a 'nepo baby germaphobe'— to my face might I add— I'd honestly be a little miffed too."

"I was not gossiping! I was relaying office information to a colleague."

"Rather insulting information involving said colleague," She giggles.

I jut my lip out. "I thought he was someone else."

"Have you considered apologising?"

"Yes!" I stress. "I tried, so many times. But he's so *mean* about it and he shuts me down every single time. I had his already overpriced jumper expensively *dry-cleaned* as a peace treaty but he didn't even spare it a second glance. He took my favourite lint roller, Gigi."

Gigi blinks. "The fancy one?'

"Yes."

CHAPTER 13

"I'm sure he'll give it back to you, if you ask for it." She reassures me. "What's a grown man going to do with a vintage lint roller?"

As we approach the restaurant, I notice the long line for walk-in customers outside. It's understandable, considering it's a Friday evening and people are eager to unwind after a busy week of work.

I'm pushing past the glass doors of the restaurant when I spot a familiar head of platinum-blond hair by the front desk.

"Gigi," I walk to an abrupt halt. "Let's have dinner somewhere else."

Pausing, she turns to me, her eyebrows knitting together. "You don't dine anywhere else."

"Perfect reason to start!" I respond, pasting on a smile, but I can tell she's not convinced.

"No, you don't *like* to dine anywhere else." She interjects. "You're very particular when it comes to your taste buds, Hals."

"Oh, well, I'm feeling adventurous today." I ramble. "And it's hardly fair that I'm the one always deciding where we should eat."

"I'm craving *palabok,*" She says. "Besides, we're already here."

"I know but it looks full," I reason.

"We made a reservation." She raises an eyebrow, studying me closely.

"We can cancel and find another place, I'll just ring them and—"

"What's the issue?" She interjects, seeing right through my attempt to change plans.

"Issue? There's no issue."

Gigi looks at me, unconvinced. "Spill."

"Nepo Baby Germaphobe at 10 o'clock," I whisper, signalling as discreetly as I can. "I don't–"

"Ate Hallie!"

Marc's voice rings loudly inside the restaurant floor despite the already noisy chatter inside.

Ahead, I catch the light, wavy blond locks turning towards my direction and I quickly avert my gaze to avoid eye contact.

Marc is walking over to Gigi and I, menus at hand. "Are you dining in?"

"We made a reservation," Gigi replies as Marc greets her in acknowledgement. "Half six."

"We're a bit busy," He comments, scanning the restaurant floor of all the occupied tables. "Do you guys mind waiting for a table to clear?"

Warily, I glance at Gigi who seems to understand my discomfort.

"We can dine somewhere else," She responds.

"Thank you anyway." I nod towards Marc.

We turn to leave when, out of nowhere, Hero appears next to Gigi and I.

"Ladies!" He nods in our direction. "Dining with us tonight?"

August is beside him, a nonchalant expression on his face, as they stand by the front desk.

"We were just leaving," Gigi says, shaking her head.

"The restaurant is full," I reply. "Gigi and I are thinking of eating somewhere else."

Hero pauses, scanning the restaurant floor before looking down at the seating plan at the front desk.

"Sit with us," He suggests. "We have a booth reserved."

August's grey eyes are fixed on me and I glance over at Gigi, my hesitation evident.

"We wouldn't want to impose," She adds. "Thanks for the offer though."

"I'm sure Snaps doesn't mind, do you?" Hero turns to August.

I can still feel his gaze towards my direction and I stare at Gigi to avoid eye contact with anyone else.

"Fine with me." He responds.

I let out a quiet exhale, realising that arguing would only make *me* seem unreasonable if I decline.

"It's been a while since I last saw you," Hero says, addressing me. "You need to tell me what it's like working for this insufferable prick."

"*Tu es une merde*," August retorts, rolling his eyes.

Hero bats his eyes in reply, "*Juste pour toi, joli garçon.*"

Next to me, Gigi is watching the entire interaction, clearly intrigued with August and Hero's dynamic.

Hero leads us to the booth at the back, Gigi and I closely following, but I made sure to maintain a few steps distance behind them.

CHAPTER 13

"Hallie," Gigi whispers, her voice carrying a tone of amusement. "He's bloody *gorgeous*."

"Gigi."

"I definitely see the appeal."

"By all means," I wince. "He's all yours."

"Not for me," She snorts. "For you."

"No thanks," I shake my head firmly. "There's no appeal. There is absolutely no appealing."

"He looks so different from his playboy days," She comments in jest. "He was such a boy, back then. His pictures do not do him justice now."

"Indoor voice, Gi."

I notice August looking back a couple of times as we walk behind him, trying to catch snippets of our conversation.

"What happened to your crush on him?" Gigi snickers.

I pull a face. "That was before I found out who he is."

"Surely that should *encourage* you?"

"Absolutely not," I lower my already hushed voice. "More than anything, it's a deterrent. I know his type."

"Really?"

"Yes," I nod. "Not me."

We finally reach the booth at the back, Hero setting down a few menus on the table before promptly excusing himself to go to the kitchen.

Even on his day off, he's still running around the restaurant.

August settles into one side of the booth whilst Gigi and I slip into the opposite end. Gigi, well aware of my preference for the outer seat, sits down first leaving me to sit on the outside. I catch the familiar assessing glint in August's eyes, a look I had grown accustomed to since our first meeting during my interview.

Feeling a bit unsure about how to interact with my pseudo-boss outside of a formal work setting, I glance at Gigi who's nudging me.

Right, *introductions*.

"Gigi, this is August." I clear my throat. "August, Gigi."

She extends a polite smile. "Nice to meet you."

"You too." August nods in acknowledgement but doesn't say anything else, his focus shifting to the menu in front of him.

"So," She begins. "How do you know Hallie?"

I turn to her questioningly as she plays doltish.

"Through Hero," He answers, disinterestedly. "We met at the restaurant."

I frown at his answer, Gigi sending me a similar look.

"We work together," I clarify, although she already knows this. "He's, um, my boss, I guess."

"You guess?" August narrows his eyes at me.

Just as I'm about to explain further, the loud ringing from Gigi's phone interrupts me.

"Oh no," She winces.

In all caps, HENRIETTA flashes on the screen.

I turn to her wide-eyed.

"Is that-?"

"The Editor-in-Chief of MODUE Magazine calling me on a Friday evening, yes." She responds quickly, shuffling out of the booth. "I need to take this, I'll be right back."

With Gigi disappearing outside of the restaurant and Hero still in the kitchen, I find myself fidgeting restlessly as I'm left alone in August's presence.

It's still a little unsettling to be around him, even more so out of a work setting.

Eyes trained on the menu, I focus my concentration on the words even though I have the entire menu memorised back to front.

"What's wrong?"

August's voice prompts me to lift my head and I look around, expecting Hero to be back. I grimace when I realise that no one's returned to the table and August is, in fact, talking to me.

"Huh?" I turn to him, finding his grey eyes already fixed on me.

He narrows them slightly as he reclines against the cushioned booth, the physical embodiment of cool and composed.

"You're frowning." He observes. "What's wrong?"

CHAPTER 13

I'm the one frowning?

Ironic coming from the man with a permanent scowl on his face.

"This is my natural expression," He answers.

Inwardly, I wince.

I desperately need to learn to restrain my thoughts and not just blurt them out unknowingly.

"I'm not frowning." Though I feel the knot sitting between my eyebrows a little more consciously now. "It's my..."

"Thinking face, so I've heard."

"Is it a crime to concentrate?" I mutter to myself.

August's assessing eyes continue to linger in my direction and I try not to fidget under his gaze.

"You'd think after nearly 4 years of working here, you'd know the menu by now." He comments.

I press my lips together, choosing not to say anything. Today had already been jam-packed at Holmes. I hadn't anticipated social interactions after work and I'm exhausted.

"Are you upset with me?" August probes.

"What?" I stammer, my eyes widening.

"So that's a yes," He concludes.

"N-no." I stutter out my reply. "It's not..."

Attempting to compose myself, I rack my brain for the most appropriate response. Confrontations have never been my forte and neither is fabricating lies to cover them up.

"It's not..." August repeats, looking at me expectantly as he waits for me to finish my sentence.

"It's nothing," I sigh.

"Your silent treatment says otherwise."

Feeling cornered, I cast my eyes around, hoping for Gigi, Hero or anyone else to come back to the table and rescue me from the stifling conversation.

"There's no silent treatment," I say quietly.

He responds without hesitation, "You usually make conversation."

"Okay..." I mutter, confused.

"But you haven't said a single word to me since your friend left," He adds, studying me.

I wrinkle my nose in confusion. "I updated you with everything at work today."

"I'm not asking for updates," He states, straight-faced. "We're not at work."

It irks me how impassive he is, even more so how attractive he looks doing it.

"We aren't at work," I repeat. "I don't need to make conversation."

I cringe at how childish my answer is.

"So you are upset."

"I didn't say that," I argue.

"You didn't have to," He counters. "I can read between the lines."

"I don't know what you want me to say."

He exhales a mocking breath. "You seem to have no trouble saying whatever gossip-fuelled nonsense you wanted before that meeting."

The Friday morning prior to the studio meeting to welcome August as the new Director of Communications comes to mind.

"I've been trying to apologise for that," I say, urgently.

He stares at me, unflinching. "Have you, though?"

"Yes." I stand my ground, albeit nervously. "But you seem to be set on doing everything but accepting my apology and making my work at Comms hard."

He blinks lazily. "Were you expecting the work to be easy?"

"I'm not naive," I argue, feeling the frustration seeping into my voice. "I *know* it's going to be difficult but you're not exactly being cooperative."

He raises an eyebrow. "*I'm* not being cooperative?"

"It's just a little…" I exhale quietly, struggling to articulate my thoughts. *Tough.*

"Tough." He repeats, eyebrows furrowing.

Mentally, I grimace, not realising until a split second later I've said my thoughts out loud again.

"If you're finding it *tough* then maybe Holmes isn't for you," August

CHAPTER 13

asserts.

Ouch.

That was like a punch in the gut.

"I'm giving you the benefit of the doubt because you're new but I know this industry better than the back of my hand," He states. "This business can be brutal. It can tear you to pieces and you're expected to make something out of the fabric scraps thrown at your face and wear it."

I blink at his overly metaphoric explanation and bite my tongue.

"Suddenly finding it difficult to communicate?" He looks pointedly at me. "That's going to be a problem since you're now working in *Communications*."

My eyebrows knot.

"I was hired for *Design*," I remind him, tone firm. "I *applied* for Design, I was *interviewed* for Design and I got the job as *Design Intern*. You're the one who shifted me to the Communications Assistant role. You're the one making me run around doing non-Communications Assistant-related responsibilities. A new role, in a new department with a new team. So forgive me for asking for a little bit of breathing room from your suffocating corset of Communications, Director."

My fists are clenched on my lap and I feel my nails digging into my palms so I splay them out on top of the menu.

But now that I've started, I can't stop.

"I specialise in Design. That's what I spent over two-thirds of my life doing. I've been sewing fabrics and making clothes since I could loop a thread into a needle. Design is something I've been practising for as long as most people have been *working* in the industry. Since my foot touched the pedal, I haven't stopped. You might have more years of experience in the business than I do but that doesn't grant you the authority to disregard my craft and discredit my place in the industry."

A heavy silence hangs between us, tension thick and smothering in the air. Part of me wishes the ground would open up and swallow me whole right now.

His gaze shifts downwards to the table at my hands. I hastily unclasp my clenched, shaking fists before hiding them back under the table.

"I didn't say you don't belong in the industry," He replies, his voice quieter.

"You didn't have to." I throw his words back at him, tucking my hands under my thighs to stop them from trembling. "I can read between the lines."

Chapter 14

After the heated, verbal altercation with August at Tito Boy's, I was fully anticipating another email from HR regarding the official termination of my employment, this time.

August and I already started Holmes on the wrong foot and he didn't seem like the type to keep giving people second chances. So I was surprised when I came into work the following Monday to find my inbox devoid of any emails.

Instead, just the usual press inquiries, invitations to fashion week events and numerous ticket requests for the Holmes catwalk show.

As well as a gift bag containing my brass-plated fabric roller on my desk. And a brand new, electric lint remover.

Part of me thinks it's a parting gift. Something to soften the blow of being fired from Holmes, ever the catastrophic thinker that I am, but an entire week passes and no such email came.

Despite me compulsively refreshing my inbox.

August ended up cancelling our usual in-person updates for the week due to conflicting conference calls with Grayson. He only allocated one slot at the week's end for our update— a session I'm running late for due to a meeting that overran with Comms.

5:02 PM.

I'm half an hour late.

Quickly saying goodbye to Ymir and Saoirse, I rush to the fourth floor where August's office is, just in case he's still there. Although I did email him ahead of time to let him know about the situation, I'm still anxious about the possibility of being reprimanded.

I knock on the door.

No response.

My fingers tap on the glass wall this time as I attempt to peer through it. The blinds are half drawn but I can see the faintest red light coming from the back of his office. I squint, not recalling the room ever being open during any of our in-person meetings.

Grabbing the handle of the door, I'm surprised to see it glide open.

"August?" I call into the room, stepping into his office. "I'm here for our daily update."

Turning on the light, it flickers to the lowest setting. His office remains dimly lit, even with the lamps scattered across the room.

"Sorry I'm late, the meeting with Ymir and Saoirse ran over. I just wrapped things up with them five minutes ago."

Still no response.

I walk towards the back of his office, where the red glow of light is emitting behind the door.

"I can stay if you need me to?" I offer, still unsure of his presence.

I'm half expecting him to be lurking in the shadows but I'm struggling to see anything properly.

Sliding the door open, a room bathed in dim, crimson light comes into view. It takes a moment for my eyes to adjust before I realise I stepped into a decently sized photography studio of sorts.

"So there *is* a darkroom up here," I mutter to myself.

Shelves lined the walls, stacked with meticulously labelled boxes of photography equipment dedicated to processing film and traditional prints. As expected from someone like August, the room exudes an extraordinary level of organisation— with rolls of film, contact sheets and discarded prints all labelled accordingly.

Stepping further into the room in awe, my eyes land on a large, sturdy table filled with an assortment of old cameras, various lenses and film canisters. Aside from the equipment, there were photographs *everywhere*. Neatly arranged on the table, clipped onto a wire, framed on the wall,

CHAPTER 14

blu-tacked on the cabinets.

I gaze up at the images of London clipped on a metal wiring. From the well-known landmarks to the hidden corners of the city. Market stalls and antique stores of Portobello Road in Notting Hill, trendy cafés, hipster bars and quirky boutiques of Brick Lane in Shoreditch.

Portrait shots of strangers and fashion-styled images are arranged neatly on the table and I approach it, intrigued. Careful not to touch anything, I look down at each photograph, admiring the subtle interplay of light and shadow as well as the intricate subtleties that make each image stand out.

August's discerning eye for creative detail is undeniable.

"Must be nice being a talented nepo baby," I whisper to myself.

Shuffling towards the safelight, I find more images, this time of familiar faces. Candid shots of heterochromia-eyed model Valentina de Hauretto and Japanese heiress Sakura Saito are captured, their tall figures juxtaposed against the backdrop of New York City streets. I recognise the latter from the articles I read about August's close-knit circle at MIDAS.

The next cluster of photos captures an event showcasing London's social scene with appearances by Alfie Dalton, a prominent British bachelor and who appears to be Romeo Conti, the eldest son of the renowned Casa de Conti fashion house in Italy. The assortment of images extends to include snapshots of various cuisines, some of which I recognise from Tito Boy's menu. There are even a couple of photos of Hero in his apartment in Chelsea.

A photo taken in a familiar-looking exhibition catches my eye. At first glance, the subject is unrecognisable. The image is slightly blurred and washed out due to the lighting. My eyes narrow at the girl with long wavy hair, standing next to a glass display wearing a distinct tweed suit. I pause for a moment before realising that the girl in the photo is *me*.

Although the image could have portrayed any visitor at the gallery showroom, specific details confirm its context for me. My large black portfolio and vintage suitcase along with the signature mess of wavy hair and my upcycled blazer co-ord adorned with heart-shaped patches on the sleeves, all serve as evidence that this photograph was taken a couple of months ago before my interview at Holmes.

I blink, reaching out to further inspect the image when I hear a voice call out behind me.

"What are you doing here?"

Caught off guard, I turn around and quickly apologise.

"The door was open," I reply, flustered. "I'm here for our update."

August's presence immediately registers beside me. Standing adjacent to his worktable, he places a small cardboard box of film rolls on the desk before he begins removing photographs from the wire.

"I sent you an email," I explain. "About the Comms meeting running late."

"I know," He responds, coolly. "To which I replied that we'll catch up tomorrow instead."

"You did?" I inwardly wince, completely forgetting to check. "Sorry, I didn't see that. I headed straight to your office after wrapping up with Ymir and Saoirse."

He lets out a low hum as he carries on with his work.

Curiosity gets the better of me as I watch him organise the film-developing tanks, chemical trays and various print processing solutions. There's a natural finesse to the way he moves around the studio that conveys his expertise as he does maintenance checks, inspecting equipment and properly calibrating them.

August is finishing up with clearing his workspace, picking up the stack of photos on the table and storing them in archival sleeves when he turns to me.

"Did you need anything?" His voice disrupts the quiet in the darkroom.

My gaze shifts to the photographs he bundled up, trying to catch a glimpse of the one of me for confirmation but it ends up being piled under the rest of the photos he developed.

"No," I shake my head, a little awkwardly. "But I just want to say thank you for, um, returning my lint roller. You didn't have to get me an electric one."

"Saves you carrying around your vintage one, you might end up losing

CHAPTER 14

it," He comments. "Or worse, letting someone borrow it and forgetting to give it back to you."

I shuffle awkwardly at the reminder of how last Friday night concluded. Gigi and I didn't end up eating at the restaurant. Instead, we had to leave straight after her phone call since she needed to do revisions on an article she was writing for MODUE.

I was glad we had to leave before I made the situation with August a lot worse.

"I want to apologise," I begin. "About the other night at Tito Boy's. I didn't mean to lash out."

August shrugs nonchalantly. "It wouldn't be the first time you badgered me at the restaurant."

Eyebrows furrowing, I tilt my head and blink in confusion. Our 'breakfast date', as Gigi calls it, was perfectly pleasant in my eyes. We got along like two needles in a pin cushion. In my years at Tito Boy's, I have never even so much raised my voice at–

"Sunnies?" I gape.

"Ah, so you are a little oblivious."

My eyes widen. "That was *you*?"

"I was supposed to meet Hero," He elaborates.

"He called in sick that morning."

I pause, remembering the chaos of four members of staff taking the day off due to a bug that was going around.

"I apologise for the verbal lashing out," I say quietly. "Both times."

He stills for a moment and I take the opportunity to continue my apology.

"And I'm also sorry for implying that you're, um, incompetent. Blatant nepotism aside, you're actually really good at your job. I wasn't trying to be... malicious about you or the situation at all." I frown, biting my lip. "I thought you were someone else and I was just..."

I pause. There's nothing more frustrating about not being able to express myself and articulate myself well enough.

"You were just..." he prompts, waiting for me to continue.

"Running my mouth whilst trying to process everything," I grimace. "All of this is still so new to me. Getting a job at Holmes, working as an intern, moving from Design to Comms. I know it might seem like a graceful strut on the catwalk for you but for me? I'm crawling on my hands and knees here."

He lets out an amused exhale. "Walking on the runway is *not* easy."

"My point still stands," I nervously fiddle with the film canister on the table. "I'm sorry."

"Better late than never, I suppose." He comments. "Apology accepted."

I raise an eyebrow at him. "That's what you wanted? An apology?"

August shrugs, casual and boyish, as he reaches towards me to retrieve a storage box from overhead. A fresh scent of something woody and citrusy filters through my senses, my nose twitching in appreciation as he continues organising the photos.

"I did try to apologise," I point out quietly. "Multiple attempts were made on my part."

"Wasn't the time nor the place," He says, expression unchanged.

I gaze up at August, noting the way his pupils have adjusted in the dimly lit room.

"When *did* you expect me to apologise then?"

"Over lunch, maybe?" He suggests, tilting his head. "Like the one you so graciously abandoned me at."

"What?"

"A little forewarning would have been nice, by the way." He states. "I sat in that café for almost an hour expecting you to come back. Ended up running late for the rest of my conference calls. Had to reschedule my meeting with Design."

My jaw drops.

"You agreed to lunch," He reminds me.

"Yes, but you— I mean—" I stammer. "You didn't say *anything*."

"You hardly gave me a chance," He counters. "And you seemed very adamant in avoiding me."

"Sorry, I was…" I trail off, unsure how to accurately convey my feelings. Stressed?

CHAPTER 14

Nervous?

Overwhelmed?

Any of those descriptors from a high-strung design intern trying to find her footing in the fast-paced fashion industry isn't likely to be well-received.

"I mean, you're…" I hesitate, struggling to find the right words.

"I'm…" He prompts, waiting for me to elaborate.

"*Intimidating.*"

"I'm intimidating?"

"Well, you're not exactly sunshine and rainbows," I mutter, my hands twitching to start fiddling with the canisters on the worktable again.

"Yes, I'm difficult to work with and *disproportionately hygienic*, I've been told."

His remark makes me visibly wince as I reply, "Sorry."

"While I'm likely more hygiene-conscious than the average man," He starts speaking, tone tinged with a hint of humour. "I'm not a full-blown hypochondriac. Despite the rumours swirling around the office."

I stand there, speechless.

"Your verbal lashing was justified," He says. "I'm sorry if I made you feel like I'm disregarding your work and your place in the industry."

There's a shift in August and he suddenly feels like he's Jean-Luc.

"I've seen your portfolio," He continues. "You're good at what you do, Mahalia. And other people know it too. So never let anyone tell you otherwise."

A warmth crawls up my neck at his praise and I'm grateful that the red light in the darkroom is concealing the blush on my cheeks.

"Do you prefer film over digital?" I ask, after a while.

I studied a module in Fashion Photography, spent an entire term behind a camera so I knew a thing or two about the genre and some technicalities of the medium.

"I think most photographers do," He responds.

"Oh?" I press further. "What's your reason?"

"My reason?"

"For preferring film over digital," I reply. "Every photographer has their deep, earth-shatteringly profound rationale behind their choice of style or method. At least, that's what my lecturer taught me at uni."

He releases a quiet, almost amused sound.

"Just personal preference," He answers. "Nothing deep. Or earth-shatteringly profound."

"Which is also the typical response from photographers who actually *do* have deep and earth-shatteringly profound reasons but they just don't want to disclose it," I remark with a knowing nod. "Another nugget from my lecturer."

He pauses for a moment, as if contemplating his next words.

"Film is timely." He settles.

"Timely?"

"Or rather, has a certain timeliness to it. And also timelessness."

"You sound like the beginning of a public speaking presentation," I muse, looking around the room and taking everything in. "Do you have a favourite camera?"

I gesture towards the devices hanging on the wall.

"Leica M6," He replies.

Picking up the rangefinder camera, he hands it to me, almost like a peace offering of sorts. Inspecting the camera and feeling the weight of it between my hands, I realise it's the same one he had with him on the day of my interview.

I look through the viewfinder even though it was impossible to see anything in the darkroom.

"I've never used a film camera before," I say.

Curiously, I fiddle with the dials on the top plate and on the back of the camera, running my thumbs over. I startle at the clicking noise, promptly handing the camera back to him.

"Sorry."

"It's empty, don't worry."

August lifts a knob on the side which opens the back cover.

"I know I'm still getting the hang of everything at Comms," I begin,

CHAPTER 14

clearing my throat. "But I'm committed to making sure that preparations for Men's Fashion Week are smooth sailing. I understand what it means for everyone here at Holmes."

August turns to me, gaze assessing.

"You're a glittering ball of tinkering talent." His mouth quirks up, just slightly. "I have no doubt you'll do just fine."

Chapter 15

Working a 9-5 job?

Hard.

Working a 9-5 job in fashion?

Even harder.

Working a 9-5 in fashion whilst simultaneously completing projects on the side?

The hardest.

And only getting four hours of sleep is the result of staying up late to finish the quilt for my grandma's birthday on a work night.

"I need you to go through the names and organise them accordingly." August's voice filters through my sleep-deprived brain. "Saoirse has the list of all the people attending. We need a spreadsheet of seating arrangements for the runway show as well as time slots for the presentations at the flagship store."

It's barely even lunchtime and I'm already on my fourth cup of coffee, struggling to keep my eyes open at my desk.

"I'd like it completed today," He adds. "Seat the guests based on their influence in the industry. There should be notes or highlights on the list differentiating them. Front row is reserved for our brand ambassadors as well as well-known industry figures with substantial social media followings."

I nod again, my mind drifting distractedly.

"Remember to seat prominent journalists from established publications on the front row for press coverage," August continues. "Similarly, well-

CHAPTER 15

known influencers and high-profile buyers should also be seated at the front."

Eyeing the cup of coffee August is drinking, I pull a face as he takes a sip. I can never take my coffee black. I need at least half a cup of milk and four teaspoons of sugar.

"Second and third row would be appropriate for lesser-known publications and individuals seeking press coverage– be it under a publication or their personal accounts or blogs."

Humming to myself, I nod in acknowledgement.

I decided I like August's voice. It's grounding and affirming with the ability to cut through mental fog.

"Mahalia," He addresses me firmly. "Are you even paying attention?"

There's a crease between his brows as he regards me with a puzzled expression and I have to fight the temptation to reach up and iron it out with my fingers.

"Of course," I respond with a slow nod. "Mr. August Vante, sir."

I punctuate my response with an overly exaggerated thumbs up, hoping to convey enough energy in his presence. Our professional rapport has been doing well so far and I'm determined not to ruin it.

August gives me a final onceover before leaving me to focus on the spreadsheets of names and continue with my tasks at hand.

I find myself in a peculiar state of being half-asleep and half-awake, time a seemingly nonexistent concept in my brain.

There's a nudge on my shoulder as someone calls out my name but my surroundings are a blur, colours fading in and out along with the soft echoes of voices.

Out of nowhere, my sleep-idled brain conjures up two distinct individuals and I frown.

August and Jean-Luc.

They're sitting side by side in a booth, chatting idly with each other as they have breakfast at Tito Boy's. My lint roller and his camera are placed in front of both of them and I stare at their figures, perplexed. One is dressed in athleisure whilst the other is dressed in formalwear.

Confusion persists as I blink, consciously aware they are one and the same person.

"Mahalia."

It's the same voice. Deep, familiar. But my dream self seems to be struggling to differentiate between them. Even if there shouldn't be a distinction.

Two pairs of eyes are blinking at me.

A set of steel grey, the other molten silver.

"August?"

"Mahalia."

The voice sounds nearer this time, less distant.

They turn towards me.

One with a scowl on his face whilst the other smiles softly at me.

"Jean-Luc?"

"Mahalia."

The scene fades to white and I jolt awake at the sound of my name. There's a hand on my shoulder, shaking it firmly.

"What— Uh—?"

The familiar sight of the Comms room appears in my line of vision as I push off my desk, jerking out of reflex. My chair wheels backwards, bumping into the body standing behind it and I wince apologetically.

"Why are you still here?" August's grey eyes are staring down at me and I glance around at the empty office, feeling disoriented.

"August?"

"It's 11 PM," He states, checking his watch to confirm the time.

"What?" I gasp, scrambling for my phone. "Oh my god, our daily update."

My phone displays 23:04 on the screen and I press my fingers to my eyes, realising I've fallen asleep.

"Nevermind that," He says. "I cancelled it anyway since I had a meeting with Grayson."

The information catches my attention amidst the mental fog. "As in *New York Grayson?*"

CHAPTER 15

He nods.

"How come?" I yawn.

"Why were you sleeping in the office?"

Slowly, I shrug. Even my shoulders feel heavy.

"I'm not sure," I reply, groggily. "I don't even remember falling asleep, if I'm being honest."

August looks uncharacteristically concerned as he stares at me.

"I finished the spreadsheets," I detail, now remembering how I opted to stay behind after work. "The seating plan for the runway. Presentation time slots. All done, boss. I've emailed it to you and CC'ed Ymir and Saoirse to be sure."

The weight of sleep is heavy around me and I press a hand to my mouth to stifle another yawn.

"If I didn't come back to the studio, you would have been locked in," August informs me sternly. "Security already left."

Curiosity gets the better of me, as is the case whenever it concerns him.

"What are *you* still doing here?" I ask.

"I needed to collect something from my office."

I assess August, two camera bags slung over his shoulder as well as a folder in his hand.

"You're so hardworking," I comment sleepily. "Best nepo baby boss ever."

Gravity pulls my head back down to the desk as my eyelids flutter close.

"Mahalia."

A steady hand presses against my forehead, preventing me from accidentally smacking my face on the desk.

"Yes?" I respond, voice muffled.

I shift my head, pressing my cheek against his palm subconsciously as my eyes close slowly.

"You're falling asleep," He tsks.

His fingers cradle the side of my face gently.

"Come on," He says, softer this time. "Time to go home."

"Okay," I hum, lazily pulling myself up.

August logs me out of the computer as I begin tidying my desk.

In my semi-somnolent state, I follow him out of the Comms room, apologising as I bump into him a few times.

Shifting weight between my feet, my body feels all too sluggish as I wait patiently for August to lock up outside of the building. My eyes droop heavily, watching as August scans his card and types in the security code before finally joining me on the pavement.

"See you tomorrow," I announce my goodbye as August taps away on his phone.

He raises a hand to stop me from walking.

"Where are you going?"

"To the station?"

"At this hour." He furrows his brows, lifting his gaze from his phone to meet my eyes.

"The tube's still running."

"It's late," He frowns, squinting at his phone. "It's dangerous travelling by yourself late at night."

I suppress a yawn. "It's not that late. I used to finish around midnight all the time when I worked at the restaurant."

"Oh? Were you also half-asleep?"

"Sometimes," I shrug in reply.

August lets out an exasperated sigh, tucking his phone back into the inside pocket of his blazer. "The taxi's one minute away. Just wait."

Blinking up at him, I find his grey eyes assessing me.

"You didn't have to get me a cab," I say, spotting a car approaching.

A London black cab stops in front of us and August reaches for the door handle.

"I didn't get it for *you*," He responds, opening the car door. "It's for *us*. Get in."

His tone left no room for argument and I follow his order, ducking inside the cab and sitting on the far side.

"45 Park Lane?" The driver inquires and I blink.

Of course, August would be staying in one of the most expensive hotel apartments in London.

CHAPTER 15

"Umm," I turn to August, suddenly unsure as he closes the door. "I live on the other side."

I inwardly wince at the possibility of inconveniencing both August and the driver for making a trip towards the opposite direction then back to Central London again.

"Just give him your address." He leans over to me to fasten my seatbelt and I'm momentarily struck by the smooth execution of the gesture.

He faces the driver without hesitation. "Just add it to the trip, please. And make it the first drop off."

"Of course." The driver nods.

"Leathermarket Court," I reply. "Near London Bridge station."

The ride to my flat is silent but I wasn't really expecting August to be making conversation.

Half-asleep and fully dazed, I rest my forehead against the cool glass of the window and watch the nighttime scenery. London at night is always pretty. The glow of the street lamps, the bustling city lights, the iconic landmarks illuminating against the night sky. Driving over Lambeth Bridge, I yawn quietly as I take in the stunning views of the city skyline.

"Should I be concerned about your lack of sleep?" August's voice cuts through the silence in the car.

I turn towards him, shaking my head. "It's not going to affect work, I promise."

The skepticism is evident on his face as he continues to watch me.

"I was working on a textile project last night," I explain.

August blinks.

"For Mahalia Made?"

"No, it was a gift," I answer, then further elaborate. "I was making a quilt for my grandma's birthday but I haven't had the time to put it together since I've been busy with work at Holmes— not that I'm implying that Holmes *isn't* a priority! It obviously is, considering it's taken up the entirety of my life. Not that I'm complaining about it either! I'm really grateful to be working at Holmes. The quilt is just a one-time thing and…"

My rambling gets even more jumbled in the drowsy fog of my half-conscious brain and I cringe at how unintelligible I'm expressing myself.

"I stayed up late last night to finish off the quilt so I can mail it to her in time," I say it one breath.

A silence follows in the car before August turns to face me.

"Can I see?" He asks after a while.

"See what?"

"The quilt."

"Oh," I unlock my phone and open my camera roll, handing it over to him. "Sure."

August swipes through the images, his eyes focused on the pictures as he zooms in and out on the quilt.

The patchwork project is something I've been working on since the beginning of the year for my grandma. Composed of earth-tone fat quarters, it features Baybayin, a Tagalog script from the Philippines, and traditional motifs inspired by nature in the islands stitched onto the fabric.

It's a labour of love for my Mama and losing sleep to complete is definitely worth it.

"You have a cat?"

August's mouth quirks slightly and I furrow my brows, peering over to look at the screen. A picture of me grinning at the camera as I hold Calix above my head to celebrate finishing the quilt pops up and I scramble to retrieve my phone.

"Ignore that." I flush in embarrassment. "Gigi took that photo."

He responds with a contemplative hum.

"I didn't know you own a cat."

"Calix was a stray," I begin. "He popped up randomly when I first started working at the restaurant. I used to feed him whenever he dropped by Tito Boy's but then he started coming in every day so I had to stop. He ended up following me to the flat one time and he hasn't left since."

I remember being so concerned, yet incredibly impressed, at how a tiny Calico cat managed to travel the underground without drawing attention to himself. Throughout the entire tube journey to my flat, I didn't even see Calix. It wasn't until I was outside of the gates of Leathermarket Court

CHAPTER 15

that I heard a tiny meowing.

"Did Hero know you were syphoning the restaurant's resources to feed a stray?" August tilts his head to the side.

"No!" I frown. "I never used the food at the restaurant, I brought my own."

He blinks. "You bought it cat food every day?"

"*Him*," I correct August. "I bought him *kitten* food."

August is staring at me now and I try not to fluster.

"There's a difference," I begin. "Calix was a baby at the time so I had to get him the right type of food to suit his needs. It had to be formulated for *kittens*, not *adult* cats. Higher in protein, fat content, essential nutrients for growth and development of younger cats, all that stuff."

"And you fed it—sorry, *him*— in the restaurant?"

"No, that's a workplace hygiene violation. " I scrunch my nose. "I fed him outside. He came round the back during my breaks."

Expecting to see a scowl on his face, I'm surprised to find the corner of his mouth twitching upwards.

"How long have you been working on the quilt?" He asks.

"Around a few months now," I reply. "It took a little over forty hours to complete."

"Everything was done by hand?"

I shake my head.

"The fat quarter pieces are machine-stitched but the script and the detailing are all hand-embroidered."

August blinks.

"Every single symbol?"

I nod. "Down to the last bead."

He looks genuinely surprised.

"That's really…"

"Time consuming? I know."

"I was going to say 'impressive.'"

"Oh," I blink. "Um, thank you."

A silence falls in the car but it's oddly comfortable. I glance over at

August and he looks peaceful, almost content. He looks different under the night lights, calmer and contemplative.

I look away before he catches me staring, turning back to the window and closing my eyes to rest.

"Mahalia." A voice pierces through my hazy state.

The sensation of fingers brushing against my forehead and my hair being gently swept away from my face rouses me to semi-consciousness.

"Mhm," I mumble tiredly.

Shifting my head, I subconsciously press my cheek against a palm out of familiarity, feeling the warmth too inviting.

"We're here." August clears his throat.

I blink groggily, recognising the entrance gate of Leathermarket Court as I look out of the car window.

Still in a state of semi-slumber, I move to unfasten my seatbelt but I overestimate my own mobility as my hair catches clumsily.

"Ow," I wince.

August shifts towards me, carefully releasing the seatbelt and adjusting it slowly to prevent it from further snagging my hair.

"Thank you," I murmur.

A woody, earthy scent mixed with something citrusy and almost spicy evades my senses as he leans towards me and I look up at him, taken aback by the sudden proximity between us.

"Start late tomorrow," He says, voice quiet and raspy. "No need to be at the studio until noon."

"Ymir and Saoirse—"

"I'll let them know." He clears his throat, reassuringly. "You can make up for the hours during the week. Just get proper rest tonight."

"But—"

"If it's really important, work on it from home." He offers as a compromise. "I don't want to see you physically present until after lunch."

"Rude," I mutter sleepily.

"Start at noon." His gaze carries an unspoken directive, leaving no room

CHAPTER 15

for me to question his decision.

"So demanding," I grumble, suppressing another yawn.

"12 PM, no earlier." He gives me a pointed look then adds gently, "Please."

"Okay." I nod tiredly, no energy left in me to argue.

Hopping out of the taxi, I quickly cross the road to the entrance of my apartment building. The car reversing as the window rolls down prompts me to look back, finding August's gaze fixed in my direction.

"I mean it, Mahalia." He says, expectantly. "Don't make me give you a disciplinary."

"*Yes, sir.*" I give him a half-hearted mock salute. "12 PM, no earlier."

The corner of his mouth twitches into a half smile. "Good."

"Umm," I begin. "Just let me know how much the cab is and we'll split?"

I feel a little awkward at my suggestion since it's probably pocket change for him but it feels rude not to offer since we both shared the taxi anyway.

August shakes his head, dismissing my offer as he starts rolling his window back up.

"Goodnight, Mahalia."

I offer a short wave goodbye before walking to the gate and entering the code on the intercom system. The iron fencing buzzes open but the car lingers by the road. Waving another goodbye, I start making my way inside my building. It's not until I've reached my flat and I look outside of the balcony that I see the black cab driving off.

Chapter 16

Encountering August nearly every hour of every day with his stoicism subtly shifting is a little startling. Ever since our shared journey in the cab, he's surprisingly become more lenient and tolerable in my presence. It's a change I didn't expect but a change I appreciate nonetheless.

It made traversing the torrential storm of task after task concerning Men's Fashion Week a lot more manageable because as the event draws closer, the more the workload is piling up.

And the more I'm hurtling around the office like a loose cannon.

"Christ," August grunts, steadying me as I end up barrelling towards him around the corner.

"Sorry!" I wince, keeping the folder I'm carrying close to my chest.

"You really are a tiny force to be reckoned with," He comments offhandedly. "Where are you off to in such a rush?"

"Back to Comms," I reply. "I just finished printing headshots of models."

I hold up the photo of Henry Atkinson, one of London's rising stars, next to my face.

"Isn't he dreamy?" I beam.

August blinks at me, unimpressed.

"He used to be in this spy show I watched growing up with Zander O'Hara," I continue, only to be met with silence. "You don't know *the* Zander O'Hara?"

"I didn't realise 'nepo babies' are your type," He tsks, disapprovingly.

I blink.

"Technically—"

CHAPTER 16

"*Everyone* is your type, I'm aware."

I'm about to retort when August diverts his attention to the folder I'm carrying.

"Why do we need more models? I thought we finalised the ones walking."

"For the catwalk," I reply. "Not the presentations."

Additional to Holmes' catwalk show, the five-day presentation of the collection during Men's Fashion Week required models in circulation throughout the day.

"Can we not use the same models?"

I shake my head. "They've already been booked for other shows in the week."

August and I fall into step with each other as we make our way to the Comms office. Inside, Ymir and Saoirse are trying to resolve the setback in the event.

"I've been trying to contact agencies in Paris and New York City," Ymir informs us.

"Some companies are a bit hesitant to work with us at the minute," Saoirse sighs.

No doubt the sinking reputation of the studio is enough to scare companies away and be reluctant to collaborate with us in any capacity.

"Have you tried agencies here in London?" August questions.

"I'm going through the list," Saoirse replies. "But it comes down to their willingness to work with us. We're not exactly in a position to impose conditions given our current circumstances."

Gathering around the table, they examine the list of different agencies: LDN Models, Heroine Management, Rouge Talent, Morena Management.

A thought strikes me, my mind flashing to an agency I'm familiar with.

"Wait," I interject. "I might know a modelling scout who can help."

August looks at me curiously before voicing my thought out loud. "SELDOM."

"Never heard of them," Ymir admits, her brows furrowed.

"They're not a big hotshot company," I explain. "But I know one of the talent recruits who work there, Chaewon."

"You think they'll have models for us?" Saoirse asks, uncertainty evident in her voice.

Before I can properly reassure them, August beats me to it.

"I've been in touch with them before," He says. "A friend of mine recommended them to me."

I blink, turning towards August.

Not a work colleague or acquaintance or associate or even an online mutual but *a friend.* I feel an odd fluttering in my stomach as August's gaze briefly meets mine.

"Would you be able to contact someone at the agency?" He asks.

I nod. "I'll give Chaewon a call."

"I'll draft the agreement," Ymir states.

"Guess it's another overtime for us this evening," Saoirse sighs, returning to her desk. "Late night takeaway and revising contracts, the ever so glamorous side of fashion."

Distractedly, I turn my attention to Saoirse who's calling my name.

"Food tonight?" She asks me. "Any suggestions?"

"We can have a mix of stuff," Ymir suggests. "I'm personally craving gyros."

"Ah, right." I make my way over to them. "I used to work in this restaurant in Kensington, Tito Boy's. They do Filipino food."

"Oooh, I've been wanting to try food from there." Saoirse acknowledges. "I heard it's good."

"Filipino and Greek it is." Ymir nods.

After contacting SELDOM, successfully securing the required number of models, reviewing their profiles and allocating the outfits for the presentation, we finally take a break.

Stretching my arms over my head, I lean back on the chair and let out a quiet yawn as Ymir and Saoirse both head out of the Comms room for a smoke. Squinting at the corner of the computer, I hum quietly at the time reading 8:18 PM before closing my eyes, thankful for a break after staring at screens for so long.

CHAPTER 16

"Don't tell me you're falling asleep again."

Immediately, I sit back up.

"I was just resting my eyes," I instantly reply.

Turning towards the voice, I find August hovering by the door.

"You're working overtime too?" I ask.

"I practically live in this studio," He responds, walking towards my desk. "I'm usually up in my office."

His gaze lands on the model portfolios spread across my worktable.

"Can you clear your desk?"

"Sorry, I know it's a mess but I swear it's organised chaos."

Gathering all the paperwork, I'm halfway through tidying when August places a brown paper bag on top of the space.

I blink, recognising the logo. "Tito Boy's?"

He opens the bag, the familiar waft of the restaurant reaching my nose.

"Aren't you hungry?" He asks.

Looking up at him, I nod.

"*Starving.*"

He begins taking out plastic containers from the bag, one by one. "I didn't know what you wanted so I just asked for one of everything."

My eyes widen. "There's over two dozen dishes on the menu."

"Is that a problem?" He meets my gaze, deep in thought. "I assumed they would have at least one of your favourites."

"They do," I blink at the *two* brown paper bags the size of a small cabin suitcase. "I didn't even know they did takeout bags that big."

"I dropped by earlier," August informs me. "Hinode was working."

As he continues to unpack the containers, I can't help but be surprised. Starters, main courses, desserts– every dish seems to be on my desk.

He ordered every single item on the menu.

"How are you going to eat all of this?" I ask.

"Me?" He frowns. "You mean us?"

I stare at him. "Even for four people, this is a lot."

"Four people?" He blinks, confused. "Oh, uhh, you can take some home. Share it with your flatmate."

Grateful, I nod. "Thank you."

A comfortable silence falls between us as August and I organise the containers on my desk, my mouth watering at the display of different dishes.

"This is equivalent to my grandma cooking for the weekend," I comment. "And she makes a lot."

Staring at the servings of food, I recall how my grandma would cook all my favourite meals whenever I visited over the holidays, realising all too sadly that it's been a while since I've had anything home-cooked from her. I reach for the already peeled quail eggs and pop one into my mouth.

"Did she receive her quilt?" August asks, starting conversation as he sits across the desk from me.

I nod, beaming. "She's over the moon."

"And did you also tell her you were practically a walking zombie after you lost sleep over it?" He looks at me pointedly.

Sheepishly, I shake my head. "She worries about me enough as it is."

"I hope you don't make a habit of it at Holmes."

"Of course not," I reply. "I mean, my work wasn't affected, I still managed to get everything done in time."

"And I appreciate that," He begins. "But I also appreciate the physical well-being of staff under my supervision. Overworking yourself to the point of exhaustion is not the feat you think it is, Mahalia Hartt."

I involuntarily wince at my full name.

"Now you sound like my grandpa," I comment, scrunching my nose.

August regards me for a moment, tilting his head to the side.

"You talk about them a lot," He observes. "Your grandparents."

"They're my biggest supporters," I say. "And they practically raised me, a little gremlin of a child that ran around with fabric shears and sewing needles."

A hint of curiosity dances in his expression.

"What about your parents?" He asks.

"They, um, passed away in a car crash," I answer. "Snowstorm."

"Oh," August pauses, his grey eyes flickering over me. "I'm sorry to hear

CHAPTER 16

that."

"It happened a long time ago," I clear my throat. "We were visiting Switzerland but I was a baby so I don't remember much of the accident."

August stays quiet, contemplating.

"It's not like I was missing parental figures in my life, you know?" I add. "My grandparents did a great job of stepping into the role as my surrogate parents. In fact, they *are* my parents. I've never had to think twice about that and I've never felt any differently about it either."

Although *family* is an entirely different topic, I'm grateful for my grandparents and their constant love and support for everything I do. I owe so much of myself to them and I would not be where I am today if it wasn't for my Mama and Papa.

"Do you visit them often?" August asks.

I press my lips together, feeling a sad smile take over my face.

"Not as much as I'd like to."

"How come?"

"Too busy, I guess?" I reply.

And scared.

I think to myself as I try to suppress the memory attempting to resurface in my mind. I should be over it by now, it's been years since the incident but I still feel the effects of it *slicing* through my skin.

My fingers spasm at the memory, my left hand itching.

"Why Menswear?"

The barrage of questions catches me off guard a little but August seems to be asking them out of genuine curiosity.

"It's the only place hiring," I say, half-joking but entirely serious.

The corner of August's mouth twitches upwards.

"I've seen your portfolio," He comments. "Your graduate showcase was *Disney Prince-inspired*. What made you specialise in Menswear?"

I pause for a moment.

"My grandma used to be a seamstress," I answer. "She worked at a men's tailor shop because none of the women's boutiques would hire her since they prioritised people with, let's just say, *lighter complexion*. It's where she met my grandpa. He would come in every week and request for her to repair and alter his clothes for him. It wasn't until they got together that my grandma found out that he used to purposely tear his clothes and would ask people he knew for any clothing that needed tailoring so he could come in and see her. He visited the tailor shop for years."

I smile at the memory of my grandma telling me the story when I was younger.

"When she retired, she still made clothes. Not officially or anything, it would just be for her boys. My grandpa, my dad, my uncles— she had five children."

August lets out a low whistle. "All boys?"

"All boys," I nod. "She would make clothes for the family when they couldn't afford it. It was all done out of love and, I don't know, I just really admired that about her."

The care in every thread, the love in every stitch.

It sounds like a terrible cliche but I couldn't help it. I've always looked up to my Mama in that way.

"I liked watching her on the old Singer," I say. "It was like magic."

There's a pause as August mulls over my words. He looks deep in thought as he assesses me and my cheeks heat up in embarrassment at my oversharing.

"Sorry, that was probably a long-winded answer." I laugh nervously.

August shakes his head. "Your answer was perfectly fine. There's no need to be doubtful of yourself."

I smile at him in thanks.

"Have you tried Womenswear?" He asks.

"I've applied for jobs," I smile tightly. "But it's so competitive, even more so than Menswear."

"Not for jobs. Have you considered starting your own line?" He questions. "I've seen some of your commissioned pieces on Mahalia Made."

Quietly, I let myself ponder.

Now *that* would be the dream. Starting my own fashion line, creating my own clothes, using my own patterns. Seeing my designs on the runway.

CHAPTER 16

"I think every designer's considered starting their own line." I shrug nonchalantly. "But I don't know whether I'm good enough for it yet."

I think of how difficult it is to exist in environments that aren't catered to people like me, how there's always been barriers in place unless you fit certain criteria and you're connected to the right people.

"What about you?" I clear my throat. "Has Grayson always been the goal?"

"Not Grayson." He shakes his head. "New York."

"Ah," I nod. "A place rather than a profession."

"You could say that." He shrugs. "It's always been New York."

I blink, tilting my head to the side.

"I figured that would be easy for you to do. Just get up and leave. You know, regardless of a job?"

August comes from money, after all. Not only that but also connection and reputation— the trifecta of success in the making, if one hasn't already made it, in the industry.

"I'd like something to keep me somewhere," He reveals. "When nothing keeps you grounded, you're just a floating mass of uncertainties. I need something tangible to tether me there, something guaranteed. Hence, Grayson."

My brows furrow. "The name Vante isn't enough?"

I think of the fashion empire that's been in his family for generations.

"I feel like it's too much, sometimes." He admits, quietly.

His voice is distant, despite sitting close to me.

A flicker of vulnerability flashes in his eyes before he clears his throat, changing the subject.

"You should be more confident in yourself. Those things you've got there?" He nods towards my hands. "Hands of the greats."

The compliment warms my heart, the genuine nature of it taking me by surprise.

"Exploding glitter also considered?" I laugh nervously.

"Yes, *Tinker-Talent*."

I wrinkle my nose at the nickname.

"Oh, would you prefer Glitter Gremlin, instead?" He fixes a sportive look at me. "Since everyone in this office seems so intent on giving each other questionable nicknames."

The reminder of the incident from his first day as DOC causes me to wince.

"I've already apologised for that." I jut my lip.

"Oh, have you?" He questions, tone lighthearted.

I narrow my eyes, looking through the box of scrap fabric I conveniently keep under my desk, bringing out a piece of eggshell-coloured lace fabric.

"This is my official declaration of a white flag." I wave the cloth back and forth.

August rifles through the paper bag on the table, pulling out a white napkin.

"We weren't exactly engaged in any type of warfare but…"

"Truce." I smile up at him.

"A ceasefire in a battle I didn't even realise I enlisted in."

He shakes his head, billowing the napkin side to side before reaching over the desk to grab a piece of lumpia. The spring roll breaks into two and ends up falling into the kare-kare sauce causing it to splatter on his clothes.

August curses, grabbing a handful of napkins.

"Dab, not rub!" I exclaim.

He pauses, blinking.

"And work inwards, otherwise the stain will spread," I add.

Reaching over to him, I take the napkin from his hand and gently pull on the fabric of his woollen turtleneck to assess the damage.

I glance up and meet his gaze, only to startle at our proximity.

"Sorry," I stammer, my heart rate suddenly picking up.

"It's alright." His voice lowers. "Continue."

I'm mildly conscious of how close we are, picking up on the faintest hint of sandalwood and a citrusy hint of bergamot. I can feel the heat of his palms as it hovers near mine.

"T-There," I finish nervously. "You might, um, want to let it soak in a

CHAPTER 16

mixture of water and bleach overnight to make sure the stain goes away. Kare-kare sauce is lethal."

I lift my head to meet his eyes, stepping back to create distance.

"You have…" August reaches over to brush his thumb against the corner of my mouth.

I tense involuntarily at the unexpected touch, my cheeks flushing.

"Sorry." He apologises this time.

"It's okay," I respond, slightly breathless. "Continue."

Something flickers in his gaze as my brain registers my own words and I startle, instinctively shuffling backwards as I wipe my mouth in embarrassment.

Outside, I hear the distant voices of Ymir and Saoirse in the corridor.

"Got the goods, boss!" Ymir announces, holding up a takeout bag as they enter the room.

"Ooooh! More food!!" Saoirse's face lights up, bounding over to the desk.

Ymir whistles. "That is *a lot* of food."

"It's like you ordered everything on the menu," Saoirse laughs.

I turn my attention towards August, the usually stoic expression back on his face.

"I'm going to clean this up." He signals towards the stain on his jumper before nodding towards Ymir and Saoirse. "Just send a message if there's anything anyone needs from me. I'll be in my office."

"Got it, boss." They chorus.

I manage a weak nod in his direction, trying to fight the flutter forming in my ribcage.

Chapter 17

The week leading up to Men's Fashion Week is probably one of the most stress-inducing experiences of my life. The pressure is palpable as everyone at Holmes worked tirelessly to make sure that the brand's debut collection, post-Vante's acquisition, is nothing short of perfect.

With the reputation and resources of the Parisian atelier, Holmes managed to secure a location for the event, disclosed only to the privileged who had invitations. For the runway, the show is being held at The Old Truman Brewery in Brick Lane, a rundown and edgy-looking building located in East London. It differs from Holmes' usual style but perfectly aligned with the collection's gritty and daring aesthetic for this season.

"Twenty minutes until showtime!" Ymir's voice echoes through the walkie-talkies.

Everyone is on edge, fully aware of the significance of the show. Darting towards the front-of-house where the rest of the Comms teams are currently situated, I hand the digital tablet containing all the guest names as well as a physical copy on a clipboard to Saoirse.

"I've verified all the photographers," I gesture towards the area of the runway where official photos are taken. "Front-row guests— press, buyers, and influencers— are all confirmed. Seating for frow should be full and standing should also be maximum capacity once we've sat everyone else."

Outside, attendees of the catwalk are forming a queue, eager to enter the venue and street-style photographers flock to take pictures of the social stars in attendance. It's a sea of bright spectacles and I revel in the well-put-together outfits of the people attending the show.

CHAPTER 17

Eden and Lara are taking photos for Holmes' social media account when a new wave of excitement garners my attention. A group of photographers rushing towards a black cab with the *London Fashion Week* label on the side pulls up just outside the venue and my eyes widen at who emerges from the vehicle.

Henrietta Goddard.

Dressed in a sumptuous and overly dramatic fur coat with a vibrant suit to match, I stare in awe at the Editor-in-Chief of MODUE Magazine making her way to the front of the queue. The cameras follow her movement, the flashes going wild as the photographers capture every action and every move.

In stark contrast, a modest yet stunningly dressed woman is tailing behind her. Head to toe in black, I instantly recognise her company as Tallulah Thao, a notable fashion critic known for her analytical op-eds. Tallulah's previous articles about Holmes and Sebastian's controversies were damaging to the brand's reputation but were, to some degree, a much-needed critique. I'm equally amazed to see her in attendance.

"Darlings." Henrietta greets us.

Saoirse engages in casual conversation with both Henrietta and Tallulah before they're escorted by Lara to their seats inside the venue. I'm in the middle of being briefed by Eden on the social media campaign that will follow after the show when we hear a commotion erupt amongst the photographers outside.

"Sebastian!"

"Over here, Seb!"

"Mr. Holmes!"

"Seb, this way!"

All at once, our heads turn sharply at the name being called out by the photographers outside of the venue.

"No way," Eden gapes as Saoirse's eyes widen.

A tall figure, dressed in a tailored-fit black brocade suit with golden detailing is none other than Sebastian Holmes— LIFT alumni, son of the late Sterling Holmes, and former Creative Director gone MIA.

"Ymir." Saoirse instantly wires up the walkie-talkie. "Code Herringbone."

A pause, then a crackle. *"What?"*

"Code. Herringbone."

"Sebastian's here?" Ymir sounds equally shocked. *"He RSVPed?"*

The disbelief in her voice had me scanning through the physical copy of the list of attendees on the clipboard and shaking my head frantically.

"He never came up," I comment.

I would know, of course. Considering I spent an entire day curating the guest list and seating arrangements for the show, I would recognise his name in an instant. I double-check for good measure, consulting the electronic tablet this time as my fingers scroll through the endless names.

"He's not on the list," Saoirse confirms for me with a sigh. "And it's very typical of him to turn up unannounced to these things."

"Talk about a clash on the catwalk," Eden mutters.

Ahead, we observe the flurry of activity around the resurrected senior designer. Cameras flash continuously as photographers swarm him, hollering his name left, right and centre before he begins to approach us.

"Eden, Saoirse." He nods.

With intense blue eyes and dark brown hair, he looks even more striking in person than in the pictures I've seen of him online.

"Sebastian," They greet him in unison.

"Long time no see," He acknowledges them with a surprisingly easygoing smile.

He turns his attention to me, regarding me with a puzzled look.

"Hallie." I nod, awkwardly extending my hand. "Design Intern."

His eyes flit over me for a brief moment before turning his attention back to Saoirse.

"Fantastic turnout, if I do say so myself." He comments, an edge to his voice.

An awkward pause follows as Sebastian stands in front of us and the cameras flash around him.

"Eden, could you show Sebastian to his seat?" Saoirse turns to her with a knowing look.

She forces a polite smile at him. "Of course."

I watch as Eden and Sebastian disappear inside, Saoirse groaning quietly as she rubs the side of her temple.

"August is not going to be happy."

From the corner of my eye, I see Pollux approaching us, slightly frenzied.

"We're missing models," He informs us.

The news prompts Saoirse and I to stare at each other, eyes widening.

"*What?*" I gaped.

Saoirse sighs. "How could we have possibly missed that?"

"They were at rehearsals yesterday," Pollux recalls with a loud exhale. "But they didn't turn up this morning."

"Which agency?" Saoirse asks.

"LDN Models."

Immediately, Saoirse bleeps Ymir on the walkie-talkies before we start making our way indoors. A long narrow runway stretches across the venue with rows of white rectangular boxes arranged on both sides. A modest backdrop with Holmes' logo is present at the back wall where the catwalk started and on the opposite end, the hub with the photographers and film crew.

"Code Runaway," Saoirse comments as we join Ymir by the photography hub.

Ymir turns towards me questioningly. "Were they double booked?"

"They shouldn't be," I answered. "I triple-checked with all the agencies."

I couldn't help but feel that the oversight was on my part, even though I knew I would flag something like this as soon as possible.

"Is it possible we make some models walk twice?" Saoirse turns to Estelle who's joined us.

"It is," She answers. "But we need to showcase the entire collection at the end."

We walked the distance from the entrance to backstage, perusing over the familiar faces already sitting in their seats and all mingling with each other inside the venue.

"Henrietta and Tallulah are sitting in the front row." Ymir tries not to grimace, plastering a smile as she waves at people she knows. "They're bound to pick up on it and probably mention it in the article."

Pollux joins us then, another stressed face added to the mix.

"Sebastian is sitting next to Tallulah." He winces. "Why is he sitting next to her?"

Our eyes find the designer perched next to the critic who looks less than pleased to be near each other.

Collectively, we're impossibly stressed.

I feel the familiar presence of August as he sidles up beside me, hand hovering behind my lower back.

"Are we good to go?" He asks, acknowledging everyone with a nod.

"We have runaway models," I comment, breaking the news to him.

"Literally," Pollux adds.

August's mask of stoicism remains on his face as Ymir and Saoirse update him on the news but I can tell by the slight tick of his jaw that he's not impressed.

"Have you contacted the agency?" He asks tersely.

Ymir nods. "Just tried. No answer."

All eyes turn to August as his intense gaze weighs in on the situation.

"Terminate their contract with Holmes," He says, conclusively. "Send them the email after the show."

I blink at his decisiveness, caught off guard by the abrupt nature of it all.

"August, you're going to have to walk," Estelle announces, her eyes scanning the people already sitting in the crowd. "Is that Henry?"

"Atkinson?"

I look to the front row and spot London's rising star in the model industry, Henry Atkinson, in conversation with a familiar head of strawberry blonde hair belonging to Valentina de Hauretto. Two other men accompany them, dark hair and dark eyes dressed smartly in suits.

"With the Contis too. Perfect." Estelle observes. "All four of you plus Valentina will walk."

"Alright," August agrees without hesitation.

CHAPTER 17

The show is scheduled to start in ten minutes, but with the mishap of missing models, there undoubtedly will be a delay. My eyes follow August as he strolls over to Valentina in true Parisian greeting, kissing both sides of her cheeks. He confers with the heirs of the Italian brand next, gesturing backstage.

Their gazes land on us and they all nod in understanding.

"Start seating the remaining guests," Estelle instructs. "Pollux, get them fitted."

"Got it," He replies.

"Hallie." Estelle takes the clipboard from me and passes it on to Saoirse. "Assist Pollux with the fittings. Someone from hair and makeup should still be backstage."

Nodding immediately, I follow Pollux as he begins to make his way towards the back.

"This is chaos," I murmur, loud enough for him to hear.

He replies with a chuckle, "Welcome to fashion week, baby."

Chapter 18

Backstage is awash with bright lights, rows of clothing racks and makeup stations now empty as all models stand in a queue, ready to step onto the runway. There's quiet murmuring amongst the models as the news of no-shows circulates in the line extending from the dressing rooms. Pollux and I immediately get to work, with no time for introductions and formalities as we dive into our tasks and start working to fit our last-minute models in their clothes.

"I'll handle Romeo, Mateo and August," Pollux instructs. "You fit Henry and Valentina."

I nod walking over to the clothing rack where the remainder of the garments are neatly hung.

"Who's closing?"

The estuary accent belonging to Henry Atkinson travels across the room and my gaze falls on the model card detailing the measurements.

"Valentina," Pollux answers.

I turn towards the eldest daughter of the iconic shoe designer. She's currently sat on one of the chairs, getting her makeup done.

"Is that okay?" I ask, willing myself not to look as starstruck as I feel in her presence.

She gives me a smile, wide and dazzling, and I feel my face flushing. "Of course."

"A woman closing a man's show," Henry chuckles before beginning to nonchalantly strip in front of everyone. "So progressive of Holmes."

The shirtless presence of London's It Boy would have had me blushing

CHAPTER 18

if it was in any other setting but I'm immediately in designer mode as I pick up the original model's outfit card in front of me.

"Come here often?" Henry attempts for an icebreaker.

"First time, actually," I reply, humouring him.

He grins, face breaking out into his signature smile.

Standing at 6ft1, Henry is tall and a little on the bulkier side than the slim physiques on the runway. I concentrate on pinning the garments down securely to his body, ensuring that the fabric drapes similarly to the original outfit as possible.

"You're a quiet one." Henry is watching me inquisitively. "And rather gentle."

"Oh," I laugh nervously. "This is my first time fitting models."

Though I'm more than a little nervous, I'm surprised at how steady my hands are as I continue to safely pin the denim-washed wide-leg trousers in place.

"Intern?" He asks and I respond with a small nod. "Glad to be your first." I smile up at him before grabbing the shirt and blazer from the hangers.

"The name's Hen," He winks as I stand in front of him. "Henry Atkinson."

"Hallie," I play along. "Mahalia Hartt."

"Beautiful name for a beautiful girl," He grins. "An absolute pleasure to be manhandled by you."

Across the room, someone is hollering and I glance up to find the younger-looking Conti snickering at the model.

"Keep it in your pants, Hen, you dog."

"Ignore Teo." Henry shakes his head. "I don't bite, I promise."

"Oh, that's a shame," I respond without thinking.

He pauses before flashing a grin and tapering off to a bashful chuckle.

"Wine and dine me first!" He exclaims. "Women these days, I swear."

Henry makes a show to act demure, covering himself dramatically and I couldn't help but laugh at his antics.

"Stay still!" I reprimand him lightly.

Working on fitting the upper part of the outfit, I adjust the fabric of the cropped blazer around him.

Henry reminded me a little bit of Hero, the same boisterous attitude sending me into a more relaxed state. But whereas Hero would rather drink bleach than attempt to flirt with me, Henry continues to throw lighthearted compliments my way. His easygoing attitude makes it near impossible for me to feel uncomfortable and I find myself oddly flattered by the attention.

"Okay, all done."

Tugging on the wide-leg trousers and the cropped blazer to ensure they're properly pinned, I give Henry a thumbs up.

"Thank you, gentle goddess." His eyes twinkle mischievously, clearly enjoying his theatrics. "Yours are the most tender hands I've ever had the pleasure of manhandling me."

I laugh, shaking my head. "You're welcome."

Stepping to the side, I gesture for him to join the queue of models backstage but Henry pulls back, turning towards me.

"Can I actually take you out for dinner?" He clears his throat.

The sudden seriousness in his tone paired with the hopeful look on his face catches me off guard and I feel my cheeks heat up at his forwardness.

"Oh, I—"

"Stop harassing my intern, Atkinson." August's voice rings across the room where he's having his makeup done.

Henry raises an eyebrow suggestively. "*Your* intern, huh?"

Sensing August's gaze, I steal a glance in his direction. Our eyes meet and, for a fleeting moment, he relaxes. His expression softens as he nods towards me in silent acknowledgement.

I nod back, managing a small smile.

"Yes, *my* intern." He asserts, his tone unwavering.

"My bad, Vante." Henry chuckles, holding up his hands in mock surrender. "Didn't realise you were this territorial."

With a wink, Henry joins the lineup of models. From the corner of my eye, I notice August narrowing his eyes, his gaze fixed intently on Henry.

"I sincerely hope you know what you're getting yourself into, should you take Atkinson up on his offer."

CHAPTER 18

"Mate, don't sabotage me!" Henry calls out.

August doesn't acknowledge Henry as he stands in front of me.

"Valentina's closing," He says. "Not that I don't think you'll do a good job but, best if Pollux handles the adjustments?"

I nod, agreeing with his suggestion. I'm already anxious enough and the final outfit is more elaborately constructed than the rest. I'm more than happy to let Pollux take over the final fit of the show. Noting the outfit combination for August, I retrieve the garments from the rack, grabbing the pins and the measuring tape.

August undressing shouldn't make me nervous but I find my heart rate picking up as he slowly removes his blazer and begins unbuttoning his shirt.

Trying to appear nonchalant, I focus on the fit and the details of the garment. Stealing a glance at August, I feel my cheeks flush at his deliberately slow pace of undress.

Professionalism, Hallie. I mentally scold myself. *Stop ogling your boss, Mahalia Hartt.*

August pauses midway from unbuckling his belt and looks up at me questioningly.

My eyes widen in realisation.

Did I just-?

The puzzled yet amused expression on his face confirms that I did indeed let that thought slip out of my mouth.

Mortified, I quickly avert my gaze.

"Do you know your measurements?" I stammer, attempting to regain my composure.

August is completely unfazed as he stands in front of me in nothing but his boxers.

Ever the professional.

"It's been a while since I did a fitting," He answers.

"That's fine." I work quickly with the tape, mindful of the ticking clock as I begin measuring him.

Chest, waist, hips, inseam. It feels oddly intimate, as though I shouldn't have such knowledge of my pseudo-boss in this way but I rid of the thoughts quickly as I focus.

Towering at 6ft2, August is lean and sculpted in all the right places. Broad shoulders, toned arms, well-defined six-pack. He stands still, eyes fixed on my hands as they work around the waistband of his boxers.

I keep my gaze focused and avoid eye contact, which isn't difficult considering August's tall height. Glancing up quickly, I measure the circumference of his abdomen, making sure not to stare at the sight of his chiselled torso.

He remains silent, his expression neutral.

Of course, it wouldn't affect him. He's a professional, he's used to this.

I double-check the photo of the fitting reference of the look on the original model before grabbing the correct runway garments on the clothing rack.

Masking an air of indifference, I kneel in front of him as he tries on the cargo trousers— long, well-defined legs disappearing inside the cotton-twill bottoms. My hands brush against the smooth expanse of his lower back to make sure the waistband is sitting in place when I feel him suddenly tense up.

He bucks forward unexpectedly and I let out a quiet squeak, feeling myself further flustering at his response. The movement causes me to lose balance and I shift forward, accidentally palming his crotch.

My eyes widen, looking up at him in mortification.

"S-sorry!"

August winces, eyebrows knotting as he shuffles backwards slightly.

"I'm so sorry, I didn't mean–"

"It's fine," He swallows thickly.

A warmth creeps up my neck as he looks away and the temperature in the room suddenly feels a lot warmer. I try not to dwell on how compromising our current positions look, refusing to look anywhere and at anyone else but August.

The cargo trousers hang slightly loose around his hips and I reach for the pins.

CHAPTER 18

"I need to secure the back in place." I stutter.

Rushing to get his fitting done as soon as possible, my index finger nicks on the safety pin and I wince at both the pressure of the prick and my skin being trapped on the fastener.

"Ow," I hiss quietly.

Out of habit, I instantly bring my finger to my lips, sucking on the wound as it draws blood.

"Are you okay?"

August promptly crouches down to my level in concern, the scent of his cologne, rich sandalwood with aromatic bergamot surrounding me.

Finger still in between my lips, his gaze drops down to my mouth and something flickers in his grey eyes. Releasing my finger, I bite my lip subconsciously as August reaches for my wrist.

Gently, he brings my left hand forward to inspect my finger. Though the bleeding stopped, a faint laceration marks my fingertip and I inwardly curse at my carelessness.

For a moment, he looks like he's going to press his lips to it, mouth hovering so close to my knuckles I can feel the slightest exhale of his breath.

August pauses, eyes squinting slightly before his thumb grazes the slightly puckered skin extending from my palm to the back of my hand. I hold my breath as he raises my arm to closely inspect a different injury and I almost forget where we are until the loud boom of music playing startles me to attention.

The show is about to start.

I quickly stand and pull him up with me, suddenly cautious of the outfit creasing. Standing behind him, I hurriedly pin the waistline of the cargo trousers in place.

"All d-done." I manage to say, heart hammering against my chest.

Slowly, August turns around before stepping back into my personal space. I look up at him and I almost feel my knees give under the intensity of his gaze until the frantic bustle of people rushing backstage breaks our charged moment.

"Is everyone ready?"

Chapter 19

The catwalk is a success.

With August walking after years of hiatus from the runway, Sebastian showing up in attendance after being MIA and New York City's It Girl closing, the show created a buzz and had everyone talking about Holmes' latest collection, post-Vante acquisition.

From the sidelines, the Comms team watched in bated breath for reactions from Henrietta but, most importantly, Tallulah Thao. Neither of them outwardly said anything about the collection itself but both did linger after the show to speak to August as well as Estelle and Pollux which everyone took as a good sign.

I didn't stick around at the venue. Mainly because I had work to do back in the office with the Social team but also at the fact that my head kept replaying the intimate moment between us.

"So, you're back to crushing on your photographer paramour," Gigi comments, her voice dripping with mischief. "What an unexpected turn of events."

She's comfortably seated in her usual spot by the dining table, working on fashion week articles for MODUE while I sit on the floor, makeup scattered all over the coffee table as I get ready for Holmes' celebratory dinner.

"Don't tell me you're suddenly warming up to the nepo baby again?" She teases.

I sigh quietly, choosing to say nothing.

"Mahalia Aurora Hartt." Gigi levels a pointed look at me.

"I don't–"

"You're a terrible liar," She cuts me off. "So don't even try."

"Just a tiny bit," I reluctantly admit. "Maybe."

The chances of August taking an actual interest towards me beyond a professional relationship are slim to none but I let myself indulge in the delusions.

"It's just a harmless crush," I say. "It's not like anything's going to happen. He's August Vante, for crying out loud."

"And you're Mahalia Hartt," Gigi shrugs nonchalantly. "A couple *tailored fit* to perfection, if I do say so myself."

Something tugs in my chest at the thought of August, the electrifying encounter from the fitting earlier replaying in my mind.

"I'm personally not a huge fan of portmanteau-ing first names together," Gigi muses. "I quite like VanteHartt. What do you think? Last names work, don't they?"

Her dark brown eyes glitter mischievously and I roll my own, opting to change the topic altogether.

"Are you attending any more shows this evening?" I ask her.

"Just a couple of off-schedule presentations," She replies. "Indie designers I want to interview for my blog. Their PR agencies sent me tickets last minute. Did you want to tag along after your dinner?"

I shake my head. "I don't know what time the event's going to finish."

"Are you excited?"

"Hardly." I bite my lip. "It's a little tense at the moment."

"I saw on social media that Sebastian attended," Gigi shares. "Sat front row next to *Tallulah Thao*, of all people?"

The bad blood between the fashion critic and the designer is another layer of drama I've yet to discover the full extent of. From the proverbial fashion grapevine, they don't have the best of relationships.

"Comms were hoping for Holmes to be in her good graces. Is there any chance you could convince her to write something positive about the collection?" I ask, a little sheepishly.

"The likelihood of that happening is zero," Gigi snorts. "Tallulah is

CHAPTER 19

immovable, everyone knows that. She's not called 'The Terror' for nothing."

I turn to Gigi questioningly. "Do you think Sebastian attending affected her judgement of the show?"

She pauses her typing. "I doubt Tallulah would let his presence influence her opinion. She works at MODUE for that reason, not Faux."

Though everyone at Holmes seems to be tight-lipped about the conflict between the two, I couldn't help but wonder what Gigi knows on her end since she's two degrees in separation from them both.

"By the way, does Sebastian attending the show mark his official return to Holmes?" Gigi turns to me.

"I have no idea," I admit. "No one in Comms knew he was going to attend in the first place so it's not even some power move at play on the studio's part. I don't think anyone has a clear grasp of the situation at the moment."

Getting up, I head towards my room to fetch the dress I'll be wearing for the company dinner.

"How did your photoparamour take it?" Gigi calls out.

"I didn't see them interact," I respond. "The only time I spoke to August was during the fitting."

"Oh yes, I completely forgot, you were copping a feel backstage."

"Gigi!" I poke my head out of my room in mortification, feeling my cheeks heat up.

She breaks into a fit of giggles. "I'm sure he was absolutely over the moon. Didn't you say he wanted *you* to fit *him*?"

"Oh my god, no." I groan. "I only said he swapped with Valentina. He was probably skeptical that I would mess up the final outfit somehow."

"Sounds like he wanted you to feel him up." Gigi shrugs.

"Trust me, he doesn't act any differently. He's the perfect picture of cool and composed." I mutter to myself. "Can you help?"

Walking over to her, I turn around so she can assist with the laces.

"I cannot believe you're finally wearing the Impossible Dress," Gigi beams excitedly. "I've been dying to see this stunner in action."

"I've only just finished it," I tell her. "Threading the glitter by hand took forever."

She regards the 1920s flapper-inspired glitter co-ord with a grin.

"You need to self-promote it," She suggests. "Loudly and proudly hit them with the 'Oh, this old thing?' 'Mahalia Hartt Original.'"

She pauses for dramatic effect before flicking her hair with theatrical flair and I giggle at her shenanigans.

"People might not appreciate me promoting a fashion brand that isn't, well, Holmes." I remind her pointedly, raising an eyebrow. "You know, the company I work for?"

"Mahalia isn't Menswear," Gigi nudges me. "This is the perfect opportunity. People always ask about outfits at events all the time."

I shake my head as Gigi helps me with the dress, taking nearly 20 minutes to lace up the co-ord pieces to turn it into one full halter neck dress.

"You look bejewelled," Gigi sighs, dreamily. "I will never tire of your sparkly creations."

"As long as biodegradable glitter exists, so do my glitter garment commissions."

"That's what I like to hear," Gigi beams. "Have fun at the dinner!"

The evening meal to celebrate the success of the catwalk show gathered the entire Holmes studio under one roof. Booked at a two-star Michelin restaurant, the Rose and Thyme is a contemporary British cuisine restaurant overlooking the London skyline.

After meeting Pollux outside of London Bridge station, we make our way inside The Shard where the restaurant is located to join Ymir and Saoirse who are in the middle of a conversation.

"I'm surprised nothing outrageous happened," Ymir comments with a sigh of relief. "I half-expected him to storm the runway and pull off some wild stunt, like a rabid fur protester."

"Glad I wasn't the only one who had that crippling fear." Saoirse grimaces.

"That would imply Sebastian actually standing up for something in Holmes." Pollux joins.

More and more people filter through the restaurant and everyone

CHAPTER 19

mingles as we wait to be seated by a staff member. I find myself scanning the area in search of August.

"Speak of the devil," Pollux remarks, his eyes trained on the door. "And he shall appear."

"Dressed to the nines too."

Our collective gaze falls on Sebastian entering the establishment. I couldn't help but draw parallels between him and August as he struts inside, greeting people in the room.

Both exuded an aura that made everyone glance their way. But where August commands attention with his presence, Sebastian demands it.

"I'm heading to the bar," Pollux announces, prompting everyone to laugh quietly.

"Order me two of whatever you're having," Ymir comments. "I'm going to the bathroom."

"I'll speak to the waiter about the tables." Saoirse nods. "Hallie, could you start gathering everyone in the lobby?"

"Of course," I reply, thankful I don't have to wait around.

If there's one thing my restless self often struggles with, it's being still and doing nothing. Guiding everyone to the lobby, I start doing a headcount of people, still waiting for August to appear.

My eyes scan the room, finding Sebastian standing by the rooftop overlooking the London skyline, a brooding expression on his face as he stares at the sun beginning to set.

Making my presence known, I clear my throat. "Hi."

For a moment, Sebastian pauses before he straightens himself up.

"Sebastian Holmes." He extends his hand.

"I know," I blink, confused. "We met earlier."

He regards me for a moment, mirroring the confusion on my face before realisation flashes in his eyes.

"Right!" He brushes it off with a low chuckle. "You're the Design Intern! Harriet? Hayley?"

"Hallie," I correct him, a little awkwardly. "Mahalia Hartt."

"Apologies." Sebastian studies me, eyes questioning. "I'm going to be honest with you, I wasn't entirely with it earlier attending the show."

"Everyone's gathering in the lobby to be seated," I gesture towards the congregation of people by the reception, all filtering to the entrance of the actual restaurant floor.

He nods, a terse pause settling between us before he speaks up.

"How are you finding Holmes so far?"

"Good, yes," I reply. "I'm, uhh, a huge fan of your work."

"You mean my father's?"

"Yours too," I say.

"Oh? Which one?" His tone suggests he's testing me, examining and seemingly prepared to challenge my response.

"Manic," I answer, honestly.

Sebastian blinks, unimpressed.

"Has nobody ever advised you against selecting the most recent collection?" He chuckles disappointingly. "That's an amateur's response. If you're aiming to impress people, choose a more cryptic line. Like the debut collection or something from a few years ago."

I frown at this.

"I wasn't seeking *your* approval for *my* answer."

Sebastian's voice takes a slightly condescending tone, as if lecturing a child as he responds in a deadpan manner. "The collection was unfinished."

"I thought it resonated with the theme," I reply.

Manic. Hysteria.

Holmes' most recent collection prior to the acquisition of the Parisian atelier was created during the most challenging aftermath of Sterling Holmes' passing. The death of the renowned British designer draped a dark veil over fashion. Holmes didn't showcase for two seasons and the hiatus was the start of the downfall of the brand.

Sebastian's own collection for Holmes would have been his debut in the fashion house. As the son of Sterling Holmes, he was anticipated to make an impact on the brand, only to fall short. His workplace habits were lamentable and his inability to meet deadlines made it impossible to work with him.

CHAPTER 19

To say the least, it wasn't well received by the press.

His eyes narrow. "My work isn't meant to be *performative*."

"I didn't mean to imply that it was," I respond quietly.

I need to stop running my mouth when it comes to conversations I clearly don't know how to navigate properly.

"I just thought it was fitting is all," I continue. "I can relate from a designer's perspective. You incorporate aspects of yourself into your collection a lot– whether physically or conceptually. Um, 'Oliver' for example."

Sebastian narrows his eyes at the mention of his middle name and mock-up collection at LIFT.

"A take on the 'in-between'. Your life in and out of Holmes. Both the celebration and the subversion of your name."

Another nepo baby who uses their middle name as an alternate identity flashes in my mind.

Sebastian blinks, studying me.

"I don't recall 'Oliver' being showcased to the public," He says.

"I studied at LIFT," I reply. "Your portfolio was the example used in most of our classes and our lecturers made your collection the main case study. You finished the year I started."

He regards me thoughtfully, blue eyes scanning my face and I try not to look uncomfortable at his overt staring.

"Where are you sitting?"

"I'm not sure yet," I respond, watching as Pollux approaches us, accompanied by Ymir and Saoirse.

Sebastian shifts his attention to the newly arrived members.

"Mind if I join you?" He asks.

Subtle looks of apprehension are exchanged between Pollux, Ymir and Saoirse.

"We thought you might want to sit with August and Valentina," Saoirse says.

She motions towards the duo currently being seated and I turn my head towards their direction.

Glancing over at August, I note the way his gaze flickers to meet mine before locking onto our group. Next to him, Valentina is chatting away with another person at their table.

"I don't think I'd be particularly welcome over there." Sebastian shakes his head. "What do you say? Pollux, old pal."

I stay silent, knowing I'm not in a position to make decisions for the group.

"Is there a spare seat on our table?" Pollux asks as Saoirse nods uncertainly.

"Perfect." Sebastian nods.

Judging by everyone's reactions, this isn't a regular occurrence. The atmosphere is stifling as we sit at our table, Sebastian situating himself between Pollux and I. There's an unspoken etiquette as everyone politely declines the drinks menu, likely due to a particular member's sobriety. Saoirse and Pollux exchanged wary glances as Ymir frustratingly kept reminding the different waiters tending to us that our table was abstaining from alcohol.

Throughout the evening, Sebastian maintains an air of cordiality, leading the conversation on multiple occasions as everyone responds— hesitantly but nonetheless.

We're all tiptoeing around each other, cautious not to step on any conversational landmines. I'm a passive participant at the table, with polite smiles and diplomatic replies, not fully engaging in dialogue lest I say the wrong thing.

Eventually, both Ymir and Saoirse excuse themselves to go to the restroom as Pollux mentions needing to speak with Estelle who's currently sitting over at August's table.

I sit idly, trying to think of something that will grant me a few minutes of breathing room away from the table when Sebastian speaks up.

"No need to fabricate an excuse, sweetheart." He turns to me, smiling ruefully. "Feel free to get up and leave."

Guiltily, I blink.

"I don't have anywhere else to be," I murmur, staying seated.

CHAPTER 19

Sebastian glances at me, a faraway expression on his face, and I fiddle with the glittery tassels of my outfit to keep my hands busy. Absentmindedly tugging on the metallic threads, I struggle to come up with a safe topic to discuss with him. I've learned through experience that spouting off nonsense to born-into-privilege individuals isn't the most ideal of social approaches.

"Did you make that?" He says out of nowhere, gesturing to my dress-imitating-co-ord.

"Oh, yes." I nod, then echoing Gigi's words from earlier. "It's a Mahalia Hartt Original."

In an attempt to alleviate the tension, I flick my hair behind my shoulder. I mentally cringe, regretting the action immediately but it earns a quiet chuckle from Sebastian.

"It's gorgeous," He acknowledges. "How long did it take you?"

Feeling that discussing design is a safe subject, I engage in the conversation.

"Around 120 plus hours?"

Sebastian blinks. "Holy shit."

"Threading the glitter and crafting the tassels took the most time," I explain. "I had to do it by hand."

"Jesus, my carpal tunnel would flare up." He shudders and I couldn't help but laugh lightly.

Staring at my left hand on my lap, I flex it open and close before tracing my thumb on the indentation on my palm.

"It only happened twice," I say, scrunching my nose. "Thankfully."

"Shit, you too?"

A louder chuckle escapes Sebastian this time which prompts the tables around us to glance in our direction.

"What kind of designer *doesn't* experience the phantom feeling of missing hands during their career?" I question quietly and he chuckles again.

"Very true." He nods.

His eyes skim over me, almost analytical, and I drum my fingers over my knees.

"When did you start working on the dress?"

"Last year," I answer. "It was a very lengthy work-in-progress. Carpal tunnel syndrome aside."

Sebastian takes a strand between his fingertips and pulls on it lightly.

"Very reminiscent of the flapper girl," He nods appreciatively. "The modern neckline adds an interesting touch."

Though a co-ord set, consisting of a crop top and a mini skirt, the tassels cascading to conceal my bare midriff and the elaborate lace-up detail at the back connect the two pieces, creating the illusion of a dress.

"This might sound a little inappropriate and you're by no means obligated to say yes but can I see the back?" He inquires. "From designer to designer."

"Oh," I blink, nodding. "Sure."

Twisting my body, I sweep my hair over my shoulder to reveal the back.

"Laced up too?" He blinks as I nod. "You have a lot of faith in these glitter strings holding the top together."

"As long as I don't make any sudden movements, it holds up," I comment.

"How long did it take you to get into the dress?"

"About 20 minutes," I respond, remembering Gigi and I's attempt to get me into the dress earlier.

"Wow." He whistles. "I wonder how long it'll take to get you out of it."

He says the comment in a way that is neither suggestive nor invasive, yet a warm flush creeps up my neck.

"Sorry, that came out wrong." Sebastian chuckles, noticing my reddening cheeks. "Function and practicality considered, of course. I was thinking like a designer, I promise you."

I laugh shyly, glancing around to avoid awkward eye contact.

My gaze falls on August across the room. He's staring in my direction, steely grey eyes narrowed and brows morphing in discontent. I didn't realise how fixated my attention was on him until Sebastian is withdrawing his hand from the curve between my neck and collarbone, having brushed my hair back behind my shoulder.

"Oh," I blink, the touch having barely registered, slightly discomforting that I didn't feel it at all. "Thanks."

CHAPTER 19

Glancing back towards August, I see him rising from his table, Valentina trailing behind him.

As the dinner concludes, members of the studio began saying their goodbyes to each other and slowly trickling out of the Rose and Thyme. After ensuring that everything is all in order at the restaurant, Pollux, Ymir, Saoirse and I are one of the last ones to leave the establishment.

"The dinner had no business being that painfully tense," Pollux remarks as we stand outside The Shard.

The air is refreshingly cool, a stark contrast to the warm and somewhat suffocating atmosphere inside the restaurant.

"I could sense the murderous tension between August and Sebastian and they weren't even on the same table." Saoirse shudders as Ymir laughs. "Who would've thought Sebastian would actually show up?"

"I think we're all just surprised that he's sober," Pollux comments. "Somewhat."

"Baby Vante was shooting daggers all night," Ymir observes. "He did not look happy with Sebastian gatecrashing dinner."

"We didn't even get to drink properly and enjoy it." Saoirse frowns, her face contorting into a pout.

"I was terrified of setting Sebastian off," Ymir admits.

I nod in agreement. "I think we all were."

"He didn't leave the table once," Pollux says, impressed. "For a man as restless as Sebastian, he sat on that table and played the role of the ideal fashion scion."

"What did you even talk about that kept him there?" Saoirse turns to me.

"Glitter." I scrunch my nose.

A chorus of laughter erupts in the group.

"Only you, Hallie." Ymir shakes her head with a smile.

"I mean," Saoirse starts. "The night is still young."

The three of them exchange knowing looks between each other and I squint my eyes suspiciously.

"Club?" Pollux questions the group.

"Club." Ymir confirms, nodding.

"Club!" Saoirse beams, dragging everyone to London Bridge station.

Chapter 20

The nightlife scene during fashion week is on an entirely unparalleled level of celebration. Every person I encounter seems to tower an entire head and a half taller than me with faces so stunningly symmetrical, I would have definitely felt more insecure about myself— had I not been four tequila shots, two jägerbombs, and a couple of rum and cokes into the partying.

Finally feeling like I can actually have fun out of work without the scrutinising gaze of certain nepo babies, I tag along with Pollux as Ymir and Saoirse's plus ones to an exclusive event in Onyx, a boujee bar and club in Shoreditch.

Typically, London nights out are abhorrently expensive. But London nights out during fashion week? Everything is free, if you know the right people. And I happen to know the right people (Pollux) who are the right people (Ymir and Saoirse).

As a result, I'm impulsively tossing back vodka shots in quick succession and senselessly careening around the dance floor to celebrate the success of Holmes' catwalk show.

"Bathroom!" Saoirse tugs on my arm as she yells over the heavy drum and bass blaring in the club, the music so loud I can feel it thrumming throughout my entire body.

Pollux nods as Ymir motions towards the other end of the dance floor.

"Yes!" My response is slow and slurred as I tail behind them.

An unexpected influx of bodies pushing past separates me from Ymir and Saoirse. Feeling the floor shifting under me, I trip over my own feet and accidentally collide with a stranger.

"Sorry!" The tassels of my co-ord-turned-dress catch on their watch as I attempt to steady myself.

"Mahalia?"

I blink at the familiar voice calling my name and I look up in confusion.

"August?" I hiccup, my eyes struggling to focus.

Onyx isn't the most well-lit of places, even with the heavy strobes of flashing lights, it was still hard to see. Dazed, I stare intently at the stranger in front of me bearing a striking resemblance to the 6ft2 nepo baby and I scrunch my nose in amusement.

"You look like my grumpy boss," I giggle drunkenly, inhibitions lowered by the alcohol.

August tugs away from me, inadvertently causing the threads to unravel from the back of my dress and I gasp at his attempt to detangle himself.

"Wait– don't!" Despite my inebriated state, I'm distinctly aware of my situation and I grab hold of his wrist.

The glitter tassels continue to loosen and, without thinking, I press myself against August to prevent his hands from further unravelling the top portion of my co-ord.

"What are you–"

"Sorry, I'm—!" I seem to lose all sensibility as the sensation of August's proximity overwhelms my already fuzzing senses.

Flashbacks of us backstage before the show earlier cross my mind and I swallow out of nervousness.

The ground beneath me feels even more unstable and I waver, struggling to hold myself up. Wrapping an arm across my chest, I notice the garment has significantly come undone from the back, leaving me to clumsily grasp the front portion in place.

"My dress," I mumble incoherently, pulling back slightly.

His brows furrow before his gaze travels the length of my body and his eyes widen in realisation.

August pulls me back towards him in a swift motion. The force catches me off guard and I let out a resounding 'umph' as he secures an arm around the upper half of my body to shield me.

"Shit— sorry." He mutters out an apology.

He relaxes his arm around me, shuffling us away from the inquisitive gazes of partygoers in the club.

"Are you drunk?"

Pulling back to look at my face, August carefully studies me and I shake my head, even though I am.

The last thing I want is to appear unprofessional by being a liability who's unable to handle alcohol in front of their boss. Despite the fact that I am indeed a lightweight and I may or may not struggle to hold my liquor when it comes to mixing drinks.

August regards me for a moment and I'm discernibly very aware of the warmth radiating from his palms as they rest against the uncovered skin of my lower back. He probably hates the glitter shedding from the tassels of the garment but I'm grateful his arms remain stationary to keep it in place.

The touch of his hands on my skin is strangely comforting and I feel a mixture of regret and satisfaction at my choice of outfit.

"Dress," I repeat, tugging on his arm whilst I press the unsecured piece of garment against my chest.

August stiffens for a moment and I wince apologetically.

"What?" He blinks down at me.

The floor seems to shift beneath my feet, the unsteadiness of my legs increasing.

"Retie it." I push against him, urgently.

"Which ones?" He sounds exasperated as he tugs on the tassels. In his defence, it's the 'Impossible Dress' and it lives up to its name of being ridiculously challenging to manage. "How?"

I rest my forehead defeatedly against his chest, my mind cloudy. Maybe I shouldn't make complicated dresses that lead me to even more complicated situations. The alcohol in my system isn't faring any better and I bury myself further into August, the resinous scent of sandalwood and citrusy note of bergamot filling my senses.

"Mahalia." His voice sounds gruff and distant.

"Hmm," I sigh contentedly, feeling the ground a little bit steadier as I level against his height.

Lifting my gaze, I see the doubling image of August noticeably swallow. I squint my eyes uncomfortably as they try to readjust, the liquor circulating in my system doing nothing to ease my distorting vision.

"Stay still," I frown. "You're making me dizzy."

Leaning back slightly, I reach up with both of my hands to steady his face, the multiplying vision of him causing my head to start pulsing.

A cool draft drifts across my front and August bristles.

"Fuck," He curses.

The resounding jeers and wolf-whistles around us earn a low, dangerous growl from him and I look behind to find a group of clubgoers clapping as they walk past us.

Immediately, a heavy fabric drapes over my shoulders and August guides me to a much quieter area, concealing us in the corner away from prying eyes.

"How much did you drink?" He questions me, his tone impatient.

Squinting up at him, I raise both of my hands to count the number of drinks and I blink. I've honestly lost count at this point and my own fingers seem to also be doubling.

August curses again as I accidentally drop the top section of the co-ord.

It might be the alcohol but the sound of August swearing is oddly amusing. I giggle quietly to myself, bowing my head against his chest.

"Oops," I laugh.

I'm not in the right conscious mind to feel embarrassed, finding the entire situation too entertaining in my drunken state.

"Mahalia," He warns and I purse my lips.

He quickly bends down to pick up the flimsy garment, tucking it in the pocket of the blazer before tugging said blazer close.

"Arms through the sleeves."

I pout in annoyance, simple instructions going over my head completely.

"Who did you come with?" he asks.

CHAPTER 20

"Pollux," I answer. "Ymir and Saoirse."

"And where are they?"

"Bathroom."

"Do they know where you are?"

My headache intensifies at his relentless interrogation and I shrug, blazer shuffling slightly. August jerks forward to cover up the front, buttoning it this time.

"Arms through the sleeves," He repeats, gritting his teeth.

He looks irritated. Offended, almost. I find myself disliking the fact that I'm at the receiving end of his foul mood. The incident backstage before the show was complicated enough, the dinner earlier didn't help the situation. Why does he have to give me the cold shoulder in the club as well?

We were doing so well. I think miserably. *We were getting along.*

I angle myself away from him, stumbling as I begin walking in the opposite direction.

"Where are you going?"

"Elsewhere," I wave him away dismissively, tripping haphazardly over my heels and bumping into a bystander. "Sorry!"

Hauretto high heels are stunning but they're practically a death trap when worn by an intoxicated individual.

Namely, myself.

"Mahalia." August's voice is surprisingly audible over the music and I turn sharply, almost falling to my feet again.

This time, he catches me and pulls me to him.

"What?" I huff in annoyance.

I'm already struggling enough to keep myself upright. Continuing to have a conversation with someone who looks less than pleased to be in my presence is not something my tipsy self can tolerate.

"You're drunk," He states, begrudgingly.

I narrow my eyes at the surly expression on his face.

"I am not."

The frown on his face further deepens and I reach up to smooth out the scowl between his eyebrows. His gaze falls to the opening of the blazer and he lets out a disgruntled noise before grabbing my arms and pinning it behind my back.

The action catches me off guard and my breath knocks out of my lungs. Even though my front is pressed up and hidden against him, I feel a lot more exposed than I was before.

"Stop moving so much." The authoritative tone in his voice makes me pause and I'm abruptly cognisant of our extremely close proximity, even in my state of inebriation.

"Sorry," I withdraw meekly, my awareness acutely returning.

His grip on my arms loosens and his hands travel down to my waist, slipping under the blazer.

"Arms through the sleeves," He grouses.

I'm now fully aware that underneath the garment, I'm technically half-nude. The top counterpart of my co-ord is tucked in the pocket of his blazer and whilst the bottom piece is still intact, I can feel it gradually sliding down from my waist, and I know it won't be long until it follows.

Wardrobe malfunctions are not fun.

"August," I murmur, barely hearing myself over the discord of noises around us.

His hands fall on my waist, fingers ghosting the bare surface of my skin and the touch is timid, as if asking for permission.

The grey in August's eyes is visibly a lot darker. Even under the dim lights at the club, I can see how dilated his pupils have become. His gaze falls on my lips, the tiniest hint of his tongue peeking out to swipe his bottom lip and something inside me *snaps*.

A sudden urge, primal and almost blazing, rushes through me and I impulsively push forward, standing on my tiptoes as I press my lips against his.

Soft. Warm.

Characteristically *unlike* August.

The electrifying current that sears the entirety of my body is enough to physically startle me and I part from him almost instantly.

CHAPTER 20

The music in the club is loud but my heartbeat ringing in my own ears is even louder. There's a pause between us, both of us shocked into silence at my bold action.

August is staring at me, wide-eyed, a hint of something unrecognisable flashing across his features. My eyes mirror his, my jaw dropping as I realise the situation.

"I am so–"

The apology doesn't make it past my lips as he surges forward, crushing his mouth against mine.

All at once, August is *everywhere*.

A hand grasping the back of my neck, the other trailing under the blazer, touching my bare skin. The kiss is permission as he brings me closer to him, his tall figure caging around me.

His normally level-headed composure vanishes and suddenly he's unrestrained, coaxing me into his mouth as his hands roam with reckless abandon.

Reaching up to tangle my fingers in his hair, I bite his bottom lip as he begins to pull away, dragging him back towards me with open-mouthed kisses. August groans, hands moving to grip my waist as he pushes me up against the wall. The moan that involuntarily leaves my lips as I press against him douses him into reality and he pulls away to look at me.

It's the first time I see August's eyes borderline black, the usual grey of his irises almost non-existent, and heat prickles my skin.

Suddenly, I'm aware of everything, every single one of my senses heightening astronomically.

"Shit," He pants, voice ragged. "You're drunk."

"I'm not," I whisper shakily.

Even though, yes, I'm 100% drunk.

But I'm absolutely thinking straight.

His breathing is heavy as he closes his eyes and presses his forehead against mine.

I want to kiss him, my entire body urging to draw towards him again, but the unreadable expression on his face stops me.

"Fuck." There's a sense of hesitation in his voice and my chest tightens at the implication of it. "I shouldn't have."

August recoils, avoiding my gaze and I find myself being submerged by an engulfing wave of rejection.

"Oh." My fingers twitch as I untangle them from his hair, my stomach tying in knots. "S-sorry."

I turn my head, eyes casting downwards as I step away from August. The stinging sensation in my chest intensifies as the feeling of shame creeps in.

"Don't you dare," He grabs my arm gently before I can walk away, enclosing me against the wall again. "Mahalia, don't do that."

My name shouldn't sound so heavenly from his lips, given how sinful his mouth can be.

"Do w-what?" I stammer, nervously.

"Look at me like that."

The sound of August's voice, low and scratchy, sends butterflies in my stomach. He leans down to run the tip of his nose along my jaw before peppering soft kisses on my neck.

"I won't be able to stop myself," He murmurs.

He leans back, eyes hooded and lips swollen and I reach for him almost instantly, winding my arms around his neck.

"Mahalia," He husks, voice pained but firm, as he keeps me fixated between his arms. "No."

"O-okay." I choke back a heavy swallow. "I'm sorry. I-I thought–"

To be quite honest, I don't know what I thought. I don't know what I'm thinking at all. A million different things are currently running through my head and they're all to do with August.

The conflicted look on his face pricks at my heart like a needle and I blink back the tears blurring my vision.

"I'll just–" I turn away from him defeatedly, shifting to create some distance from where he's cornered me against the wall.

"No," He grunts, keeping me in place. "You're drunk. We're not doing this when you can't even think straight."

"I'm thinking straight," I argue breathlessly.

CHAPTER 20

All day I've been thinking about you.

"Mahalia." His voice is shaky, akin to a plea.

"August." I mirror him.

His gaze flickers between my eyes before they land on my lips. "God, please don't say my name like that."

August's thumb trails the bottom of my lips and I part them slowly, my tongue rolling out subconsciously to draw the slender digit into my mouth.

"Fuck," He rasps, grey eyes wide and in a trance-like state as I release him from my lips.

There's a brief pause before his head falls on the crook of my neck and he nuzzles into me, teeth grazing over my erratic pulse.

"Please."

I couldn't identify whether the request came from me or August. My mind is overwhelmed and my body overheating at the sensation of being around him.

August draws back but his hands remain firmly on top of the garment covering my hips, fingers careful not to touch any part of my exposed skin this time. I stand unmoving, feeling my resolve slipping. The scent of him around me, the feel of him on my skin, the taste of him on my tongue.

It's all too much yet not nearly enough at the same time.

August meets my gaze and I hold it, determined. He's tugging me towards him and leaning back in when a sudden, hurtling sensation in my stomach starts making its way up my throat.

Panic rises in me as I push past August and dart away immediately. Even I'm impressed with how quickly I make it to the bathroom, in high heels no less, as I keel over the porcelain bowl.

My dinner from the Rose and Thyme is completely unrecognisable as I violently vomit it back out in the toilet. The undeniable pounding in my head and the burning sensation in my throat are grim reminders of overindulging in shots and excessively mixing one too many drinks.

Sitting on the floor of the cubicle, I lose track of time in the bathroom as I purge out the contents of my stomach.

"Oh my god, Hallie!"

A voice that sounds recognisably like Saoirse's echoes within the stall and I look up to find bleach blonde hair and pretty blue eyes staring at me.

"We've been looking everywhere for you." I turn my head to find Ymir crouching down next to me as she holds my hair away from my face.

"Are you okay? Did you get everything out?" Saoirse asks as I nod, still feeling uneasy even after expelling my guts.

"That is a surprisingly great shade of orange," Ymir comments casually and I can't help but find it slightly comical at how unfazed she is.

This must be a regular occurrence for everyone.

"We nearly had an aneurysm searching the club for you. You were gone for nearly an hour," Saoirse adds, sitting down next to me. "Do you need any—"

"Whose is that?" Ymir's voice cuts through Saoirse's questioning and I look down at the expensive-looking blazer I'm wearing, thankfully untouched by my gastro-reflux.

August.

The situation sobers me up, embarrassment crashing down on me almost instantly.

"Oh god."

Unsteadily, I rise to my feet with both Ymir and Saoirse's assistance. Hobbling over to the sinks, I cringe at my dishevelled reflection in the mirror. Wild, unruly hair and smeared makeup courtesy of a certain platinum blond.

In an effort to keep the whirlwind of emotions under control, I exit the bathroom to find Pollux standing outside waiting for us.

"Oh thank god." He rushes to me, eyes scanning for any signs of injury. "You're alive."

"I had to tactical chunder," I answer grimly, glancing around for August but he's nowhere to be seen.

"You will never guess who I saw loitering around the women's bathroom," Pollux snickers. "A certain nepo baby of ours looked like he had a raunchy rendezvous in the club. He had *lipstick stains* all over his–"

He stops abruptly, catching sight of me in the light as I'm wiping the

CHAPTER 20

smears of lipstick from my mouth.

"What is it?" The feeling of nauseousness is still vaguely present in my system, despite having just emptied my stomach.

Pollux's eyes widen. "No way."

I blink at him. "What?"

"You and Baby Vante?"

It takes me a moment to figure out what Pollux is implying, hands wildly gesturing at my face.

Note to self: invest in smudge-proof makeup.

Without delay, I begin to shake my head. "It's not what it looks like–"

"You're wearing his *blazer*," Ymir interrupts me.

Saoirse blinks, almost in awe. "You're *wearing* his blazer."

There's a beat before Pollux's mouth dramatically hangs wide open in realisation.

"*You're wearing his blazer.*" He bounces around me enthusiastically. "That's essentially him asserting ownership."

I pull a face, shaking my head incredulously. "I don't think that's how it–"

My words are cut short as my stomach protests, prompting me to make another frantic sprint towards the bathroom.

Chapter 21

The whirring sound of the coffee machine is what stirs me into consciousness. There's a soft throbbing in between my eyes and I groan, feeling the ache stretch all the way to the back of my head.

Slowly, I open my eyes.

"Good morning, sunshine." Gigi choruses as she waltzes into the living room, drawing the blinds apart and flooding the room with sunlight.

The unexpected brightness makes me wince, my eyes squinting at the clock on the wall.

07:09 AM.

"God, I feel awful." I groan, dragging a pillow over my face.

My voice is hoarse, my tongue heavy in my mouth.

"I'm surprised you made it back in one piece. You were pretty out of it last night," Gigi comments. "How was dinner?"

Sluggishly, I sit up, swinging my legs over the side of the sofa bed. It takes me a moment to ground myself, despite my bare feet brushing against the cool wooden floor.

"Tense," I answer. "Sebastian was there."

"Did Rose and Thyme set on fire?"

Recollections of the previous night float back into my head, fragmented and blurred, as I rub the sleep from my eyes.

Visions of platinum blond and steely grey pop into my memories, a wave of realisation washing over me as I gasp loudly.

"I kissed him."

Gigi blinks, her expression morphing into mortification. "Sebastian?"

CHAPTER 21

"No," I grimace, shaking my head. "August."

Her jaw drops in shock. "No way."

The overwhelming realisation pulls me under this time as the memories replay much more vividly in my head.

I didn't even make it to the bathroom, immediately throwing up all over the floor by the bar and being kicked out soon after. Everyone else was gracious enough to leave the club with me but I felt bad at having to cut the evening short and I wince at potentially being blacklisted at Onyx.

The thought of my face being plastered across tabloids and gossip columns makes my stomach lurch. I'm already anticipating the stern lecture I know I'm bound to receive from August because what happened last night crossed so many lines and stepped over so many boundaries.

"Wait." Gigi eyes me up and down. "Did you go home with him?"

"Of course not!" I sputter. "He's my *boss*, Gigi."

She laughs sheepishly. "You didn't get back until this morning, I thought you would have walk-of-shamed your way out of his penthouse apartment or something."

I try not to blush, feeling the heat creeping up my neck.

"Although, it would have been interesting to know how long it would have taken him to get you out of the Impossible Dress," She giggles.

"Oh my god, my dress." I groan, cursing what started everything off.

I scramble up, eyes scanning around the living room to find my dress on the armchair.

"I'm assuming that belongs to August?" She points towards the navy blazer next to the dress. "I swear you're stockpiling his clothes like you're making a collection."

Clumsily, I collapse onto the bed as my mind struggles to recount every detail from last night.

"I think this is it. I'm going to lose my job." I drag the pillow over my face to muffle a quiet scream.

"You're catastrophising." She tugs the pillow away from my face. "Hals, if August dislikes you as you claim he does, he would have fired you a long time ago. Not necked you off in the dark and questionable recesses of

Onyx."

"What am I doing with my life?" My voice is muffled as I bring the pillow back over to my face.

"Schedule your existential crisis for later," She laughs lightly. "Don't you have the Holmes presentation today at Regent Street?"

Rolling over to my side, I hug the pillow to my chest, wanting nothing more than to crawl back under the duvet covers.

"Yes." I sigh.

The flagship store in Regent Street is buzzing with excitement as the presentation of Holmes' latest collection is showcased throughout the day. Attendees of the event freely mingled around the open space, their attention drawn to the models wearing the garments. It differed from the usual hecticness of a catwalk, the presentation allowing the guests to admire the clothing up close instead of the fleeting performance of the runway.

My job for the day is relatively straightforward. Distribute the press releases to attendees, make sure that everyone adheres to their designated time slots and keep track of all the glass champagne flutes being given out throughout the day. It didn't take a lot out of me which my lingering hangover is grateful for.

I'm standing passively at the back of the store after finishing another round of press releases, clipboard in hand, when a flash of platinum catches my attention.

Standing by the entrance and making idle conversation with guests is August, looking effortlessly dressed in a casual suit.

My heart stumbles at the sight of him.

He isn't intentionally avoiding me but I can sense his reluctance to engage in conversation as he mingled with the other guests. He'd been present in the store since the presentations started and we'd awkwardly skirted around each other all morning.

Our eyes meet again and his gaze lingers longer than usual.

Taking this as a sign, I summon all my courage and take a deep breath as

CHAPTER 21

I begin making my way towards August.

He glances in my direction as I approach him, eyes flitting quickly to look me up and down. I see the faintest hint of apprehension before it hardens over.

"August," I call his name out quietly. "Are you free to talk?"

He hesitates for a moment, gaze flickering, and I nervously fidget with the clipboard.

"Snaps!"

A bright and cheery voice bounces off the walls of the store and a cluster of heads turn towards the sound. A woman with dark brown eyes and sleek black hair cascading down to her waist approaches August and I.

"Sakura?" August blinks, clearly surprised to see her.

"In the flesh."

Sakura Saito is the youngest of five, the only daughter of one of the most renowned jewellers in Japan. I stare at the Japanese heiress, stunned by the dimples adorning her symmetrical facial features.

"What are you doing here?" August asks.

"Your beloved *girlfriend* was the one that dragged me out," Sakura replies, nodding towards Valentina.

Smiling brightly, the heterochromia-eyed model approaches us with a shy expression on her face.

My breath catches in my throat as I glance at August.

Girlfriend.

Valentina laughs then, her tone light.

"We wanted to show our support, silly."

It dawns on me.

His hesitation. The avoidance, the conflicted look in his eyes. Last night's event is a hazy blur and I can barely recall what he said to me but I do remember his *refusal*.

"Mahalia." A pause. "No."

August didn't mention *having* a girlfriend. But he didn't mention *not having* one either.

My mind flashes back to the day of my interview at the gallery showroom

191

at Holmes, his casual comments about Valentina. August doesn't strike me as the kind of person to openly discuss his personal life with strangers. So understandably, he would keep certain aspects of his life a secret.

Of course, *the* August Vante would have a girlfriend.

And of course, it would be *Valentina de Hauretto*.

"Sakura and I studied photography in MIDAS," August begins to explain.

"I majored in Business and did my minor in Photography," Sakura nods, glancing over at me. "The opposite of Snaps here."

"We were in the same academic year," August continues but his words barely register in my brain.

My head suddenly feels all too light whilst my chest feels heavy as I grapple with the fact that I kissed August when he's involved with Valentina.

"You should see his work!" Sakura nudges August playfully. "He's good in front *and* behind the camera."

My stomach lurches as I nod robotically, not entirely sure how to navigate the conversation.

"She already has," August adds, clearing his throat.

Everyone's gaze falls on me.

"Oh?" Valentina and Sakura chorus.

Their attention shifts to August, expressions carrying a mix of surprise and curiosity before their gaze lands on me again.

"Just... some cityscapes of New York and London," I reply, delicately. "Some portrait work too, you both looked stunning in the black and white photoshoot."

I turn towards Valentina who flashes me a warm smile, my hands twitching anxiously.

"You're so sweet, thank you." She grins and I almost want to cry at how genuine she is. "That shoot is one of my all-time favourites."

Sakura watches me intently, her gaze flickering between August and I.

"So you've seen both past *and* present work," She deduces. "Interesting."

I try not to panic, stealing a glance at August and wondering if I've said the wrong thing.

CHAPTER 21

"Mahalia, isn't it?" Valentina acknowledges me, her smile unwavering. "You were backstage at the Holmes show. I saw you at the dinner."

I nod, my throat tight. "Hallie."

"She's one of our designers," August adds.

Sakura is still watching me, eyes assessing. "Vante?"

"Holmes," I reply. "I'm a Design Intern."

"You've worked with Sebastian?" She asks.

I shake my head. "I only started last month. I'm helping out with the Comms side of things at the moment."

"So you're working with August," She muses, directing her gaze towards him.

Sakura gives him a knowing look which August returns with a hardened gaze. Valentina is nothing but polite, including me in conversation as the three of them chat like old friends. It's stifling as I stand by, feeling like a spectator in a situation that I don't fully comprehend.

"Oh, Lulu's here!" Sakura points out excitedly, tugging on Valentina's arm. "Babe, let's go."

"That woman has been *impossible* to reach lately," Valentina adds.

She leans over to August, her voice low as she whispers something and I avert my gaze, feeling the jagged realisation prick itself further in my stomach. It takes them more than an instance to break apart and I do my best not to intrude in their intimate moment.

"Vee!"

Sakura marches back over, dragging Valentina to where the fashion critic is currently in conversation with another familiar face belonging to the heir of the Italian fashion house.

Dazed, I turn towards August.

"Mahalia, last night–" he begins.

"I didn't know, I swear." I rush to interject, my voice betraying my distress. "If I did, I wouldn't have– I didn't mean– I'm so sorry."

God. I'm such an idiot.

My mind races, each thought vying for attention as I consider the possible ramifications of my actions.

August looks puzzled, eyebrows knotting as he opens his mouth to speak but I cut him off, my words tumbling out.

"I'm not that kind of person. I-I know it's my fault and I take full responsibility for initiating the kiss but I swear I didn't know," I continue. "I don't want any trouble, August. It won't happen again. I'm not... The last thing I want is to cause any problems. I won't— I'll stay out of your way, I promise."

The expression on August's face morphs into confusion and concern.

"What are you—"

"Hallie, can you come help in the back?" Ymir's voice crackles through the walkie-talkie and I'm thankful for the diversion.

"I really am sorry, August." I swallow, feeling my chest tighten even more.

Without hesitating, I dash towards the back office of the store.

Chapter 22

Guilt and rejection are the two worst feelings combined but I somehow manage to compartmentalise my feelings, knowing that I still had work to do at Men's Fashion Week and last-minute events to attend to.

Namely, the after-party hosted by MODUE Magazine to conclude London Fashion Week.

Gigi managed to secure an invite for me as her plus one, as the editorial assistant covering the event, but her presence was required to be at the venue before the guests so I find myself arriving at the function without her.

The celebration is already in full swing by the time I arrive in Soho and I'm taken aback by the throngs of people gathered by the entrance, the thumping music audible even from outside.

The line for the entry stretched around the corner, with frighteningly bulky security guards turning people away who aren't on the guest list.

Checking my phone, I see a message from Gigi.

Message me when you're here so I can come get you!

I send her a quick text to let her know I'm outside, standing metres away from the entrance as I people watch. Everyone is dressed to the nines, which comes as no surprise– bold patterns and stylish ensembles making up the crowd outside of the five-star hotel where the after-party is being held.

In fashion, there's no such thing as being overdressed so I can't help but feel significantly underdressed in my mini, red slip dress and matching Hauretto high heels.

I'm hovering awkwardly at the front as I wait for Gigi's reply when I hear a voice call out behind me.

"Hallie?"

I turn to find messy dark hair and intense blue eyes belonging to none other than Sebastian Holmes himself. He's dressed more casually than the first couple of times I've seen him, wearing a blazer over a white t-shirt and black dress trousers.

"You're not going in?" He signals toward the entrance and I shake my head.

"I'm waiting for my friend to come get me," I reply. "She's already inside."

I gesture at the queue, already feeling a little more overwhelmed than usual. Waiting for Gigi would also save me the embarrassment of being turned away if my name *isn't* on the list.

"I've got you, don't worry."

He walks towards me, offering me his arm and I awkwardly grab on to his elbow. The fabric of his blazer is tactile under my fingers, the raised ridges and valleys of the twill weave slightly coarse to the touch.

Approaching the security guards by the door, Sebastian doesn't even give his name but they lift the rope nonetheless, allowing us access through the VIP entrance.

"See?" He smirks. "Easy."

"Thank you." I nod as we ascend a flight of stairs.

"Did you make the dress you're wearing too?" He nods towards my outfit.

He helps me out of my long, beige trench coat as we reach the cloakroom and I respond with a silent nod.

From the outside, the roar of music is discernible making it difficult to register his words clearly.

"I need to head upstairs real quick." Sebastian leans over to me, motioning towards a set of double doors. "The main room is through there, will you be alright on your own?"

CHAPTER 22

I nod my head. "Yes, I'm going to find my friend."

"Alright, I'll see you in there."

Sending Gigi a quick text, I watch as Sebastian heads up another flight of stairs.

Inside now!

Entering the main room, I'm greeted by a sea of people and bright lights flashing overhead. There's a dance floor in the middle of the room with a DJ spinning tracks but I skirt around it, finding it a little too overwhelming for my senses, especially with the photographers who are continuously taking photos of people around.

In an attempt to search for Gigi, I make my way to a calmer, more subdued lounge area next door. The atmosphere is a lot more relaxed with its jazz ambience and mood lighting so I find myself able to breathe a lot easier.

My eyes scan the room, flitting across various faces when I spot someone familiar.

Jet black hair and dark brown eyes that should really belong in the kitchen at Tito Boy's.

"Hero?" I question.

He turns at the sound of his name. "Hallie!"

"What are you doing here?"

"Snaps invited me!" He beams. "I'm his plus one."

He tilts his head across the room, revealing the unmistakable form of platinum-blond hair and intense grey eyes surrounded by a group of very tall and very gorgeous *models*.

August is wearing his signature navy suit with a black formal shirt underneath, the first few buttons undone. Valentina is next to him, an arm wrapped around his torso as she pulls him in a side hug.

As if sensing my gaze, he looks up and a prickling sensation settles in between my ribs the moment our eyes meet. He maintains his usual air of nonchalance as the people around him chatter eagerly.

My chest tightens and I avert my gaze.

"You're not going to say hi?" Hero questions.

"He seems busy." I shake my head, feigning indifference. "Shots?"

Turning to Hero, I watch as his face immediately lights up at the mention of alcohol.

"I heard it's open bar too," He grins.

Even though I have no intention of drinking, especially after last Friday, I indulge Hero and his company.

"You're a bad influence, Mahalia Hartt." He laughs, immediately following me as I start making my way towards the bar.

"How's everyone at the restaurant?" I ask.

"Good. Same as always." He takes one shot after the other. "We've had a few new hires. The masterclasses Rowan hosts every other weekend is a hit. You should come by more often. Everyone's missing you."

"Work has been so busy," I grimace.

Hero nods. "I can see why though, fashion week seems intense. It's back-to-back shows, one after the other, I can't keep up."

"You've been attending the shows?"

"Thanks to Snaps," He chuckles. "He's been dragging me out to every event but I'm not complaining. I didn't realise the fashion scene in London is so diverse."

"It didn't use to be the case," I laugh airily. "But now foreign talent does make up a significant portion of London's lineup."

"When am I going to see yours?" Hero inquires.

"Holmes showcased on the first day," I reply. "You've already missed it."

"Not Holmes." He shakes his head. "*Hartt.*"

I sigh wistfully. "A girl can dream."

"There you are!"

I sense a presence come up behind me and I watch as Hero's smile fades. Turning around, I find Sebastian standing beside us at the bar, sipping on a glittery purple liquid in a glass.

"Try this, it's a drink they made specifically for the event," He offers, passing me his glass.

CHAPTER 22

Sebastian watches me curiously and I take a small sip of the drink out of politeness.

"What do you think?"

"Too sour," I reply.

Though the taste isn't completely unpleasant, I find it too tangy for my liking.

He chuckles, wrapping his fingers around my hand as he reaches back for his glass. I try not to visibly flinch at the contact, finding it a little too close for comfort as he brings the drink back to his mouth and takes another gulp.

"This is my friend." I step away to gesture awkwardly towards Hero. "Sebastian, this is–"

"*Hiroshi Hinode*," He smiles but it doesn't reach his eyes. "Good to see you, chef."

"Sebastian," Hero nods impassively.

I can tell by the way he visibly bristles that, despite being acquainted, they are *not* friends.

"How do you know each other?" I ask curiously.

"August." Hero responds bluntly.

He doesn't elaborate further, my eyebrows furrowing as I sense the tension growing between them.

"I did a foundation year at MIDAS before attending LIFT," Sebastian reveals.

In the corner of my eye, I see the familiar head of platinum blond hair walking over to us. Panic rises in me as I turn sharply towards Hero and Sebastian.

"I'm going to the bath—"

I underestimate how long August's strides are because he is over to us within an instant.

Sebastian greets him first, squaring his shoulders.

"Vante."

August looks him over with a blasé expression.

"Holmes."

The same tension at the dinner is apparent between the two of them, further heightening the already tense atmosphere. I suddenly feel a lot smaller in their presence so I keep my eyes trained on the drink in my hand, avoiding everyone's gaze.

"It's been a while," Sebastian comments, shifting back towards me. "Didn't realise you're back in the party scene, *playboy*."

He brings an arm around me to take his glass, unsettlingly close.

"I'm not," August responds curtly.

"Oh yeah?" Sebastian asks. "Heard you took Vee home after the company dinner."

At the mention of the heterochromia-eyed model, my gaze flickers towards August.

"Sakura and I made sure she got back to her hotel okay," He replies bluntly, eyes fixed on me.

Guilt chords itself around my chest, squeezing my heart.

"Last season was a bit messy." Sebastian takes a long, leisurely sip of his drink. "Keep it clean this time, yeah?"

The statement is like a lashing against my heart and the tightening feeling around my chest intensifies.

Sebastian reaches over, handing the half-empty glass back to me.

"All yours, doll."

He gives everyone a nod of acknowledgement before leaving.

Glancing over at August, I watch as his gaze briefly falls on the drink in my hand before it trails after Sebastian's retreating figure.

"I'm going to the bathroom," I announce quickly, leaving August and Hero by the bar.

An unpleasant feeling eats away at me as I speed walk towards the restroom, my hand gripping the glass.

I had absolutely no idea of August and Valentina's involvement with each other, of course, but maybe I should have known *better*.

Placing the glass by the sink, I walk the length of the bathroom to calm my nerves. My fingers twitch involuntarily, tapping restlessly on my thighs as a group of brightly dressed women stumble into the bathroom.

CHAPTER 22

"I love your dress!" One of the girls drunkenly comments before beelining for a cubicle.

The tell-tale sign of retching can be heard before two other girls scurry over to tend to their friend. It triggers a flashback of when I was throwing up at Onyx and my heart sinks at the memory, feeling even more guilty.

"Just stay out of it, Hallie." I mutter, staring at my reflection in the bathroom mirror. "Do *not* get involved, Mahalia Hartt."

Glaring at my reflection one final time, I pick up Sebastian's glass and down the rest of the drink, the burning sensation of liquor tasting oddly bitter this time.

It doesn't counteract the tightening feeling of guilt in my chest.

If anything, it makes it worse.

Coughing loudly, my eyebrows furrow at the much darker remnants of the glass before gathering myself and exiting the ladies bathroom. I'm two steps out when I feel a hand wrap around my elbow and I'm suddenly tugged into a corner.

I look up to find grey eyes staring sternly at me.

"You're avoiding me."

The statement catches me off guard and I swallow out of nervousness, the minimal distance between us causing my heart to flutter.

He hands me a bottle of water and my brows knot in confusion.

"You were drinking with Hero," He states.

"I took a shot," I reply, the irony not lost on me.

"And Sebastian's drink, clearly." He responds in an irritable tone.

I take the bottle from him. "I had one glass."

"Did nobody ever advise you against drinking with strangers?" He grouses.

His voice takes on a condescending edge, as though he's scolding a child and it makes me feel even worse.

"Sebastian isn't a stranger," I comment.

Something flickers in his eyes as he takes a step towards me.

Flashbacks of the club flood my mind and I chug down the water, hoping to wash away the bitter taste of rejection and the guilt lingering in my mouth.

I hand the bottle back and take a step away from him.

"Thanks. If you'll excuse me—"

August doesn't give me the opportunity to leave as he reaches out and gently grabs my hand.

"Mahalia."

His touch sends tingles down my spine, goosebumps erupting on my skin.

My vision blurs slightly as I feel his hand brush against mine longer than necessary and I restrain the impulse to intertwine my fingers with his. Out of the haze, my mind conjures up a vision of blonde hair and a pair of different-coloured eyes.

Instantly, I pull away.

"I'm going home." I assert.

I don't give August the chance to stop me this time as I stumble back to the bar, my legs unsteady.

My surroundings spin slowly and I frown, finding it difficult to move as the floor is suddenly pulled from under me.

"Woah!"

I look up at the body I collided with, tall and imposing, and I mumble a breathless apology.

"You alright?"

I shake my head, blinking rapidly at the blurring figure as I try to focus. I feel the familiar texture of the twill weave against my fingers and I blink at the black and blue slanted parallel lines.

Herringbone.

"Sebastian?"

My tongue feels heavy, my mouth oddly dry.

"Easy there, sweetheart." His hands try to steady me as I push against him to stand upright. "Wait, hold this."

He hands me a glass of clear liquid and I clumsily reach for it, taking multiple gulps. I choke on the sudden burning sensation down my throat and shake my head.

CHAPTER 22

"Water."

"Oh shit," His hands are cold as I feel his touch on the exposed skin of my shoulders. "That's not water, no."

The drink spills as I stumble backwards, the glass slipping out of my hands.

"S-sorry," I wince. "I want to go home."

"Alright, I'll call you a cab."

I try to keep my vision focused as I nod, stopping when my head starts to feel heavy.

"Hallie?"

Disoriented, I turn towards the familiar sound of a woman's voice.

"Gigi?" I frown, my eyes losing focus.

Everything around me is painfully overwhelming, enhanced colours and distorted shapes, as I reach out towards her.

"What the hell do you think you're doing?"

I flinch at the irritated voice belonging to August.

"Relax mate, I was just helping her." Sebastian's voice is aloof, his grip around me loosening.

"Hallie, what's wrong?"

Gigi's voice is muffled. Too distant sounding despite her being so close to me.

"I don't feel too good," I answer. "I want to go home."

The room is starting to spin again and I ungracefully sway with it. I duck my head down to ground myself when I feel myself being led away by an all-too-familiar touch. I look back up to find August holding me now, Sebastian nowhere in sight.

"Wait, I'm still on the clock." Gigi's eyes meet mine before she looks around. "I need to let one of my colleagues know so I can leave—"

"No," I interrupt. "You're staying."

She frowns. "I'm not leaving you by yourself."

"It's your event, Gigi." I hiccup, struggling to speak clearly.

"Hallie—"

"You're not leaving." I shake my head firmly. "*I'm* going home."

203

"Stop, Hals—"

I stumble forward, into Hero this time, and I blink languidly.

"How much did you drink?" His eyebrows knot in apprehension.

"Hallie," Gigi frowns. "You're drunk."

"I'm not drunk," I argue.

There's a pressure in my chest that feels foreign, almost like a cramp, my heart beating so rapidly I can hear the blood pulsing in my ears.

"I had one drink. And a shot. Is that drunk? I don't think that's drunk. That's not drunk at all." I'm babbling now but I can hardly stop, suddenly feeling all too jittery.

August steps in front of me abruptly and takes my face in his hands.

For the briefest moment, I think he's going to kiss me, but he only fixes his gaze on my face, grey eyes examining me closely. I stand frozen in place as he pulls gently on my eyelids, the faintest touch on my skin.

"What did you take?" His tone is stern as he stares into my eyes.

I blink quickly, the question scrambling around in my head and throwing me off guard.

Did I take what?

"I didn't take anything," I protest, my body beginning to tremble.

"She took something," He asserts, eyes trained on me.

"I didn't."

August doesn't say anything else as he cups my chin with his fingers, tilting it to the side and observing my face from different angles. He slides his thumb under my jaw before tracing it down to the hammering pulse point on my neck.

I hold my breath as he inspects me, my body warming up at his touch.

"Hallie?"

I turn toward Gigi who's looking at me now, eyes full of concern.

"I didn't take anything," I repeat, feeling like my knees are about to give in. "I would never."

"I was with her earlier, I would know if she took…" Hero's sentence trails off, his eyes landing on someone from across the room.

My head turns towards the bar where I see the hazy yet unmistakable

CHAPTER 22

silhouette clad in a blazer and tailored trousers. The air around me prickles as a wave of anxiety washes over me and I falter under August's touch.

"I don't know what I took."

There's a pounding in my head as I struggle to recall every drink I had tonight. Concentrating is a battle, thinking clearly seems nearly impossible.

"Snaps." Hero turns towards August, worry etched on his face.

"I don't know what I took," I repeat, turning towards Gigi with a whimper.

A high tide of nausea pulls me under this time, the feeling of paranoia engulfing me within an instant. Panic flashes across Gigi's face but she does her best to mask it for my sake.

"Do we need to go to the hospital?" Gigi asks.

August hesitates, attention steadily on me.

"Open your mouth," He instructs.

I comply, quickly parting my lips.

August curls his index finger under my chin, lifting it more gently this time as his thumb pulls on my bottom lip. Our eyes meet and my head clouds over as I resist the overwhelming temptation to kiss him again.

"She'll be okay," August says, reassuringly. "We just need to keep an eye out on her."

I feel clammy, my body alternating between hot and cold flushes as the dizziness forming in my head intensifies with each passing second.

Hero lets out a sigh. "I'll take her home."

"I'll go with you." August offers.

"Snaps, it's fine."

I don't need to be fully within my headspace to notice that it's most definitely not fine and Hero is most certainly far from happy.

"We'll take her home," August tells Gigi. "Book the taxi. I'll meet you both outside in 5 minutes."

Chapter 23

Lethargy starts to take over my body and my movements become listless as I follow Hero out of the venue. The streets of Soho are a blur of lights and I'm overwhelmed by the music and the sea of bodies pushing past me.

"Hero," I mumble. "Wait–"

The ground beneath me shifts and I wait for the impact of the pavement only to feel an arm securing itself around my waist.

"Careful," August says, hoisting me back up.

"S-sorry," I mutter out an apology.

My trench coat is wrapped around me shortly after, the familiar scent of sandalwood and bergamot filling my senses. August tugs me towards him and I lean my forehead against his shoulder, feeling too lightheaded.

I don't remember how long it took for the taxi to come but I do remember warm hands guiding me in and being pressed up against a hard body under a silky exterior, the feeling of the material under my fingertips easing my discomfort.

"Hallie, your keys." Hero's voice wades through my muddled consciousness. "Where is it?"

"Purse," I reply weakly, burying my face into soft, silky fabric.

I feel the absence of my clutch bag as it's pulled from my hand, registering the sound of someone rummaging through the contents inside.

"Does she have everything?" The sudden beam of light from Hero's phone causes me to wince and I feel a hand raise to shield my face from the blinding brightness.

"Hinode," August hisses. *"Light."*

CHAPTER 23

"Shit, I forgot, sorry." Hero mumbles. "What's the code to the gate, Hals?"

I lift my head as I strain my ears to hear, suddenly realising that I'm still in the taxi, wedged between Hero and pressed tightly against August.

"The what?"

"The code," Hero repeats. "To your gate."

I blink. "I can't remember."

"*Hallie—*"

I flinch at his harsh tone, turning my head away and hiding my face in August's shirt.

"Gigi knows," I mumble. "Call Gigi."

"Where's your phone?" Hero questions, voice stern. "I don't have her number."

"Purse," I hiccup. "No passcode."

An exasperated sigh leaves Hero as he begins rifling through my bag again.

"Snaps, can you help her get-"

The sound of the car door opening prompts me to crawl to the opposite side. I stumble out of the taxi, a sharp pang shooting through my ankle and I lose my footing, landing ungraciously on the ground.

"*Hallie,*" Hero reprimands me. "What the hell are you doing?"

"Getting out of the taxi," I answer, feeling a headache forming in between my eyes.

"You're on the *floor*," He hisses. "Get up."

From the disapproving tone of his voice, I can tell that Hero is losing his patience.

"You can both go home," I say quietly. "I'm fine now."

"Like hell you are," Hero argues, exasperated. "Don't be difficult."

His voice is firm, almost admonishing, and I suddenly feel like a child being chastised.

"I'm not trying to be."

"Then get up and walk."

"W-wait," I request, feeling a strain on the foot I twisted earlier.

There's a burning pressure on my ankle and a dizzying weight in my

207

head as I try to blink back the tears forming in my eyes.

"Hallie, *hurry up*."

I can see Hero's agitated figure standing by the gate from a few metres ahead. He's holding my phone by his ear with one hand whilst keeping the gate open with the other. Rising to my feet, I'm suddenly struck by a faint spell of vertigo and my legs give out from under me.

"I c-can't," I whimper in response.

"Stop wasting time, Hals." Hero yells towards me.

"I'm not," I grimace. "My head hurts... and my foot..."

"Hallie, I swear to god—"

From my crouched position on the floor, I can see a faint trickle of blood from where the strap of my heel chafed against the skin of my swollen ankle.

"Hinode, stop." August calls out to Hero. "She's hurt."

Hero walks back over to me, clearly disgruntled. "How *the hell* did you manage to do that?"

"I don't know," I sob quietly, reaching out for the railing as my head continues to spin.

The gate buzzes close and Hero curses, rushing back over to open it again.

"Mahalia."

I hear August call my name this time as he approaches me but I refuse to look over, already feeling overwhelmed by the situation.

"I'm getting up," I sniffle, tired. "Just give me a moment."

Feeling him standing beside me, I swallow down the hurt and ignore the throbbing pain in my ankle as I attempt to straighten up.

The last thing I need is for August to start scolding me as well.

"Arms around my neck," He instructs.

I turn to him with a questioning look and blink. Before I can respond, he slides his arms under my knees and lifts me bridal style.

"Take it easy on her," August says, holding me tightly against him. "She's disoriented."

Hero's response fades into the background as my surroundings blur

CHAPTER 23

once more. I don't recall being this sensitive to my environment when I'm drunk but I don't think alcohol is the only thing in my system right now.

The familiar ding of the lift and the sound of the doors opening is what draws me back to reality as I glance around and realise I'm back in my flat. The lights are dimmed in the living room and I'm thankful that only the lamps are on.

"Where's her room?" August asks.

"She sleeps in the living room," Hero replies. "I need to sort out her bed, you can set her down on the armchair."

"She's fine, I've got her."

It takes Hero a good few minutes to set up the sofa bed. The sounds of the frame unfolding, the mattress extending and the bedding being arranged echoing in the living room.

August eventually sets me down on the bed, fluffing up a pillow under my head.

Slowly, I push myself up to a sitting position, the dizzying feeling beginning to fade which I'm grateful for.

"Stay in bed, Hallie. You'll end up hurting yourself somehow," Hero scolds me before muttering towards August. "She bruises like a peach."

The irritation in Hero's voice weighs down on me and I purse my lips, feeling worse and worse about the entire evening.

August squats down to my level tucking the loose corner of the bed sheet under the mattress.

"Are you okay?" He asks me.

"I want soft clothes," I mumble, disliking how the dress I'm wearing is beginning to feel.

It's suddenly scratchy and rough and all too uncomfortable on my skin.

"Can you watch her?" Hero sighs. "I'll grab something from her closet."

"Sure." August nods.

He sits on the armchair in the living room as I slowly swing my legs to the side of the bed. August watches me intently as I reach for my heels and struggle to undo the strap.

"Do you need help?" His voice is unusually soft and it tugs on my heart.

209

I shake my head, resenting the idea of being a further imposition in his presence, considering everything that's happened between us recently.

Hero returns to the living room, handing me a familiar-looking jumper and I grimace. Out of all the items of clothing he could have picked from my closet, it would be the jumper August gave to me.

"Change here, I don't trust you to be in the bathroom by yourself." Hero's voice takes on an assertive tone. "August and I will be in the kitchen. I'll make you something for tomorrow."

The opening of cupboard doors and pans clattering in the kitchen followed by hushed whispers as Hero and August converse between themselves reverberate in the kitchen.

"You sure she doesn't need to go to the hospital?"

"She just needs to ride out the high," August answers. "Preferably conscious."

"How long is the comedown?"

"Usually a few hours."

"Do you know what she took?"

"No, but I don't think it's anything too serious," August replies. "She's probably not used to the effects."

I hear Hero sigh.

"She's fine, Hinode." August says. "She could have taken something a lot worse."

A longer pause settles between them.

"I was with her earlier. I didn't even realise."

"It's not your fault. And it's not hers either." A pause. "I take it she's never done drugs in her life?"

My eyes widen.

Drugs?

The revelation sends me into a small spiral.

I was drugged?

My chest constricts and I claw at the straps of my dress, desperate to pull the garment off my body.

A soft meowing catches my attention as Calix jumps up on the sofa bed

CHAPTER 23

next to me.

"Hi Cal," I sniffle, stroking his head.

Purring softly, Calix nuzzles into my hand before headbutting my palm affectionately. I let out a watery smile, watching as he stretches lazily before laying on his back and exposing his belly.

"I've got somewhere to be tomorrow morning before my shift at the restaurant," Hero says with a wince. "I'm gonna have to cancel."

There's a silence between them before August speaks.

"You can trust me with her."

"I do," Hero responds. "It's her I'm a little skeptical of."

August lets out a low chuckle. "What is she going to do? Attack me?"

"Yes," Hero deadpans. "Probably with her mouth. She *kissed* you?"

"I don't think it meant anything. She was drunk."

My stomach sinks, the feeling of guilt seeping back into my gut.

Hero chortles. "Snaps, your *girlfriend* is not going to be *happy*—"

"Christ, not you too." August's voice sounds exasperated. "I left you alone with Saito for *five* minutes."

The seeping sensation travels up to my chest and I press a hand to my heart to alleviate the ache.

Calix seems to sense what I'm feeling because he kneads my leg for a short while before curling up in my lap.

"Look, I know Hallie," Hero begins. "She isn't someone who goes around—"

"Can..." I call out meekly, purposely interrupting them. "Can someone help?"

"Are you decent?" Hero's voice responds from the kitchen.

"Yes."

The sound of hushed conversations filters the air before the clamour of clanging pots and pans rings loudly in the kitchen. Expecting to see Hero, I'm puzzled when platinum blond hair and grey eyes crouch down in front of me.

"The heels?" He questions me and I nod. "Is this Calix?"

Standing alert, Calix puffs up his fur before jumping down and curling around my legs protectively.

"Hey kitty," He begins. "I just need to have a quick look at your *maman*'s ankle."

Calix stares at August, golden almond eyes unblinking for the longest moment before meowing resignedly and bouncing back on my lap.

August helps me remove my heels, his movements slow and his touch careful, as he examines my ankle.

"I don't think you've broken anything," He reassures me. "The swelling should go down in the morning."

He brings a bag of frozen peas out of nowhere and gently places it on my ankle as tears begin to well up in my eyes.

"I'm so sorry August," I apologise tearfully. "I didn't know about you and Valentina."

August blinks. "What?"

"I would never try to ruin your relationship," I sniffle, feeling a different burning sensation in my chest. "I promise, I'm not like that."

"What?" August repeats, confusion marring his features.

"If I had known you were with Valentina, I would never have tried to kiss you. It was a drunken kiss and–" I falter.

I couldn't bring myself to claim it was a mistake and that it didn't mean anything because that would be far from the truth.

"You…" August's gaze lingers on me, contemplative, before he exhales slowly.

"I didn't know." I swallow, voice strained. "I'm sorry, please don't—"

"Sleep, Mahalia." August interrupts me, rising from the bed. "Don't burden yourself with overthinking. You've had a long night and you're not feeling too good. We can talk about it in the morning when you're a little more yourself, okay?"

I'm about to argue when Calix meows loudly in my lap.

"Listen to Calix," August reaches down to pet him, the Calico cat purring in content. "Get some rest."

I watch as August gets up and heads back to the kitchen, fully anticipating him to be gone the next morning. In the next room, I can hear August

CHAPTER 23

and Hero talk quietly, their incoherent sentences and disjointed phrases blurring together into a stream of white noise.

Exhaustion eventually envelops me and, before long, I find myself drifting off to sleep.

Chapter 24

My mind is a jigsaw puzzle of fragmented memories that aren't quite fitting correctly when I wake up the next day.

"God, my head is throbbing," I groan, feeling an awful sense of déjà vu. "Who parties in the middle of the working week?"

The haze of sleep still lingers and there's a pressure inside my skull, the events of the past 24 hours catching up to my conscience as I wake up.

"Welcome to the world of fashion."

I turn towards Gigi to find her already sitting down in the living room and wearing sunglasses indoors with her laptop in front of her.

"How are you feeling?" She asks me.

"Not great," I answer honestly. "But surprisingly better than last night."

My eyes scan the clock on the wall, finding it difficult to concentrate.

11:38 AM.

"Oh shit!" I scramble up immediately. "*I'm late for work.*"

The movement causes me to sway and I nearly tumble out of bed.

"Take it easy, Hals." Gigi is beside me almost instantly. "You might still be on a comedown. August told me for you to take the day off."

"He did?"

"He was here all night," She nods. "Hero left when I got back from the after-party but August stayed until about an hour ago when his phone started blowing up."

I wince at the thought of August staying behind to watch over a highly strung-out, drugged-up liability when he undoubtedly has more pressing obligations.

CHAPTER 24

"He was awake when I woke up this morning but you were still out of it," Gigi continues.

"Why didn't you wake me up?" I ask with a wince.

"August told me not to," She replies. "He said to leave you to rest and to take the day off. I think he was waiting for you to wake up."

We'll talk in the morning.

I slap my forehead with my hand.

"I don't think he slept, you know." Gigi adds.

My stomach knots.

"This is a nightmare," I groan.

"Do you remember what happened last night?" She asks.

"It's all a blur in my head," I reply. "But I know I was *drugged*, somehow."

I pinch the bridge of my nose, massaging the space between my eyes gently as my head begins to throb again.

"I need to go to the studio," I sigh.

The intermittent bursts of raised voices and sharp, heated exchanges can be heard as soon as the lift doors open to the fourth floor. Clipped arguments echo down the corridor as I approach August's office.

"Stop jumping to conclusions, August." Sebastian's voice reaches my ears. "I didn't touch your precious intern."

I pause, eyebrows furrowing at the topic of conversation.

"What is your fucking problem?" It's August's voice this time.

"*You* are my problem, you prick." Sebastian seethes. "You fucking punched my face in after accusing me of drugging someone. I was trying to *help* her."

"Help her what? Get into your fucking trousers?"

"Jesus." A loud, derisive laugh echoes inside. "Never thought I'd see the day *the* August Vante gets jealous of something under *my* name."

A threatening tone tinges August's voice. "She isn't yours."

"Who knew you could be so protective, *playboy*." Sebastian scoffs. "This is new. Are you changing your roster of playthings? Thought that a nice, little romp in the sheets with an intern was a lovely change in scenery, did you?"

August's voice drops dangerously low. "Leave her alone."

"Oh, but she's such a doll! An absolute gem, if you ask me," Sebastian taunts. "Fancy breaking her in together? You know, for old time's sake."

There's a momentary pause before a thunderous crash resounds in the room. Startled by the sudden noise, I rush inside without a second thought and I blink at the sight of August and Sebastian squared up against each other, the former with a firm grip on the blazer lapels of the latter.

"Hallie!"

Sebastian's posture changes completely as he sees me, August immediately releasing him as he notices me stumble inside his office. The blinds in the room, usually drawn in, are pulled wide open casting an unsettling brightness in the area. It's a little disconcerting to see his workspace in broad daylight, given my familiarity with its typically dim environment.

"I heard about last night," Sebastian begins, straightening his blazer. "How are you doing?"

He walks over to me and my mouth hangs open in shock at his marred-up face.

"I'm fine," I reply, trying to stay impassive as I take in his bruised eye and split lip. "Are you?"

"Oh, this?" He points to his face before waving a hand dismissively. "Nothing to worry about, doll. Just a little tiff between old friends."

The tension between August and Sebastian is almost tangible, the air prickling with an energy that feels like imaginary pins piercing my skin.

August, normally stoic, doesn't hide his disdain as his eyes pore over Sebastian.

"I'll see myself out." Sebastian nods towards me, completely ignoring August. "Lovely to see you as always, Hallie."

Sebastian exits without another word, leaving August and I in his office. My eyes linger momentarily at the door before I turn towards August, gasping as I take in his facial features. There's a gash on his cheekbone, early signs of a bruise forming on the right side of his face.

"August," I swallow.

CHAPTER 24

His normally steely eyes are molten silver as they stare at me with concern.

"How are you feeling?" He asks quietly. "I told Gigi to tell you to take the day off."

An ache forms in my chest as he walks towards me.

"I'm feeling well enough," I say. "What happened?"

My fingers twitch as it reaches up to touch his face and his eyes flicker to my palm. The uncertainty in his gaze prompts me to force my left hand back down to my side.

Instead of answering my question, he counters it with one of his.

"Can you remember anything last night?"

"Fragments," I answer. "It's a bit of a blur."

My memory recollects moments in between, playing snippets that distort themselves, like an overexposed film negative— too dark in the shadows, too dense in the highlights.

"How's your ankle?" He inquires.

His tone takes on the same softness from the night before and it tugs on my heart.

"It's fine," I reply quietly. "Just a slight swelling but it's nothing I can't handle. I'm wearing flats today so—"

Unexpectedly, August crouches down to inspect my ankle. The gesture catches me off guard and I shuffle nervously as his fingertips brush against my poor attempt at bandaging my ankle with a compression wrap.

"You fell quite hard," He says, his touch gentle on the bruise. "Are you sure you don't want the rest of the day off? Get your ankle checked at the hospital?"

His voice somehow manages to be even softer as he looks up at me, his gaze all too intimate.

I nod wordlessly, feeling the room warming up all of a sudden.

"Let me redo the bandage at least," He says gently.

"I-I'm okay," I stutter. "Thank you though, I appreciate it."

He doesn't say anything else as he slowly shifts into a standing position. The familiar scent of sandalwood and bergamot overwhelms me and the mental fog in my brain clouds over even more at his closeness.

"Do *you* need anything?" I look up at him. "An ice pack? Some painkillers? I can go out and get it for you."

"I should be asking you that."

August moves back to his desk, reaching for a remote that begins drawing up the blinds of the room, the lighting dimming with it.

"Well done on everything you've done for fashion week, by the way." He says.

"Just doing my job," I reply.

"You'll be happy to know you're being assigned back to Design." He nods towards me. "There's some paperwork that needs completing but it should come as no problem for you. You're back in the studio on Monday."

"Thanks, August." I say.

He gives me an aloof nod, a signal to take my leave but I linger a little longer.

"Are you sure you don't need anything?" I ask. "I can, um, fetch you pomegranate wine? It won't be the exact one from that Mediterranean island but it'll still be fermented pomegranate juice?"

The corner of his mouth twitches ever so slightly.

"I'll be fine," He nods. "Just… Please look after yourself."

Something flashes in his grey eyes and he appears torn, almost sad. My mind clears suddenly, a different lurching in my gut as I remember something.

"I'll explain everything to Valentina," I say. "I'm sure she was wondering where you were last night. Gigi told me Hero was already gone when she got back to the flat but you stayed with me until you had to leave for work."

August turns to me, eyebrows furrowing.

"I'll talk to her and let her know she has nothing to worry about," I continue. "You can tell her it was a drunken mistake on my part. I got intoxicated, which I did. And that it was my fault, which it was."

I wring my hands nervously behind my back.

"It didn't…" I hesitate for a moment.

It didn't mean anything.

CHAPTER 24

The statement gets lodged in my throat. Nothing has ever tasted more sour in my mouth and I turn my gaze away from him.

"Val and I aren't together."

My head jerks up, horrified.

I can almost see the headlines now.

HOMEWRECKER HARTT!!
Fresh-Faced Fashion Designer Destroys Relationship on the Runway

"Oh God. Let me explain to her," I plead. "I'm sure she'll take you back if she finds out the truth. I'll tell her *everything*, she'll—"

"Mahalia."

"I can fix it, I promise." I swallow. "If you let me talk to her, I can-"

"Will you please let me finish?" August shakes his head, somewhat amused. "Nothing is going on between Valentina and I."

I frown. "What?"

"Valentina has never been my girlfriend," August says. "Nor is she interested in ever being one. Sakura teases me about it all the time because she knows it will never happen. You and her have more of a chance with Valentina than I do."

I blink at that.

"Whatever's going in that tinkering talented head of yours, get rid of it. You're not a home wrecker, you haven't destroyed anyone's relationship."

"I still want to apologise," I say. "About the club. I don't want to be trouble for HR or PR or anything like that. I don't want you to—"

"File a complaint for harassment?" He asks. "What makes you think I haven't already?"

My eyes widen and I turn to August, panicked.

"I'm kidding," He quickly backtracks, clearing his throat. "I won't be reporting any issues. Besides, I kissed you back, remember?"

My brain short-circuits as I feel a blush travel up my neck.

"Oh…" I nod awkwardly. "Yes, you did. Thanks."

I pause. And then, a realisation.

"Wait, I meant—"

"You're welcome." The corner of his mouth quirks up slightly. "I'll try not to take offence at the fact you ended up vomiting in the bathroom straight after."

My mouth drops in mortification at the memory.

"That was not your fault." I shake my head. "I mixed one too many drinks and—"

August releases a breath, similar to a quiet chuckle.

"Would you have kissed me, a *third* time, if you didn't?"

"In a heartbeat!" I answer automatically before the question fully registers in my head.

His grey eyes twinkle in amusement, the corner of his lips twitching into a small smile.

"Wait, I mean–"

"Relax, Tinker-Talent." His voice is gentle, the nickname slipping effortlessly from his lips. "If you're not taking the day off, at least work from my office. Hero will kill me if he finds out I didn't keep an eye on you."

His tone, this time, leaves no room for argument and I nod, making my way to the small seating area.

"Do you want the blinds drawn or?" He asks me.

I look up to find him standing by the window and I shake my head, aware of his preference for working in low-lit environments.

"I'm okay with working in the dark," I answer. "I still have a headache from last night."

A strange stirring materialises in my chest, the feeling of something untangling as I watch August walk back to his desk.

There's a newfound softness to him as he works behind the computer in the dim lighting of his office, eyebrows furrowed in concentration. He glances in my direction and the unwinding intensifies. I quickly look away, tamping the feeling down before I can put a name to it.

Chapter 25

The conclusion of Men's Fashion Week marked the end of my temporary contract as Comms Assistant and working with August.

After finalising the completion reports and sending them off to the team, I officially went back to working in the Main Studio with Pollux and Estelle.

Thankfully, I was able to catch up as they both briefed me on everything I've missed and provided updates on upcoming collections.

For the next couple of weeks, encounters with August have been far and few between and I saw very little of him since I no longer worked under his supervision. His office being located on the fourth floor meant our paths rarely ever crossed either.

It's amusingly contradictory now, how I found myself wanting to be more and more in his presence.

I'm in the middle of doing my usual morning tasks of reading up on news in the industry and responding to emails when Estelle walks into the studio, tablet in hand and a mug of coffee in the other.

"Holmes has been contacted by a high-profile client," She says in greeting as she powers up the computer on her desk.

"Oh?"

I peer over to Estelle and rise from my swivel chair.

"They want us to design a line of suits tailored for special occasions and festive celebrations for a royal clientele," She expands as I approach her desk. "Regalwear."

"Regalwear?" I echo, the concept new to me.

"Haute couture for aristocracy, if you will." Estelle nods. "Patent pending by Vante."

I sift through my knowledge of anything regalwear.

I've known of royal attire of course. Clothes designed and custom-tailored to fit the unique style and preferences of the individual royal, with garments typically made of luxurious materials and also incorporated specific symbols or designs associated with monarchy.

"The clients wanting to work with us are the Royals of Toussaint. It's a small country by the borders of Europe and the Mediterranean," She explains. "Have you heard of them before?"

I tilt my head as I try to recall where I've encountered the name previously.

"Did MODUE include them in an article about the Royal Bachelors of Europe?" I ask.

Estelle nods in reply. "Yes, both Prince Elias and Prince Tobias were featured before Prince Elias' engagement."

Gigi's mention of the article comes to the forefront of my mind and I vaguely recall the details of both heirs in line to the Toussaint crown.

"Vante usually takes on any projects requested by the Toussaint royals," Estelle continues. "They've had a longstanding relationship that dates back to King Theron and Sir Leverett Vante."

My eyes widen as I turn to Estelle.

"*The* Leverett Vante?" I gape. "As in the founder of Vante Atelier?"

"Cedric's grandfather, yes."

I sit in amazement.

That makes August his *great-grandson*.

The history of Vante Atelier is rich. A local tailoring business turned global fashion empire. Vante has a legacy of over 100 years, the fashion lineage extending as far as the late 1800s. One of the case studies at LIFT focused entirely on the empire created by a young Parisian tailor named Leverett Arsène Vante in 1881. Vante is essentially the founding father of fashion.

"Often it's been under the radar," Estelle continues. "Toussaint isn't one

CHAPTER 25

to exclaim from the parapets, so to speak. But shifts are occurring in the way public affairs are being managed by the royal institution, hence why there's been a consistent stream of news and engagements being done internationally."

I contemplate Holmes' struggle to hold its territory, how it's barely out of the fashion trenches, and whether forming a coalition with the company is the best tactic for the other party involved.

"Cedric believes it would be advantageous for the brand to spearhead the project as an inauguration for clientele work since Vante's acquisition," Estelle says, as if reading my thoughts. "Holmes' comeback collection during fashion week was successful. But we need a steady traction of good designs *and* good press."

"So our design team would be taking on the project?"

"Half of us," She replies.

I blink in surprise. "We're hiring more people?"

"Not at the moment," She shakes her head. "We need to make do with the team we have. Pollux and I have already discussed that our main focus would be prioritising the core collection. He's very intent on seeing through and completing the work for next season since he's been involved with it from the beginning. Less disruption with the workflow."

I nod in understanding.

"Having said that we did consider you a more appropriate fit for what's being requested by the Royals of Toussaint."

My eyebrows knit together in confusion.

"Your Disney Princes collection that went viral last year," Estelle mentions.

"My final major project at uni?" I blink.

Estelle hums, her attention back on the computer as she types away on the keyboard.

All things considered, it makes sense. The silhouettes of the collection are based on the traditional tailoring of men's royal attire with pattern variations for contemporary blazers and trousers. However, the scale of my university project is minor in comparison to the quality of production that Holmes and Vante generate.

"Would you be able to bring your Disney Princes' portfolio on Monday? I'd like to have a proper look and further discuss it with the staff at the Royals of Toussaint's communication office."

"Of course." I nod.

"And if it all goes well, I'd like for you to be the supporting designer for the project."

My mouth drops at the proposition.

"For the regalwear collection?" I ask skeptically.

"The Holmes collaboration with Toussaint, yes." She nods. "Pollux and I are still available to assist in whatever capacity needed of us but dividing the work is our best course of action until we've recruited additional designers."

Excitement surges in my chest, a warm buzz coursing throughout my entire body at the prospect of working on such a high-profile project.

"So, what are your thoughts?" Estelle turns her attention back to me.

"Yes," I beam, trying to contain my enthusiasm. "That would be an amazing opportunity, I would love to."

"Perfect." Estelle smiles warmly at me, further elaborating, "You'll be assisting the Lead Designer."

The distant whirring of the printer in the corner of the room catches my attention and I watch as Estelle walks over to retrieve some documents. She hands me a sheet of paper with information about the client details and the project overview.

The Royals of Toussaint Regalwear Collection.
In Collaboration with Holmes London.

I blink at the name under the title of Lead Designer.

Sebastian Holmes.

II

Part Two

"In difficult times, fashion is always outrageous."

— *Elsa Schiaparelli*

Chapter 26

The news of Sebastian's return to Holmes travelled fast in the company and it quickly became public knowledge soon after. It seemed like every single employee had something to say, receiving a variety of reactions from everyone at the studio.

Naturally, August's position as Director of Communications heightened the gossip. Given their rocky relationship, it sparked debate about the potential challenges that could arise and people were more than skeptical with the idea of Sebastian reclaiming his position as Creative Director and Senior Designer. By lunchtime, word circulated that the previously missing-in-action son of the late CEO was officially accounted for, turning the on-site cafeteria into a buzzing hub of gossip.

"Two neurotic nepo babies under one fashion roof?" Ymir quips as we queue up for lunch. "This is a fashion disaster waiting to happen."

She grabs a platter of sushi and I opt for my usual salmon poke bowl. Despite returning to the Design department, I still have lunch with Ymir and Saoirse whenever our schedules align.

"They can't be that bad, right?" I ask curiously, picking up a bottle of coconut water.

"Individually, maybe not," Ymir replies. "But together?"

"Way worse," Saoirse comments, joining Ymir and I in the queue as she grabs a salad from the counter. "You saw them at the dinner."

Considering all that transpired at Holmes since I started working here, the studio's reaction is hardly a surprise.

"It's one struggle after another in this company," Ymir shakes her head as we walk towards our usual table.

"We need you back in Comms, Hallie." Saoirse sighs, taking a seat opposite me. "We're going through new hires like mad. We've had half a dozen interns come in and quit in just under two weeks."

My eyes widen at the numbers.

"August is impossible to impress." Ymir shakes her head, echoing Estelle's words. "And so *particular*."

"His daily in-person meetings can be a little intimidating." I nod in agreement.

Saoirse frowns. "Daily meetings?"

"The end of day face-to-face updates?" I clarify. "They sometimes clashed with our meetings. Detailing how every hour of my day is blocked was intense."

Ymir and Saoirse share a confused look.

"He doesn't... He doesn't do that with you?" I question.

They both shake their heads.

"We email him updates and have a catch-up meeting every Friday morning," Saoirse elaborates. "But other than that, nothing so intense as an hour-by-hour run down of tasks every single day."

"That's brutal," Ymir remarks. "No wonder the interns are all quitting."

"It's impossible to pass his infamous Tinker Test," Saoirse says.

I choke on my coconut water. "His what?"

"Thinker. Tinker. We have no idea." Ymir shrugs. "We overheard him talking to someone on the phone about it. He gives the new interns a few days and if he doesn't *think* they're the right fit..."

"Faith, trust and pixie dust right out of the studio," Saoirse finishes.

A grimace forms on Ymir's face. "The legal team is on standby as we speak."

"I'm surprised HR hasn't mentioned anything about any of them wanting to sue," I add quietly.

"*Yet*."

I look up to find Pollux making an appearance, sitting down next to me with a tray of fish and chips.

CHAPTER 26

"It's official," He groans, picking at his food. "We're back in Herringbone hell."

None of us need to ask further about what, or rather who, Pollux is referring to. The entire office hasn't stopped talking about the highly anticipated comeback of the designer.

"I take it you're excited," I comment.

"Bursting at the seams," He deadpans.

I recall the few and far between interactions I've had with Sebastian– the dinner, the after-party. He'd been tolerable enough *alone* in my presence but things always seem to go south whenever August is involved.

Their altercation from that morning replays in my mind. Some of the things Sebastian said were provoking to August, almost like he knew how to get under his skin.

"Sebastian is a wolf in sheep's clothing," Pollux discloses. "A fantastic designer, don't get me wrong. The man is talented, like his father, naturally."

"But?" I question.

"He can be a sadistic fucking sociopath," He stresses. "I was working as a junior designer for over a year when he just started as a senior and when it's going good? It's great."

"And when it's bad?" I ask.

"*Herringbone hell,*" He states. "Sebastian is hot and cold. Even before he started working at Holmes, he was already unpredictable. I mean, our *Dandy Designer* essentially grew up with the *Peroxide Prince* in the industry."

Everyone at the table winces.

"In fairness," Ymir begins. "Baby Vante isn't actually that bad. Definitely cleaned up his act from his playboy faring days."

"I wonder how the two are going to get on," Saoirse comments, voicing the thought in my head.

Like a fashion house on fire, I bet.

I bite my lip to keep myself from saying anything, knowing better than to indulge in gossip. With so much news regarding August's past and

Sebastian's future, it was hard to keep up with it all. At present, a lot of it is lost in translation.

"They might be caught in the same net of nepotism but they're hardly cut from the same cloth," Pollux says. "And you know what the bible says about mixing fabrics."

We turn towards him, curious.

"Thou shall not wear leather and lace, ladies."

"Isn't it wool and linen?" I blink.

Ymir turns to Pollux. "I thought you were an atheist."

"When did you become religious?" Saoirse shakes her head, trying to suppress her laughter.

"Since I saw God in August Vante," Pollux replies, seriously. "Speaking of divinity himself."

He motions towards the entrance of the canteen and our heads turn collectively.

It's the first time I see August in over two weeks.

Wearing a dark plum suit with his usual black turtleneck underneath, August strides effortlessly inside the canteen. His hair is a little longer, styled in its usual tamely tousled, slightly slicked-back look with the undercut peering through.

Just like everyone else at the table, I openly admire his appearance.

"He's been doing nonstop overtime for Holmes and Grayson," Ymir reveals.

His signature Peroxide Prince glower sits prettily on his face as he peruses the selection of drinks in the beverage area.

"We think he's planning on moving to New York once Holmes finds a permanent DOC," Saoirse adds.

My gaze drifts to the half-eaten poke bowl in front of me and I begin to prod it mindlessly.

It's not surprising that August would be leaving soon, his role as Director of Communications here at Holmes is only temporary. Everyone expected it. But still, my heart couldn't help but sink to the bottom of my stomach at the news.

CHAPTER 26

A slight commotion erupts around the table and I frown in confusion at everyone trying to look inconspicuous. Feeling a set of eyes on me, I look up to find August staring in my direction.

Our eyes meet and I watch as the dip between his eyebrows softens slightly. He gives me a small nod of acknowledgement and, without thinking, my hands twitch up into an awkward wave. He pauses for a moment before the side of his mouth quirks up slightly.

"What was that?" Pollux interjects, a mischievous glint in his eyes.

I blink. "What was what?"

"That." His tone is teasing as he nods towards August, now exiting the canteen.

"I have no idea what you're talking about."

"Uh-huh," He eyes me knowingly. "That has your Hartt-eyes written all over it."

I turn to him, perplexed. "My *what* eyes?"

"This thing you do where you stare at something like you're head over heels in love with it," Pollux reveals. "You look at *toile de jouy* fabrics in exactly the same way."

A noise of collective agreement ripples around the table and I flush in embarrassment.

"The print is *pretty*." I reason, continuing to stab at my poke bowl, a little more purposefully now.

Pollux snorts and gestures towards August's departing silhouette.

"And so is that upholstery fabric of a man."

The entire table frowns in confusion at Pollux's endless fashion euphemisms.

"You know, because he's a little rigid but durable and comes in surprisingly different patterns," He explains. "Plus, you can sit on him."

I gasp as Ymir shakes her head and Saoirse throws a napkin in his direction.

"Pollux!"

He meets our incredulous stares with a pointed look.

"What? We were all thinking it!"

Chapter 27

Royals of Toussaint x Holmes London Collaboration:
The Regalwear Collection
Lead Designer: *Sebastian O. Holmes*
Design Assistant: *Mahalia A. Hartt*
Support Team: *Estelle N. Li-Young, Pollux L. Okusanya*

Reviewing the brief for the regalwear collection and finding my name listed as part of the team made everything more real. The project deviates from the standard process of a collection, the Toussaint Royals only requesting for a set of samples to present at the annual Winter Gala at Cionne, the capital city of Toussaint, before the official tailoring for each royal could begin.

This meant that if I did well, I could continue working on this project in the foreseeable future. And even explore future projects surrounding it, should the opportunity present itself.

With the brief in my inbox and an introductory meeting scheduled for next week with *an actual member* of the Toussaint royal family, I feel the nervous excitement building. Contributing to a high-profile project for a distinguished client is a remarkable milestone and I still can't believe I've been given the opportunity.

My first official project.

A Regalwear Collection.

The initial task I've been assigned before starting actual work is clearing

CHAPTER 27

out the secondary studio on the fourth floor, where I'll be working with Sebastian on the collection. It was a way to keep the main collection downstairs separate from special client work.

I immediately get to work as I reach the second studio, drawing the blinds open to let natural light in from the outside. I look around the space appreciatively, taking note of the stacks of cardboard boxes and haphazardly placed mannequins in the room. It's not as big as the main studio downstairs, only half of its size really, but the space is more than adequate since it would only be Sebastian and I working here rather than the usual team of five.

If he ever decides to actually work in the studio, that is.

Pollux warned me of Sebastian's tendency to work from home days at a time and then deliver results last minute and I've mentally prepared myself for any hiccups along the way.

Quietly humming to myself, I'm wiping down the surface of the worktables in the middle of the room when I hear voices out in the corridor.

Puzzled to know who else is on the fourth floor, I peer outside of the door and freeze as I spot the recognisable head of platinum blond hair. August is in the middle of a conversation with another person, their voices filling the empty corridor. I do a double-take because they look strikingly similar at first glance.

Same height, same stature. Same facial features, almost.

One could easily mistake them for twins, if it wasn't for the stark contrast between August's platinum head of hair and the honey-brown locks of his companion. They walk past the secondary studio, completely unaware of my presence inside.

"Why didn't you go to Vante?" I instantly recognise August's voice as he speaks, an urgency in his tone.

"We did," Comes the reply. "You turned us down."

"What?" August sounds taken aback.

A pause. "The Palace received an ever so gracious email of rejection from *the* Cedric Vante himself. Redirected the Royal Comms to Holmes instead to take over the project, putting in good word of the studio team led by a certain Sebastian Oliver Holmes."

"*What?*"

"I figured your knowledge would be limited since I didn't hear anything from you firsthand."

"Limited?" Annoyance laces his voice. "More like *nonexistent.*"

"Clearly."

"I'm sure the work of your favourite designer will help."

Intrigued, I poke my head further out of the door, noticing them standing in front of his office.

"I'm not worried about *her,*" August says, almost defensively. "She's perfectly capable. She can take over the entire project if she wants to, in fact, I encourage it."

His companion hums in acknowledgement.

"It's *Sebastian,*" August continues. "Leading the team, of all people. I thought my father wanted good press for Holmes but this move just sends us back to the not-so-high graces of the press. This is going to be tabloid fodder."

"Are you sure your concerns aren't a personal matter?" The stranger asks. "Sebastian can be... a little neurotic but he still delivers excellent work. Aside from what happened with the spring/summer collection last year."

"It's complicated." The exasperation in August's voice is evident. "When exactly did my father approve of this?"

"Last week." Came the answer from his company. "Uncle dearest not only approved of the switch, he *endorsed* it."

My eyes widen.

Uncle?

Their conversation continues to echo down the empty corridor, making it clear I'm not privy to their discussion.

I retreat to the studio room in an attempt to stay hidden, quietly pushing the sliding door into a close lest they know that there are actually other people (ie. me) on the same floor.

The quiet sound of the lock clicks shut and I breathe out a sigh of relief.

CHAPTER 27

Slowly backing away from the door, my triumph is short-lived when I accidentally bump into a mannequin.

Like a domino effect, it sends the rest of the dozen mannequins crashing onto the laminate flooring.

"No!" I whisper-gasp, dust erupting around the heap of dressmaker dummies. "Damn it."

I cover my mouth to prevent the cough from coming up my lungs but I accidentally inhale the dust through my nose, making me sneeze loudly instead.

"*Atchoo!*"

There's a brief pause before I hear the rapid approach of footsteps. I inwardly curse, breaking out into a coughing fit as the sliding doors open, revealing a pair of light grey eyes. His gaze carries a mixture of surprise and confusion as it locks on to me.

"Mahalia?" August blinks.

"Hi," I cough, waving awkwardly as dust floats around the room.

I pull on the mannequins in an effort to stand them back up, my attempt feeble as the dressmaker dummies continue to topple over.

August narrows his eyes as he glances around the dusty studio and I see him hesitate for a few seconds before he and his companion step inside the room.

"What are you doing here?" He asks.

Curiously, I eye the person trailing behind him.

Tall, like August. If not a little taller due to his much straighter, much more rigid posture. Whilst August is a little more relaxed, the stranger exudes an *uprightness* to him. He's stylishly dressed, too, wearing a white button-up shirt underneath a caramel-coloured two-piece suit and tan Oxford shoes.

"Estelle told me to set up for the regalwear collection," I explain, glancing over at the third party in the room. "She wants Sebastian and I to use the secondary studio."

At the mention of the project, the tall well-dressed stranger perks up.

"Oh!" Honey-coloured hair and warm hazel eyes greet me with a regarding look. "You're working on the Holmes collaboration with Toussaint?"

"I'm assistant to the Lead Designer," I confirm, offering my hand. "Mahalia Hartt."

There's a knowing twinkle in the stranger's eyes as he looks over me quickly. "*The* Mahalia Aurora Hartt?"

I blink at the full mention of my government name.

"Umm, yes."

Glancing over at August, I see him silently watch me interact with the unknown stranger bearing an uncanny resemblance to him.

"Tobias," The stranger introduces himself with a warm smile as he shakes my hand. "Of Toussaint."

My mind blanks, brain short-circuiting as I take a moment for his greeting to process.

"Your Highness," I gasp, eyes widening as it finally does so.

"You may curtsy," He instructs with a charming nod, causing me to nearly trip over my feet in awe.

"Tobias," August addresses him, cautiously.

Still reeling from the unexpected encounter, I forget all sense of decorum regarding royal protocol as I bow my head and dip slightly into a curtsy, accidentally bumping into the mannequins again.

August is quick to react as he reaches out towards my direction. His hand grabs my arm to steady me, but completely misses the toppling dressmaker dummies behind.

I wince at the loud crash that follows. "Sorry."

"Be careful," August turns to me, his expression softening. "Are you okay?"

I nod wordlessly, a fleeting recollection of soft grey eyes and intimate encounters flashing through my mind.

My flat, his office, the bar, the fitting, the club.

Neither August and I have spoken properly to address the events that happened between us during Men's Fashion Week, becoming lost in translation as we gradually got busier with our jobs at Holmes. It almost

CHAPTER 27

feels like a fever dream, a distant memory left unspoken, now that we're back to working in our respective roles.

A slow and deliberate cough interrupts my thoughts and I straighten up, glancing at the hazel-eyed prince behind August. The nervousness I feel grows tenfold at the sight of my first client in the same room as the man I may or may not be still harbouring a little crush on.

Prince Tobias smiles kindly at me.

"It's a pleasure to meet you, Miss Hartt."

"Just Hallie is fine," I stammer, bowing forward again and mentally cringing at my anxious behaviour. "And likewise– Your Highness, sir."

"Tobias is here to see the studio," August says.

This time, I notice the lack of title in his acknowledgement of the second-in-line to the Toussaint crown.

"August is kindly showing me around," Prince Tobias adds, eyes shifting attentively as he scans the secondary studio.

I gesture awkwardly around the room.

"This is, um, one of the smaller studios. I'm tidying it up and clearing it out. It's going to be 100% spotless for the collection, rest assured."

Nervously, I glance over at August who appears to be hyper-focused on the fallen mannequins on the floor. He seems tense, as if he'd rather be anywhere else.

"I don't doubt that for a moment," Prince Tobias replies with a look of congeniality, most definitely fit for a royal. "I look forward to seeing the collection."

"Thank you, sir." I nod, remembering *not* to curtsy this time. "Your Highness."

"Just Tobias will do." He clears his throat, casting a sideways glance at August. "Since we are in the company of my dear cousin."

I blink at this information.

Cousin!?

Wide-eyed, I turn to August.

"Tobias," He warns, once again omitting any formal title when addressing the royal.

"Ah," Prince Tobias gives August a, far too polished, look of atonement. "Apologies."

August sighs, shaking his head, as I stay quiet. My mind is working overtime as I make the connection with August and one of the crown princes of Mediterranean Europe.

Of course, he would have associations with royalty, *of course*.

"Do you need any help?" August turns towards me.

My mouth opens in alarm. "N-no! It's alright, I've got it all under control."

Both men, all sharp angles and tall stature, glance over at the toppled mannequins on the floor and exchange a look.

"Right," August frowns as I offer him, what I hope to be, a reassuring smile.

"I'm sure I'll be fine," I continue. "Thank you though."

August doesn't reply straight away. Instead, he shares another look with Prince Tobias. They seem to communicate almost telepathically, the faintest rise of the prince's eyebrow prompting the most not-so-subtle of eye rolls from the nepo baby himself.

"I suppose I have nothing else in my schedule today," The royal responds. "I am here to see the studio after all."

I shake my head towards August and send him a pointed look, hoping he reads between the lines.

"Your Highness, it's fine," I say. "Thank you sincerely for the offer but—"

"We'll give you a hand." August decides, eyes roaming around the unkempt studio.

Inwardly, I wince.

So much for reading between the lines.

"August, it's dusty and grimy and *not clean*," I stress, hoping his semi-hypochondriac tendency will make him reconsider.

"Then the sooner we tidy up, the better." He replies, taking one last sweeping look around the studio. "I'll grab one of the humidifiers in my office."

He leaves without saying anything else and I can only watch as he exits the room. From the corner of my eye, I see Prince Tobias moving to upright the fallen dressmaker dummies, prompting me to scramble towards him immediately.

"Prince Tobias, truly. There's no need to—"

"I insist, Miss Hartt." The prince interjects with a warm smile. "It's only a little bit of organising. Perhaps it will distract my dear cousin from having an aneurysm over the latest news regarding the Holmes collaboration."

"Oh," I swallow, not entirely sure how to approach the conversation I so happen to have been eavesdropping on. "I, umm, was made aware that Holmes wasn't your first choice for the regalwear collection."

"Yes," Prince Tobias nods, a slight hesitance clouding his cheerful expression. "We initially pursued a collaboration with Vante. Family ties and whatnot."

My mind is still reeling from the revelation of August's connection to aristocracy, leaving me unable to contribute much to the conversation. The extended silence that follows is stilted as I struggle to think of things to say.

As if sensing my anxiousness, Prince Tobias continues.

"But no matter, we have faith in Holmes since uncle did hand the responsibility over to the studio," Tobias reassures me, the gracious smile back on his face. "Also, if you are indeed *the* Mahalia Aurora Hartt then I've seen your work."

"You have?" I gape.

"Estelle sent us your portfolio," He details. "Your Disney Prince collection is a work of fantastic craftsmanship, Miss Hartt. You most certainly have the eye and skill for design."

"Oh, t-thank you, sir." I stutter out a response. "I appreciate that."

I find it slightly disorienting that Prince Tobias, second in line to the Toussaint crown, is engaging in actual conversation with me as he helps clear out a dusty room at Holmes let alone complimenting my portfolio.

"I can see why my cousin is a big fan of your work," He muses. "Have you considered women's clothing? Or is your work strictly menswear?"

"I do commission work for womenswear," I nod. "But I specialised in men's tailoring at uni."

"You're LIFT alumni, correct?"

"Yes, sir." I reply.

Though he doesn't seem that much older than I am, if anything he seems to be around August's age, my excessive politeness in the presence of new company naturally kicks in.

"Please, call me Tobias." He insists. "Prim and propriety is only for the public eye after all."

I nod, laughing out of nervousness. Even though I'm certain I'm still going to address him every other formal variation of his royal title and not just simply *Tobias*.

August returns, a contemplative look on his face as he meets me in the middle of the studio.

"Here." He reaches out towards me, his touch gentle as he places the humidifier in my hands.

My heart rate picks up as his fingertips brush against my skin, the touch lingering much longer than necessary. My gaze falls to our connected hands and I look up to find August's grey eyes staring intently at me.

"Thank you." I nod, breathless.

Another purposeful cough resounding in the studio brings me out of my trance.

August drops his hand and I turn towards Prince Tobias peering over at us with an inquisitive look.

"Am I correct to assume you have a structure in mind as to where everything should be?" Prince Tobias asks.

He continues to haul up the rest of the mannequins as August walks over to the worktable stacked with cardboard boxes of different sizes.

"She has a system with everything," August answers for me.

It shouldn't affect me how August seems to know my working habits but I find my heart fluttering at his attentiveness nonetheless.

Prince Tobias sends August a knowing glance before turning to me.

"We're at your disposal, Miss Hartt."

Chapter 28

"He's related to *royalty?*"

Gigi's voice echoes in the flat as she calls out to me from her bedroom.

It's a Saturday evening, both Gigi and I are getting ready to attend an event on behalf of MODUE Magazine as I simultaneously detail the events that transpired over the past few days at Holmes.

"Like legitimately?" She questions.

"I don't know how exactly but yes," I reply, grabbing my black strappy heels from my closet. "Legitimately."

Opting for all black, since I feel far more comfortable blending in rather than standing out in events I have very little knowledge on how to network in, I decided to wear a black lace bandeau with matching black wide-leg silk trousers and strappy heels.

Making my way to the living room, I walk over to the armchair and sit down, securing the straps of my heels around my ankles.

"Your man is like an 18th-century Rococo mantua dress," Gigi comments. "Elaborately decorated with so many layers."

I shake my head at the accurate description. "Not my man."

Standing up, I grab my black clutch bag, double-checking I have all my essentials.

"Your man who isn't your man, sure." She laughs. "I've never met someone so…"

"Overly embellished and complicated?"

"I was going to say multifaceted but that works too."

I've always been a relatively straightforward person. Particular, sure.

But I know what I like and I'm happy with what I like.

August is still an enigma to me. A complicated one at that.

Involving myself with him would be like wearing something that's two sizes far too big. I simply wouldn't fit and it would not be flattering.

Gigi struts into the living room moments later, dressed in a black diamante studded playsuit with matching black stilettos.

"Are you catastrophising?" She questions, voice filtering through my thoughts.

"No," I reply, sheepishly.

Gigi playfully rolls her eyes at me before checking her phone. "Schedule your catastrophic thinking for later, Hals. Taxi's downstairs, let's go."

The event I'm attending with Gigi is a collaboration between Babble, the online dating app, and The Duke & Dalton, a private gentleman's club in Mayfair. Gigi had been tasked with writing up an article of the press event in place of the junior editor who abruptly left Entertainment. It's a non-fashion PR function and that's as far as I know.

The moment we're outside of the establishment, Gigi is instantly in work mode as she struts towards the entrance.

"Hi, Mason." She nods towards security. "Genevieve Winters and Mahalia Hartt."

"Of course, G." The guard replies, stepping aside to let us in.

Entering the private club, I'm immediately in awe at the elegance of the interior. The fusion of Art Deco extravagance and continental charm is evident, with walls adorned in velvet curtains of deep emerald and sapphire, accentuated by intricate gold-leafed mouldings. Plush leather chairs and divans, upholstered in velvet fabric decorate the entrance room, as crystal chandeliers cast a warm and inviting glow to the interior. Every detail is meticulously curated, from the fancy parquet flooring to the hand-carved wooden panelling.

Gigi and I settle at the bar, my eyes perusing the expensive drinks menu.

"Hals," Gigi whispers to me. "That's the co-founder of Babble right there."

I turn my head. "The one you're supposed to be interviewing?"

CHAPTER 28

"Jack Montgomery," She confirms.

Her eyes are assessing as she gives the tall stranger a few metres across from us a quick once over.

"Will you be okay on your own for a bit?"

"Yes," I nod in reply. "Don't worry, I'll behave."

Sensing how important this is for Gigi, I push away the drinks menu and turn to her.

"Go," I usher her quietly. "Do your thing, Miss Winters."

Gigi flashes me a grateful smile before striding over to a man in his late twenties with dark blond hair, currently in conversation with William Dalton, the man who owns The Duke himself.

I sit by the bar, content with people watching and admiring the decor. It's obvious that the bar is a central focal point of the gentleman's club, boasting an impressive selection of top-shelf spirits. I'm not a huge fan of rare whiskies and elaborate cocktails but I know an expensive alcohol menu when I see one.

My eyes fall to the tiny intricate glass water bottles in the display and I reach for one, admiring the ornate label detailing the glass.

Perks of attending fancy events? Freebies. I'm about to sneak another bottle into my purse when I hear a voice calling out to me.

"Hallie?"

I turn my head to find a familiar figure approaching the bar.

"Fancy seeing you here, gentle goddess!" Henry grins at me.

My nose scrunches at the nickname as he pulls me into a side hug, the stool I'm currently sitting on is elevated so I'm just coming up to within eye level.

From head to toe, Henry is brightly dressed. A short-sleeved, white canvas button-up shirt patterned with brush strokes and paint splatters, low rise wide leg trousers and pristine white boat shoes to match.

"Did you come with August?" He cranes his head over the bar as I shake my head.

"No, I came with a friend." I turn to gesture in Gigi's direction only to find the spot vacant. "Or she was here, she's around somewhere."

I scan the well-decorated room full of exquisite paintings from across the continent gracing the walls. It's an overwhelming display but it boasts the rich cultural heritage of Europe that The Duke & Dalton are very much associated with.

"Wanna come join me at my table?" Henry asks. "I'm here with a few friends."

"Oh, I don't want to bother you," I answer with a small smile. "But thank you."

"Don't be daft," Henry insists. "It's only the boys. You've met the Contis already, right? They walked at the Holmes show."

I briefly remember dark hair, dark eyes and tanned skin at the fitting and I nod.

"Perfect, we're over by the private booths on the first floor. I just need–" He pauses as he looks behind me and recognition flashes in his eyes. "Actually, Sebastian will take you. Seb!"

Following his gaze, I turn to find a figure with dark brown hair and intense blue eyes approaching us. Sebastian's wearing a white button-down, with the first few buttons of the shirt undone, and black trousers paired with loafers.

"Evening," He nods at me, aloofly.

There's no animosity between us professionally. At least I'm hoping there isn't, but there is a slightly undisclosed tension on my end, being an extended associate to August.

"Will you show Hallie our table?" Henry says to Sebastian. "I need to go to the bathroom."

I smile politely. "It's fine, I don't–"

"Be right back." Henry gives a two-fingered salute before disappearing into the crowd of people making their way towards the bar.

Sebastian regards me for a moment but he doesn't say anything, walking past me completely.

I pause for a moment, before turning my head to watch him. I expected Sebastian to continue walking up the stairs to their private table but I'm surprised to find him standing at the bottom of the stairs waiting.

CHAPTER 28

"Are you coming?"

Sensing there's no escaping the situation, I nod wordlessly before sliding off the bar stool.

Neither of us have seen each other since that morning in August's office and there's a slightly standoffish energy to Sebastian as I follow him. We haven't discussed what happened but I don't feel like I know him well enough to. Sebastian and I aren't necessarily friends. We're acquaintances at most, even moving to colleague territory since we'll both be working on the regalwear collection.

Whenever he decides it's convenient for him to come to the studio, that is.

The first floor of The Duke & Dalton is warmly lit. Separated into a bar and booths, there's a walkway by the bar that overlooks the ground floor. Peering down the railing, I sigh in relief as I spot Gigi sitting in conversation with Jack Montgomery in one of the seating areas in the corner.

Sebastian leads as we walk down the walkway that separates the VIP tables into private booths.

"I sincerely hope an angelic thing like you isn't coming home with a spawn of the devil like him." A voice teases as Sebastian and I approach one of the booths in the corner.

"Prick," Sebastian calls out good-naturedly and the faces around the table erupt in quiet peals of laughter.

I blink at the stranger's comment, glancing towards Sebastian.

"This is Alfie, that's Benji." He begins motioning towards each person around the table. "And you know the Contis, Rome and Teo."

There's a chorus of hellos before Sebastian continues.

"This is Hallie," Then, as if pondering what to call me, he settles for: "My partner."

All four of them choke on their drinks and I turn towards Sebastian at his introduction, a bemused expression on his face.

"In Design," I quickly add. "I'm assisting with the regalwear collection at Holmes."

"Bloody hell, mate." Alfie chuckles.

"You could've started with that." Benji shakes his head.

"Lovely to see you again, Hallie." Romeo nods towards me. "Hen will be glad to see you."

"He's the one that found her," Sebastian comments.

I feel a little out of place, to say the very least.

"How are you finding the event?" Mateo asks, politely making conversation.

"It's a nice change in environment," I answer. "I spend a lot of time cooped up in a studio so…"

I trail off, not entirely confident standing in front of a table full of testosterone-fuelled nepo babies.

"We're not really big on these events either," Benji comments. "But we know Jack and there's free alcohol."

"And Alf basically forced everyone," Romeo adds.

"You mean my dad and his PR team," Alfie rolls his eyes, before turning to me. "They've been wanting some press for Duke and these so-called influencers are decent eye candy apparently."

Benji shoves at him playfully, thick American accent as he comments. "Dude, we're doing this for free."

"Please do not call me an influencer," Mateo scoffs. "It's insulting."

"Might have to agree with him there," Sebastian says, nudging Alfie so he can sit down.

Hovering by their table, I glimpse down at the ground floor, mentally sighing in relief to still find Gigi by the corner with Jack Montgomery.

"Sit with us." The eldest Conti offers.

I'm about to decline their invitation and head back down to Gigi when I feel a presence behind me.

"What did I miss?" Henry drapes an arm over my shoulder as he looks over the table, his other hand holding a whiskey glass. "Let the lady sit, boys."

He gestures wildly around the booth for everyone to shuffle, sitting me down before I can protest. He shuffles in after me, essentially sandwiching

CHAPTER 28

me between him and Sebastian.

"Drink?" Romeo motions towards the champagne cooler on the table and I shake my head politely.

"No, thank you."

"The fact that she came up here willingly with Seb, completely sober, tells us everything we need to know," Alfie jibes.

Playful snickers erupt around the table as Sebastian scoffs before leaning back on the booth and taking another swig of his drink.

"Aren't you with August?" Mateo questions unsuspectingly.

There's a record scratch as the table pauses, animated chatter falling into silence.

"He came with you?" Alfie blinks, looking over his shoulder as if expecting August to materialise out of thin air.

I shake my head.

"No, I came with a friend," I pipe up, craning my neck over the balcony to see Gigi. "She works for MODUE Magazine."

"You know her, Benj?" Romeo turns towards the young chief executive of the New York brand.

"I don't automatically know every single person that works for MODUE," Benji rolls his eyes before looking over in my direction. "Henrietta is my godmother."

I nod in acknowledgement because, of course, everyone would be connected to someone here. I can probably play people association with one person in the room and end up connecting every single person in the establishment to each other, one way or another.

"It's a shame August couldn't be here tonight," Alfie shakes his head. "Would have been the first time the infamous Fashion Four are all under the same roof."

"Nothing ever keeps him interested long enough," Benji snorts. "The playboy's difficult to please."

The sound everyone makes in agreement with the statement somehow makes my stomach turn.

"I'm sure he'd come running once he finds out his favourite designer's in attendance," Henry teases me, bumping my shoulders and I force a smile. "You should have seen his face when I asked Hallie out to dinner, the man was ready to gut me inside out."

Everyone is looking at me as I stiffly sit next to Sebastian.

"If looks could kill," Henry visibly shivers. "He has it down pat."

"It's the Peroxide Prince glower." Benji snorts.

There's reshuffling in our seats as Sebastian gets up.

"Bathroom," He states before walking away.

"Maybe don't bring him up so damn much." Romeo sighs before following Sebastian.

Henry holds his hands up placatingly as Mateo gets up to order more drinks at the bar and Benji excuses himself to take a call.

"So, you and August, huh?" Alfie regards me as I end up sitting next to him, hazel-green eyes curious.

"No, we're just..." I pause.

Work colleagues? Friends? Certainly nothing more but I don't know what to refer to him as, especially in this setting.

"Oooh, she hesitated." Alfie chuckles.

"Friends of friends," I answer.

It's the safest option, I suppose. Not too disconnected as work colleagues but not close enough to be actual friends.

"Is that what we're calling it nowadays?" Henry snorts. "Do friends of friends kiss each other on the mouth?"

I blink.

"There are eyes and ears in Onyx," Henry reveals. "And a lot of lips, apparently."

Taken by surprise, I try not to react to his comment.

"It's nothing like that." I shake my head. "August and I aren't... like that."

Of course, I wasn't expecting anything to come out of a drunken kiss. August had been gracious and understanding enough, even sparing my feelings instead of flat-out rejecting me.

"So I still have a shot?" Henry winks at me.

Alfie cuts in. "I wouldn't entertain this little man-slag if I were you, babe."

CHAPTER 28

"Not you too," Henry groans. "What is with everyone cockblocking me?"

"Lads!" The booming voice belonging to Jack Montgomery echoes on the first floor. "They want pictures downstairs."

I look to find him making his way over towards the private booth I'm in, Gigi trailing behind.

"There you are!" Gigi sighs with relief. "I thought I'd lost you."

"Told you she's in safe hands," He comments, holding his arm out towards me. "Jack Montgomery."

I nod nervously, shaking his hand. "Hallie. Mahalia Hartt."

"Ah yes, Gi was ready to call out a search party for you," He quirks a smile before turning his attention to the rest of the table. "Hen, photo op by the entrance. Alf, don't forget to smile."

They all excuse themselves downstairs, leaving Gigi and I by ourselves in the VIP booth.

I turn to Gigi. "*Gi*, huh?"

"Don't ask." She scrunches her nose.

"That took a while," I comment as Gigi sits opposite me.

"He wanted me to play matchmaker," Gigi snickers. "Apparently, a certain London It Boy has his eye on you."

I frown. "Gigi..."

"Don't worry," She winks at me. "I told him there's a particular heir to a Parisian fashion house that's already vying for your attention. Jack is sending Henry thoughts and prayers."

"I really don't think that's the case." I sigh.

If the company he keeps is any indication, I'm confident August Vante is not the type of person who would be interested in someone like me.

Sebastian returns, gaze hardening as he assesses the empty table.

"Pictures," I supply stiffly. "They've gone downstairs for a photo op."

There's a pause as he studies Gigi and I.

"I'll be in the studio next week," He informs me. "To go through the schedule and workload with you for the collection."

I clear my throat. "We're using the studio on the fourth floor."

He nods in acknowledgement but doesn't say anything else as he leaves, not even sparing a second glance as he descends the stairs.

Chapter 29

Following the conclusion of the initial meeting with the Royal Comms and the design team, I'm immediately plunged into the research and ideation phase of the regalwear collection.

While it might seem tedious to some, it happens to be my favourite part of any project. I actually enjoy the process of immersing myself in the background and history of an assignment.

Deciding to stay behind after work, I began researching information on Toussaint's royal fashion, traditions and ceremonial wear for the regalwear collection.

With music blaring and my third cup of coffee in hand, I'm sliding over to the printer to collect the images being printed for the moodboard. I've forgone wearing my platform Mary Jane shoes out of comfort as I walk around the studio, gliding across the hardwood flooring in my knee-high socks instead and dancing clumsily to the songs playing as I go. Silk ribbons wrapped around my neck and lace fabric draped over my shoulders, I'm twirling around the room with a mannequin in my arms when I catch a glimpse of a figure standing by the door.

"August?"

I skid to a stop, nearly tumbling as I straighten myself up.

"The door was wide open," He explains. "And your music was hard to ignore."

My cheeks flush in embarrassment at being caught candy dancing with a dressmaker dummy to some alt-indie band and I quickly reach towards the speakers to turn the music off.

"Sorry, I didn't realise you were working overtime."

August's office is always dark from the outside so it's hard to tell whether or not he's actually in. It's just past 7 PM and, whilst the rest of the studio left two hours prior, the design team sans Sebastian decided to stay behind to do much-needed work.

"What were you listening to?" He asks, gesturing towards the speaker.

"Umm, medieval rock?" I reply sheepishly. "I'm not sure, it was on a playlist with different artists from Toussaint."

I slide the mannequin back over by the sewing machines, removing the ribbons and fabric around me and draping them over the dressmaker dummy instead. Walking back to the computer, I suddenly feel oddly nervous about August's presence as he enters the studio.

"No wonder it sounded familiar," He muses. "You were listening to music by Saintians."

I blink. "Saintians?"

"People from Toussaint," He adds. "Toussaintians, technically. But they shorten it to Saintians. Less of a mouthful."

"Oh *that's* how you pronounce it," I mutter to myself, jotting down the name on my notepad before turning to August. "*Sahn-tee-uns*. How did you know that?"

"I was born there."

"You're..." I blink up at him. "*Toussaintian?*"

"Half," He nods. "My mother's side of the family is from Toussaint."

He doesn't elaborate, ever the enigma.

But it makes a lot of sense. How he's related to the Toussaint royal family. August has that refined air about him too, gaining the attention of people in the room with his presence effortlessly.

Even now, with just the two of us.

"Is there anything you need from me?" I ask curiously.

"No," He replies. "I just wanted to see the source of the deafeningly loud music."

"Sorry," I wince. "I'll be camping out on the fourth floor over the next couple of months to work on the collection but I'll make sure to close the

CHAPTER 29

door and keep the noise down."

"You're fine," He shakes his head, eyeing the box in the middle of the worktable of silk ribbons and lace fabric. "What are these for?"

"Oh, they're mine," I answer. "I have a commissioned piece for Mahalia Made. But it doesn't interfere with studio work, don't worry. I work on it during my breaks."

He pauses, staring at me. "You *work* during your *breaks?*"

"I get restless when I'm not doing anything," I laugh nervously.

He narrows his eyes, concern marring his features. "Do you ever not work?"

"When I'm sleeping," I reply jokingly.

August sends me a serious, scolding look this time. "Working yourself to the point of exhaustion is concerning behaviour, Mahalia."

"Blame my hands, they don't like being still."

His grey eyes sweep over my left hand, almost assessing, and I retract it from his view out of self-consciousness. There's a subtle shift in his expression as he redirects his focus, scanning his surroundings.

August's attention flickers to the humidifier stationed in the corner before his gaze drifts around the room, briefly settling on various homeware accessories. I grimace at the random bits of decorative pieces I've scattered around the room to make it feel cosier since I'm practically going to be living in this studio for the next couple of months.

"Is that supposed to be a thimble?"

He squints, evaluating one of my peach-coloured plushies sitting on top of a thick blanket haphazardly thrown over the sofa in the back of the room.

"Oh, yes." I nod, slightly embarrassed. "It's a comfy pillow."

He turns back to me. "Please don't tell me you sleep in the studio too."

I eye him hesitantly. "Are there rules for taking naps in the studio?"

"You're impossible," He exhales a breath, shaking his head. "How's the regalwear collection coming along?"

"Good," I nod. "Really good, actually. I met Prince Tobias and members of the Royal Comms of Toussaint earlier this week. Sebastian and I discussed the official brief and we're just doing the research phase at the moment."

"By 'we', do you mean 'you'?"

"Sebastian's working from his home studio," I explain.

"I'm very familiar with Sebastian's work practices," He mutters disapprovingly.

"He was at The Duke & Dalton a few nights ago," I glance over at him, hoping to catch a glimpse of a reaction but his face remains stoic. "Babble hosted a PR event."

"You attended?"

"I was Gigi's plus one," I reply.

A beat.

"Did you drink?" He asks.

"Yes," I nod. "The fancy glass bottles of spring water from the Swiss Alps were very refreshing. I sneaked about half a dozen bottles in my purse."

At this, he chuckles.

"They were looking for you." I attempt a conversation. "The boys? Alfie, Benji and the Contis."

"Ah," he nods. "I was... working."

August looks like he doesn't want to expand further, like he's unsure of the answer himself.

"What are these for?" He motions towards the early stages of a moodboard, printed images scattered all over the table.

"Research," I answer. "I had no idea Toussaint was on par with Great Britain when it came to textile manufacturing during the Industrial Revolution."

A small island nestled between the coast of the Mediterranean and Europe, Toussaint is renowned for its expertise in fabric production spanning centuries. The country's history is rich in power looms, cotton gins and carding machines, even rivalling Britain which is impressive for a small country by the Mediterranean Sea.

August nods. "Toussaint *is* known for its textiles."

Listening as he effortlessly provided more information about the country, I expected a more business-oriented conversation so I was

CHAPTER 29

genuinely surprised when he shared little anecdotes, recalling nostalgic details of his time there.

"Cionne is teeming with culture," He continues, referring to the capital city. "And it's beautiful in the summer."

From my research, the island's capital is a picturesque city, boasting cobblestone streets, vibrant houses and breathtaking views of the Mediterranean Sea.

"It looks it," I sigh dreamily, looking down at the images I've collected. "It would be amazing to conduct primary research to see the textiles in person."

Standing in front of the computer, I continue to scroll through more research on the island, momentarily falling into a daydream of warm sand, saltwater hair and sun-kissed skin.

"–so we'll go." August nods at me.

"Huh?" I turn to him, missing part of what he was saying during my daydream.

"To Toussaint," He replies as he casually surveys the images on the table.

"I, um, don't know how long HR will take to approve work trips." I begin, still uncertain whether or not I heard him correctly. "Not to mention going through it with Sebastian. He told me his schedule is really busy over the next couple of weeks so I'm not sure if he'll find the time."

I've already been warned by Pollux that working around Sebastian and his erratic schedule will be challenging. The senior designer doesn't seem to adhere to the usual 9-5 routine, often working from home and responding to emails at 3 AM. Despite holding a senior role, he spends more time outside the studio than in it and suggesting an international trip doesn't necessarily align with my typical duties as an intern.

"I said *we* will go," He repeats, firmly. "We can plan it for this weekend. Are you busy?"

I blink. "I'm not but..."

"Great." He nods, sliding the photos of a fancy-looking building as well as the exterior of a mill factory towards me. "We can pay a visit to the National Museum of Cionne and go to the textile factories at the Toussaint

Foundry. You'll have plenty of source material and inspiration for the collection."

"Are they even open during the weekend?" I ask.

He shrugs. "I'll see what I can do."

Before I can voice any objections, August retrieves his phone and begins typing, his laser-focused gaze fixed on the screen.

"So," He begins, sliding his phone back into his pocket. "This weekend in Toussaint. I'll email you the details of our itinerary before Friday."

"Do you need me to help with anything?" I ask.

He shakes his head.

"Just leave it to me."

Chapter 30

I wasn't quite sure what to expect regarding the work trip that August is supposed to be organising. So receiving a meticulous schedule for our research trip in Cionne over the weekend, planned entirely by himself, was something I most definitely did not anticipate. The itinerary was itemised down to the last hour– from our flight to Toussaint on Friday night to the plane back to London on Monday evening, even taking into account a free day on the last day.

The email concluded with a note:

> Itinerary is only an outline and is subject to change depending on additional material you might need for your research.
> – AV

It's currently Thursday and I'm once again staying behind at the studio to work on the Holmes x Toussaint collaboration when the email about the trip to Cionne comes through. The two-page PDF document detailed all the timings, locations of establishments as well as potential alternatives and I couldn't help but be amazed by August's thoroughness.

"I figured you'd still be here."

I look up to find the very same head of platinum blond hair I'm thinking about, now standing in front of me.

"No concert tonight?" He inquires, the corner of his mouth quirking.

Warmth travels up my neck.

"I saw your office door open earlier," I reply, quietly. "I didn't want to disturb you."

"That's a shame. I enjoyed the front-row seats to your performance." He gives me a onceover, his gaze almost teasing as he scans the studio. "Where's Sebastian?"

"He's attending networking events in Amsterdam this week."

August frowns.

"Amsterdam," He echoes emptily. "Has he even stepped foot in the studio?"

"He was here Monday," I reply. "Our focus is still primarily on research which I'm responsible for."

It feels oddly reminiscent of my time working under August as I update him on the work I've been doing and log every task in detail.

"We're back and forth via emails," I add. "But Sebastian said he should be back by the end of next week."

"End of next week," August repeats, stiffly. "Is he expecting you to do the majority of the work?"

"It's only research," I assure him, sensing his souring mood. "It's the boring stuff that not many people want to do but I like research so I don't mind."

August maintains his stoic composure despite his growing agitation.

"You didn't specify which airline we're flying with," I comment, trying to change the topic. "I don't know how much, or how little, to pack."

"As much as you'd like," He replies. "You can bring your entire wardrobe if you want. We're taking the jet."

I stare at him, unblinking. "The jet?"

"Yes, the jet."

"As in…" I press for clarification.

"A private plane."

"To Toussaint?"

"Yes."

My eyes widen. "We can't finance a business jet to the Mediterranean

CHAPTER 30

for a small *research* trip."

"Why not?" He turns to me. "It's on the company card."

"But not on company time!"

"Technically, we're on the clock."

On a private jet.

August turns to me. "Is this another nod to your attempts of saving the environment?"

"Well now that you've mentioned it, yes—"

"This is actually the first time I'm taking my private jet out this year," He says. "Comparative to last year, my carbon footprint is practically non-existent."

"That's technically impossible," I mumble.

"Flying commercial is too inconvenient," He begins to explain. "There's too much waiting around. Check-in lines, security lines, boarding lines. Time is money."

Hesitantly, I turn to him.

"August, we can't—"

The beginning of my argument is cut short by a ridiculously loud growling.

August and I stare at each other for a moment before his gaze dips to my stomach.

"That… did not come from you." He blinks.

"Sorry." I duck my head, flushing in embarrassment. "I forgot to eat lunch today."

"Mahalia, it's 7 PM." August squints disapprovingly. "Losing sleep, forgetting to eat– do we need to schedule a session with a wellness coach for you?"

"No, no." I visibly wince. "I'm fine, I've just been so hyper-focused on starting the project that it slipped my mind."

He doesn't look convinced and I feel a tugging at my heart at the display of concern on his face.

"I picked up an order at the restaurant earlier," He says.

I tilt my head curiously. "I didn't realise you've become a regular at Tito

Boy's."

"Hero doesn't want me to order anywhere else."

"Sounds about right," I laugh then add playfully, "You ordered food from my favourite place of all time and didn't think of getting me any?"

August pauses, hand reaching up to rub the back of his neck. The action is oddly boyish, almost a little shy, and it looks somewhat out of character.

"I, uh, did actually." He clears his throat. "It's in my office."

I blink at him curiously as he gestures behind him.

Not entirely convinced, I follow him to his office and sure enough, there's a brown paper bag with Tito Boy's logo perched on his desk. Looking inside, my eyes widen at the plastic containers with August's initials as well as mine.

"Wait, you actually ordered me food?"

My stomach flips excitedly at the kind gesture, or maybe it's the hunger taking effect.

"I saw you making your way up to the fourth floor before I left the studio earlier," He provides. "I didn't order the entire menu but I did double-check your preferences with Hero."

I try not to read into it, the somersaults in my stomach cartwheeling upwards to my chest.

"Eat," He urges gently, rummaging through the paper bag to retrieve the plastic cutlery and setting it down in front of me. "You're not leaving my office until you finish a dish."

August watches me intently as he makes his way to the chair behind his desk and plops himself down. He retrieves his own food as we make idle conversation.

"Were you being August or Jean-Luc?" I question.

He turns to me inquisitively as I purse my lips towards the darkroom, the familiar red glow peeking out from underneath the door.

"Comms work or photography?" I inquire.

"Ah," He nods understandingly. "Photography. London's becoming one of my favourite muses."

"Don't let New York hear you say that," I tease, feeling the ease growing

CHAPTER 30

in our interaction. "Can I see?"

"After you've finished your food."

Speedily, I devour the bowl of sopas, grinning as I show him the empty container.

He shakes his head before getting up and I follow him into the darkroom, noticing that it's slightly more cluttered compared to the first time I've been inside but it only highlighted how much work August has been doing in the meantime.

"When do you find the time to do all of this?" I ask, my eyes widening.

He shrugs in response. "I make time."

My gaze remains fixed on the images clipped to the wire, imagining how difficult it must be to navigate the work between two fashion houses whilst still managing to make time for his photography.

"August, these are incredible." I stare in awe at the various photos of, what appear to be, couples in Hyde Park. "Are they recent?"

He nods, a subtle excitement in his eyes. "I started a series where I take pictures of, uh, couples I come across when I'm out."

My attention is drawn to the label taped to the corner of each photograph.

"Lovers in London." I read out loud.

The candid snapshots of each couple are eye-catching, each photo expertly framed with varying compositions including wide angles and close-ups. One particular portrait shot of an elderly, interracial couple sticks out for me, reminding me of my grandparents.

"They've been married for over 50 years," August details.

Just like Mama and Papa.

A warmth spreads throughout my chest as I stare at the photo of the couple with their arms around each other. They're both beaming at the camera, eyes bright, with laughter lines decorating their faces. August captured them in a way that made the viewer *feel* the emotion. I admire the image, the memory of my grandparents tugging at my heart.

"Taking pictures of the elderly is probably my favourite." He comments.

"Oh?"

"They lived through life." He shrugs in way of explanation. "I like hearing their stories, their experiences. Plus, it's refreshing to just be Jean-Luc, the 'nice young man with the camera' rather than August Vante the—"

"Peroxide Playboy Prince of Paris." I finish.

He shoots me a mock glare. "That sounds like the title of a smear campaign that Faux ran against me."

I laugh lightly. "If it's any consolation, you were firstly Jean-Luc to me, the 'obnoxious photographer who mansplained sustainability to a designer'."

"I'm glad," He chuckles quietly. "Certainly beats Baby Vante the 'Nepo Baby Germaphobe'."

He continues to share stories of the photographs he's taken and I listen attentively, finding myself clinging to every word he says. August looks different under the glow of the red light, his features seemingly softer and his voice more gentle, like he's sharing secrets of the world he's discovered for himself.

He's in the middle of recalling a photo of a couple he took in one of London's Royal Parks when something catches my eye amidst the cluttered space of his worktable.

The photograph of me at the gallery.

It wasn't hidden under the pile of endless photos anymore. Neither is it clipped on a wire like I originally saw it. It wasn't even tacked on the wall like some of the other images are.

This time, it's propped up in a frame on top of his desk.

Chapter 31

Packing for the weekend trip to Toussaint turned out to be moderately straightforward. I opted to travel light, given the short duration of our stay, bringing along only a medium-sized suitcase. August and I arrived in Cionne late in the evening and it was already 10 PM local time by the time we reached the hotel, well past the usual check-in hours.

The accommodation we're staying at is The Royal Maisonette of Toussaint, although the term 'maisonette' hardly did justice to the lavishness of the establishment. It's a grand building located in the capital city, drawing inspiration from French architecture. The hotel's exterior boasts intricate mouldings, wrought-iron balconies and large windows. Stepping into the lobby, I'm greeted by an expansive area adorned with crystal chandeliers, marble floors and the most sumptuous seating arrangements– definitely velvet.

Having travelled straight after work, August is dressed in his signature attire: a navy suit with a black turtleneck and a pair of black oxford shoes.

"Master Vante, Mademoiselle Hartt." The receptionist warmly greets us. "Welcome to The Royal Maisonette."

I can only smile and nod in acknowledgement, still stunned by the extravagant design of the establishment.

"Laurent," August regards him. *"Bonsoir."*

"Delighted to see you always, *monsieur.*" Laurent tilts his head in greeting. "Your preferred suite has been prepared as per your request. All three rooms are accounted for."

I'm too busy admiring the interior of the hotel to pay attention properly.

It feels like stepping into a palace with its ornate columns, baroque carvings and gold accents.

"Do you require assistance with your luggage?" Laurent inquires.

August turns towards me in question and I politely decline with a shake of my head.

"I'm fine, thank you for the offer."

"We'll manage, *merci*." August adds.

"*D'accord.*" Laurent nods. "*Deux cartes-clés pour la suite présidentielle.*"

August hands me a metallic gold card embossed with the letter P on it before gesturing towards my luggage.

"Pass me your suitcase."

"My suitcase? What for—"

He doesn't let me finish as he walks over to me and drops his weekender bag on top of my luggage, effortlessly wheeling our bags away from the reception area.

There's a certain refinement to August's movements as I follow him towards the lift. He operates almost like clockwork, tall and striding with a purpose as we manoeuvre around the hotel. It's not until we're both standing outside the door labelled 'Presidential Suite' in embossed writing on a golden plaque that I clear my throat, catching his attention.

"Where is my room?" I question, glancing behind me as I fail to spot any other door on the floor.

August glances down at me, eyebrows furrowing in confusion. "In here."

I look up at him. "We're sharing the same suite?"

"Is that a problem?" He asks.

My mind blanks. "Is there, umm, more than one bed?"

"Yes." The corner of his mouth quirks into a faint smile. "There are three."

He scans the room key, the double doors opening automatically and I gasp as I step inside.

The Presidential Suite is huge, probably the size of the entire first floor of our office back in London. If I thought the lobby was grand, it's nothing compared to the sheer extravagance of the suite August and I will be staying

CHAPTER 31

in over the weekend.

"*Trois chambres.*" August comes up behind me, gesturing towards the smaller set of double doors inside the suite. "Take your pick."

I'm too much in awe as I survey the interior design of the accommodation. Much like the lobby, it seamlessly blended French sophistication with art deco, a reflection of Toussaint's culture and heritage, no doubt.

"Sorry, this is just…" I eye the exquisite decorations of the suite, the high ceilings and the crystal chandelier suspended in the centre of the room. "Wow."

"It's comfortable," August replies with a shrug.

That's what rich people say. I think to myself, walking towards the windows.

"What, no balcony?" I joke.

I peer out of the enormous glass windows intricately framed by detailed plasterwork. It's already nighttime so the view outside is obscured but, from my research of the city, I can imagine the breathtaking scenery it boasts during the day.

"In your room," He responds. "Whichever one you choose. Each bedroom has a balcony."

"Of course it has." I nod, disbelievingly.

It was beyond anything I could have imagined for a small Mediterranean island just off the southern coast of France. Lavish is definitely an understatement. Well-equipped with a kitchen, workspace and a living room, my mind still can't fully grasp the fact that the suite contained *three* separate bedrooms– actual rooms within a room.

"Decided which one yet?" August inquires.

I notice his bags already placed in front of a set of double doors close to the entrance. Thinking he's claimed that room for himself, I point to the farthest doors across the suite.

"I'll take that room?"

He pauses for a moment, eyeing his suitcase and weekender bag by the double doors before moving.

"Alright."

I watch as he strolls towards the room next to the one I've chosen, carrying his belongings into the space. He leaves his doors open as he settles inside and I'm mildly cognisant of how he beelines straight towards the bedside light, switching it on and then dimming it down.

"Should we only keep the lamps on?" I ask, eyeing the smaller lights scattered around the living room before gazing up at the chandelier above.

"What do you mean?" He calls out from his room.

"The lights," I squint pointedly at the lighting fixture attached to the ceiling. "Isn't the chandelier a bit too bright for you? Can we dim it down?"

Gazing up, I blink at the layers of crystal cascading down in tiers and clusters refracting off the multifaceted surfaces. The soft, ambient light diffusing through the glass created a warm glow as it hung suspended from golden, intricately designed metal arms.

"What?" He questions.

August emerges from his room, sans blazer and his sleeves rolled up to his forearms.

"Aren't you sensitive to bright lights?" I turn towards him.

He looks a little perplexed, a knot forming between his eyebrows as he glances between me and the chandelier.

"Sorry, I just assumed…" I pause. "Your office is always dim. You've mentioned your eyes before… I thought…"

I trail off, suddenly feeling like I shouldn't have said anything at all.

"No, that's right." He nods, clearing his throat. "You just… caught me off guard. No one really comments on it."

"Oh," I blink. "I'm sorry, I didn't mean to sound insensitive by pointing it out."

"You didn't, it's fine." He shakes his head, meeting my gaze. "The light is adjustable."

He points towards the entrance, my eyes following the direction to the digital control panel on the wall.

"Ah," I nod.

Turning my attention back to August, I'm surprised to find him still

CHAPTER 31

standing by his door, watching me.

"So, tomorrow's schedule," He begins. "We have an 11 AM start at the museum. The foundry is a little overwhelming so the exhibitions should be a nice easy introduction to Toussaint before we actually visit the textile factories."

"Sounds good," I comment, giving him an awkward thumbs up.

"Are you hungry?" He asks.

I shake my head.

"In case you do end up craving food, there's room service so feel free to order from the menu." He signals towards the kitchen. "The hotel also stocked up the pantry and the fridge so just grab whatever you like."

I blink at the huge complimentary basket filled with fruits, chocolates and pastries of, what I'm assuming is, Toussaint's homegrown produce and baked goods on the kitchen counter.

"I need to do work for Grayson," He informs me, motioning towards his room. "I have a couple of calls I need to take tonight."

"Got it," I nod. "I'll be sure to keep quiet."

"Alright." He gives me a quick onceover. "I'll see you tomorrow."

"Bright-eyed and bushy-tailed."

Chapter 32

It's fast approaching 11 AM when I'm stumbling out of my suite, feet hobbling as I readjust the white knee-high boots I'm wearing. Sleeping through my alarms was not something I was expecting, forcing myself to prepare for the day in less than 30 minutes even more so.

"Sorry, I didn't mean to oversleep!" I skitter to a stop as I enter the living room, hoping that my heels haven't scratched the hardwood flooring. "Those silken sheets have ruined me, that bed is quite positively the comfiest thing I've ever slept on."

Granted that I don't actually have a proper bed.

My hair is still slightly damp, having had no time to dry it, and August watches as I adjust the eggshell-coloured beret atop my unruly mop of hair. The extra accessory might be a bit much but it matched my off-white turtleneck and knee-high boots perfectly and I'm not about to miss the opportunity of a colour-coordinated outfit.

"Does one of us have to change?" He questions.

I turn to him, his comment momentarily confusing me before I realise.

We're both dressed almost alike.

The tan-coloured co-ord I'm wearing, consisting of an oversized, checkered print blazer with a matching checkered mini skirt, is nearly identical to his taupe, two-piece suit.

We're even matching turtlenecks underneath.

"I'm wearing this co-ord to test if it's manageable in Toussaint's weather," I comment.

He eyes my outfit. "You made it?"

CHAPTER 32

I nod.

"Gabardine is great." I gesture towards his suit. "But it can sometimes be uncomfortable in warmer weather, especially with a thick lining. I think suits for every season will be ideal for the collection and I want to test the practicality of the fabric in the country's climate."

Linen, although not revolutionary, is lightweight and less stiff to navigate in. It's ideal for spring and summer and can be designed without the need for extra lining.

August blinks at me before asking, "How did you know this suit is gabardine?"

I eye the diagonal ribbed texture, tight weave and slightly structured draping properties of the material he's wearing.

"Lucky guess." I shrug.

As I anticipated, the National Museum of Cionne is normally closed during the weekends. But as similarly expected, August somehow managed to book it open for the day, even arranging for the Head of Curation of the Textile Museum to give us a personal tour of the building and the current exhibitions in the gallery.

I've always been fascinated by the different techniques used in textile design so I couldn't wait to learn more about Toussaint and how the culture has influenced their fashion. The museum is yet another ornately decorated building, much like all the architecture I've seen of Cionne so far. It featured colourful exhibits including fabrics, clothing and accessories that spanned over *decades*. I'm struck by the vibrant displays showcasing the country's textile traditions.

August and I spend the next several hours under the guidance of Corrina, the museum's Head of Curation. We explored numerous exhibits, taking in everything from intricate embroidery and delicate beadwork to stunning applique techniques used in creating the fabrics for the island's traditional clothing. I quietly marvel at the interactive displays which allowed guests to touch and feel various textiles.

As someone with a slight fixation to textures, it was like a treasure trove of tactility.

Surprisingly, spending the day with August turned out to be quite enjoyable. I hadn't anticipated him to be an active participant in the tour, half-expecting him to simply stand around whilst Corrina guided us around the museum. But to my surprise, he consistently engaged in every conversation, pointing out things he knew and asking Corrina questions about subjects he was unfamiliar with.

Throughout the entire tour, I was sketching and taking notes. Online research is one thing but seeing everything in person gave me a deeper understanding of the island's textile history and I'm eager to incorporate some of the research I've found into the garments for the collection. My sketchpad is already halfway filled with design ideas and technical sketches by the time we reached the end of the tour.

After being granted permission to freely browse the museum, August and I were left to wander around by ourselves.

I'm standing on my tip toes and leaning over a glass display, straining to read the information when I hear a quiet chuckle and a shutter of a camera behind me.

Shuffling in my knee-high boots, I look over my shoulder. "Did you just take a photo of me without my consent?"

"I took a picture of the display that you just happened to be standing in front of, yes." August nods, walking over to me. "What are you doing?"

"I'm trying to…" I attempt to examine the notes before giving up entirely. "Can you read what it says?"

"Here." He takes a photo of the display and shows me a zoomed image of it.

"Thank you, I think I have enough notes to—"

A loud clanking echoes throughout the building, followed by lights dimming, and I look up, confused. The only source of light filtering through is from the windows high above the ceiling as the entire floor we're on is submerged in semi-darkness.

"Merde," August mutters. "Not again."

"Again?" I turn to him. "What's going on?"

CHAPTER 32

August looks up at the windows, eyes squinting slightly before glancing at his watch.

"They're closing," He explains, not the least bit surprised.

"Do you make a habit of getting locked in museums?" I eye him suspiciously as he gives me a somewhat sheepish look.

"We just need to get to the gallery entrance before the security guards lock each floor," He responds, nonchalant. "Otherwise, we might end up being stuck here over the weekend."

"Please tell me you're joking." I search his face for any sign of humour. "*August.*"

"How quickly can you walk in heels?"

"We're on the *third* floor."

"A fast stroll it is then." He winks.

Leaving me no chance to argue, he takes my tote bag and slings it over his shoulder before darting out of the room.

"August!" I exclaim.

I can hear the sound of his shoes against the concrete floor as he sprints down the corridor. Glancing at my knee-high boots, I shake my head before dashing after him.

"Catch up, Tinker-Talent!" He yells. "Or else you'll get locked in!"

I watch as August rushes down the stairs, skipping steps to reach the landing below.

"I didn't sign up for this!" I exclaim.

The sound of his laughter echoes throughout the second floor and I couldn't help but smile at the deep and hearty resonance as it reverberates around me. I bolt past each exhibition room, laughing alongside him at the absurdity of our situation.

Two grown adults, racing through an empty museum like school children.

"I'm pretty sure we're not allowed to run in here!" I call out.

Echoes of our shoes– my boots and his brogues– fill the museum halls, echoing after each flight of stairs and every dash across one end of the building to the other. The natural light from the windows provided just enough visibility for me to trail behind August as he led the way, a good few metres ahead of me.

He eventually slowed his pace, and I underestimate my own speed, stumbling to a stop right in front of him and colliding with his tall frame.

"Sorry!" I squeak, the air physically being knocked out of my lungs. "Sorry."

August wraps an arm around me to prevent me from further faltering as I clumsily grab onto the lapels of his blazer.

"Mr. Vante?" Corrina questions, eyes widening. "Oh my goodness, we're so sorry. We thought you and Miss Hartt left the museum a while ago."

"No harm done, Corrina." August replies, steadying me as I regain my balance. "We lost track of time whilst we were browsing."

His hand is poised on my lower back, the lightest pressure of his fingers as it curls around my hip. The familiarity of his touch brings back memories of the night at the club and I shake my head to clear it.

"I can't believe you made me run in platform boots," I exhale, feeling the adrenaline rush still in my system.

"You run in heels better than you walk in them," He chuckles, gently pressing me to him. "I'm impressed."

"It's a skill," I laugh breathlessly.

Looking down at my boots, I mentally grimace at the ache beginning to form on my right foot.

"I might have *re-sprained* my ankle though." I wrinkle my nose.

Behind us, the security guards are emerging after completing a thorough check of the museum, one of them holding a cream-coloured fabric in his hand.

"Oh, that's mine." I shuffle out of August's grasp as he releases me, awkwardly hobbling towards the security guard to retrieve my beret. "Thank you."

After expressing our gratitude for the tour and bidding Corrina and the security guards goodbye, August and I exit the building, me lagging slightly behind as I concentrate on avoiding putting too much pressure on my injured foot.

CHAPTER 32

Trust me to injure myself, again.

We're descending the stairs and I try not to wince at each step, pausing when August stops abruptly in front of me.

"On my back."

I blink in surprise. "What?"

He turns around, assessing me quickly before removing his blazer and tying it around my waist. I realise he's still carrying my tote bag when he turns back around and pats my pleather-covered calves.

"Up." He instructs.

"No, it's okay, I'll just—"

"I'm not asking, Mahalia." He says, bending down slightly. "You're limping."

Nervously, I shake my head.

"It's fine, the walk to the car park isn't that far, I can—"

"Don't make me throw you over my shoulder."

I pause in an attempt to call his bluff.

"You wouldn't."

August immediately turns around, crouching to shoulder me up and I take a step back.

"Oh my god!" I exclaim. "Okay, I'll get on your back."

The corner of his mouth twitches up slightly before he turns back around.

"Good."

I try to control the flush rising to my cheeks as he adjusts my tote bag on his shoulder and resumes his earlier position. Wrapping my arms around his neck, I'm attempting to figure out the least awkward way to climb onto him when his hands grip my thighs and he lifts me on his waist.

"August!" I squeak as he shifts to haul me up higher on his back. "I might be heavy—"

"You weigh next to nothing." He tsks.

"Be careful!" My voice pitches higher than usual as he bounds down the stairs, a little too quick for my liking. "Slow down, you might trip and end up—!"

August jolts forward and I tighten my grip around his neck, preparing for us to stumble down the stairs.

"Just kidding." His entire body shakes as he chuckles and straightens himself up. "You good?"

He turns his head to check on me and I tug on his ear to scold him.

"*Not funny,*" I huff.

"Do you really think I'd let us fall?"

"Yes," I answer without hesitation, earning another chuckle from August.

Returning to our suite, I managed to organise the research I gathered along with additional materials from leaflets and books August bought from the museum. All of my notes as well as the initial rough sketches are on the coffee table when August appears from his room wearing grey sweatpants and a matching oversized grey hoodie.

"Trading your turtlenecks for hoodies," I comment. "Never thought I'd see the day."

I'm still in the same outfit as earlier sans my knee-high boots, choosing instead to wear thick socks and the fluffy white slippers that came with the suite to give comfort to my ankles.

"You've seen me wear athleisure before," He replies.

I eye his hoodie, my fingers twitching at the urge to tug on the aglets to level the drawstrings.

"I think I just got used to you wearing turtlenecks every single day to work," I laugh lightly.

He strolls over to the sofa, room service menu in one hand and his laptop in the other.

"London is bleak," He sighs. "I don't take kindly to cold weather."

He places his laptop on the coffee table before sitting next to me.

"Are you okay with room service tonight instead of going out for dinner?" August asks, rifling through the hotel's carte du jour. "I have extra work I need to cover this evening for Grayson that they sprung on me last minute."

"Of course," I nod. "It'll give my feet a break too."

We exchange small talk about the trip to the museum, August comment-

CHAPTER 32

ing on the notes I've taken and the quick sketches I've done before I head back to my room to change into something more comfortable since we're staying in for the evening.

Dressed in a cosy fleece crop top, baggy sweatpants and an oversized fluffy cardigan, I step out of my room and back into the shared living space.

I expected August to retreat to his room to do work like he did last night so I'm surprised to find him still sitting on the sofa. This time, his laptop is in front of him, his eyebrows knotted in concentration as he talks to someone on the phone. Conscious of disturbing him, I quietly walk towards the coffee table and retrieve my research materials.

"Everything okay?" August glances up at me, eyebrows furrowing slightly.

I nod before gesturing towards his phone and whispering, "I don't want to disturb you."

"You're fine," He says with a shake of his head. "Come sit."

I can still hear the voices over the phone as he takes my sketchpad from my hands and tugs me back down to sit on the sofa.

"Order us room service," He signals towards the menu. "I trust your judgement."

August gives me a small smile of encouragement, a comfortable silence settling between us before the voice on the phone started calling out his name.

"Hello?" He answers. "Yes, sorry, I'm still here."

Chapter 33

Getting up the next morning was surprisingly easy as I found myself naturally woken up by the sunlight streaming through my window. The schedule for today included a visit to the actual textile factories to see the manufacturing practices and the production of the fabrics firsthand.

Today, I've decided to wear a soft baby pink maxi slip dress complemented by a cream-coloured cropped cardigan. My ensemble prioritises comfort and practicality this time, with lightweight and breathable fabrics ideal for Toussaint's warmer climate *and* the environment of a textile factory.

I make my way to the living room, matching pink ballet flats in hand, glad I'm the early one out of August and I this time.

Sitting on the couch to slip on my flats, I hear a set of double doors opening and I look behind me to find August walking into the living room. I blink at his outfit, a loose-fitting cream sweater paired with baby blue twill chinos and off-white moccasins.

"Your hair's caught," August comments.

"Oh," I stand up, twisting my body to untangle my hair from the straps of laces on the back of my dress. "I was rushing."

"You're impossible," He remarks, reaching over to me. "What is it with you and complicated dresses?"

August tugs lightly on the ends of my curls, his attempt to free my hair from the tangled criss-cross design of my dress causing his watch to snag on the loose strands.

"Ow," I flinch, craning my head towards him awkwardly. "What is it

CHAPTER 33

with your watch getting caught in everything?"

"Wait," He fusses over me. "Stay still."

"I *am* staying still."

"You're *moving*."

"I am not."

"You are." He chuckles quietly.

Despite his careful efforts, my hair strains painfully against my scalp and I wince. Being hypersensitive to touch makes situations like this less than ideal and I squirm at the ache forming on the back of my neck.

"August," I whine.

"*Mahalia*," He chuckles again, louder this time.

A warmth spreads across my chest as he shuffles close to me to manoeuvre us.

"Hold steady," He comments.

"I *am* holding steady."

His free hand wraps around my waist and my heartbeat quickens as he pulls me flush against his front. The laces of my dress extend all the way down to the bottom of my spine and I can feel the soft texture of his sweatshirt against my back.

Holding my breath, I wait nervously as he untangles my hair from his watch and eventually releases me.

"Done." He nods.

"That hurt," I mutter, pursing my lips as I rub the back of my head. "But thank you."

Above me, I sense August shift, his hand reaching out to gently stroke the top of my head before I feel a pair of lips press against my crown.

My body stills.

Thinking I've just imagined the gesture, I slowly look up at August who's staring at me, unblinking. He looks equally stunned, as if surprised by his own actions and he clears his throat.

I awkwardly brush my hair behind my neck, the strap of my dress falling from my shoulder.

August's gaze flickers down to the thin piece of material.

"Did you make this?" He queries, fingers reaching out to gently tug the strap back on my shoulder.

Wordlessly, I nod.

His thumb grazes along the hem and my breath hitches as I feel his fingers trail along the seam of the dress.

"It feels nice." The sudden lower register of his voice causes my skin to erupt in goosebumps. "Mulberry silk?"

Flashbacks of every intimate exchange we've had in the past replay in my mind and I nod, distracted. If August noticed the goosebumps on my skin, he doesn't comment on it.

"How's your ankle?" He asks, instead.

"Better," I answer. "I used an ice pack on it before bed."

"We'll take it easy today," He says. "No marathon race around the foundry, I'm afraid."

"Not even a quick sprint?"

"You do enough running around in my head," He mutters, passing me my cream cardigan. "Let's go."

Located on the outskirts of Cionne, the Toussaint Foundry consisted of vast complex buildings, each dedicated to a different stage of the fabric manufacturing process. It operated on a daily basis and I'm immediately struck by the scale of operation as we walked around the premises.

Once again, Corrina served as our guide for the tour. This time accompanied by Hector, the seasoned chief manager of operations at the foundry. They provided us with a succinct overview of the facilities before leading us on a comprehensive physical tour.

I observe as raw fibres are converted into yarn which are then transformed into a wide range of fabrics, each unique in texture and design. The weaving machines were vintage in aesthetic but they functioned with surprising speed and accuracy, despite the old-fashioned look of them.

Although I've witnessed something similar through documentaries, seeing everything in person is a completely different experience. From rigorous quality control measures to meticulous equipment inspections,

CHAPTER 33

the commitment to make sure that the final products meet the specifications is expertly executed. I couldn't help but marvel at the attention to detail at every stage of the manufacturing process.

"This is amazing," I whisper to August, eyeing the intricately designed machines. "Isn't it amazing? Are you taking photos? Make sure you get photos."

"Yes, ma'am." He nods.

There's an amused glint in his eyes as he begins snapping pictures of the carding machines and the roving frames.

The tour continues as August and I are introduced to a team of workers dedicated to ongoing research, innovation and product development at the foundry. I'm surprised to find Toussaint's integration of new technologies in their textile customs while simultaneously keeping the traditional practices of the country's artisans, particularly those specialising in decorative stitching and ornamental sewing.

Watching as the skilled workers use delicate embroidery techniques to add intricate details to the fabrics and garments on display by hand, I turn to August.

"Am I allowed to ask about the labour?" I whisper discreetly.

"Toussaint is known for being one of the most ethically employed textile manufacturers in Mediterranean Europe," August replies, quietly. "They're ranked number one."

"We also have The Artisan Initiative," Corrina reveals. "Arts and cultural funding are working with the museum and the foundry to nurture local talent. It's a work-in-progress but it's well-received by everyone involved."

"We prioritise the well-being of our employees," Hector adds. "The facilities dedicated to workers are closely moderated to make sure that our working conditions are above standards."

I nod, appreciating their efforts.

If only other existing clothing factories followed suit.

"We work strictly with companies and brands who share the same values as we do. We understand the importance of moral labour practices and ethical employment when it comes to textiles, hence our longstanding reputation working with Vante."

Hector tilts his head respectfully towards August who mirrors him in thanks.

"What about the environmental impact?" I ask quietly, gesturing around the room.

August pauses, a playful glint in his eyes before shifting his gaze towards me.

"They're ranked as number one in the *worst* textile manufacturing CO2 emissions in the world." He replies, flatly.

I turn towards him, my eyebrows furrowing as my mouth drops in horror.

"I'm kidding," He smirks, tapping on my frown lightly.

"Don't joke about the environment." I narrow my eyes at him. "We are in a *climate crisis*."

"Don't worry, Little Miss Sustainability," He chuckles. "Cionne's working towards sustainable practices, energy efficiency improvements, and supply chain optimisations. They're hoping to reduce CO2 emissions by 50% come 2030."

"*By half?*" I remark, astonished. "That's ambitious."

"It's Toussaint." August shrugs.

Hector chimes in. "We are nothing, if not ardent and ambitious."

I nod in acknowledgement as we enter an area where dyes are being created. I'm expecting the smell of chemicals and toxins but I'm surprised to find sweet, almost fruity, scents permeating the room.

"Are those pomegranates?" I point towards an area in the corner.

"Toussaint's national fruit." Hector nods as he takes us closer to the workstation. "We're reintroducing the use of natural dyes to our fabrics."

My eyes widen, recalling a similar idea I suggested during a brainstorming session with the Design team.

"That's what I suggested!" I whisper excitedly, tugging on August's arm. "Natural and non-toxic."

"The pomegranates grown in Toussaint are more vibrant in colour than in any other country," Hector continues. "The lightfastness of the natural dye is very potent here so the colour is less likely to fade when exposed to sunlight over time. We're experimenting with different qualities of mordants to achieve lasting results when fixing the dye to the fabric."

I nod in understanding, remembering my research on natural dyes.

"How long does it take for the factory?" I ask. "Preparation, dyeing, mordant-ing as well as drying and curing stages considered."

"Several days to a week," Hector replies. "It's labour-intensive and time-consuming. Achieving consistent and predictable colours is also challenging as the results can vary based on the dye bath and the fabric material."

I stare at the barrels of pomegranate dye, already considering the idea for the collection. One of the only downsides would be the colour range since, compared to synthetic dyes, it would be very limited. But natural dyes would be an advantage for the collection because they'll be manufactured on a much smaller scale.

"What fabrics do Toussaint pomegranates stick to most effectively?" I inquire.

"The ones made from natural fibres," Hector answers.

"Cotton and linen?"

He nods. "As well as silk and wool."

I consider the time it would take. Sebastian's tendency to outsource fabrics entirely from scratch comes to mind and I frown. The smaller scale of the dying process is ideal but it's the question of practicality versus practicability.

"Do you think it's ideal?" I turn towards August.

"What?" he responds, looking distracted.

"To use natural dye."

"For?"

"The collection."

"Oh." He tilts his head forward. "Very pretty."

I blink, confused.

"Not *pretty*," I shake my head. "*Practical*."

"Yes?" He blinks back at me. "You're both."

Tilting my head to the side, I squint my eyes at him. "What are you talking about?"

"What are *you* talking about?" He questions me.

"The dyes."

"Ah," He nods. "Smells fantastic."

I stare at August before turning to Hector. "I think the fumes are getting to his head. Are you sure it's non-toxic?"

Beside us, Hector is chuckling as he continues to walk to get to the other side, August following promptly.

"Wait, what were we talking about?" August quietly whispers to Hector.

I lag slightly, scribbling notes on my notepad as well as drawing sketches of little pomegranates, before finally catching up to them.

"You were discussing how Miss Hartt is both *pretty* and *practical,*" He answers and August blinks, casting a sideways glance at me.

My cheeks warm as I pretend not to overhear their conversation, absentmindedly doodling on my notepad instead.

The tour concludes and before I knew it, August and I are heading out of the foundry.

"I managed to organise a visit to the Imperial Boutique," August informs me as we get into a taxi. "I think you'll enjoy it there."

"Well, I've enjoyed every single aspect of this trip so far." I nod.

"I'm glad to hear that."

I turn to him excitedly. "Did you see the needlework in some of the fabric? I can't believe they do embroidery to that scale. It must take *months* to finish. And Toussaint's own *toile de jouy*? The timeless aesthetic! The historical significance! It might not appeal to the contemporary minimalist but the *classical charm* of it? I need to get my hands on every single design they have, you don't understand."

August blinks.

"I have never met anyone so passionate about printed textiles." He shakes his head, the corner of his mouth tugging upwards.

"*It's an art,*" I gesture wildly. "I'm 100% going to incorporate a *toile de*

CHAPTER 33

jouy suit for the collaboration. I'm surprised that Holmes— and Vante actually— *haven't*. I mean, I would like to know, why hasn't your dad considered an entire collection of printed textiles? Can you ring him to find out? Actually— no— that would be odd. Don't do that. He probably wouldn't care, I'm an intern for crying out loud, nevermind. But still. I can't believe Toussaint has their very own *toile de jouy* fabrics."

The sound of August's laugh, deep and dulcet, prompts me to stop my endless rambling.

"God, I didn't realise you could be so *chatty*," He comments. "Listening to you talk endlessly about textiles with Hector all day was something I didn't expect."

I flush, embarrassed. "Sorry."

"No, don't apologise," He chuckles. "You really know your stuff, it's actually very impressive."

"Right," I nod, suddenly feeling all too self-conscious about the mindless babbling I've been doing.

"Keep talking, Tinker-Talent." He gives me a pointed look. "You mentioned ringing my dad. Do you want to speak to him? Should I give him a call?"

He reaches into his trouser pocket to retrieve his phone and my eyes widen.

"No!" I shake my head. "Oh my god, your dad is extremely busy overseeing a fashion empire, August. Don't disturb him with mindless questions from silly, design neophytes!"

"That's not a very nice way to talk about yourself." He responds, brows furrowing in disapproval.

"Oh," I blink, turning sheepishly towards him. "I was talking about you."

He pauses for a moment, staring intently at me before throwing his head back and letting out another loud laugh. Eyes crinkling at the corner, his face breaks out into a wide grin and my stomach somersaults.

It's overwhelmingly staggering how impossibly handsome August looks when he smiles.

"You really are something, Mahalia Hartt."

My stomach does another flip at the genuine expression on his face.

"Thanks," I comment offhandedly, the flutter travelling throughout my entire form.

Chapter 34

Containing my eagerness as we arrived at the Imperial Boutique was a considerable effort on my part. My excitement was through the roof and I was practically buzzing as we reached the location.

Nestled within the castle grounds of the Toussaint Grand Palace, the three-story boutique was something straight out of a movie. It was a goldmine of gorgeous garments and stunning suits. Everyday wear and special occasion attire worn by The Royals of Toussaint, past and present, were stored at the opulent establishment.

Two tailors, Pippa and Armand graciously guided us on a tour around the luxurious boutique.

"What is it with Cionne and crystal chandeliers?" I quip as I gaze up at yet another ornamented fixture on the ceiling.

"They have a deep-seated animosity towards me, clearly." August comments, squinting up slightly.

His response makes me laugh as we're led inside the lavishly decorated surroundings of the grand fitting room. In a well-lit space adorned with luxurious drapes and intricate tapestries, I find myself standing amongst rows and rows of clothing racks and gilded mirrors.

"These dresses are stunning," I comment.

The soft click of a DSLR camera catches my attention and I turn to find August taking a picture of me in the middle of the room.

"You look like a kid in a candy store," He remarks, a boyish smile appearing on his face as he looks through the camera. "Twirl for me."

I humour him, spinning slowly as I strike the most ridiculous poses.

"Beautiful." He praises as he snaps away on his camera.

Bounding back over to him, I couldn't help but laugh as he shows me the images.

"Oh god, this is why I design and not model." I shake my head, swiping through the photos. "You're not even taking pictures of the dresses in the background!"

"Photography 101, dear Hartt," He begins. "The subject must *always* be in focus."

Zooming in on one picture, he's captured me mid-laugh, my eyes crinkled and my hair slightly dishevelled from my impromptu spinning. He's looking at the image of me on the viewfinder, grey eyes almost twinkling and the fluttering feeling cages itself in my chest.

Before I can say anything else, another voice echoes in the room.

"Well, look who finally decided to grace us with his presence."

I turn towards the source of the familiar voice.

Prince Tobias stands by the entrance wearing a white button-up shirt and a pair of tan-coloured trousers. Behind him, two security guards as well as Pippa and Armand are all talking animatedly between themselves.

Remembering royal protocol, I instantly straighten up, preparing myself to curtsy as he walks towards us.

"How did you know we were here?" August questions, a hint of suspicion in his voice.

Tobias shakes his head at August disapprovingly.

"No 'hello'?" He tuts. "Your manners around royalty are appalling, dear cousin, truly. I should have you hung, drawn and quartered at the square."

August only grunts in response, grey eyes narrowing as he speculates the presence of the prince.

"Miss Hartt." Tobias extends his hand towards my direction, greeting me in acknowledgement.

"Your Highness." I bow my head, curtsy and shake his hand all at the same time.

So much for being less anxious.

"A pleasure to see you again," He smiles warmly at me. "How are you

CHAPTER 34

finding Toussaint?"

"It's beautiful, sir." I reply. "Cionne is a wonderful city."

"*Tobias*, mademoiselle, please." He laughs. "Calling me 'sir' makes me feel so senile."

I nod, smiling politely. Addressing royalty by their first names feels inappropriate, even with his encouragement.

Tobias observes us both, hazel eyes shifting between August and I with amusement.

"I quite like the colour palette of your outfits," He comments. "Very *his and hers*."

August frowns before clearing his throat, seemingly unimpressed by the royal's observation. A pause settles between them as Tobias regards him with a knowing, almost teasing smile on his face.

"I was informed about your little research trip by your dearest Genevieve," Tobias discloses.

I turn to him, blinking. "Gigi?"

From the corner of my eye, I see August narrow his eyes at Tobias suspiciously.

"Since when were you and the editorial assistant close?" He questions, tone dry.

"We're well acquainted," Tobias replies with a nonchalant shrug of his shoulder that bore similarities to August. "I believe she's working on an article about Toussaint for MODUE Magazine. And she was rather concerned for her best friend's safety, gallivanting off in another country with a man she barely knows."

"We're on a *work trip*." August's expression shifts to one of irritation. "What did she think I was going to do? Kidnap her?"

Tobias only shrugs, expression somewhat smug.

Next to me, August openly glares at the sibling of the crown prince– as if trying to communicate with him.

"Her friend only had the best intentions," Tobias chuckles. "She wanted to make sure that you weren't going to do anything... unseemly."

"*Unseemly?*" August deadpans.

Tobias ignores his comment as he turns to me.

"I was rather surprised to find Miss Winters in my inbox, detailing your little trip. Though it was slightly more frightening how she acquired my *personal* email," He chuckles. "Quite a character that one, your Genevieve."

I laugh nervously.

Only Gigi would track the private information of a prince to make sure the person I'm travelling with doesn't have psychopathic tendencies.

"I thought nothing of it at first," Tobias continues, turning his attention to August. "You haven't visited Toussaint in years, despite my persistent invitations. So you can imagine my astonishment and *utter delight* when I received word of a certain *Peroxide Prince's* private jet landing in Cionne. Not to mention the weekend booking of the presidential suite at The Royal Maisonette as well as access to the Toussaint Foundry *and* the Imperial Boutique."

There's a teasing lilt to Tobias' voice, almost like he knows a secret he's itching to reveal. August glances over to him, doing nothing to hide his increasing agitation.

"A little heads up would have been nice. To welcome you in noble fashion." Tobias concludes.

"I figured you'd be occupied," August replies, unimpressed. "You know, with royal duties."

"Actual royal obligations fall on Elias." He speaks of his older brother. "I'm never too busy for my favourite cousin."

"I appreciate that, Your Highness." August replies, voice dripping with sarcasm.

Another silence falls as they engage in a staring contest and I can only watch between the two.

"How is the regalwear collection faring, *mademoiselle*?" Tobias turns to me.

"It's going well," I reply. "We're in the ideation phase at the moment so we've been gathering a lot of primary and secondary research, hence why we're in Toussaint."

Tobias regards an indifferent August with a bemused look.

CHAPTER 34

"Rather strange how *you* are in company, dear cousin," Tobias' eyes are gleaming as he assesses August. "I expected Sebastian to be in charge of this work trip. He is the lead designer, after all."

"He's busy," August replies in a tone that left no room for further elaboration.

"Well, I do hope that this trip will be beneficial with the research for the collection." Tobias nods towards me. "Have you visited the trousseau?"

I shake my head. "It isn't on the schedule."

Tobias redirects his gaze to August.

"Cousin!" He exclaims over dramatically. "You cannot possibly have a designer step foot in the Imperial Boutique and *not* visit the Royal Trousseau."

I turn towards August excitedly to find him already watching me.

"Alright," He sighs.

"Excellent!" Tobias grins. "It's been a while since I was present at a garment fitting. Elias is very adamant he will not be trial fitting his wedding tuxedo until he meets his bride-to-be."

"I'm not playing dress up, Tobias." August deadpans.

"Aren't you here for research?" Tobias clicks his tongue disapprovingly. "You've come all this way to Toussaint's very own wonder of the world."

"No," He deadpans.

Glancing over at August, I deflate at seeing his aversion to the fitting.

"Miss Hartt?"

"Oh, it's okay." I shake my head, disheartened. "We don't have to if–"

"Cousin, how cruel!" Tobias turns to August. "Are you genuinely capable of rejecting these doleful puppy dog eyes?"

He makes an elaborate gesture towards me and I blink, about to retort when August's loud sigh cuts me off.

"Fine," He concedes with a glare.

Tobias winks at me with a knowing smile.

"You as well, *mademoiselle*."

Being fitted into one of the dresses feels like the scene in the movies where the main character goes through some wild transformation. The dress I'm wearing is a beautiful floor-length ball gown, the skirt cinching in at the waist and flaring out in layers and layers of shimmering tulle. The upper half of the dress is a beautiful halter neckline with a detailed design of lace and embroidery. It's backless too, the sheer fabric dipping just below my spine.

I feel an odd tugging at my heart as I stare at myself in the mirror.

The choice of colour sends me into a nervous frenzy: white.

Stepping out in four-inch high heels, I walk slightly off balance as the ball grown grazes the floor.

"It's rude to stare, dear cousin." Tobias calls out and I spin to see August standing by the velvet-upholstered chaise in the back of the room.

Dressed in a classic black tuxedo, August is wearing a blazer with satin peak lapels and matching buttons. His crisp, white shirt is tucked into black sleek, slim-fit trousers giving the outfit a polished look. On his feet are black leather shoes, completing the ensemble.

In moments like these, it's so *fitting*.

There's a reason for his title as the Peroxide Prince.

Cautious of keeping the dress in its pristine condition, I tread carefully as I make my way towards August.

"You look…" He trails off as he meets me in the middle.

"Sparkly?" I motion towards the abundance of twinkling tulle of the dress, marvelling at the skirt's airy feel despite the seemingly endless layers of fabric.

"It's…"

"Glitter, I know." I laugh, feeling skittish for some reason. "You hate glitter."

Nervousness coils and settles in my stomach as August fixes his gaze on me. His grey eyes flicker with an urgency of sorts but he turns away before I can properly place the emotion.

"But look," I tilt my body away from him slightly. "No laces. Just zippers."

"Oh?"

"It's on the side, you just pull it down here…" I gesture to my waist. "And

CHAPTER 34

it comes straight off apparently, Pippa told me."

August swallows and I realise too late at the very suggestive implication of the design.

An intense flicker of light brings me out of my fairytale daze and August winces slightly. He turns his attention towards the source, eyes narrowing as Tobias takes another photo with a brighter flash.

"Tobias," He hisses, shaking his head in annoyance as multiple flashes of the camera continue to go off. "Are you done?"

"Not quite." He chuckles. "Pose for the camera, *les jeunes mariés!*"

August frowns, pressing his fingers to his lids and I instantly remember his sensitivity towards intense lighting.

"Are you okay?" I position my hands above his to cover his eyes.

Even with the high heels, I still have to look up at August.

The frown on his face deepens as his gaze drops down to the dress I'm wearing. It's probably making his discomfort worse, with all the white tulle and glitter reflecting the brightness of the lights in the room.

"You both look absolutely stunning," Tobias comments. "Tailored fit to perfection, if I do say so myself."

I turn to the hazel-eyed blond standing just a few feet away, a quirk of a smile on his lips. His comment is strikingly similar to Gigi's and my heart skips a beat.

"You're a royal pain in my ass, Your Highness." August mutters.

I face him, worriedly. "Are you—"

"Done here? Yes." He turns sharply towards Tobias. *"Tu perds mon temps."*

I blink.

You're wasting my time.

August steps away, barely glancing at me as he disappears back into the changing rooms with Armand. I furrow my brows at his abrupt shift in behaviour, uncertain if I might have unwittingly said or done something that could have triggered the sudden change.

"I would apologise for his actions," Tobias starts. "But you're probably aware of how temperamental he can be."

"He's not that bad," I reply, wringing my hands nervously. "I enjoy spending time with him. Professionally, of course. He's a great person— great boss, even. Very considerate and, um, competent."

My eyes remain fixed on where August disappeared as I stand rooted to the spot, trying to calm the fluttering inside my chest.

Tobias tilts his head, looking at me with a curious expression.

"My gravely ill-tempered and *cantankerous cousin*, are we talking about the same person?"

"I can hear you." August's deadpan voice echoes from behind the curtains of his fitting room.

Recalling the events of both yesterday and today, it's obvious to me that I appreciate August's presence and thoroughly enjoy his company. I find myself enjoying our time together more than I'd care to admit, though I'll certainly never confess that out loud– especially not to his cousin.

"Do you know what Toussaint is known for?" Tobias asks out of the blue, pulling me out of my thoughts. "Aside from textiles, of course."

"Umm," I blink, racking my brain to think. "Pomegranates?"

Tobias turns to me, chuckling lightly.

"Though we are the main importers of pomegranate supply in Europe and the Mediterranean, no." His mouth quirks into a warm smile, pausing for a brief moment before continuing. "Toussaint is the country of lovers."

He says the statement matter-of-factly, straightening himself up as playfulness forms in his expression.

"Lovers?" I respond, a little obtusely. "I didn't know that."

"Saintians are very passionate people." He nods. "We're terrible cliches but I'm afraid that's the only way we know how to express ourselves. *In ardore et in ambitione.*" He continues in a somewhat lecture.

"Of course," I nod, though I'm struggling to understand why the conversation is heading towards this particular topic.

"I'm sure you're aware of his past reputation in the media." Tobias gives me a knowing look as he tilts his head towards the changing rooms. "My cousin, though only *half* Saintian, is full of heart. His intentions are genuine, please know that. All that is required is a small measure of patience extended to him. A modicum of tolerance, if you will. Despite his

CHAPTER 34

endless list of *fashion faux passes*, he means well *en amoureux* and I would like to think that he's deserving of it."

The oddly heartfelt conversation throws me off guard as I try to think of an appropriate response. I think of the beautiful women August has been involved with in the past that the media has written about and my mind trails off to the ones in his company that he doesn't openly disclose at present.

"August is admired by a lot of people," I say, trying to maintain professionalism. "I don't think there's a scarcity of women or men interested in him nor is he lacking in female and, um, male companionship, Your Highness."

"And are *you* one of those companions, mademoiselle?"

My eyes widen.

"N-no!" I blanch. "Well, yes but not really. I mean, I think August is fantastic. I really admire him and the work he does. I mean it when I say he's a great person. But we only work together. Well, *worked*. Past tense. I would never— We haven't—"

A flashback of the club enters my hazy mind and I mentally veer away from the topic completely.

"I don't think August sees me like that," I continue. "N-not that I want him to or anything. We aren't— like that. Our relationship is… strictly business. Just work colleagues. I'm just an intern, after all."

I'm rambling out of nervousness now, telling myself for my own peace of mind, more than anything. I don't want to end up saying something I'll regret but, at the rate I'm going, I most likely will.

"I should probably change back." I gesture towards the fitting rooms.

Tobias nods, humming as he steps aside and I bow awkwardly before taking my leave.

Slipping back into my pink silk dress, I rid myself of the thoughts of even comparing myself to the people August has been involved with in the past. Actors, models, actors *and* models.

Sitting on the velvet chaise in the middle of the room, I watch as August quietly emerges back into the main room.

"Here," He says curtly, handing me a tote bag. "Books and secondary sources you might be interested to read through. I bought a few copies."

"Thank you."

Taking the bag from him, I couldn't help but notice the distracted look on his face as he avoids my gaze.

His slightly standoffish behaviour is apparent but I refrain from saying anything as we begin to walk over to Tobias.

"Thank you, Armand, Pippa." The hazel-eyed prince nods towards the royal tailors. "You've both been a tremendous help. I'm more than happy to accompany my cousin and his guest for the rest of the tour."

They both bow and take their leave, Armand pausing for a moment before turning to me.

"It was very lovely to meet you, Hallie." He smiles, curly brown hair bouncing as he nods towards me.

"You too," I smile politely. "Thank you so much for your help."

"I'm excited to see what you design for the collaboration," He continues, shuffling on the heels of his feet as he stands in front of me. "Are you in Toussaint long?"

His gaze is curious, long lashes framing bright blue eyes and I couldn't help but wonder what they would look like if they were shades lighter—softer and more muted, almost grey.

"Just one more day," I answer.

"Did you like seeing the sights?"

"We didn't really look around." I turn towards August, expecting him to elaborate but he stays silent. "Aside from the boutique, we only visited the museum and the foundry."

"Ah, that's a shame." Armand shakes his head. "Toussaint has fantastic historical landmarks beyond the city and the castle grounds. They reopened the waterfalls of St. Valentine just last week. And Tussore Beach is gorgeous at this time of year. You must visit The Gardens of Dimitrus and Lyra, it's our very own version of Romeo and Juliet."

Slightly overwhelmed by the outpour of new information, the places Armand lists go over my head completely so I just nod in response.

CHAPTER 34

"I'm assuming you have a busy schedule in the morning?" He asks.

I blink, remembering that August hadn't actually planned anything for the day.

"It's actually our free day tomorrow."

Once again, I turn towards August but he still doesn't respond. Instead, he's schooling the most aloof expression on his face.

"Would you be interested in seeing more of Cionne?" Armand asks excitedly, glancing over at August before settling in my direction. "The sunsets in Toussaint are beautiful. The trail up to Paramour's Point is perfect for a leisurely stroll and it overlooks the city so you can see the stunning skyline in the evening."

I glance quickly at August, an irritation flashing in his gaze.

"Oh, I'd love to but…" I try to think of the most polite way to decline. "August and I are actually heading back early so we'll be short on time. Thank you for the offer anyway."

Armand nods in understanding.

"If you're ever back in Toussaint for leisure, do let me know," He says. "I'll be glad to show you around."

He reaches into his blazer and takes out a small rectangular card before taking both of my hands and placing it in my palm. Turning towards August in recognition first, he then bows at Tobias.

"Your Highness."

Tobias nods at him in acknowledgement, signalling for him to take his leave.

Next to me, August's expression remains impassive and unmoving as he stares at the business card embossed with the Imperial Boutique logo.

Armand Dubois.
Royal Tailor of Toussaint.
+707 9704080

"Since when did your tailors have their own personal calling cards they give to customers?" August questions, watching as the curly-haired tailor disappears out of the room.

He swipes the card from me and eyes it with a gaze so nettled, I can almost *feel* the pricking sensation.

"It's a business, cousin." Tobias chuckles then adds to taunt him, "Mixed with a little bit of pleasure, it would seem."

August lets out a disgruntled sound and I'm reaching out for the business card when he diverts it from my reach and pockets it inside his blazer.

Tobias eyes him attentively before whispering to me, though loud enough for everyone to hear.

"I think he's upset Pippa didn't give him *her* contact details," He says.

August rolls his eyes.

"Clearly she's the more *professional* one out of the two," He scoffs, revealing his disapproval. "This is a business trip, not a sightseeing jaunt in Cionne. Did he expect us to be gallivanting around like tourists? We're here for *work*. Christ, Tobias, what possessed the Boutique to hire inexperienced individuals? And ones who shamelessly make inappropriate advances towards my staff, no less?"

Staff.

"I see someone's not in the best of spirits," Tobias observes, meeting August's narrowed gaze.

"This is a waste of my time," He mutters, his irritation much more evident now.

His statement hurt more than I expected it to and the disappointing feeling lingers in the pit of my stomach.

Dejectedly, I lift my head to meet his gaze but his narrowed eyes are fixed on Tobias.

"I'd extend an invitation for dinner tonight but am I correct to assume you already have plans?" Tobias asks.

"Yes, we do," August answers abruptly, still avoiding my gaze.

"Reservations where?" Tobias inquires, hazel eyes shifting between August and I.

The room falls into a heavy silence, prompting Tobias to blink at August.

"Come now, cousin. I'm not one to *gatecrash* your evening engagements." Tobias rolls his eyes. "I'm well aware that three's a crowd."

"The Edelweiss," August responds, voice clipped.

CHAPTER 34

"A choice as charming as it gets in Cionne," Tobias remarks with a smile, as he shifts his gaze toward me. "You're in for a delightful experience there."

"Are we done here?" August glares at Tobias. "We're already running behind schedule."

"August…" I begin but he immediately steps to the side, gesturing for me to lead as we head towards the exit of the changing rooms.

Behind me, I catch snippets of hushed conversations between August and Tobias.

"Follow your *heart*, dear cousin." Tobias chuckles, just within my hearing range. "She is quite literally leading the way."

Chapter 35

After the visit to the Imperial Boutique, August appeared even more affronted. I refrained from discussing it during the journey back to The Maisonette and he retreated to his room almost immediately, claiming he needed to sleep off a headache before dinner so I spent the rest of the afternoon organising the notes I took at the boutique.

By the time it was 7 PM, I assumed we'd be spending the evening in the suite so I was surprised when August quietly knocked on my door, reminding me to start getting ready for our dinner reservation at The Edelweiss.

Changing into a black slip dress and sling-back heels with a long black cardigan to match, it's the most simple outfit I packed for the trip. All black with no glitter, no laces, no intricate fastenings or over-the-top embellishments.

There's an almost uneasy tension in the air as we meet in the living room. He doesn't comment on my clothes or the fact that our outfits are, once again, matching. Like me, August is dressed in all black, with his turtleneck tucked into slim-fit trousers, sleeves rolled up, and sporting black loafers.

He hardly makes conversation, seemingly deep in his own thoughts as we call a taxi and wait. The entire car journey to the restaurant was quiet. Despite my attempts to steer the conversation, his responses were curt and it was clear to me that he was in no mood to engage in any discussions.

By the time we reached The Edelweiss, it's apparent that August's mood isn't going to improve. He hasn't said more than a sentence since leaving the hotel, his eyebrows in a perpetual knot.

CHAPTER 35

"If you're not feeling well, we don't have to stay," I say to August as the waiters guide us through the restaurant. "We can order room service again like last night, I don't mind."

Our table is further out from the main dining space which I'm thankful for as the area is heavily decorated in sconces and pendant lights. The waiter seats us in a private dining space by the window on the second floor with a gorgeous view of the Cionne night sky.

"We're already here," He turns to me, brows furrowing. "If you didn't want to go out for dinner, you should have said something earlier."

"That's not what I meant," I explain, hastily. "I want to be out for dinner. I just thought you might still be feeling unwell after earlier."

"I told you," He bristles. "I'm fine."

The dismissive tone in August's voice makes my stomach sink. His mood is still off and I can't help but also be affected by it.

We sit in silence, August's eyes scanning the menu but I can tell he's not actually reading it. His gaze is sombre as his eyes slowly dart across the list of dining options.

Under the table, I fidget with my hands nervously. It's unsettling how sour the mood has become, especially since I may have been the inadvertent cause of it.

"August," I clear my throat, tugging gently on his menu to get his attention.

He sighs. "What?"

I bite my lip, sensing the irritation in his voice.

"I'm sorry," I say.

His eyebrows tug into an even deeper frown.

"What?"

"At the Imperial Boutique," I remark. "I didn't mean to waste your time."

Anxiously, I continue to wring my hands on my lap, aware that my tendency to get a little more enthusiastic than the average person can cause people to feel a little harried.

"I shouldn't have entertained the idea of trying on the dresses, I know we only came here for research on the suits," I continue. "I'm sorry for assuming it was okay."

My nose crinkles as a sensation of discomfort prickles my chest.

"I understand it's a work trip and I'm here as an employee. I should have been more mindful that we were on a strict schedule so I'm sorry if I overstepped any boundaries or if my behaviour was unprofessional." I finish, quietly.

"Mahalia, that's not…" He trails off.

"I really didn't mean to waste your time. I'm sorry."

Feeling my eyes well up, I keep my gaze fixed on the menu in front of me. What I'm not going to do is cry in public.

"Mahalia, look at me." August's voice prompts me to meet his gaze. "You have nothing to apologise for. You worked incredibly hard this weekend, I'm really impressed."

His praise makes my heart flutter, warmth spreading across my chest.

"I apologise for *my* behaviour earlier," He sighs. "I didn't mean to imply you were wasting my time nor did I think you were being unprofessional for wanting to sightsee. Hell, I want to sightsee around Cionne too. Tobias was just trying to get under my skin. He might be a prince but he's still my absurdly aggravating cousin. The way he was being more *vexing* than average, it usually means he's up to something."

"Oh," I blink, frowning. "I see."

"If you…" He hesitates, contemplating his next words. "If you want to take the tailor up on his offer to show you Cionne tomorrow, here."

He slides the card with Armand's details across the table and I tilt my head to the side, confused by the sudden offer.

"The latest the jet can leave is at 8 PM so you can have the entire day with him," He adds, an incisively distant look on his face. "But do be mindful that we have work the day after and I will not wait around if you decide to stay out late."

"Oh, I'm okay," I assure him.

"Mahalia," He warns. "Losing sleep over a *boy* is not something that you—"

"No," I interrupt him, shaking my head. "I mean, I'd rather go by myself."

CHAPTER 35

I slide the card back to him before looking outside the window at the Cionne skyline. Whilst the idea of sightseeing is appealing, I scrunch my nose at the thought of spending a full day with a person I've only just met and who'd probably end up getting tired of my company.

August blinks at me, confused.

"I like doing things at my own pace," I explain, turning my attention back to him. "I have a feeling he'd want to show me everything in such a limited amount of time and I don't really fancy overwhelming myself. I don't want to underwhelm him either, I don't think he'd enjoy my company very much."

August frowns. "What do you mean? Did he say something to you?"

"No, nothing like that," I laugh nervously. "I just... I feel like all I'd talk about is work. I don't have much of a personality outside of making clothes, unfortunately."

I try not to let my insecurities resurface but I've been on enough awkward first dates and forced social interactions to know that people get tired really quickly when all a person can talk about is work. I've picked up enough of those social cues to understand that.

After a pause, I turn to August questioningly.

"Are we okay?"

"We're more than okay." He nods. "I apologise for my mood. My migraines make me irritable."

"Does it still hurt?" I ask, concerned.

"I slept it off and took some painkillers earlier," August replies. "I feel a lot better now."

"I didn't realise camera flashes would be so triggering for you," I comment. "Did it happen a lot when you were modelling?"

"It's not..." He trails off, pausing momentarily before sighing. "It had nothing to do with the flashes."

I wait for him to elaborate.

"Not entirely. My royal pain in the ass cousin and his scheming ways are triggering."

"Scheming?"

"Tobias likes to meddle whenever women in my life are involved." He rolls his eyes. "Especially since we're on *his* turf. Full-blooded Toussaintians are territorial like that."

"Oh," I blink in realisation. "It must happen with all the women the Peroxide Prince brings to Toussaint, huh?"

"Seeing as you're the only woman I've ever brought to Toussaint," He starts. "He's more than thrilled."

"Don't worry," I reassure him. "I already told him it's not like that."

Something flickers in August's eyes.

"I heard," He nods. "Any chance I can change your mind?"

I blink at his question, unsure whether or not I heard him correctly.

"Change my mind?" I stare at him. "About—"

Before I can finish asking, the waiter approaches our table, my question getting lost and fading into the background.

"Ready to order, *monsieur? Mademoiselle?*"

August and I are well into the dinner, two courses out of the five done, as well as an entire bottle of Merlot finished when August orders another bottle. I blink at how easily he drinks wine like it's water but then remember his party-centric days as the Peroxide Prince.

"Do you really need alcohol to tolerate my presence?" I ask.

He responds with a nod. "It blurs you."

I gasp audibly, taken aback by his reply. "That's so *rude*."

"Well, you are kind of…" He gestures flippantly, hiding a smile as he sips into his glass of wine. "Disorienting."

"Excuse me?" I blink, not quite sure how to react.

"Yes, visually." He nods, a teasing glint in his grey eyes. "Painfully glaring, almost."

I narrow my eyes at him.

"That *isn't* any better, August."

He hums in mock thought.

"Blinding, then?" He turns towards me and nods, as if content in his choice of wording. "Fitting, I think. Given my condition."

CHAPTER 35

"That makes it so much worse." I grimace, struggling to find anything complimentary about rendering someone devoid of vision.

"You're *positively* blinding because you leave me in a daze," He continues. "How about that?"

"Is that supposed to be a compliment?" I glare at him before looking away, trying not to draw attention to the heat rising to my cheeks.

"I'm telling you a *fact*, dearest Hartt." He says, modest smirk transforming into a wider smile now.

The influence of alcohol is starting to show, causing him to be more playful and less reserved.

"You're so dazzling, it physically hurts my eyes." He pauses, his voice lowering to a murmur. "Yet it's *impossible* to look away from you. I have to *force* myself most of the time."

He shakes his head, says the statement in a way that sounded like it was meant solely for his ears to hear.

"Seeing you in that dress?" He continues, speaking in such hushed tones that I almost miss it. *"Blinding."*

He takes another sip of his wine.

"I think it was the tulle," I reply quietly. "And the glitter."

August shakes his head.

"It was you." He looks at me sincerely, foregoing any attempt to hide his smile now. "Brilliant and beautiful and so damn blinding."

My heart stutters in my chest.

The tips of my fingers twitch involuntarily and the overwhelming urge to reach over and kiss him surges through me. His eyes flicker down to my mouth and it almost looks like he's going to lean over when our waiter walks over to refill our glasses.

He takes the wine bottle and pours it over August's glass and, just as August reaches out for it, I quickly swipe it across to me.

"Uh-uh." I shake my head. "Pace yourself."

He lets out a low chuckle, gazing at me in a way that's all so new yet all so familiar.

"Stop looking at me like that," I mumble.

I sweep my hair behind my shoulder, in an effort to discreetly fan myself at the sudden rise in temperature I feel in August's presence.

"Why?" He leans forward, continuing to openly stare at me. "Am I making you nervous?"

Yes.

"You're so unreserved." He smiles easily then, reaching out to take a loose curl from my face and tucking it behind my ear. "It's refreshing."

I frown, realising I've replied out loud and say nothing else, choosing to gulp down the rest of my wine.

"Tinker-Talent, pace yourself." He mimics me this time. "No more alcohol for you."

Sliding the empty glass towards his direction, he gives me a playful, reprimanding stare.

"Yes, well." I huff, blinking at him. "Now *I* need to blur *you*."

August chuckles, the sound sending my chest in a flutter. I try not to think of how the sound of his laughter seems to be the soundtrack of our trip, wanting nothing more than to keep hearing it outside of our time here in Toussaint.

Chapter 36

"Why are you still up?"

A low, raspy voice echoing in the dim space of the Presidential Suite startles me and I press a hand to my chest out of fright. The living room is in complete darkness except for the small lamp on the table and I see the vague outline of August emerge from his room.

I'm currently sitting on the sofa, idly sketching on scrap pieces of paper after finding myself unable to sleep due to the eventful day *and* evening with the man now standing across from me.

"It's 2 o'clock in the morning, Mahalia."

His voice is ladened with sleep, as if he's only just woken up moments before.

"I was finishing some sketches." I motion towards the coffee table.

All the tension and worries I feel usually ease up when I keep my hands busy.

"In the dark?" He asks.

August's figure becomes more discernible as he steps into the glow of the lamp on the coffee table and I blink. He's wearing nothing but a pair of grey joggers, the waistband hanging low on his hips.

"I didn't want to trouble you," I say, looking away and focusing my gaze on the sketchbook on my lap. "In case you woke up."

He walks over to the table, eyeing the sketches as he adjusts the lamp so he can see better.

"These are good." He picks one up and squints his eyes, letting it adjust to the dim light. "Very impressive."

I wrinkle my nose. "It's just a sketch."

"Your sketches belong in a museum," He chuckles.

Rising from the sofa, I reach across the glass surface to collect the scattered pieces of paper. From across the coffee table, August is watching me, eyes roaming my figure and I feel myself flush in the dark.

His grey eyes linger where my hands are nervously fiddling with the hem of my top. I'm currently in my sleepwear, dressed in a grey lace camisole and grey frilly shorts to match. I hadn't bothered dressing more reservedly since August had gone to bed already and I wasn't expecting to see him until the next morning.

The intensity of his gaze rekindles an all-too-familiar flutter in my stomach and I refrain from making eye contact.

"I don't remember coming back to The Maisonette," August clears his throat as he walks to the fridge in the kitchen. "Nor do I recall finishing dinner."

"We got kicked out of the restaurant," I say, schooling a serious expression as I sit back down on the sofa. "For being too loud."

"*Merde,*" August curses, running a hand over his face as he walks back over to the living room, a glass of water in hand. "We did?"

"I'm kidding," I shake my head, grinning. "But we were close. You kept cursing the chandeliers."

I stifle a giggle at the memory of a slightly drunken August complaining far too loudly about the hanging light fixtures on the ceilings as we were exiting the restaurant.

"I forgot that would be normal for you," I begin. "Being dragged into and getting kicked out of lavish places like the party animal that you are."

"*Were,*" He corrects me. "Those days are behind me. I'm far too old for that shit."

"You're *twenty six.*"

"And I feel like I've aged two decades in the past two months."

August plops himself next to me on the sofa, sitting so close I can almost feel his body heat. My eyes trail down from his neck to his bare chest and I quickly look away.

CHAPTER 36

Gripping the edge of my sketchpad, I focus my attention on drawing, the light scritching of my pencil on paper is the only sound that can be heard in the quiet atmosphere of the living room.

"I've never met anyone who works like you do." He comments, taking a sip of his water.

I pause my sketching, looking up to find him staring at me.

"Your father is *Cedric Vante*," I declare. "I'm pretty sure he works ten times as much as the entire fashion industry, August."

"Not *'as much'*," He shakes his head. *"Like."*

I tilt my head to the side, waiting for him to comment further.

"I know people who work nonstop in this industry, I'm not oblivious." He says. "But not quite like you."

"And how might that be?"

August downs the rest of his glass in one, looking nonchalantly suave as he does so.

"With your heart on your sleeve."

Closing his eyes, he leans his head back and brings the arm closest to me on the back of the sofa. It's unfair how effortlessly cool and attractive he is. His devilishly handsome face, his charmingly blasé attitude. I tried not to openly stare at him during the fitting because it would have been unprofessional but seeing him now, all sprawled out next to me in all his shirtless glory?

Well, he isn't called the *Parisian Playboy* for nothing.

My throat dries and I swallow quietly, trying not to fidget on the sofa.

"You're staring," He states, eyes still closed.

I blush, diverting my eyes.

"Yes, well." I begin then blurt out obtusely, "You're shirtless."

He chuckles, grey eyes flickering open as he rolls his head in my direction. *"Stop ogling your boss, Mahalia Hartt."*

A wave of embarrassment floods my system as he echoes the statement I subconsciously spouted out during the catwalk fitting backstage. Of course, he would remember that humiliating incident.

"I'm going to finish my sketches in my room." I clear my throat, getting up to leave. "Goodnight."

"Wait, I was just teasing." August reaches out for me, gently grabbing my wrist. "Sorry, I'll stop."

So much for professionalism.

The thought slips out of my mouth before I can stop it.

"I think we're past the point of professionalism here, Tinker-Talent." He chuckles, the sound deep and resonant. "You've literally grabbed my dick through my pants and I've had my tongue down your throat."

My brain short-circuits at his crass remark.

"That was an accident!" I sputter, blushing furiously. "I wasn't trying- I didn't mean to-"

"Didn't mean to what?" August looks at me intently, a boyish smirk on his face. "Inappropriately touch your boss?"

My eyes widen in mortification.

"I'm not complaining," He shrugs, the smirk on his face transforming into a grin. "I'd like a bit of a head's up though. I'm honestly struggling to keep up with your rather *lewd advances*, Miss Hartt."

I can feel my face overheating, my mouth gaping like a fish as I struggle to think of an appropriate response to his apparent teasing. Being awake at 2 AM in Toussaint is yielding no favourable outcome for me, clearly.

"I'm leaving," I announce instead.

Holding my sketchbook close, I make a move to head back to my room when August grabs my left hand, interlocking it with his.

"Okay, sorry, I'll stop." He holds his free hand up placatingly as his grey eyes pore over me. "Please stay, I want to share some news."

Curious, I turn back to him.

"A confirmation came through about my transfer to Grayson."

I gasp, immediately sitting back down next to him.

"Oh my god, congratulations!" I grin. "I mean, not like I— or anybody else for that matter— expected a different outcome, being a nepo baby and all. But congrats!"

August rolls his eyes playfully.

"You'll be back in New York before you know it." I tug on our hands

CHAPTER 36

excitedly, offering him a genuine smile.

"Except," he starts, eyes flickering down to our intertwined fingers. "I think I've grown to like London. Never thought I'd grow so attached to the city yet here I am."

There's an unreserved softness to his gaze, echoing the expressions he exhibited at the dinner earlier.

"London would love to keep having you," I say sincerely.

"Would she?" He stares at me. "Would she really?"

Something pulls at my chest, pushing me towards him. I have a feeling he isn't talking about the city anymore but I nod anyway.

"She would," I affirm.

"God, what I'd give to have London." He mutters, eyes flitting down to our hands before looking back up at me again. "She's unlike anyone I've ever met."

His grey eyes bore into mine, warm and seeking, as he searches my face.

There's a frantic tugging on my heartstrings and I bite my lip.

August's eyes flicker down to my mouth, my throat tightening as I swallow.

"Mahalia?" His voice is gentle as he whispers my name.

"Yes?"

A pause.

"Can I kiss you?"

My breath hitches, my stomach fluttering at the question as August raises his gaze to meet mine before slowly trailing his eyes back down to my lips.

I nod, exhaling quietly.

"Please."

Slowly, he leans in, the scent of sandalwood and bergamot invading my senses as my eyes flutter close and his lips meet mine.

The kiss is soft, slow and searching.

August is gentle as his hand travels to my neck, cupping my jaw to pull me closer to him as he coaxes me into his mouth in a delicate caress.

There's a gentleness to his kiss that differed from the ones at the club, a tenderness to his touch.

It's light yet assuring— certain.

August begins to pull away but I find myself gravitating towards him as I wrap my arms around his neck and press my lips against his, imploring.

I feel him smile against the kiss, biting lightly on my bottom lip before he gently nudges me backwards until I'm lying flat on the sofa, my hair sprawled out around me.

August leans back to look at me, grey eyes trailing the length of my body and I'm suddenly all too conscious of the amount of skin I'm showing.

The flimsy top I'm wearing does nothing to hide my decency, one strap falling down my shoulder as the hem rides up my stomach. All the while, the waistband of my shorts has shifted low on my hipbones, exposing the lace trim of my underwear.

August inhales slowly, eyes transfixed.

"You're fucking mesmerising," He exhales.

His large hands skim over my pelvis, fingers tracing the lace detailing before settling on the exposed skin of my waist. Heat simmers in the pit of my stomach as his palm slides under my camisole, my body burning at his touch.

"August," I whisper, a newfound craving coiling within my core.

He hums, grey eyes roaming appreciatively before his lips surge forward for another kiss.

It's heavier this time, urgent and demanding.

His teeth gently graze the bottom of my lip before his tongue parts through and licks eagerly into my mouth. The taste of mint is subtle, along with something fresh and crisp and I resist the urge to bite into him.

"I love hearing my name from your lips." His words are murmurs against my mouth. "Say it again."

"*August.*"

He reaches for my leg, wrapping it around his lower back and my breath catches in my throat as he presses his hips against mine. Reaching up to wrap my arms around his neck, I pull him down for an onslaught of hurried kisses.

"Mhm—" His voice is deep, gravelly as he groans into my mouth. "Fuck."

CHAPTER 36

August traces his fingers over the hem of my tank top, snaking his hand under the fabric to firmly settle on the bare skin of my stomach and I moan, finding myself sensitive in places I didn't even know existed.

"Please," I whimper into his mouth.

My mind is too hazy for me to fully comprehend what it is I'm begging for.

"—lia." The shaky exhale of my name coming from his lips brings me back to reality. "What are you doing to me?"

August is fervent, grip tightening around my waist and his head tilts back to look at me.

"You're in everything, you're everywhere." He begins, dazed. "I can't get you out of my head. You're on my mind all the time, I can't think straight when you're next to me but I can't function when you're not around either. I'm so fixated on you— the idea of you, the *reality* of you. I can't get you out of my head no matter how hard I try. You're constantly in my thoughts, you occupy every corner of my damn mind. I see you in everything, everyone, everywhere. Ever since I met you— fuck, you're all I think about, you're all I want."

His confession is an urgent unravelling, threading its way to my heart.

"August," I swallow shakily, blinking up at him.

He groans, turning away. "God, don't look at me with those eyes."

I push myself up on my elbows as he shifts to a sitting position. Even in the dim lighting, his profile is still striking, wavy locks tousled as he lolls his head on the back of the sofa. There's a slight flush to his face, neck exposed and bare chest tinted the lightest pink as he breathes raggedly.

He looks beautiful, God-like.

Feeling brave, I crawl over to August, straddling him between my legs.

"Mahalia," He sounds winded, almost tortured.

He grips the cushioned sofa underneath him, so much so that his knuckles are turning white. My own fingers twitch, nerves and adrenaline rolled into one.

"Please," August swallows as he tugs on the hem of my top, the strap slipping off one shoulder.

My heart stutters at the insinuation, my stomach curling with desire.

"I'm not..." I begin, shakily. "I haven't..."

I don't know what I'm doing.

"We don't have to do anything you don't want to."

He slides the fallen strap back over my shoulder, tracing the dip of my collarbone before placing a gentle kiss on the base of my throat.

Goosebumps erupt all over my skin as he trails his lips upwards and gently nips at my neck. The singes from my fingertips course throughout my entire body, every fibre of my being set ablaze by August.

Every muscle, every nerve— down to the last synapse.

"August," I breathe out. "I want you."

Pressing myself down on his lap, I roll my hips against his, tugging clumsily on the drawstrings of his sweatpants.

"Are you sure?" He asks, straightening me up to look me in the eyes.

The grey of his irises is almost non-existent. Only a thin layer of silver surrounds his enlarged pupils as they search my eyes for confirmation.

"Yes," I nod my head. "A-are you?"

I can't contain the vulnerability in my voice at my question as I bite my lip and stare at him.

August's gaze is unwavering, eyes locked on mine as he draws me closer to him.

"*God, Mahalia.*" He responds, leaning his forehead against mine. "I've never been more certain of anyone in my life."

Chapter 37

There's a dreamlike state to my surroundings as my eyelids flutter open, the morning light filtering into the room in a soft haze.

My body is oddly tender, an unfamiliar ache rooting itself in my bones.

With a quiet yawn, I stretch languidly on the bed, the thick material of the duvet covers sleek against my bare skin. There's still a noticeable warmth in the sheets and I hum in content, basking in the cosiness around me despite the gentle throbbing all over my body.

Inhaling deeply, I bury my face into the silken pillows, murmuring in appreciation at the rich scent of sandalwood and bergamot as a slow breath escapes me.

I pause.

Sandalwood and bergamot.

Immediately, I shoot up.

This isn't my bed.

An acute soreness accompanies my harsh movement and the tingles I often feel on the tips of my fingers are everywhere now.

The sound of the shower hums in the background, the rush of water nothing but white noise as my eyes survey the room and I take in my surroundings properly this time. Despite the identical layout, glaring details confirm that it isn't my room— August's suitcase by the door, his weekender bag next to the wardrobe, his clothes draped over the sofa.

My eyes catch his grey sweatpants on the floor by the bed and a warm flush crawls its way up to my neck, the events of last night washing over me in torrent flashbacks.

We don't have to do anything you're not comfortable with.
My cheeks burn even hotter.

His playboy image and reputation should not be underestimated, we did everything regardless of comfort and it was *sensational*.

Another startling realisation hits me.

I scramble for my phone without delay, finding it on the bedside table next to August's, and quickly scroll through my contacts.

"Hello?" Gigi's voice, muffled and sluggish, promptly picks up.

"Gigi," I breathe.

Her groan sounds over the phone.

"*It's 5 AM on a Bank Holiday Monday, Mahalia Hartt,*" She says. "*You better have a good reason for interrupting my beauty sleep.*"

I glance at the clock on the wall and wince, forgetting that Toussaint is a few hours ahead of England.

"Sorry, it's just..." I trail off, unsure how to approach the topic. "I'm in *August's room...*"

The line goes still for a while and part of me thinks she's disconnected the call until the sound of her voice breaks the silence again.

"*Oh my god!*" Her loud gasp is audible over the phone, sounding more awake now. "*Did you just lose your virginity to August Vante?*"

I blush, the delicate discomfort between my legs a confirmation.

"Well..."

The shower turning off prompts me to turn my head towards the bathroom.

"Gigi, I have to go," I say quickly. "He just finished showering and—"

"*Mahalia Hartt!*"

"I'll speak to you later, love you, bye!"

I quickly hang up just in time as the door opens. August emerges from the bathroom, freshly out of the shower with only a towel wrapped around his torso. It hangs low on his hips and leaves absolutely nothing to my imagination, not when I already experienced the reality of what's underneath it last night.

"You're awake."

CHAPTER 37

There's a softness to his voice as he acknowledges me.

"Good morning," I greet him quietly.

A silence settles between us, neither awkward nor uncomfortable, just a quiet lull blanketing over the events of last night.

Holding my breath, I pull the bedsheets a little higher over my chest as I observe August closely for any subtle signs of unease, or worse, regret.

"How are you feeling?" He asks, gently.

A twinge of nervousness coils in the pit of my stomach.

How do people navigate the morning after?

"Good, yes." I swallow, clearing my throat. "You?"

Something flickers in his eyes as he watches me from the doorway of the bathroom and I try not to fidget under his gaze.

"You look like you want to bolt out of my room," He chuckles, the sound a soft rumbling from his chest.

"No," I squeak, visibly flinching at my nervousness.

August walks towards me, settling himself on the edge of the bed.

"Did I–uh," He pauses, concern colouring his expression. "Did I hurt you?"

I blush, feeling the tenderness everywhere. "I-I'm fine."

His eyes are warm, molten silver.

There's something intentional in his gaze as he watches me, like he's trying to commit something to memory.

The chime of a doorbell echoes in the suite and I turn towards the sound, frowning.

"Room service," August answers, reading my confusion. "I ordered us breakfast. Figured you'd be hungry."

He reaches out to brush his thumb on the knot between my eyebrows before cradling the side of my face into his palm. The softness of the gesture makes my stomach flutter and I reflexively lean into his touch.

"I didn't order too much," He says. "I had no idea whether you'd prefer to eat in before we go out. But we can always grab food later when we're sightseeing."

"Sightseeing?" I blink up at him.

He nods. "Touristy spots, local places. Whatever you want to do, Tinker-Talent."

My heart flutters with excitement at the idea of spending another day with August in Cionne.

"There's extra towels back there." He signals towards the bathroom. "Feel free to shower in my en-suite."

He leans down for a moment, his grey eyes contemplating, before tucking my hair behind my ear.

"I'll sort out breakfast." He clears his throat before exiting the room.

I shower quickly in August's bathroom before getting ready in my own room, my mind inundated with the events over the last 24 hours when I hear a knocking on my door.

"Come in," I call out.

August strolls into my room, wearing a light blue linen shirt, white chinos and a pair of light brown loafers.

"I wanted to see if I needed to change," He says.

I blink down at my own outfit, deciding on a simple beach outfit with a white corset top, a light blue pinstripe high-lo maxi skirt and some tan gladiator sandals.

Now this is just ridiculous.

"I can change if you want," I clear my throat. "I brought other outfits."

"No need," He shakes his head amusingly. "We've already made it this far."

He looks over me for a moment, grey eyes intentional before extending a hand towards me.

"Ready?"

Shyly, I reach out for his hand. "Ready."

August laces his fingers through mine, before tugging me close to him and pressing his lips on the top of my head. The action is similar to yesterday but he lingers longer this time, the gesture intentional, and something stirs in my chest.

Looking up at him, I watch as the corner of his lips quirks into a soft smile.

CHAPTER 37

"*Allons-y, cher cœur.*"

Cionne is teeming with Toussaint's culture. The sun-kissed city is a tapestry of elegant European architecture and the allure of Mediterranean lifestyle.

After exploring the city the whole day, August and I found ourselves sitting in a quaint café, one of his favourite local spots. Tucked away in an unassuming part of the city, it's a modest building with a wrought-iron gate adorned with trailing ivy that leads to a sun-dappled terrace. Warm hues of aged wood and exposed brick walls provide a rustic backdrop for the antique bistro tables and matching chairs that are dotted around the terrace, the air infused with a rich aroma of freshly brewed coffee.

August is relaxed and ridiculously radiant as he sits opposite me by the outdoor seating area, his hair practically glowing under the golden hour sun.

"I spent a lot of my summers in Cionne," He shares. "A place to get away from it all. Not so much when I was, uh, more involved in the industry. But this place definitely has a special place in my heart."

He doesn't talk about his sordid reputation as the infamous playboy, skimming over it entirely. Whether it's in the past, I'm not too sure.

Instead, August continues to share stories about his time in Toussaint, opening up about a part of his life that's rarely talked about in the media. It feels strange to hear things from his point of view, rather than the tabloids.

August talks in a way that makes you listen. It makes sense, I suppose. Under all the stoicism is a warmth about him— a reserved softness, almost always hidden.

"*C'est bon, monsieur?*"

The server approaches us.

"The bill, *s'ilvous plait.*" August says, sliding his Black Amex card out of his wallet.

I blink, shaking my head.

"August, no."

"It's just coffee, Mahalia."

"With two main meals and a shared side." I give him a look.

"Exactly, so let me pay."

"August."

"Mahalia."

"I haven't spent a *single penny* on this trip."

"Good." He nods towards me approvingly. "You're being smart with your money."

"*August.*" I glare at him.

Glancing over at the waiter as he presses a button and gestures towards the card machine, I reach out instantly, tapping my card on top of the reader and listening to it beep.

"*Merci.*" I nod awkwardly.

Blinking, the waiter turns to August who only shakes his head, amused.

"*C'est bon,*" August comments, waving a hand dismissively. "*Elle est mon petit cœur têtu.*"

"Cœur?" I ask, having heard the word a few times now. "Heart?"

August clears his throat before lifting his cup of coffee to take a sip. "I said you're stubborn-hearted."

"Oh," I nod before narrowing my eyes and crossing my arms. "I am *not*."

He looks at me pointedly then, a small smile hiding behind the porcelain cup. "I rest my case."

"I'm not stubborn," I repeat. "I'm just... immovable in my convictions."

A chuckle escapes his lips. "That's a rather ornamented way to say 'stubborn.'"

"I am not–"

"*Stubborn.*" He interrupts me teasingly, putting the cup down and looking at me in a sprightly uppity manner.

His overt playfulness is something I didn't expect, considering I've grown so accustomed to his impassive attitude. Deepening my glare, I grab the Polaroid camera on the table to take a picture of him in retaliation, a flash erupting from the device.

"ARGH!"

August shouts in surprise and I draw a sharp breath as he jerks backwards,

CHAPTER 37

covering his eyes. My stomach twists, not realising that the flash on the camera was switched on.

"Oh my god!" I scramble over the table to reach for the hand covering his face. "I'm so sorry!"

He lets out a sharp hiss and my heart lodges itself in my throat.

"Are you okay? Does it hurt?" I question, holding his face as gently as I can.

His entire body tenses as I attempt to examine his closed lids and he lets out a groan.

"Should I call an ambulance?" I ask, beginning to panic. "Do you need the hospital?"

In another effort to see his eyes more clearly, I carefully grasp his head in between my palms but the back of his hand remains firmly covering his lids.

The distress I feel heightens as his eyebrows furrow and I gently intertwine my fingers with his.

"A-August." I swallow, my voice wavering.

He stills, one eye suddenly opening as he peers over to look at me above our interlocked hands.

I pause, staring at him as he looks up at me wide-eyed and blinking and optically unharmed.

"You–!" I visibly recoil, swatting his arm before sitting back down. "That was *not* funny."

The rapid beating of my heart begins to slow and I breathe a sigh of relief, thankful that I didn't send him to a focal seizure.

"Sorry," He draws back slightly, face apologetic. "I couldn't resist."

I narrow my eyes at him. "I thought I temporarily *blinded* you."

The corner of his mouth curls upwards as he sits upright.

"You blind me every day, Tinker-Talent."

My heartbeat picks up again and it most definitely has nothing to do with the little spectacle he just put on. There's a familiar fluttering in my chest as I recall our conversation last night at the restaurant.

Brilliant and beautiful and so damn blinding.

"Not funny." I scrunch my nose in disdain.

He turns towards me. "The hospital though, really?"

"I don't know the severity of your condition," I reply, huffing. "You were *bedridden* yesterday afternoon. Not to mention, *intoxicated* in the evening. I don't know how many factors there are to consider. Migraine, alcohol, drugs. Slight discomfort or genuine pain."

"Worried about me?" He teases.

I look at him, seriously.

"*Yes.*"

He blinks, gaze softening.

There's a familiar fondness in his grey eyes— the warmest shade of molten silver.

"Photalgia," He shares. "Light sensitivity."

Tilting my head, I make a mental note of the condition.

"It's mainly flashes and flickering lights," He continues. "Glare from reflective surfaces, high-contrast lighting in certain environments, staring at bright screens for too long."

"Does it hurt?"

"It used to," He answers honestly. "It was a lot worse when I was a kid. Being in front of the camera when I was younger probably didn't help, I don't think. But it's tolerable nowadays."

Wearing sunglasses, working in dimly lit rooms— it makes sense.

"Don't worry," August teases. "Your tiny, little camera won't disorientate me."

He grabs my Polaroid, motioning it towards me.

"Okay, your turn. Smile."

I narrow my eyes at him, turning my head away. "No, thank you."

"Oh, *now* you're camera shy?"

"We're not all photogenic." I look at him pointedly. "And literal models."

"Ex-model," He quips.

"As if *that* makes any difference."

I glower at the lens as he points it in front of my face and takes a picture, flash erupting.

CHAPTER 37

"Smile, Tinker-Talent," He coos. "Frowning doesn't suit you I'm afraid, come on now."

I make an exaggeration to deepen my glare.

"There are many expressions I adore on your face but frowning isn't one of them, sadly." He shakes his head. *"Souriez, mon cœur."*

"No," I continue scowling at him. "I'm channelling my inner Peroxide Prince."

At the mention of the moniker of his modelling days, August chuckles.

"You should channel this one," He says, picking up the developing Polaroid of me. "I call it the *Glitter Gremlin*."

He holds up the photo he took moments ago, me scowling at the camera with my eyebrows furrowed into a deep V and my lips pursed into a small pout.

"You are so rude!" I gasp, flipping him off.

It earns me another laugh from him, the sound of his deep, baritone chuckle distracting me momentarily.

"Stop wasting the film." I roll my eyes at him, giggling.

"Photography 101, Tinker-Talent." He starts. "There's no such thing as wasted film."

Picking up his Leica M6, he begins to take photos of me with his film camera and I retaliate by taking photos with my Polaroid.

The images pile up as we continue our photo battle, switching cameras with each other every now and again. I watch in real-time as the film photos of us begin developing, my own feelings for him mirroring the same sentiment.

Chapter 38

For the next two weeks, my routine at the studio consisted of design concepts, fabric selection and pattern making.

The trip to Toussaint was useful and I was able to determine the overall style and theme of the collection. I sketched out a dozen designs for Sebastian to look through, the silhouette being the most important part to pay homage to the previous royal attire.

Sebastian favoured working out-of-office which nobody questioned but it made communicating with him a lot more difficult.

His working practices are questionable, at best.

Pollux wasn't joking when he said that Sebastian would ring in the ungodly hours of the night— emailing, messaging, and even calling. I found myself having to adjust my sleeping patterns, just so I don't miss any important updates or requests from him.

I've just finished wrapping up for the day at the studio, saying goodbye to Estelle and Pollux on the second floor when my phone buzzes with a text.

In Paris until the end of next week.
Then flying to New York on Monday.
Should hopefully be back in London by Friday.

I'm about to reply when another text comes through.

I'll be all yours next weekend.

CHAPTER 38

The familiar fluttering in my stomach surfaces as I type my response.

Can't wait to see you!

I send the text to August, not dwelling too deeply on it.

He's currently working between all three cities as he wraps up his responsibilities here at Holmes, and transitions over to Grayson whilst still maintaining his commitments at Vante.

We haven't seen each other since our trip to Toussaint and we've yet to have the conversation on where we stand, if we're standing *anywhere* at all so I've been doing my best to keep my emotions levelled.

Neither of us is skirting around our newfound dynamic but we're not exactly scrambling to put a label on anything.

I'd much rather have the conversation in person.

But with August's balancing act between London, Paris and New York, it feels nearly impossible to discuss it with him face-to-face.

"Your deliveries are *not* a fun workout, Mahalia Hartt!"

Gigi's voice echoes down the hallway as the lift doors open to the flat.

Absentmindedly, I step into the living room. Clusters of intricately designed wooden chests on timber pallets and bolts of fabrics on clapboard frames have taken up the entire floor space of the flat.

I turn to Gigi curiously. "What's all this?"

"You tell me!" She huffs. "I've had to run up and down the building, orchestrating half a dozen delivery men to bring in these medieval-looking shipments in our tiny apartment."

The logo of the Toussaint Foundry catches my attention and I blink.

"I thought it was a PR package from the monarchs in the Middle Ages," Gigi continues to comment, pushing the boxes around to make a pathway. "Care to explain?"

"These should've been sent to the studio," I reply. "Why are they–"

The sound of my phone ringing cuts me off and I quickly grab it from my pocket, seeing August's Caller ID pop up on the screen.

"Hello?" I answer.

"*Sorry for not calling sooner,*" August's voice, rushed and apologetic, filters through the line immediately. "*I've been in back-to-back meetings all day. Conference calls are such a pain in my ass, I've forgotten how tight of a ship my dad runs at Vante.*"

The background noise of blaring cars and French-accented chatter can be heard on his end and I instantly know he's in Paris.

"It's alright," I answer. "Don't worry, I know you're busy."

Walking over to a hulking mahogany chest, I blink at the label 'EMBELLISHMENTS' under the foundry's logo. Out of curiosity, I open the clasp, my eyes widening at the massive compartments containing various decorative elements for garments. Embroidery beads, sequins, buttons and ribbons are all neatly arranged inside.

"—*lia?*" August's voice cuts through my awe.

"I'm here," I reply. "Sorry, there's just..."

I open another chest, this time labelled 'SEWING SUPPLIES'. An array of thread assortments is placed in the middle with needles, pins, chalk, fabric markers and tailor's pencils packaged neatly around it. There's also a dedicated section for fasteners and closures, smaller boxes containing zippers, buttons, snaps and hook-and-loop fasteners.

"*You sound distracted,*" August comments. "*Is everything okay?*"

"Yes," I respond. "I just– a lot of deliveries from the Toussaint Foundry came today."

"*Oh, already? That was quick.*"

"So it was you? You placed the order?" I ask to clarify.

"*Of course. Should I not have?*"

"No, it's fine. But the foundry accidentally sent it to my address. I have an entire living room's worth of fabrics and sewing supplies when it should have been sent to the studio."

"*Oh, it's not for Holmes,*" August responds. "*The textile supplies are for you.*"

I blink. "What?"

"*It's for you.*"

I stare at the various lengths and widths of fabric rolls neatly secured on cardboard bolts as well as the mahogany chests of various sizes scattered

CHAPTER 38

around the living room.

"To use for the samples?" I ask.

"*To use however you'd like,*" He answers. "*Although, I did place a separate order for the regalwear collection. That should be sent to the studio.*"

"Are you sure there isn't a mix-up?" I question. "There are far too many deliveries here."

"*There shouldn't be. I requested the foundry to dispatch your order first,*" He replies. "*Everything sent to your apartment is yours.*"

Walking to my studio, my eyes widen at the half a dozen rolls of *toile de jouy* fabrics propped up against a wall, all varying in themes, motifs and colour palettes.

"August," I gasp aloud. "I can't afford all of this!"

"*It's alright, I've put it down as company expenses.*"

I blanch. "You just told me it isn't for Holmes!"

"*Alright, you got me.*" He sounds sheepish. "*It's under Vante.*"

"You're putting my expenses under the Parisian atelier?!" I squeak.

"*Under my name, Tinker-Talent.*"

Overwhelmed, I press a hand to my chest.

"August…"

Tailoring materials like the ones from Toussaint are not cheap. I didn't even bother asking the prices for anything during the tour at both the foundry and the boutique because I simply knew that I wouldn't be able to afford it.

"*Don't worry,*" He reassures me. "*Just think of it as compensation.*"

"Compensation?" I repeat in disbelief. "*For what?*"

"*For putting up with me throughout the whole trip.*"

"August—"

"*Don't overthink it.*" He cuts me off gently.

Though it's impossible not to overthink anything when it concerns August.

"*I have it covered, cher cœur.*"

His tone leaves no room for argument.

"Thank you," I say. "Really, August. I'm so grateful. But I can't possibly—"

"*Uh-oh, I can't hear you.*" August interrupts me once more. "*Tinker-Talent, you're breaking up. Sorry, what did you say?*"

"Funny," I deadpan. "You need to stop spending so much time with Hero."

August's deep chuckle echoes over the phone and the sound tugs at my heart.

"*I'll be back next week,*" He says, clearing his throat. "*We'll talk properly then, okay?*"

The call ends after we say our goodbyes and I feel a lot lighter at having spoken with August.

Walking towards one of the smaller mahogany crates in my studio, I open it up to find different ribbons slotted into a wooden rack. A particular section of white glittery tulle ribbons catches my eye and I smile, the fabric reminding me of the dress I tried on at the Imperial Boutique.

Chapter 39

"I'm scrapping the sample suits."

It's a Thursday afternoon when the proverbial fashion bomb drops, tanking the work I've been doing for the collection over the last few weeks.

Hovering by the mannequin I'm currently pinning fabrics into place, the statement goes over my head completely as Sebastian walks into the secondary studio.

"What?" I blink.

"The Spring/Summer line." He points towards the dressmaker dummies with my half of the samples.

A knot forms in my stomach.

His assessment throws me off guard and I stare at him, still unsure whether or not I heard him correctly.

"It's not Holmes' standards," Sebastian states.

"What do you mean?" I try to keep my voice level as he approaches me.

"It needs revision."

"Revision?" I repeat, stunned.

I try not to panic. The deadline for the collection is in less than two weeks and I've been working on my half of the lineup for twice as long.

"It's too..." Sebastian trails off, looking around the room to search for the right word when his eyes land on me. *"Hartt."*

I continue to stare at him, waiting for further elaboration.

"It isn't Holmes enough. It's too reminiscent of *your* collection and holds far too many similarities with *your* designs. Didn't you use the patterns from your graduate showcase?"

"Loosely," I answer. "I made alterations to the patterns to incorporate silhouettes that *you* requested for the collection."

"But the designs themselves feel too much of Hartt, instead of Holmes." He says with a disapproving tone. "There's a glaring contrast when compiled next to the Autumn/Winter line. It looks like two separate collections instead of one. There's no cohesion between the two. As if two different designers have worked on the project."

I blink at this.

Technically, we did.

"You approved the initial designs," I argue, numbly. "Sebastian, your concerns should have been addressed during the early stages of the project, not when we're two weeks away from our deadline. You couldn't have given this feedback earlier on?"

Sebastian narrows his eyes at me.

"Are you questioning the *Lead Designer* of the project, Hallie?"

"N-no, of course not. But–"

"I'm well aware that the deadline is in two weeks." He replies nonchalantly.

Blindsided is an understatement. I feel an unease growing in my chest as the reasoning hardly makes any sense.

"Then what... what am I supposed to do?" I ask, voice strained.

"Work on the revisions for the Autumn/Winter lineup," Sebastian answers. "I brought half of my samples with me today. You can pick the rest up from my flat at the end of the week."

I try to remain as calm as possible about the whole situation but I feel the panic escalating steadily.

"Less Hartt," He demands. "More Holmes."

Discarding half of the lineup so close to the deadline is one of the worst-case scenarios of any fashion collection. I've encountered a lot of countless mental breakdowns during my time at university but nothing quite prepared me for the harrowing situation of experiencing it myself in the world of work.

CHAPTER 39

It's a sartorial nightmare, to say the very least.

A knock on the door brings me out of my spiralling thoughts.

"Working hard, Tinker-Talent?"

I should have been more excited to see August again after over two weeks. My chest should be fluttering with all the newfound emotions for him but all I feel is a tightening sensation around my ribcage as I stay seated by the sewing machine.

"What are you doing here?" I blink, distractedly.

"Things finished up early in Paris so I thought to come see you before New York," He replies. "How's the collection doing? Are these your samples?"

At the mention of the Spring/Summer suits, I feel another wave of anxiety sweeping over me.

"N-no." I shake my head. "They're not."

I focus my attention back on the sewing machine in front of me, changing the needle for the fourth time. Since finding out my half of the sample lineup is being pulled, I've broken three machine needles within the past hour.

The thread catches on the latch again and I huff, agitated.

"Mahalia," August calls out to me.

"Sorry." I shake my head. "Did you say something?"

"I asked if you wanted to grab dinner after," He replies, looking at me expectantly. "Thought we might get the opportunity to talk?"

I stare at August, the taut feeling in between my ribcage intensifying, like a corset tightening around my chest.

"Whenever you're done," He motions to the sewing machine. "I'm free for the evening."

"I can't," I shake my head before I backtrack, "Not that I don't want to. Just not today. I'm really busy right now. I have a lot of work to do."

The machine whirrs as the fabric snags and bunches up under the presser foot. Frustrated, I pull on it before it finally starts working again. I can hear distinct voices calling my name but I want to tune it out, the sound of the needle stitching the fabric is loud but I need it to be louder.

Pressing the pedal faster, I block out everything around me, focused on finishing the lining seam of the blazer.

"*Mahalia.*"

The needle breaks as it catches on the sleeve of my cardigan and my breath hitches.

"Shit," I swallow, coarsely.

The realisation of how close the needle had been near my hand, just missing the tips of my fingers by a thread, makes my stomach turn. In front of me, the sewing machine rattles in protest and I immediately take my foot away from the pedal.

My hands begin to tremble and I feel the odd singes on the tips of my fingers, like tiny electric shocks as I look up to find August's gaze fixed on me.

"Are you okay?"

"Yes," I answer, voice strained. "I'm just…"

The imaginary corset wrapped around my chest winds impossibly tighter, boning digging into my ribcage.

"You're shaking." His grey eyes flicker across my face. "What's going on?"

A look of pure concern etches itself onto August's face and my heart catches in my throat. The pressure on my lungs bursts as I let out a strangled breath.

"I messed up," I answer, winded. "Sebastian is scrapping the samples I've been working on. He was here— earlier— and he told me… He told me—"

My breathing comes out in staggered gulps.

"Mahalia," August says softly.

"It's *half* of the lineup, August." I choke out. "The one *I'm* responsible for. The turnaround time would be impossible to meet. Alterations to garment silhouettes and modifying patterns should have been done at the very *early stages* of the project. It doesn't make any sense. He was greenlighting everything from the very beginning."

"Mahalia," August says my name again, firmly this time. "What does Sebastian want you to do?"

CHAPTER 39

"Finish up the Autumn/Winter samples," I answer frantically. "He said he's going to revise the Spring/Summer ones."

August frowns. "He wants you to work on *his* half of the collection whilst he fixes yours?"

I nod.

An unpleasant feeling lurches at the bottom of my stomach and I feel it crawl up my chest. There's sudden pressure in my lungs as tears prick my eyes and I shut them tightly.

"Tinker-Talent," August tries again. "Breathe."

My hands begin to tremble and I ball them into fists to ground myself.

He wraps his hands around my own, thumbs pressing gently against my fingers as he tries to pry them open.

"None of that now," He urges calmly. "You'll make yourself bleed."

I didn't realise how badly I was digging my nails into my palms until I see maroonish crescent moons forming.

"S-sorry." I wince.

The room suddenly feels smaller, I feel far too faint and all too dizzy.

"Up," He instructs softly, tugging me to him and away from the sewing machine. "Tell me what works for you. Distance or distraction?"

"What?" I blink.

His question confuses me.

"I think you might be having a panic attack," He says quietly.

My eyes widen.

The apprehension I feel heightens as my body begins to shake uncontrollably and I press a hand against my chest. It's one thing to feel the panic but it's another for someone to point it out and solidify it, I suppose.

"I'm—" Imaginary bile rises in my throat. "Oh God. I'm having a panic attack."

"It's okay, you're okay," August reassures me, grey eyes assessing my face. "Distance or distraction?"

"I don't know," I answer, my voice quivering. "I don't know."

My mind blanks as I stare at my jittering hands, no longer feeling like they're attached to my wrists.

August reaches for them, interlocking our fingers and I watch as my nails dig into the back of his hand, burgundy crescents marring his skin. He makes a move to get up from the chair, hands slipping from mine and I let out a quiet noise of distress.

"August," I cry out quietly, shaking my head.

"Alright, not distance." He nods, drifting back over to me as he brings both my hands to his face. "I'm here."

Repeatedly, I blink as my vision blurs, trying to focus on August and not the nauseating feeling coursing through my entire body.

"I just need to get you water first, *mon cœur*, I'll be right back."

He takes his blazer off and wraps it around me as my heart races, the erratic pulsing loud in my ears. The feeling of the chair underneath me is the only thing grounding me as August leaves and I close my eyes to focus on the warmth of his blazer draped over me.

... wasting her time...

Pins and needles stab at my lungs and I blink away the dark spots blurring my vision.

"I'm here." August is back in front of me, plastic cup in hand from the water cooler outside. "You're okay, drink this."

My hands convulse with tiny tremors as he hands me the plastic cup, water spilling on his trousers.

... won't get anywhere ...

"I'm sorry," I croak out. "I'm so sorry."

He wraps his hands around my trembling fingers, guiding the cup to my lips. The liquid is cold as it travels down my throat, the feeling distracting me.

... such a disappointment...

My focus blurs and I choke on the water.

"I'll do better," I sputter. "I'll be better."

August gently manoeuvres me, pulling the chair I'm sitting on closer to him until I'm positioned in between his legs.

"What are you talking about?" He tuts lightly. "You're doing exceptionally well, Tinker-Talent."

CHAPTER 39

His voice is calming as it penetrates through the bedlam of negative voices in my head.

August takes my hands again, the pads of his thumb rubbing soothing circles on my knuckles. I feel him trace the slightly raised and rough texture on the back of my hand and I recoil slightly.

"*Mon cœur*, look at me." He requests, voice soft. "It's okay, you're okay."

His lips brush over my knuckles, pressing a reassuring kiss and my eyes flutter at the gesture, similar fluttering erupting in my stomach.

"Give me something for each sense, quick."

Hands still connected with mine, he lifts my chin up with a gentle nudge, his gaze never leaving mine.

"Huh?"

"Name me something each of your senses can detect," He instructs gently.

My brows furrow. "I don't…"

He leans forward, planting a gentle kiss on the furrow in between my eyebrows.

"What do you see?"

I stare at him, dazed.

You.

"August."

"Okay," He chuckles, the sound taking over the loud thrumming of my heartbeat. "What do you hear?"

"Laughter," I respond and he nods, mouth quirking into a small smile.

"What about smell?"

My eyes flicker down to the blazer wrapped around me, breathing in the scent of August's cologne. I crinkle my nose in appreciation as I hone in on the woody-citrusy scent I've grown so familiar with.

"Fifth by G&S?" I sniffle, mentioning the perfume brand. "2022, His Edition."

"That—" August blinks. "— is surprisingly accurate, *holy shit.*"

Heat rushes to my cheeks as I open my eyes, blearily blinking. "Sorry."

"Nothing to be embarrassed about." He smiles, affectionately tapping my nose.

"Touch?"

His hands find mine again, intertwining our fingers and giving them a reassuring squeeze.

I look down. "Hands."

"Good." He nods. "Taste?"

My eyes flicker to his mouth and I'm distracted by the urge to suddenly kiss him.

"Tinker-Talent," He hums. "What do you taste?"

I swallow. "Water?"

"Perfect."

There's a gentleness to August as he tucks my hair behind my ear, eyes trained on me the entire time.

"Now take deep, slow breaths," He says. "In through the nose, out through the mouth."

I inhale unsteadily, exhaling just as shakily.

"Have you eaten?" He asks after a while and I shake my head in reply. "What food would you like? Tito Boy's? Or someplace else?"

I purse my lips and frown, wanting more than anything for the comfort of Filipino food.

"Words, *mon cœur*." He guides me gently.

August is patient, soft grey eyes watching me.

"Tito Boy's," I reply with a sniffle.

"Good girl," He says, eyeing the clock on the wall. "I'll give Rowan a call. I don't think Hero's working tonight."

He lets go of one of my hands as he takes his phone out of his blazer pocket. The urge to sink my nails back into my palms returns and I spread my fingers across my kneecap to stop myself from curling my hand back into a fist.

Without August's hand to hold mine, it suddenly feels impossible.

"You talk to Rowan?" I manage to find my voice.

"From time to time," August confirms with a nod, scrolling through his contacts. "I've attended a few of his cooking masterclasses with Hero."

I peer at his phone, my eyes blinking at the contacts when I see Tito

CHAPTER 39

Boy's name as well as the letters 'MH' on the list.

"You have the restaurant on your Favourites?"

"Of course," He says. "We order there so much, I had no choice."

An overwhelming sense of fatigue washes over me, my entire body feeling all too heavy after my panic attack. August's voice is like a blanket I want to wrap around myself, curl up into and fall asleep in as he talks on the phone.

"We just need a pick-me-up."

August holds his phone between us as he puts it on speaker, the quiet questioning of *'we?'* from Rowan on the other end of the line crackling.

"Tink— uh, Mahalia's here."

"Hi." I make my presence known.

"Hallie?" Rowan says slowly, a hint of suspicion in his voice. "It's 10 PM."

I stare at the clock on the wall. It didn't even register in my mind that it's already so late in the evening.

"Dare I ask what you're both doing together at this hour?" His tone is somewhat teasing as he speaks.

"We're at the studio," August answers, voice sombre.

There's rustling on the line before I hear Rowan ask, "Is she okay?"

"I'm fine," I reply faintly. "Just doing overtime at work."

A dense haze clouds my thoughts as I attempt to focus, the exhaustive aftermath of my panic attack pressing heavily on me.

"August Vante," Rowan says, a warning tone to his voice. "I swear if you're overworking her."

I press my lips together, feeling them tremble at his concern.

"I'm okay, Rowan."

August reaches towards me, fingertips delicately swiping away the strands of hair from my face before tucking it behind my ear.

"I think she just needs a little bit of home."

The softness in August's voice is a contrast to the familiar harsh clattering of pans that can be heard on the phone over on Rowan's end.

"Got it," Rowan affirms. "Will you still be at the office? Or at your place?"

August pauses, contemplating. "The office should be fine."

They wrap up the conversation, me adding a faint goodbye as I slump on the high chair, exhausted. I haven't had a panic attack, at least not anything close to the one I've just had, in years. I'm quickly learning that the comedown isn't the most pleasant feeling.

"How are you feeling?" August asks as he pulls the chair closer to him.

"I don't know if I can do it, August." I swallow thickly. "The deadline is in two weeks."

"Of course you can." His eyes meet mine with reassurance. "You're Mahalia Hartt. You're good at what you do and other people know it too. Don't ever doubt yourself, you have no reason to."

I nod, absentmindedly playing with the sleeves of his shirt and tugging on the cufflinks.

"Come on." August takes my hand as he tugs me down from the counter stool.

"Where are we going?"

"I want to show you something," He replies.

August guides me down the hall, our fingers interlocked the entire time as we walk towards his office.

As usual, the room is low-lit and my eyes take a bit longer to adjust, even more so as he leads me into the darkroom. Rows and rows of printed photographs hang across the room and it takes me a moment to register the images dangling on the thin wire lines, my eyes widening.

The photos taken during our trip to Toussaint.

"I was going to put the pictures into a photo album," He shares, clearing his throat. "Thought it might be useful for reference if you need it."

The darkroom looked like a mini exhibition of sorts, with developed photos of various sizes meticulously arranged and hanging on the wires around the room. I recognise so many images of our tour at the museum, the foundry and the boutique. Our sightseeing day in the city. The photos of us at the café. I didn't realise August took so many, there were at least over a hundred images all around the space.

A new, fluttering sensation spreads throughout my entire body and I feel tears welling up in my eyes.

CHAPTER 39

"Shit, what's wrong?" August asks, concern evident in his voice as he looks at me.

My reply gets stuck in my throat as I blink up at him.

"You're crying." His eyes scan my face quickly before shifting to lead us out of the darkroom.

I shake my head, tugging him back towards me and wrapping my arms around his torso.

"Thank you."

My voice is muffled as I bury my face against his chest. A calmness washes over me as August wraps his arms around my shoulders, pulling me closer to him.

"Are you sure you're okay?"

His voice is quiet, whispering against the crown of my head and I nod.

"Much better, thank you."

I look up to meet his gaze, the warmth and concern of his eyes undeniable. There's a light unravelling in my chest as I feel the invisible corset loosening.

A photograph catches my attention and I withdraw from August, slowly reaching up to take the developed photo just by his shoulder— already with the label 'Glitter Gremlin'.

"This is an awful picture of me," I comment.

He glances down at the image before chuckling.

"I strongly disagree. It's my second favourite picture of you on that trip."

"I'm afraid to ask what the first one is." I purse my lips disapprovingly.

He readjusts his arms around me, hand falling to my waist. The soft unravelling between my ribcage manifests into a flutter as a small smile appears on his face.

He nods his head just above me and I shift, turning around to see.

The image of me wearing the white dress.

Chapter 40

Attempting to get the regalwear collection back on track was a Herculean effort on everyone's part.

Sebastian was more demanding than usual, almost hysterical, in every obscure and minute change needed for the sample suits. Adjustments to embellishments and trims, modifications to closures and fastenings, tweaks to details such as pockets and pleats and even *ruffles.*

Neither Estelle nor Pollux were surprised. In fact, they were anticipating it. They could only reassure me to wade through the tide of the lead designer's last-minute demands.

Nobody knew what was going on with Sebastian but it became increasingly difficult to work with him. He was unpredictable, swinging between extremes, with outbursts seemingly triggered by the most minor details and I often found myself bearing the brunt of his erratic behaviour.

Hence how I ended up dropping by his flat in Chelsea after he requested I collect the Spring/Summer lineup samples.

Loud music and distinct chatter can be heard from outside the door, and I furrow my eyebrows as I ring the doorbell. It's nearly midnight on a Thursday evening and although I'm aware of Sebastian's penchant for hosting parties and attending social gatherings, I didn't expect him to be indulging in celebrations with deadlines just around the corner.

A girl with dark brown hair and pale skin answers, green eyes smudged with dark makeup.

"Hi," I blink at her in greeting. "I'm here to see Sebastian?"

Glaringly, she looks me up and down and I try not to shuffle uncomfort-

CHAPTER 40

ably under her intimidating gaze.

"Who are you?" She asks me.

"Hallie," I answer, uncertainly. "I work at Holmes."

She narrows her eyes at me before turning her nose up. "He just popped out. He'll be back soon."

"I can come back," I reply. "Do you know how long he'll be?"

"No idea," The girl responds before opening the door wider to let me in. "But he mentioned you were coming so."

Stepping inside, I'm instantly greeted by an atmosphere overwhelming to all my senses. The thumping bass of EDM music echoing through the walls, pulsing lights in various colours filling the room, the pungent smell of weed and smoke as well as the faint scent of perfumes and colognes permeating the air. There's a murmur of chatter from the people in attendance, beautiful faces belonging to impossibly tall models. My eyes quickly scan the room but I don't recognise anyone at this party.

"Sit." She motions towards the expensive-looking leather couch where people are already crowding around and all I can do is follow her instructions. "Line?"

My gaze falls on the glass coffee table. Lighters. Cigarette packs. Rolling tobacco pouches. Credit cards. Pills in plastic bags. Crushed white powder.

I shake my head, hoping my smile isn't as forced as I feel it.

"I'll pass, thank you."

"Smoke then?"

The girl holds out a cigarette.

"I don't, um, smoke."

She pulls a face. "What about a drink?"

"I have work tomorrow, sorry."

There's a vacant look in her eyes as I answer and she blinks at me slowly. "Suit yourself."

She kneels by the coffee table and I watch as she does a clean line on top of the glass. Sniffing loudly, she presses the back of her hand against her nose before turning to me.

"What do you do again?" She questions, though she never even asked me to begin with.

The room is all too warm and all too loud and I feel all too out of place.

"I'm a Design Intern," I reply. "At Holmes."

"Seb's type?" A voice asks, snickering.

An instant answer from someone else, "Nah, that's *Vante's girl.*"

The energy in the room shifts as the women exchange knowing glances between them. They eye me up and down, catty expressions evident on their faces as they openly scrutinise me.

"Is he coming?" One of them asks, voice nasal and biting.

"I'm— I'm not sure." I fidget uncomfortably on the sofa.

"How do you know him?"

"We worked together," I answer.

Mocking giggles echo in the living room as knowing whispers and hushed conversations overlap each other.

"I used to work with August," A blonde girl with blue eyes grins at me. "He used to keep me up, *working.*"

The implication isn't lost on me and I sink into the sofa, the room feeling a lot stuffier.

"Oh," I swallow.

"All night, all the time." Someone else adds.

It was getting difficult to keep track of all the different people in the room, their voices blending into one.

"You're not his type," Another girl comments and I turn to her, taken aback by her blunt remark.

"They just have to be *pretty,*" A guy, this time, retorts. "All his playthings need to be."

"You're the latest fad he's fucking?"

The question strikes me unexpectedly, a critical lashing across my chest.

Someone lights a cigarette in front of me and I will myself not to be overwhelmed. The music is too loud, the smoke in the room is too heady. I feel like there's cotton everywhere— my lungs, my throat, my mouth.

The presence of someone leaning over me, hand grabbing onto my shoulder, jolts me out of my heightened sense of emotions.

CHAPTER 40

"Hey, gentle goddess."

Vaguely recognising the voice over the loud music, I turn my head to find Henry behind the sofa.

"Fancy getting some air?" He signals towards the balcony.

I nod, getting up quickly to join him.

"Thank you," I smile gratefully as I step out into the brisk Autumn night. "It was getting a little stuffy in there."

"Not really your scene?"

I let out a nervous laugh. "Unfortunately not."

"Don't mind them," Henry nods his head towards the group of women milling around the coffee table in the living room. "They're normally easygoing but they get catty when they're coked up. Bit brassed off that they're waiting around for the Peroxide Prince, I think."

"August is coming?"

"Isn't that why you're here?"

I shake my head, confused.

August hasn't mentioned anything, but then again, communication has been a little rocky between us since I've been so focused on the collection. I know that his flight back from New York to London is due in the evening but I haven't heard from him since this morning.

"Put everyone out of their misery, Hallie." Henry chuckles but it sounds strangely empty, distant. "Are you and the Parisian Playboy an item, then?"

The nickname makes me shuffle uneasily.

"We're not... like that." I trail off, shaking my head. "Just friends of friends."

I don't elaborate further simply because I don't really know how to. August and I haven't actually discussed it properly and I know better than to make assumptions on my part, or worse, *catastrophise* the situation.

After my panic attack at the studio, August avoided any topic of conversation that could overwhelm me and potentially trigger me into another breakdown so we spent the rest of the evening talking about his photography work. He was called into New York the following morning so we didn't even get a chance to have the conversation the next day.

"I thought that would have been the case." Henry nods. "You're not August's type."

"His type?" I question.

"Power hungry," Henry answers with a chuckle. "Obsessed with her image, obsessed with his name."

My eyebrows furrow. "I didn't realise that's what August liked."

"It's what he attracts." Henry shrugs. "It's who can keep up with him, really. Every single woman in that room wants to sleep with the Peroxide Prince, half of them he's probably slept with already since being in London."

The playboy has a plaything in every city he poses in.

A tight knot forms itself in my chest.

"Do you know where I can find the samples for the collection?" I ask. "I think I'll just grab them and head out."

Henry points towards the corridor across the living room. "Seb's studio is just down the hall."

"Thank you," I nod.

Avoiding the crowd of bodies tipping themselves over each other, I walk towards the hallway and hurriedly enter the studio.

Sebastian's workspace is like a luxurious bachelor pad. Industrial loft vibes with exposed brick walls and concrete floors. Large windows with sleek, dark curtains which are currently drawn shut. There are high-end fashion sketches and moodboards of every collection he has ever worked on framed and displayed on walls. In the middle of the room, Edison bulbs hang from the ceiling and hover over his worktable which is surprisingly void of any clutter.

"No wonder he prefers working at home," I mutter to myself.

It's cooler in the studio, less suffocating and I'm thankful for the breathing space. The chaos of the party in the other room is far too much for me to handle, the comments made about August lingering in my mind.

Frankly speaking, I'm probably nothing more than the countless passing presence of people he encounters in the industry. Someone he can conveniently revisit whenever he finds himself in London, *if* he chooses to. A piece of clothing he can slip on and off.

CHAPTER 40

A trend he'll be over with next season.

Reflecting on the exchanges I've had with August, it occurred to me that I had been the one to initiate most of our intimate interactions— how I essentially threw myself all over him at Onyx and the way I was practically begging for him at The Maisonette.

I inwardly wince.

Of course, he would entertain that. It's what he's used to. It's the norm for him. If I hadn't shown interest, he wouldn't have bothered.

He would have never looked in my direction, he wouldn't have given me a second thought.

But his confession that night in Toussaint-

The door clanking shut pulls me out of my thoughts and I blink, not even realising that someone else entered the studio.

"Did you find what you were looking for?"

I look up to find Henry standing by the entrance, the sound of the lock clicking into place echoing in the room as he walks towards me.

His presence suddenly makes the space a lot smaller, despite the considerable size of the studio.

"No," I shake my head. "I think I'll just wait for Sebastian."

I head towards the door but Henry grabs my arm before I can walk past him.

"Hallie, wait."

Turning to him, I frown at the unexpected pressure around my bicep.

"There's something I've been meaning to talk to you about," He states.

I register the faint scent of alcohol as he attempts to pull me close to him but I press my feet firmly on the ground.

"What is it?" I ask.

"You," He replies. "I think you're great. Really great, Hallie."

"Oh," I blink, taking a cautious step backwards as he advances towards me.

Staring up at Henry, I notice how his eyes are red and glazed over. He looks distracted, a little frenzied almost, as I attempt to ease myself out of his grasp.

"I can be good to you, Hallie." He murmurs, tightening his grip around my arm. "Better than August."

My skin prickles as his other hand trails up my neck, fingers grasping the back of my head forcefully.

"Henry," I begin, panicked. "I'm not—"

My mind blanks as I feel the force of his lips against mine.

Henry's mouth is crushing, the hand wrapping around the nape of my neck bruising as he pulls me against him. Every muscle in my body locks up and I press my lips together, closing my eyes tightly.

He backs me into the worktable, the corner digging into my hip and I grimace. Resisting against his grip, my body goes into panicked overdrive as my mind finally registers what's happening.

"Henry," My voice is muted as I push against his chest but he's immovable. "Stop."

His teeth sink into my bottom lip and I gasp, the skin tearing as the taste of copper bleeds into my mouth. I thrash against his hold in an attempt to shove him away from me, my hands curling into fists. His teeth catch on my busted lip and I wince, pounding frantically against his chest.

"Hallie," He rasps as I finally break away from him.

Hand outstretched, Henry takes an unsteady step towards me but I quickly beeline for the door before he can reach me. His fingers latch onto the sleeve of my blouse and I gasp at the loud tearing of the fabric from my shoulder, the delicate buttons at the front clattering on the floor.

"Stop, Henry!" I choke out.

A sickly sensation forms in the pit of my stomach and I feel it burning up my throat. Henry's eyes are glassy as he stares at me, a disoriented expression on his face.

My fingers tremble as I touch my mouth, my eyes watering at the sight of blood.

"Fuck, I'm sorry." His apology is muffled as he runs a hand across his face.

Grasping my blouse shut, I wrap my other arm around me as I fight to keep the noxious feeling down my stomach.

CHAPTER 40

"Shit, Hals, I didn't—"

Henry inches towards me but I shake my head forcefully.

"No," I swallow, teary-eyed. "Don't."

Outside, I can hear the indistinct sounds of loud cheering as faint voices near the studio. A rattling noise from the other side prompts me to immediately reach for the door to unlock it.

The handle twists from the other side and the door swings open.

"I'm telling you she's—"

The light from the hallway illuminates the dark space of the studio and I'm instantly met with Sebastian's face.

"—here." He blinks in confusion as he looks over me before his eyebrows shoot up in surprise at seeing Henry. "Are we interrupting something?"

He steps inside the studio and I see another familiar figure by the door, just behind Sebastian.

"August," I exhale, my voice strangled.

There's a long pause as he assesses the scene and I blink through my blurring vision. His grey eyes study me intently, briefly falling to my lips before flickering towards the ripped fabric on my shoulder and the hand clutching my blouse shut.

Something dark and dangerous flashes in his gaze before it lands behind me.

"Mate, it's not—" Henry attempts to explain but he is immediately cut off by August.

"We're leaving."

His jacket is wrapped around me in an instant, the garment engulfing me. Before I can respond, August grabs my wrist and pulls me to him as we head towards the door.

"Hallie, wait." Henry trails after us, clasping a hand around my forearm underneath the jacket.

I freeze in place, flinching against his touch. The air around us charges with a prickling energy. August tracks Henry's movement at my reaction, his gaze hardening.

"Let go, Atkinson." He grits his teeth. "You have no business with her."

"Neither do you," Henry challenges him.

August watches Henry through steely grey eyes.

"She *is* my fucking business." He counters, voice dripping with a possessiveness.

There's a furious, almost frightening glint in August's eyes as he stares at Henry.

"I'm not going to ask again," He warns, his voice low and threatening. "Let. Go."

Henry holds his gaze for a tense moment before a look of defeat flashes across his face and he releases me.

August pulls me back to him almost immediately, wrapping an arm around me as he leads me out of Sebastian's studio and down the hallway. He doesn't say anything else as he rigidly charges back into the living room, his posture tense.

"Are these all of your things?" He asks, jaw tightening.

I nod silently as he moves to grab my coat and bag on the sofa.

Around us, excited chatter erupts but I'm too focused on August to pay anyone else any attention.

"Leaving so soon?" Someone comments coyly from across the room.

August barely glances in their direction, his entire body rigid as his hands close into fists.

"Aw, come on, Vante." Another joins. "You're no fun anymore."

His face doesn't budge, clear-cut stoicism etched on his features as he completely ignores everyone at the party. Draping my coat and bag across one arm and grabbing my wrist by the other, he drags me out of Sebastian's flat without saying another word.

"August," I falter, struggling to keep up with his pace.

The strides of his legs are long and I almost trip a few times but he doesn't let go, not until we make it to the end of the corridor where the lifts are.

"What the hell are you doing here, Mahalia?"

He turns to me sharply, the accusatory tone in his voice making my skin

CHAPTER 40

prickle.

"I came to pick up some samples," I respond with a strained voice.

"*Late at night?*"

"Sebastian said to collect them, I didn't realise there was a-"

"Did you take anything?"

"Of course not." I blink up at him, brows furrowing. "Why would I-"

He grabs my chin to assess my face, staring down at me with intense, angry eyes.

"I didn't take anything, August."

My eyes tear up as his thumb harshly traces my swollen lip, the memory of Henry in Sebastian's studio making my skin crawl.

"Did you kiss him?"

I whimper against his touch, shaking my head. "It wasn't-"

"Don't lie to me, Mahalia."

"*Henry* kissed *me.*"

Rage sparks dangerously in his eyes but he douses it before it manifests into a fire. August doesn't say anything else as he walks away but he doesn't need to. I see the tick in his jaw and the crease between his brows as he paces up and down by the lift.

"It isn't what it looks like," I sniffle, feeling a pressure between my ribcage. "Not like it makes a difference but we didn't do anything-"

"*Not like it makes a difference?*" He interrupts me, eyes flaring. "What the hell is that supposed to mean?"

"Henry was *drunk-*"

August turns to me in disbelief. "You're defending him?"

"No!" I shake my head, exasperated. "I'm *explaining* to you— he just kissed me and-"

His eyes flicker to my blouse and his expression shifts back to a quiet rage.

"He *just* kissed you," He laughs then, the sound hollow, almost mocking.

"You're not listening to me, August." I swallow, feeling a burning sensation in my throat.

"Because that's how it always starts right?" He grits his teeth. "Someone's a little too *drunk*, a little too *high*. Let me guess, it didn't mean anything, right?"

August is heated, almost frantic. His normally nonchalant and cool composure is set ablaze by a slow-building rage inside. I reach for his arm but he recoils before I can touch him.

"What the hell were you thinking? Entertaining those crackheads? Fucking around with Atkinson?"

I blink at the spitefulness of his words.

"Are you really this naive?" He snaps, turning harshly towards me. "It's not all sunshine and rainbows and fucking glitter here, Mahalia. Do you even know any of those people? Did you even stop to ask yourself what you're actually doing here? Don't involve yourself with people who could care less about you and stop inserting yourself in places you don't belong in."

His words puncture before they cleave, blades cutting my sutured heart wide open and my eyes well up with tears.

... *a waste of time* ...

... *won't go anywhere* ...

... *so disappointing* ...

The comments are bleeding out before I can stop them, muscle memory wounds splitting open, and I take an unsteady step backwards as my vision blurs.

"Wait, that's not what I meant," August sighs defeatedly.

He drags a hand through his hair, accidentally dropping my things in frustration and I quickly gather my coat and bag from the floor, my own hands trembling.

"Let me explain–"

I shake my head, my eyes beginning to water as I press the button to call up the lift.

"Mahalia—"

"No," My voice cracks and I bite down on my lip, the sharp sting surging. "I'm not stupid, August."

A rotten feeling seeps into my already bleeding heart.

CHAPTER 40

"I know what all of this is– or rather, what it *isn't*." I say, furiously blinking away my tears. "I know what we are…"

And what we're not.

The sentiment manifests into a sizable ache, welling up and growing heavy, and I press a hand against my chest to suppress the overwhelming emotions threatening to overflow.

"I'm not…" I take a deep, shaky breath. "I'm not one of your *playthings*, August."

The lift dings open and I immediately step inside.

"Mahalia–" His arm reaches out to stop the doors from closing.

A cacophony of female voices echo in the corridor, the burst of giggles and loud chatter prompting me to look away.

"Where did he go?"

"Oh, playboy!"

"Told you he's still here."

The ache spills over, bleeding out of my heart and into my lungs.

"I know who I am to you," I say, my throat constricting. "I also know who *you* are…"

And you're not who I thought you were.

"Mahalia—"

"No, August." I swallow. "I don't want any part in any of this."

His expression turns blank as he stays rooted to the spot.

"Come on, *pretty boy*." A voice calls out from down the hall. "For old time's sake."

August's gaze falters and I watch as he turns to look behind him.

My heart sinks to the bottom of my stomach and I duck my head, clutching my belongings tighter to my chest.

"Goodnight, August." I say quietly, pressing the button to the lobby once more.

His eyes search mine for the final time, cloudy and obscure, before he straightens up and takes a step backwards.

I wipe my eyes with the sleeves of his bomber jacket, the blurry silhouette of August as he walks away being the last thing I see before the lift hums to a close.

Chapter 41

The weekend came and went with not a single word from August.

Part of me had hoped he would reach out but given how things ended at Sebastian's, I can understand why he wouldn't. I'd been the one to stand my ground and he had been the one to walk away.

The case of the Monday blues is far too taxing as I make my way up to the secondary studio. After a Design team meeting this morning, sans Sebastian, about the next stages of the regalwear collection, I feel oddly detached.

The lift doors open and I step out into the hallway. Even though the fourth floor hardly housed anybody, it feels even emptier.

I see August's office at the other end of the corridor, hoping to find the tiniest faint of red glow as a beacon of light, but my heart sinks in disappointment to find the entire room submerged in complete darkness.

A tiny part of me also considered knocking to confirm whether or not he's in but I realise there's no reason for him to be.

According to Pollux, who received the information from Ymir and Saoirse, they've already considered a new Director of Communications and they're in the beginning stages of transition planning. August had been gradual with handing over his responsibilities, which everyone at Comms found strange since they were expecting to see him gone as soon as he received confirmation from Grayson a month ago.

After the Comms team received formal word from him this morning through an early conference call, it became definite.

August is officially done at Holmes.

I cast one final glance at his office, wondering if I'll ever cross paths with him. My stomach churns and I try not to focus on the ache forming in my chest at the thought of never seeing August again.

Entering the secondary studio, an unusual emptiness invades the space. Even though I'm accustomed to working by myself, there's something strangely hollow about being up on the fourth floor on my own.

Shaking the feeling off, I begin my morning task of going through my emails.

> From: sebastian.oliver@holmes.co.uk
>
> To: estelle.li.young@vante.fr
> cc: ymir.yassin@holmes.co.uk, saoirse.campbell@holmes.co.uk, pollux.okusanya@holmes.co.uk, mahalia.hartt@holmes.co.uk
>
> Subject: Winter Gala Press Content and Regalwear Presentation
>
> See attached the revised press content and official presentation for the upcoming regalwear presentation in Cionne.
>
> For any changes, please contact me before the end of the week.
>
> Sebastian O. Holmes
> Creative Director, Holmes London
>
> [Regalwear Collection - PRESS KIT.pdf]
> [Regalwear Collection - PRESENTATION.ppt]

Glancing over at the finished samples of the Autumn/Winter lineup of the regalwear collection on the mannequins, I feel anxious at suddenly having no excitement at reaching this stage.

CHAPTER 41

Biting my lip, I begin reading through the official presentation being shown at the Winter Gala next week.

The Regalwear Collection is a collaboration between the illustrious Royals of Toussaint and the esteemed fashion house, Holmes London.

Designed by Sebastian Oliver Holmes, the exclusive collection is a seamless fusion of the cultured elegance synonymous with Toussaint and the refined sophistication characteristic of Holmes London's designs.

Furrowing my brow, I stare at the last slide.

I quickly view the presentation again, skimming through the segments until I reach the Collection Overview. My eyes sweep over the key pieces of the Spring/Summer lineup and I blink.

There are barely any alterations from the original designs I created.

In fact, it looks *exactly* the same.

My fingers twitch out of anxiousness.

Clicking the PDF file of the press kit for the regalwear collection, my eyes dart along every word of information.

A lurching feeling twinges in my stomach as realisation sinks in.

My name is completely omitted.

The sound of the sliding door opening brings me out of my spiralling thoughts and I look up. A glimmer in me hoped it would be August so I deflate at the sight of Sebastian by the entryway.

"Did you receive the press kit for the Winter Gala?" He asks, stepping into the room.

"And the presentation." I nod, hesitantly. "Some things need rectifying though. The Spring/Summer lineup still has the old design sketches and final samples I made and there are no signs of the ones you've been working on."

"Oh, that wasn't an oversight," Sebastian replies. "It wasn't feasible to revise the Spring/Summer lineup due to time constraints."

I blink. "So you're still using my samples?"

Sebastian nods. "Yes, is that a problem?"

I shake my head, the new development unsettling me. My eyes catch the Autumn/Winter lineup I'd been restlessly working on for the past two weeks and turn to Sebastian.

"What about my name?" I ask quietly. "It isn't mentioned anywhere in the press kit or the official presentation."

"I didn't think it was necessary," He answers with a nonchalant shrug of his shoulder. "Since I'll be the one presenting at the Winter Gala."

The lurching in my stomach worms its way up to my chest.

"I won't be presenting with you?"

"Your attendance isn't necessary."

I frown. "I'm not going to Toussaint?"

"Why would you need to?" Sebastian questions.

"For the gala," I reiterate. "As part of the regalwear collection I've been working on for the last few months. The one you're using all of my samples and revisions for."

Sebastian eyes me up and down, almost bored.

"You work at *Holmes*," He says, dismissively. "Under *my* supervision."

"But it's not just *your* work." I fire back at him. "It's also my research, my ideas, my designs. Research you assigned *me* to do, ideas I've had to work on by *myself* and designs *I* had to create from scratch."

My hands begin to tremble and I curl them into fists behind my back.

"All this talk about me, myself and I." He tsks. "This is a *collaborative* effort, is it not?"

And where was your effort in this collaboration?

My vocalised thoughts cause Sebastian to narrow his eyes and I falter under his sharp gaze.

"Hallie, you're an intern." He states, punctuating every syllable. "I don't expect you to understand since you're new to the industry."

Frustration roots itself in my chest at his reply.

"What's not to understand? You're taking credit for work I've done." I

CHAPTER 41

say shakily, trying to keep my voice level.

"*I'm* taking credit?"

Something flickers in Sebastian's eyes as he stares at me, glaring.

"Do you really think anyone would care about your designs if it wasn't under *my* name?"

The question slaps me in the face and I feel myself physically recoil at the sharp sting of Sebastian's words.

"Be serious now, sweetheart." He shakes his head at me, a mocking lilt to his voice. "You're hardly anybody in the industry."

I find myself unable to reply, my own words lodged in my throat as his comments sucker-punch my gut.

"You might be talented," Sebastian continues, the compliment a sugar-coated, sour-centred sentiment. "But talent hardly carries any weight in the business if you don't have the influence. You're a design graduate with very limited industry experience whose only claim to fashion fame is a viral re-imagining of an already *existing* concept."

My left hand spasms uncomfortably.

"Virality doesn't equate to vigour." There's an icy edge to his tone. "And I just don't think you have the capacity to advance beyond those limitations. Your designs wouldn't be able to carry itself without the label. Best not waste anyone's time."

Each word spoken is a weight on my chest, growing heavier and heavier in Sebastian's presence.

"The Winter Gala is for influential individuals only, Hallie." He continues, adding further affliction to my already heavy heart. "Know where you stand and sit this one out."

His closing criticism is the final lumbering load and my heart crushes under the pressure as it parallels a sentiment I'm already familiar with.

Stop inserting yourself in places you don't belong in.

Chapter 42

Work is starting to feel like *work*.

Every interaction at Holmes leaves me increasingly exhausted and I feel less and less excited about coming into the studio. I'm restless, but not in a good way, fraying at the edges and unravelling in the worst ways possible.

Commissions feel like a chore, so much so that I've had to put Mahalia Made on hiatus. I'm either procrastinating or postponing things, losing interest in starting and even finishing any type of design work. Even pursuing personal projects feels of very little significance to me.

The opposite of love is indifference, people say.

And I'm slowly falling out of something I used to be so passionate about, watching myself nosedive into the indifference.

The sound of the lift whirring echoes down the hall and I hear the lift doors ding open.

"Hallie?"

I feel Gigi's presence first before I see her, standing by the door of my studio with a hesitant look on her face.

"How are you doing, doll?" she asks, watching as I begin grabbing hangers of clothes from my closet.

"I'm leaving for Switzerland tomorrow morning," I tell her.

Running away from my problems is probably not the most ideal approach but being in London is far too suffocating.

Everywhere I went, there was a connection to Holmes.

And every little thing reminded me of August.

I open the door to my closet wider, shoving away the assortment of

CHAPTER 42

fashion books and reference materials piled up by the floor in front of it. Leaflets and reading resources from my research trip at Cionne catch my eye, causing a sudden lurching in my heart.

"What?" She asks. "Just like that?"

Silently, I nod and watch as she reluctantly steps inside the room.

The current state of my studio is a mess.

Piles of fabric scraps scattered on the floor, partially crumpled sketches and torn design drafts strewn haphazardly across worktables. Unfinished garments that I haven't touched in months hang from clothing racks and every single mannequin of mine is pinned with half-finished garments from postponed commissioned work.

My worktables are cluttered with spools of thread, fabric swatches and random trimmings and embellishments that I haven't bothered putting away.

There is nothing controlled about the creative chaos I used to pride myself on. There's no artistry thriving in the messiness of my design studio.

Opening my closet to retrieve my suitcase, my stomach sinks at the sight of mahogany chests with the logo of the Toussaint Foundry.

I roll my suitcase out of my closet, sidestepping around pattern pieces and templates littering the floor before grabbing an armful of clothes and heading out into the living room.

"What about Holmes?" Gigi asks, trailing behind me.

"I'll be handing in my notice after Christmas," I reply.

Hauling the empty luggage on top of the sofa bed, I begin to remove my clothes from the hangers and dump them inside.

"You're quitting?" She asks in disbelief.

"I requested time off in the meantime," I say quietly. "But I'll be leaving in the New Year."

One by one, I messily fold my clothes to make them fit in the suitcase. Cream-coloured fabric peeks out from the disorderly pile and I pause.

August's jumper.

My fingers twitch as I tug on the delicate material and pull it out from the pile. It's soft to the touch but I find no comfort in it like I used to.

Eyes watering, I bite my lip to stop it from quivering.

"I've done all the work needed on my end for the regalwear collection," I say. "I won't be needed at Holmes anymore."

Gigi's eyes flicker to the jumper in my hands.

"Have you spoken to August?"

The question hangs heavy around us, the mention of his name a deadweight on my chest.

"No," I swallow. "I don't think he wants to hear from me."

"*That prick,*" She seethes, shaking her head.

"It's not his fault," My voice sounds oddly distant, hollow to my own ears as I speak. "I told him I didn't want to involve myself with him."

I was delusional to think that I actually knew August. Even more so to think that everything that happened between us was more than what it was. In reality, I was nothing more than a fleeting face in the industry.

The latest fad he's fucking.

A stinging sensation lurches in my chest.

"I thought he liked me," I say quietly.

I fold his jumper neatly but I don't put it inside my suitcase.

"Oh, Hallie..." Gigi's eyes flicker with a sadness.

"It doesn't matter," I shake my head. "He was right, Holmes isn't for me."

"That's total fucking bullshit, Mahalia Hartt."

The frustration in her voice about the situation is evident, I know because I feel it too. I turn towards Gigi who's looking at me with glossy, dejected eyes.

"Didn't you also try to dissuade me from joining Holmes?" I joke, trying to lighten the mood. "Consider me defected from the fashion frontlines, General Winters."

Gigi rolls her watery eyes at me. "This is different and you know it."

There's a pause between us, my heart beginning to feel heavy.

"I've never had to question what I love doing, Gigi." I say, voice shaking. "Sure, I question *myself* so many times. Everyone in the industry is far more qualified, far more experienced than I am. My mind is in a state of

CHAPTER 42

constant comparison to other people. I question myself a lot but I've never had to question *my passion*. Despite people telling me otherwise, I've never had a single doubt on what it is I love to do."

I can feel the tears gathering in my eyes, threatening to spill over.

"Oh, Hals." Gigi sighs.

Her gaze is downcast, dark brown eyes brimming with unshed tears as she moves to hug me.

"But lately, it's all I think about," I sniffle. "It's all I *feel*. The uncertainties that come with the territory. It makes me wonder, who am I doing this for? When am I going to see results? Where am I going with all of this? What am I actually doing?"

Everything is just so… *grey* again.

But not the kind of grey that melts into silver and provides me with a sense of security whenever I look into them.

It's an overcasting, cloudy grey— unpredictable, indecisive.

"There's just so many rules to all of this, I'm struggling to keep up." I continue. "Being in the industry, being in fashion. Why is it so unnecessarily difficult? Why do things have to be so stupidly complicated? All I want to do is be in my silly little studio, make my silly little clothes and maybe kiss a silly little grey-eyed photographer every now and again."

Gigi chokes on tear-filled laughter.

"Adulting is fucking hard," I complain, scrunching my nose tearfully.

There's a slight tremor in Gigi's voice as she speaks.

"First of all," She begins, letting out a shaky breath. "There's no need to put so much pressure on yourself, Hallie. You're 22 years old. You're a baby adult. You've been trying to navigate the godforsaken adult world for like, what? Two years? That's nothing. You're at potty training stage."

I burst into a cheerful sob.

"You say that as if we're not *the same age*." I shake my head, wiping my eyes. "I wish I had your brain."

"I wish I had your heart," She responds, sniffling. "And your hands. You're talented, Hals. Don't ever let anyone tell you otherwise."

You're good at what you do and other people know it too.

August's voice rings in my head.

Don't ever doubt yourself.

I turn to Gigi, giving her a watery smile as I pull her into another hug.

"No crying, Genevieve."

"I will attend as many of these sorrow soirées with you as I want to." She dismisses me with a playful eye roll. "Will you be okay? Going back to Switzerland?"

I nod.

"I think a change in scenery would do me good," I say. "And I really want to see my Mama and Papa. I miss them both, so so much."

As of this moment, the thought of reuniting with my grandparents is the only thing providing me a sense of comfort and I want nothing more than to be in their company, especially after everything that's happened.

"If you need anything, I'm here, okay?" Gigi says to me.

"I know." I smile at her. "Thank you."

She gives me a reassuring smile before enveloping me in another bone-crushing hug.

"Have a safe flight to Geneva. Send Lola and Lolo my love."

III

Part Three

"Fashion is about dreaming. And making other people dream."

— *Donatella Versace*

Chapter 43

Travelling to Switzerland was like being on auto-pilot mode. From packing my bags, getting a taxi to Heathrow and Gigi seeing me off at the airport to checking in, going through security then finally boarding.

Two hours on the plane felt like two days as I finally land in Geneva. The airport buzzed with activity, intensified by the Christmas holidays and navigating the rail network was even more hectic.

Sitting on the train by the window, I watch in real-time as the Swiss landscape, normally bright and vibrant in greenery, is covered in white as it begins to snow.

An untouched canvas, a clean slate.

The thought of seeing my grandparents in person for the first time in almost half a decade left a warm feeling in my chest despite the anxiety-inducing notion of spending the holidays in Switzerland.

A lot of time has passed but the memory of Christmas from four years ago continues to cast a shadow over my thoughts. Resting my head against the glass window, a heaviness settles in my ribcage and I find myself drifting off to sleep.

"She's wasting her time."

The exasperated voice from one of my uncles can be heard in the living room as I sit by the top of the stairs.

"It's not too late," Another voice replies, this time from one of aunts. "She can defer and then apply again next year."

"We're not asking for solutions on the matter." It's my grandma this time. "Lia

is fine."

There's a quiet frustration in her voice as she speaks and I feel a tug on my heart at my grandma defending me.

"She is delusional." The voice of my Uncle Jeremiah is the one I hear the most. "Always making things so difficult for herself and for everyone else around her."

He's speaking in Tagalog but I can loosely translate and comprehend what he's saying, despite his attempt at lowering his voice.

"She won't get anywhere with a degree in fashion," He emphasises. "That boarding school should have disciplined her, not fed into her delusions. I can't believe she had the audacity to go against our wishes and apply for that art school nonsense."

"Fashion school," My grandmother corrects him tiredly. "She applied and got accepted to one of the most prestigious institutions in London. A school she has consistently expressed interest in attending and has equally spent a lot of her time dedicating work to. Her decisions are not on a whim, Jeremiah. Give your niece a little more credit."

"Why are you entertaining her mindless fantasies?"

"Jericho and Cassandra would have wanted their daughter to choose what she loves to do most." My grandma states, an air of finality in her voice.

At the mention of my parents, the growing ache in my chest intensifies. I bite my tongue and blink back the tears blurring my vision.

"She is not your daughter, Remy." It's my grandpa this time. "Your expectations are not hers to uphold."

"If she were my daughter, she wouldn't be such a disappointment."

I jolt awake as the memory slowly fades from my mind, a familiar knot forming in the recesses of my chest.

This time, four hours on the train felt like four minutes as I reach Interlaken station.

Heavy snowfall starts to form, my hands twitching involuntarily at how the cold has suddenly frozen them over. Driving through the snow-covered streets, I'm grateful that the taxis are still operating as I see the recognisable sights of the picturesque town I spent so much of my

CHAPTER 43

childhood come into view.

Festive decorations adorn the wooden chalets and the quaint, cobbled streets as twinkling lights and garlands hang on lampposts and storefronts. The usually crystal-clear waters of the lake have frozen over, the snow-capped mountains adding to the atmosphere of the holiday season.

Everything looks the same and, somehow, changed.

I finally arrive at the house belonging to my grandparents, a three-floor traditional Alpine-style structure with a sloping roof and overhanging eaves. Nestled on a hill and surrounded by towering pines, the chalet is located further out from the main commercial area of the town, my grandpa preferring the peace and quiet of nature rather than the hustle and bustle of the high street.

Though it towered over me, it felt a little smaller than what I was used to back then. The water fountain in the small courtyard at the front is surprisingly still functioning, even in the cold weather. The festive lights and bright display of ornaments that decorated the outside is typically Filipino and I couldn't help but smile.

Every year, my grandparents always go above and beyond with the Christmas decorations and seeing it all in person again is making me a little emotional.

Slinging my backpack over my shoulder, I wheel my suitcase towards the front door, the nervousness I feel growing with each step I take. Pausing by the porch steps, I stare at the ornament hanging on the door.

A star-shaped lantern made up of bamboo sticks and craft paper.

My heart warms at the display as my eyes begin to water.

It's the parol I made when I couldn't have been more than 10 years old.

Knocking on the door, I wait patiently as the noise of keys jangling can be heard on the other side of the wooden frame before it swings open.

A surge of emotions courses through me as my grandma comes into view.

"Hi, Mama." I greet her, voice quivering. "Surprise?"

My grandma blinks at me, big brown eyes widening in realisation as she takes in my presence by the front door.

"Lia."

My vision blurs as I move to hug her, an overwhelming feeling washing over me as she hugs me tightly.

The dam of emotions I've been barricading since landing in Switzerland bursts as the waterworks begin. I've always been an emotional person and I prepared myself for the tears but I didn't realise it would be as soon as I step foot *in front* of the house, not even inside it.

"Who's at the door?" The gruff voice belonging to my grandpa echoes from inside.

Peering over my grandma's shoulder, I see my grandpa in the hallway, wearing a familiar-looking Christmas jumper with bobbles all over it. My grandma pats me on the back before releasing me and I scuttle over to my grandpa.

"Papa," I give him a watery smile.

It takes him a moment to realise before he envelopes me in the warmest bear hug I haven't felt in years. My grandma's presence is instantly next to me as she hugs both of us and I bite my lip to prevent myself from ugly crying in front of them.

"Lili?" The nickname I haven't heard in person for *years* tugs on my heart.

"Yes, *po*." I respond with the Filipino honorific.

My grandpa chuckles affectionately. "Well, if it isn't our little Christmas miracle."

His words pull on my emotions and the next thing I know, I find myself bawling my eyes out like a baby as he envelops me in another bear hug.

"Are you well?" I ask him, my voice muffled.

"Why are you crying?" He pats my shoulder twice then scratches my head, something he used to always do when I was younger to stop me from crying and I weep even harder.

"I've missed you both so much."

"Come inside, it's so cold out!" My grandma exclaims, ushering me in and closing the door behind us.

My grandpa assesses me for a moment, "Have you eaten? You look so

CHAPTER 43

skinny."

Next to him, my grandma lightly swats his arm and I let out a watery giggle.

"Don't mind him, hija." She shakes her head, turning to me. "What would you like to eat?"

"Anything, ma."

"Your favourite?"

I nod. "Yes, please."

Chapter 44

Spending the day with my grandparents by catching up and preparing food reminded me of when I used to visit them regularly during my time at boarding school. My Mama would be the one telling stories as she fussed around in the kitchen and my Papa would just sit back with a soft smile on his face, quietly listening and clinging on to her every word as he sips on his coffee by the island.

"Your Mama's on a mission to collect fruits that are, once again, out of season for Christmas." He shakes his head, gesturing towards the centre of the dining table.

My eyes catch the pomegranates inside the massive fruit basket and I'm momentarily reminded of August.

"Hush, Josef." The playful tone in my grandma's voice carries from the kitchen.

She returns to the dining room, placing a bowl of cut mango pieces in front of me.

"Thanks, Mama." I smile at her, grateful.

Conversations pick up again, the topic of my job inevitable. I tell them about the outcome of the regalwear collection, how I won't be attending the Winter Gala after a disagreement with the lead designer, even though I worked the extensive bulk of the project. I briefly skim over the details but I did disclose to them that I'll be quitting Holmes.

I avoid any talk about August, still feeling like I can't even mention the slightest bit of information about him without getting emotional. I left London for a change in environment and talking about him, no matter

CHAPTER 44

how small the discussion, will put me right back where I'm trying not to be.

In my feelings and out of my mind.

It's well into the night by the time I head up to my childhood bedroom, feeling even more nostalgic as I take in the little sanctuary of an aspiring fashion designer in her teenage years.

An entire wall of my room is dedicated to a moodboard of the life I wanted to manifest with fashion sketches, magazine cutouts and vintage posters of my favourite fashion icons and runway shows.

The standard sewing machine and mannequin occupied the corner of my room. Next to it, a workstation that is neatly organised with sewing materials from yesteryears. Running my hand across the crafting surface, I expected it to be collecting dust so I'm surprised to find it spotless.

Stacks of cardboard boxes tucked underneath the table with the label 'Lia' taped on them grab my attention and I blink.

Kneeling down, I pull the boxes from under the table and begin opening them to find textile materials and crafting supplies, from fabrics and embellishments to equipment and tools.

Clothes that I used to cut up and reassemble, outfits for my dolls and teddy bears, life-size garments assembled together from scraps of fabric. I carefully pick up one of the pieces, a tattered dress made from fat quarters my grandma used to buy in the market. Sentimental memories flood my mind— countless hours spent and all fingers pricked as I sit in my room, needle in one hand and thread in the other, fabric markers in my pockets and a measuring tape around my neck. Nothing compared to the joy I felt when I finished a piece and the look of pride on my grandma's face when I showed it to her.

Lost in my thoughts, I'm gently brought back to reality by the soft voice of my grandma standing by the door.

"Did you find anything useful?" She asks, walking inside.

"I can't believe you kept all of these," I reply quietly. "I thought you would have thrown them out by now."

My grandma smiles, patting my hands as she picks up a fabric with hand-embroidered sequins and beads. "Why would I do that?"

"The stitches on that are awful." I wrinkle my nose disapprovingly.

"It did quite nicely for a *10-year-old,*" She chides, voice filled with warmth. "You were such a restless little thing. Nothing calmed you down more than seam rippers and scissors."

"Dangerous for a hyperactive child," I snort.

"*Ayy nako,*" My grandma laughs, shaking her head. "You were always sneaking into my sewing room to steal equipment."

"I cried every time you locked me out of it." I nod, cringing at the memory.

"You threw the biggest temper tantrums." She shakes her head, affectionately. "I remember how excited you were when you got your first sewing machine. I don't think I ever heard it stop when you were here."

I recall the summers I spent here in Switzerland, hunched over the sewing machine. I couldn't have been older than 12 years old when my Mama and Papa gave me my first Singer. I created clothes *constantly*. Mostly DIYs and upcycling old clothes when I first started and then fully functional garments when I got better at operating the sewing machine and discovered clothing patterns.

I stare at my hands.

I never stopped sewing, I couldn't. Nothing fuelled me more than creating something and bringing it to life.

Hands of the greats.

August's voice rings in my head, my heart fluttering in my chest.

"This is probably my favourite," My grandma comments, carefully retrieving a piece of clothing hidden beneath the endless layers of fabric.

The first jumper I knitted when I was 14.

My fingers gently caress the soft woollen garment. It's a vibrant lilac adorned with red heart-shaped patches hand-embroidered on the sleeves. Memories of my younger self come flooding back and I vividly remember the countless hours I spent knitting the jumper, frustration and determination in every stitch.

"You were so excited to show it to us," She smiles at me. "The little girl with restless hands, proudly wearing her heart on her sleeves."

CHAPTER 44

She holds it up against me, chuckling at how it looks like it could still fit me.

It probably could, to be fair.

"I think I stopped growing at 13," I say seriously and my grandma laughs, eyes turning into half moons.

"Physically, yes." She grins at me teasingly. "But you grow every day. You learn, you live, you laugh, you love. And you lose, sometimes, too. But that's okay. That's life, anak. You grow from it and you continue to grow with it."

Tears well up in my eyes as I take in my grandma's words. She's always been the one to encourage me to dream big and follow my artistic pursuits ever since I was a little girl.

The only person, along with my Papa, who believed in me without question.

"I'm very proud of you, Lia." My grandma shares.

The statement comes out of the blue and I turn to her, blinking.

"I can sense you're struggling with something, hija." She continues. "Do you not think your Papa and I will wonder why you've decided to visit in person, so out of the blue?"

I stay quiet, hesitant.

Despite the concerned expression on her face, an understanding flashes in my grandma's eyes.

"I'm not going to force you to tell me anything," She says gently. "We can talk about it when you feel like it— *if* you feel like it. I won't push you but I'd like for you to know that whatever it is, I'm here to listen. And whatever you're feeling, it's completely valid."

"Thanks, Ma." I reply, sniffling.

My grandma reaches for me, patting my cheek affectionately.

"Your work for that fashion company might be under a different name but it's still you, hija. It's still Mahalia Hartt, don't forget that."

Chapter 45

The sound of a distinctly upbeat ringtone and loud clattering against my bedside table is what wakes me up the next morning. Still half-asleep, I reach for my phone, my voice groggy as I answer automatically.

"Hello?"

Normally, I'm not one for sleeping in but the hecticness of the last few weeks has finally caught up to me and returning to the familiar comfort of my bedroom in Switzerland has heightened my natural habit of being a recluse.

"*Did you see the articles I sent you?*"

It's Gigi.

"Articles?" I mumble, disoriented. "What articles?"

Glancing at the time on the corner of my phone, I blink. It's just after 1 PM which means I've slept for over 12 hours.

Yet I still, somehow, feel so tired.

I press a hand over my mouth to stop myself from yawning loudly over the phone.

"*Check your messages, Hallie.*" Gigi urges. "*I sent you links.*"

Slowly I sit up and put my phone on speaker as I swipe on my notifications. My brows furrow at the flurry of messages, not only from Gigi but also from Pollux as well as Ymir and Saoirse. My phone continues to ding as more notifications come through, this time from my socials for Mahalia Made.

I tap on Gigi's message, scrolling through links and screenshots, swiping to access each one in succession. I frown, unable to understand the articles

CHAPTER 45

as they're in different languages.

"Gigi, they're in French and Italian and— why did you send me an article in Korean?"

I couldn't help the yawn that escapes my mouth this time.

"Read the first one, Hals." She says pressingly. "The one in English for MODUE."

Rubbing the sleep from my eyes, I blink blearily as I read the headline.

"Rags to Royal: An Insider's Look at the Toussaint x Holmes Regalwear Collection by Upcoming Designer..." I pause, jolting alert. "Mahalia Hartt?"

My brows shoot up at the title and I rub my eyes again for good measure. I blink at my phone screen, not quite sure whether I'm hallucinating.

Skim reading through the rest of the links, my mouth hangs in disbelief. Sure enough, it contained different articles but it's all about the same topic.

The Holmes collaboration, the regalwear collection, Toussaint's aristocratic fashion. The languages may be different due to the translations but one thing stayed the same– my name.

Mahalia Hartt.

On every article.

Emerging Designer.... Promising Fashion Talent... Newcomer in Design...

"Gigi, what is this?"

"It's an article published on the MODUE website." She replies.

"Wait– what?"

My eyes quickly read through the article featuring an interview with His Royal Highness, Prince Tobias of Toussaint detailing his thoughts on the regalwear collection.

"I don't understand."

"*I wrote different articles about your work as one of the designers for the Holmes x Toussaint collaboration,*" Gigi answers. "*I interviewed Prince Tobias as the source for one of them.*"

"You wrote multiple articles?"

"*I did the exclusive interview as the main one, then a review and an opinion piece. All translated into different languages and posted on a variety of publications."*

I blink, in awe.

"Won't you get in trouble for this?" I ask, voice thick with emotion as I continue scrolling through the articles from various websites.

"Nope," Gigi responds. *"Head of Digital approved it."*

Her reply stuns me. "How?"

"August." She answers.

My heart skips at the mention of his name.

"Not only was he able to pull some strings and get the articles published but he also had it translated to get wider reach." Gigi continues.

A whirlpool of emotions stirs in my chest.

"He helped?"

"As August and Jean-Luc," Gigi confirms.

"What?"

My eyes sweep over the pictures in the articles. The majority of the photos are from the research trip to Cionne but there were plenty taken of me working at Holmes. Candid images of me in the studio, behind-the-scenes of the samples being assembled— all photographic evidence of my involvement throughout the entire project.

I look at the Copyright tagged at the bottom right corner of every photo and I feel the maelstrom in my chest ground itself to the eye of the storm.

Jean-Luc Photography.

"He orchestrated the entire thing," Gigi reveals. *"And before you say anything, I'd like to clarify that I did not contact him whatsoever. August reached out to me. Granted that I might have written a strongly worded email to Prince Tobias regarding the worrying malpractice of a certain studio that they're currently working with but I digress."*

"Right…" I reply with a laugh, my voice shaky.

"I genuinely had no idea he would use his connections as a nepo baby," Gigi remarks. *"August managed to get the articles published in all the well-known publications of every fashion capital— West and East."*

Eyes watering, I couldn't help but laugh at the absurdity of the situation.

"Does Holmes know?" I ask.

CHAPTER 45

"Internally, I can imagine they're having a field day with this coming out of nowhere," Gigi comments. "Externally, it's good media coverage for the brand. Like genuinely good exposure. Holmes needs all the positive publicity they can get."

"This is insane," I reply, shaking my head.

"It would be very difficult for anyone at Holmes to challenge it since it's been approved by Vante," Gigi says. "It puts your name back in the project where it belongs, Hallie. August made sure of it."

My mind wanders to August. Even through the rollercoaster of the last few months, he managed to put his personal feelings aside and still be professional when it comes to work.

"Was he angry?" I ask quietly.

"Who?"

"August," I reply, clearing my throat.

Even saying his name sends my heart into a flutter.

"*He was* livid."

I swallow. "Oh."

"But not at you," She backtracks. "At Sebastian."

"Really?"

"Tobias told me they were both at the Winter Gala and that August was expecting to see you there," Gigi shares. "He was not happy when he found out Sebastian essentially removed you from the project and stopped you from attending the presentation."

My fingers twitch anxiously at the memory of my confrontation with Sebastian which ultimately led to my decision to leave the studio.

"*Hence,* Operation: Headlines for His Hartt," Gigi adds. "*Tobias'* surprisingly catchy name for August's quest to distribute the articles as quickly, and as widely, as possible. Your man was on a mission, Tobias said that man did not sleep."

My heart tugs at the information.

"Thank you, Gigi," I comment, then add after a realisation. "Since when were you on a first-name-no-title basis with the spare heir?"

She answers without missing a beat, "*Since the first email I sent him regarding your little research trip to Toussaint."*

I laugh loudly, feeling significantly lighter.

Only Gigi would conspire with a literal prince.

"Sorry for gatecrashing your little sorrow soirée all the way in Switzerland," She says, lightheartedly.

I smile. "I can't think of anyone better."

"Not even your shutterbug sweetheart?" Gigi sing-songs.

"Huh?"

"Nothing!" She clears her throat.

After quickly catching up and informing me of her own plans for Christmas, Gigi and I hang up.

A sense of relief washes over me and I feel far more uplifted than I have been over the past few days.

Staring at my phone, I begin scrolling through my contacts until I find August's number and I contemplate for a moment.

The way things ended between August and I was less than ideal. But he didn't let personal feelings get in the way. When it came down to it, he has always been nothing but supportive of me and what it is I love to do. My thumb presses the call button and I wait. Part of me wanted him to pick up but I'm also relieved when it goes to voicemail so I could leave a message.

"August. Hi. It's Hallie."

I cringe at how stilted I sound.

"Mahalia, um, Hartt." I pause, suddenly realising I don't know actually what to say. "Happy holidays? I, uhh, tried to ring but it went to voicemail. I mean, you're probably busy since it's the Christmas holidays— so I understand if… if you may not be able to answer…"

I trail off, awkwardly. I should have probably prepared in advance the sentiments I wanted to express.

"I just want to say thank you, umm, about the articles. I really appreciate the efforts you went through… I know- I know the last time we spoke wasn't the most *amicable* and I would like to apologise on my part. If you're not too busy… I'd love to meet up? Just to say thank you in person. After

CHAPTER 45

Christmas or... whenever you're in London. I know you're probably busy with Grayson... How is New York City, by the way? I bet Christmas is amazing there. Unless you're in Paris, in which case, *Joyeux Noël*..."

I inwardly wince, realising I'm rambling now.

"Just let me know? If you're interested," I continue. "B-but if you'd rather not, that's okay too. I just want to let you know that I'm really grateful. For all the help and encouragement you've given me during, um, the times we worked together. You have no idea how much it means to me to still have your support, even after everything. I wholeheartedly appreciate it and I appreciate you. Thank you so much for believing in me."

My throat constricts as I feel myself get emotional so I begin to wrap up the voicemail.

"Have a wonderful Christmas, I hope everything's going well with you in New York. Sending you my love— uhh—ly well wishes. Sending you *lovely* well wishes from London. Well, technically Interlaken, but-"

I stop myself before I start talking nonsense again.

"Thank you August, truly." I say. "I really hope to see you soon."

Chapter 46

Over the next few days, the buzz for the articles about the collaboration continued.

Mahalia Made has been at the forefront of the news, inundated with tags, comments, and shares. Even though the regalwear collection isn't due for an official public showcase until the beginning of next year for Men's Fashion Week in January, publications were eager for the latest story and emails from different media outlets asking for an interview with me overwhelmed my inbox.

Receiving correspondence about future collaborations from the Royal Communications of Toussaint also took me by surprise and I wondered if Gigi mentioned anything to Tobias about me leaving Holmes.

New and exciting opportunities have started popping up and they *feel right*. For both the brand and the business. I feel inspired, with a renewed sense of purpose, and also reconnected with Designing in a way that I haven't felt in a long time.

I find myself completely restless.

But in the best ways possible.

Similarly, the house became progressively rowdier as my uncles and their families all travelled to Interlaken.

"Everyone's visiting," I share on the phone to Gigi, hoping I don't sound as anxious as I feel.

It's always been tradition to spend Christmas in Switzerland so it comes as no surprise that family would be coming over but I haven't been to a single gathering in *years* and I'm not sure how to act.

CHAPTER 46

The incident of Christmas from four years ago is a dark cloud hanging over my mind.

"*Even your uncle?*" Gigi asks sourly.

"He's coming tomorrow with Aunt Luisa," I answer.

The severity of the incident was something that I downplayed, even when I came back to London with my left hand bandaged up. Stitches that curved from the back to the palm of my hand accompanied by a splint for my fingers due to metacarpal fractures was something that everyone dismissed as a skiing accident.

Even though I have never attempted to ski in my life.

I didn't tell anyone, not even Gigi. We weren't close at the time and I didn't know anyone well enough during first year.

Only Rowan found out when I had to take over a month off from work at Tito Boy's because my hand needed to heal and I had to catch up with uni work. Initially, I wanted to quit but he sat me down and asked about it so I ended up divulging the details of what had happened.

Gigi only discovered the full extent of it during second year when we spent the entire Christmas break working on our uni work together. I didn't end up going home for the holidays and neither did Gigi, that's when I found out that her relationship with her family is a little rocky too. Instead, she worked on her assignments whilst I focused on my coursework and we bonded over fashion trends and family traumas.

"*How are you feeling?*" She asks.

"Antsy," I reply.

It will be the first time I'll be seeing everyone again since that incident and I can feel the anxiousness in my chest brewing so I kept myself busy physically to prevent myself from being overwhelmed, mentally and emotionally.

So far, I've knitted two oversized jumpers with hand-embroidered hearts on the sleeves in different shades of grey, the colour reminding me of a certain platinum-haired nepo baby.

"Has Prince Tobias mentioned anything about August?" I ask.

"No..." Gigi replies. "*Should he have?*"

"Ah, it's fine, I just thought..." I trail off. "I called him a couple of days ago but he hasn't responded."

"He's probably busy," Gigi clears her throat. *"Tobias did mention that August has been nonstop with work in New York."*

I nod, although Gigi can't see me, and I try not to dwell on the rejection that nestled itself between my ribs.

"Lia!"

My grandma's voice calls out from downstairs.

"I have to go, Gigi." I exhale nervously. "I think my family are here."

"You've got this, Hals."

"Thank you," I say. "I'll talk to you later."

"Speak soon."

I end the call, inhaling slowly.

Now or never.

Releasing a breath, I exit my bedroom and walk out into the hallway, the telltale sound of raucous conversations between my family resounds in the living room as I walk down the stairs.

"That snowstorm is *relentless*."

"It's going to get worse over the next few days."

"Remy and Luisa's flights keep getting delayed."

I pause at the bottom of the stairs, the amount of people suddenly within my range a little overwhelming. The chattering is constant as everyone fusses over the weather and transport and I feel a little discombobulated just watching.

"Ate Lili!" A little girl runs up to me. "Do you know who I am?"

I blink at the dark-haired, brown-eyed five-year-old with two front teeth missing beaming up at me.

"Dayna?" I ask, briefly remembering the barely walking one-year-old in diapers, all those years ago.

"Lola says you make pretty dresses," She smiles brightly. "Can you make me one?"

I look over at my grandma who gives me a wink.

"I've been making clothes for boys, at the moment," I say, crouching

CHAPTER 46

down to her level. "But I can definitely make a pretty dress for you."

She grins. "My favourite colour is pink."

"Me too," I smile at her.

More and more people begin shuffling into the living room, the familiar faces of my cousins coming into view.

"Dayna, don't be bothering Ate Lia."

"Hi Russ."

"Hi, Ate." He gives me a nod, ushering Dayna away. "Sorry, she's really hyperactive."

Out of all the cousins, Russ is closest to my age. I'm only a couple of months older but he still calls me the honorific for older sister.

"That's okay." I shake my head. "How's… fourth year?"

"I'm doing a placement year," He informs me. "But yeah, technically fourth year. Medicine is a ballache. How's London?"

"Good, yes." I nod.

"Russ, Papa said to get our bags in the car." Alexa approaches us. "Hi, Ate Lia."

"Hi Lex," I give her a small smile.

"Are you still doing fashion?" She asks and I nod, not really wanting to further elaborate.

"Ate Lia said she's going to make me a dress." Dayna beams excitedly, tugging on Alexa's hand.

"How's college?"

"Sixth form," She replies. "It's good, just revising a lot. Exams in January."

There's a pause between us as she fidgets on the spot.

"I wanted to ask you about something." Alexa clears her throat, voice quiet.

She looks a little skeptical, as if she's contemplating her words.

"Will you be able to write me a reference?" Her voice is even quieter at the request.

My brows furrow and I strain my ear to confirm that I heard her correctly.

"A reference?" I repeat.

She nods.

"Are you sure I'm the right person for that?" I ask, uncertain. "I don't know much about Law to write you a reference that would be considered as–"

"Not for law," Alexa cuts me off, carefully. "For an art course. I'm applying for art schools in London."

I blink, remembering Alexa from my teenage years. Nose in sketchbooks, always drawing and always painting. Pencil in her hair, graphite smudges, paint splatters on her clothes. It's different to the Alexa in recent years. Head full of textbook knowledge. Academic essays and homework club. Future Oxbridge student. Or maybe even Harvard.

"Does Tita and Tito know?"

There's a flash of uncertainty in Alexa's eyes as she shakes her head.

Despite our five-year age difference, Alexa and I had been quite similar growing up. We were a lot closer when we were younger due to our mutual love for being creative. I recall how she'd always eagerly accompany me at every family gathering, always keen to borrow my pencils and sketch with me in my room.

"Lex," A voice calls out towards us. "Help your brother with the stuff in the car."

"Yes, Ma." She replies before turning to me, cautiously. "It's okay if not. But please don't mention anything? I might not even apply. So I don't even know if-"

"I won't say anything." I interrupt her gently. "And I'll write you a reference. Which art schools in London?"

"It's just the one," Alexa replies. "If I don't get in, I'm not going to bother with anywhere else."

She says it as an ultimatum of sorts. That's one of the bigger differences between Alexa and I. She has other things to fall back on, whereas for me, it's fashion design or nothing. As dramatic as it sounds.

"Which one?" I ask.

"Aston," she answers, clearing her throat. "The one Tita Cassie went to."

I blink at the mention of my mum but nod in understanding.

CHAPTER 46

"Aston or nothing," I affirm. "I've got you."

A genuine smile appears on her face as she looks at me.

"Thanks Ate Lia."

I mirror her smile. "Of course."

"Alexandria!" A voice exclaims.

"Coming, Pa!"

Alexa gives me another smile before walking back outside.

The whole house erupts in a familiar, homely buzz as everyone starts settling into the living room. My aunts and uncles regard me conversationally, making small talk and light pleasantries as if the incident that happened four years ago is just a distant memory to them.

In all fairness, it probably is just an obscure recollection to everyone.

It's likely they didn't find it as traumatising as I did, given the fact that they weren't the ones who ended up with a mangled hand and shattered fingers.

Lingering by the archway between the living room and the hallway, I watch as everyone chats idly between themselves— the atmosphere is pleasant, cosy.

The sound of the doorbell interrupts the comfortable conversations, prompting everyone to pause and take notice.

"Are we expecting more people?" My grandpa looks around in confusion.

"Remy and Luisa aren't arriving until tomorrow evening." My grandma shakes her head in response.

"Maybe it's a delivery," I say, turning my attention to the door. "I'll get it."

Bracing myself for the cold, I unlock the door and pull on the handle before blinking at the person standing in front of me.

Platinum blond hair and steely grey eyes.

"August?"

Chapter 47

"Mahalia."

A puff of white escapes his lips as August exhales a sigh of relief.

I blink repeatedly, scanning his entire figure as he stands in front of me.

Wearing a long khaki trench coat over a black turtleneck and matching black trousers, he's bundled up with a red checkered scarf and a brown woollen trapper hat that most definitely looks out of place for the likes of his wardrobe. The scarf wrapped around him is thick and the hat covering his head is dusted with snowflakes. I glance down at his black leather oxfords that are most definitely *not* meant for the snow.

August offers me a frozen smile, the tip of his nose tinted pink.

"You..." I look up at him, my eyes widening. "What are you–"

"Can I come in?" He interrupts me, gesturing towards the front door.

"No!" I exclaim. "I–I mean, you can't–"

"No?" He blinks at me, slowly.

I glimpse a look behind me before immediately stepping out into the foyer and closing the door.

"What are you doing here?" I turn to him, quizzically.

"Trying not to freeze to death," He replies flatly, eyelids drooping. "Can I explain inside?"

"Of course, I just—" I watch as he shivers, his entire body shuddering in the cold. "Wait here."

I disappear back inside, my mind reeling as I sneak a look out of the window. Outside, August sits shakily on the bench, puffs of white air leaving his mouth.

CHAPTER 47

Suddenly, my grandma pops up in front of me.

"Who was it?" She asks, peering over my shoulder.

I rack my brain to think of an excuse as to why my former nepo baby boss and ex-situationship, if one can even call it that, is currently outside. The thought of how unfavourable that would be from a conservative Asian household makes me wince. I can't even think of a logical reason as to why he would be in this country, let alone a believable enough excuse for why he would be standing in front of this house.

"Ma, there's–"

"It's Jack Frost!" Dayna exclaims excitedly as she climbs up the window sill ledge, pressing her face against the glass. "He's so tall!"

"The snowman?" Russ blinks.

"No!!" She giggles. "The boy!"

"A boy?" Alexa peeks her head out from the hallway.

"Lia brought a boy?" One of my aunt's questions aloud and I inwardly wince.

A gush of voices expressing approval choruses as everyone begins to filter out of the living room. Different pairs of eyes are suddenly looking at me, interests and curiosity piqued as I shake my head, attempting to block everyone from the hallway.

"No! He's..." I stall, trying to think of a convincing explanation without raising any questions. "A colleague, at work. Old workplace. Not the restaurant, the studio. I–"

"They're making you do work?"

"Over Christmas?"

"But it's the holiday season!"

Another collective chatter erupts, this time of disapproval as they attempt to look outside. Dayna and the younger children are all waving at August from the inside, my other cousins glancing over curiously as he waves back at them.

"Why is he still outside?" My grandpa pipes up. "You can't leave the poor boy out there. A *snowstorm* is on the way, Lia."

My grandma disappears into the living room as I try to keep the hallway blocked.

"Yes, Pa. I just need to—"

"Everyone in the living room!" My grandma calls out as she comes back to the front door, a swaddle of blankets in her arms.

"Wait, Ma, it's fine." I shake my head vigorously. "He's only dropping by. He probably needs to leave soon—"

"The poor boy looks like he's going to freeze to death, Lia, bring him inside!"

Before I know it, she's opening the door and gesturing towards August. He looks up from where he's sitting on the porch before scrambling to his feet.

"Madame Hartt, *bonjour*." His teeth chatters as he speaks. "*Oder guten tag*."

He takes my grandma's hand, palm downwards, and presses her knuckles against his forehead. I blink in confusion at the traditional gesture of respect towards Filipino elders.

"Oh hijo, you're freezing cold!"

She grabs his hands, gloveless and slightly tinged blue, and pats it with concern.

Outside, the blizzard is beginning to pick up, gusts of wind and flurries of little snowflakes drifting inside the house as the door stays open.

"Come in. You'll freeze to death out here."

My grandma drags August inside and he sways slightly, tripping over his own feet by the front door.

"Thank you," August nods politely as my grandma grabs the blanket and wraps it around his tall frame.

"I don't know why Lia didn't invite you in the first place." She shakes her head, sending me a look of disapproval.

"Ma, wait."

She closes the door behind her and the house is warm again. August steps into the entryway, silence taking over the household as a pair of half a dozen or so eyes all blink at him.

August, tall and towering, turns towards me and I freeze, lost for words.

CHAPTER 47

"Who's at the door?"

"He's handsome!"

"Is that your boyfriend?"

I gape in mortification as more and more faces pop up from the archway of the living room watching August and I.

Shaking my head, I move to grab his arm and pull him towards the stairs.

"August," I say. "Shoes."

He blinks at me, slightly dazed as his eyes fall on the piles of shoes by the entrance, and nods. His movements are listless, almost clumsy as he shuffles back down the stairs and begin removing his oxfords. Eyebrows knotting, his grey eyes find mine before they flutter close and he stumbles down the stairs.

"August!" I gasp.

Suddenly, the entire room erupts in wild commotion as he falls to the hardwood floor with a resounding thud.

"Oh my god!"

"Lili!"

"Is he dead?"

I glare at 14-year-old Jax hovering over August as everyone begins to crowd around him.

Pushing past the congregation of bodies, I drop to the floor next to August. My hands reach out to lift the back of his head and I gasp at how hot his skin feels against my palm.

"Mama, he's really warm." I swallow, turning to my grandma. "I think he's sick."

"Give the poor boy room to breathe," My grandpa's commanding voice booms in the hallway. "Stop crowding him."

I watch as my grandma ushers the younger kids away from the stairs and people begin dispersing back into the living room.

"Should I call an ambulance?" I stammer, the worry in my gut slowly building.

"I don't think any form of vehicle's going to make it to Lola's," Gabe, Jax's older brother, pipes up. "Look outside."

I turn my head towards the window, the blizzard fully forming.

"He'll be okay, Lia." My grandma pats my arm reassuringly.

I look down at August, assessing his face. His complexion is a lot paler than usual and dark circles are forming under his eyes. He looks exhausted but he still manages to look strikingly handsome.

"Russ, Gabe— help take August upstairs." My grandma instructs them before turning her attention towards me. "Wrap him up warm, Lia. I'll make him something to eat, he's probably just exhausted from travelling."

Crouching down next to me, Russ takes one of August's arms and drapes it over his shoulder, leaning his body against him as he pulls him up to a standing position.

"Bloody hell, Lia." Gabe heaves as he walks over to the other side of August, dragging his other arm around him. "Your boyfriend weighs a ton."

"He's not—" I begin but I'm cut off as Russ loses his balance and August sways towards me, his forehead knocking against mine.

"Shit," Russ winces. "Sorry, Ate."

"*Be careful,*" I stress.

I stand behind them as we begin walking up the stairs, keeping a watchful eye so August doesn't hit himself anywhere because the man is impossibly tall and difficult to manoeuvre.

"Which room?" They ask as we reach the top of the stairs.

I pause for a moment, cursing inwardly as I remember that all the guest rooms are now taken.

"My room," I answer, nodding towards the door just opposite the stairs on the third floor.

Moving away from August, I open the door quickly and clear my bed as best as possible, mentally grimacing at the mountainous piles of plushies by the headboard as my cousins carefully set August down on the bed.

"You should probably undress him," Russ suggests, moving August on his back.

"What?" The high-pitched sound I let out is unnatural as they look at me, puzzled. "What??"

CHAPTER 47

"His clothes, Ate." Gabe blinks at me, a confused expression on his face. "Your boyfriend's coat is soaked through. The bed's going to get wet."

I feel the heat rise to my cheeks.

"Right— right!"

I quickly remove the scarf around August's neck and the hat on his head. His hair, a little bit longer and even lighter than I remember, is slightly tangled and I can feel him burning up against my palm as I swipe the strands away from his forehead.

"Ate Lia," Russ turns to me worriedly. "He's burning up."

I try not to let my concern show through.

"I know, I know." I swallow, nervous habits kicking in as I begin undoing the belt of his trench coat. "He doesn't take kindly to cold weather."

"The guy sure has a death wish if he was travelling during the snowstorm," Gabe comments and I wince.

I quickly thank them for helping as they exit my room.

Placing my palm against the skin peeking above his turtleneck, I swallow the lump building in my throat.

His temperature is concerningly high.

"August," I shake him lightly. "Can you hear me?"

He lets out a quiet hum of acknowledgement but he doesn't open his eyes, brows furrowing as he begins to shudder a little more violently.

The worry in my gut doubles as he lays in my bed, unresponsive.

Chapter 48

My room is in complete darkness save for the tiny light lamp plugged in at the corner of my room, just above my worktable.

August is sleeping soundly on the bed, the lump of duvet hasn't moved since I dressed him in much more comfortable clothing... *almost 12 hours ago.*

But I try not to get unnecessarily anxious as I watch over him.

August is a still-sleeper. I had to keep checking on him every half an hour, just to feel reassured that he's actually breathing because he's terrifyingly quiet and seemingly dead to the world.

Tiptoeing across my room to my worktable, I begin putting my knitting needles and yarn away. I'm in the middle of organising my crafting materials for the nth time out of nervous habit when I hear a rustling on the bed.

"Mahal–?" August's voice is hoarse from misuse and I bolt up in attention.

"August," I gasp, rushing to him immediately and turning the lamp on my bedside table.

He groans loudly, turning his head away from the light.

"Sorry, sorry!" I whisper, reaching over to cover the lamp with a plushie. "Are you okay? Do you need anything?"

His eyes are closed, brows furrowed as he twists towards me slowly. The damp cloth on his forehead slips off as he attempts to sit up.

"Careful," I say. "Don't get up, just lie down."

"How long was I out?" He mumbles, words slurring.

CHAPTER 48

"About half a day," I reply, glancing at the clock on my wall. "It's just after midnight."

"Shit," He breathes.

"Are you okay?" I repeat. "How are you feeling?"

"Warm," He hums contentedly, burying himself backwards and sinking further into the bed.

I try not to let my embarrassment show at the immense accumulation of different soft toys currently occupying my bed.

"Not *too* warm?" I ask.

He shakes his head sluggishly, gaze falling at the lilac plushie beside him.

"Is that a sewing spool?" He reaches a hand towards it, his movement slow.

"Yes, sorry." I blush as he pats the head languidly before looking around my bed.

"And a button?" He chuckles, softly. "Plus a sewing needle. You have an entire collection of... sewing supply plushies?"

"They're gifts," I clear my throat self-consciously. "The guest rooms are all taken. Otherwise, I would have put you in one of the other rooms instead."

"And miss the opportunity of being introduced to your plethora of plushies?" He exhales cheerfully.

August doesn't say anything for a while, just admires the cushioned textile materials on my bed. His eyes slowly scan my room and I watch him assess my childhood bedroom, gaze surprisingly piqued with interest as he takes everything in, despite exhaustion lining his face.

Without warning, his face contorts, nose scrunching up and eyebrows knotting as he lets out a hiss.

"Are you in pain?" My heart lurches at the injured expression on his face. "Do you need medicine? I have paracetamol. Or ibuprofen. Does your head hurt? Or is it muscle ache?"

I clamber for the piles of different medicines currently on my bedside table.

Perks of having an aunt who works as a nurse.

"I'm okay," He winces, attempting to sit up. "Just need to stretch."

"Are you sure? Maybe you're hungry. You haven't eaten all day-"

"Tinker-Talent?" He interrupts me, the nickname sending a warm tingle in my chest. "Stop fussing. I'm okay."

August reaches out for my hand and intertwines our fingers, the tension visibly leaving his body as he slumps back down on the bed and closes his eyes.

I sit on the edge of the bed, watching his face, still so handsome despite looking weary with illness. The urge to reach out and swipe the hair that fell across his forehead makes my fingers twitch but I hold myself back.

"Alright," I say after a prolonged silence. "I'll leave you to it. I just wanted to make sure you're okay. My lamp isn't adjustable but I found a night light that is and I plugged it in the corner so you can turn it down if it's too bright. Let me know if you need anything."

Humming quietly, August brings our interlocked hands to his chest.

"Where are you going?" He asks as he opens his eyes tiredly.

"Downstairs," I tell him, shuffling nervously under his gaze. "We're sardining on the floor."

"Sardining?"

"There's um, not enough rooms so my cousins— there's like ten of us— we all sleep on the floor. Like sardines."

I feel a little stupid explaining it to August, the concept probably strange to him but it had been an odd tradition when we were all younger and it just kind of... stuck.

"Is there room for one more?"

I nod. "I can probably fit somewhere."

Although I'm pretty sure that all the good spots are taken. It's way past midnight now and everybody in the house is asleep.

"I meant for me," He says.

I blink, silence following.

"I'm not sleeping on *your* bed whilst you're on the *floor*." He looks at me pointedly.

"It's really not that big of a deal," I comment. "We do it all the time. It's

CHAPTER 48

comfy. There are plenty of pillows and blankets and it's actually quite fun, if you think about it. It's like one big massive sleepover and–"

"Sounds fun," August nods. "I'm sure I'll enjoy it down there."

I look at him skeptically.

"You can't sleep on the *ground*."

"I've passed out on piss-covered pavements in Paris," He deadpans. "I think I'll be fine on the carpet of your living room."

I think of the reactions from every single member of my family when they see August in the morning.

"You're not sleeping on the floor, August."

"Then neither are you." He shifts weakly on the bed, making room for me.

"Wait, I don't-" My brain short-circuits for a moment. "I can't sleep next to you."

August gives me a look.

"We've done more than share a bed, Mahalia."

My face flushes, heat flooding my cheeks.

"It's not…" I shake my head, sighing. *"You're ill, August.* You need to rest properly."

"You're here," He says. "I'll rest more than fine."

I try not to overthink his words, a jittery feeling rooting itself in my ribcage.

"I'll stay on this side of the bed." He shuffles backwards, even rearranging the soft toys on my bed so they create some sort of barricade between us. "Better?"

Sensing there's no swaying August, I sigh quietly before turning off the lamp and lying on my back.

The room is silent, far too quiet for my liking, and I feel strangely nervous.

My finger twitches and I gingerly reach out for a plushie, busying my hands to calm the slowly building anxiousness I feel at being in such close proximity to August.

"How many of these thimbles do you have?" He says into the quiet of the room.

"Just two," I answer, clearing my throat. "It's a set of twin thimbles."

He hums. "You have a pink one at Holmes."

Had.

I ponder for a moment then inwardly flinch as I realise I inadvertently said the thought out loud.

"Yes," I add, twisting my hands. "I need to pick it up from the studio along with the rest of my stuff."

The bed shifts on August's side and I feel a gaze lingering on me, even in the dark.

"Mahalia, about what happened—"

"Rest, August." I insist softly.

I don't know the extent of August's awareness about what happened between Sebastian and I regarding the regalwear collection, if he knows anything at all. And right now, I don't think I'm in the right headspace to revisit or relive any arguments, my mind too inundated with my anxious thoughts.

"Please?" I add quietly.

A long pause settles between us before he sighs, acquiescing.

I sense the heaviness of it, my own heart feeling the weight of his emotions as I slowly reach out for his hand.

"We'll talk about it in the morning, okay?"

Chapter 49

If there was a 'wonder of the world' in fashion, waking up next to the Peroxide Prince is probably one of them.

August is sleeping peacefully, a serene expression on his face.

True to his word, he maintains his distance, body curled in my direction to face me as he continues to rest on his side, a respectable gap between us.

Shifting carefully, I inch closer to him.

Up close, he looks like a work of art— porcelain skin completely void of any imperfections, long wispy lashes kissing his cheeks and Cupid's bow lips formed in a slight pout.

Sleep made him look younger, boyish. It softened the angles of his features.

There's no frown on his face, just a relaxedness in his repose.

His light blond hair, much longer and even wavier now, frames the sharp lines of his facial features that reminded me of his younger self. Tabloid pictures of the *Parisian Playboy* flash in my mind and I shake my head to get rid of the mental image of *that* August.

This version of him looks less troubled, more carefree.

His eyelids flit delicately before they slowly open and I quickly cast my eyes away before shuffling backwards, trying not to look like I've been staring at him whilst he'd been sleeping.

"Morning." His voice is thick with sleep as he greets me, the sound sending flutters to my stomach.

"Morning," I greet him quietly. "How are you feeling?"

"So much better," He answers with a soft sigh. "I told you."

Natural light peeks through my curtains and filters inside my room. It casts August in an almost angelic light as the warm light filters behind him, conveniently creating a glow around his silhouette.

August's grey eyes sweep over my face slowly, mapping out every feature of my face. It feels far too exposing and all too intimate to be so closely under his gaze like this.

Feeling myself flush, I shuffle to lie on my back and stare at the ceiling.

"You don't have a suitcase with you," I comment after a while. "It wasn't outside when I checked. Did you drop it off at your hotel or?"

I can still feel August's gaze, lingering and intentional.

"It's still at the airport, I think."

"Geneva Airport?" I glance over at him.

"Or JFK." He shrugs. "They lost my suitcase but I couldn't wait for them to find out where."

"How did you manage to get to Interlaken?" I question.

It had been a struggle for my family to travel domestically, the snowstorm cancelling international flights and limiting public transportation around the country so I'm surprised to see August here at all.

"Train from Geneva to Bern." He pauses, brows furrowing as he recalls his journey. "Rail connectivity was down in Bern for a little while so I hitchhiked with a Normandy couple to Interlaken. Public transport was unavailable when I got here so I just walked the rest."

I sit up suddenly.

"You *walked* in the snow?"

My jaw drops, recalling how the train station is at least an hour away from my grandparent's house on foot. And that's on a good, non-blizzard day.

"There were no taxis. Or buses. I tried to hitchhike a few times but people were driving in the opposite direction. Your grandparents live in the middle of nowhere."

"August, that's..." I struggle to find the right words. "Are you out of your mind?"

"Well, I was most definitely not making sane decisions, no." He chuckles.

CHAPTER 49

He sits up with me, sleepy grey eyes meeting mine with a sheepish expression.

"Why would you do that?" I turn to him, incredulous. "We could have arranged to meet up after Christmas. Or whenever you were back in London. You didn't have to go to all the trouble of travelling to Switzerland, especially since it's dangerous—"

"I didn't want to wait," He says. "I couldn't. *I tried.* But every time I heard your voice... I needed to see you as soon as possible."

There's a pause between us.

"What happened at Sebastian's..." He begins. "Fuck. It was triggering in ways I didn't even expect."

He closes his eyes, swallowing as he continues.

"Everyone knows about my reputation growing up in the industry. The partying, the alcohol, the drugs," He hesitates for a moment. "The women."

August's eyes cloud over for the briefest moment before they clear again.

"Being exposed to the industry, at such a young age too, it fucked with my head," He continues. "There were just so many expectations, far too many than I was capable of. For a kid, that's fucking terrifying. I had to live up to the Vante name. There were so many people to please, places to possess but I didn't want any of it. It did a lot of damage to me mentally so I coped the only way I could."

His voice sounds distant, almost small.

"You don't need to explain yourself to me, August." I say, reaching for his hand.

He takes my hand and intertwines our fingers, his touch warm.

"I want to," He responds, taking a deep breath. "I was in that cycle *for years*. I'm not proud of it— the reputation I had. I couldn't walk away from the industry. It's my entire life, after all. So I had to figure out how to keep it at arm's length and find something, *someplace*, to keep my feet grounded at the same time."

"New York?" I ask quietly as August nods.

It makes sense.

His fondness for the city.

"It changed everything," He states. "Studying at MIDAS, residing in Queens, learning photography. It balanced out my life, keeping things from a distance. I didn't say no to the party scene, I still went to clubs and attended socials, but I wasn't getting black-out drunk and sleeping with different women every night."

His eyes flicker suddenly, as if recalling a memory.

"Seeing you at Sebastian's studio, fuck, it messed with my head." He sighs, exasperated. "Seb and I grew up in the industry together. We got involved in the same stupid shit, played the same godawful games. Finding you with Atkinson? I saw red."

He closes his eyes, pressing his fingers against his lids as if trying to physically block the memory from his mind.

"That's what I meant when I said you didn't belong there," He replies quietly. "It wasn't about Holmes. Or even the industry. It was *those* people in *that* place."

August brings our interlocked hands to his chest and I feel the heat of his body under my palm.

"I didn't want them anywhere near you," He admits, a soft possessiveness in his tone. "You deserve far more than people who are going to take advantage of your kindness and mistreat you. I want the best for you, Mahalia. You deserve to be in bigger rooms, with better people."

His words tug at my heart.

"Gigi told me about what you did," I begin. "About the articles. You didn't have to do that."

"Yes, I did." He looks at me determinedly. "You worked hard on the collection. You deserve the recognition. I'll be damned if I just let myself watch from the sidelines as someone strings you along you and strips that away from you."

An influx of emotions lodges in my throat.

"Thank you," I swallow.

"You're not a *plaything*, Mahalia." He presses his lips together. "You're not some doll to be toyed around. I don't think you have any idea just how important you are to me."

CHAPTER 49

My eyes well up and before I could stop myself, I throw my arms around August's neck, feeling the fever of his skin. He grunts softly, sinking into the headboard and I mutter a quick apology before pulling back slightly, the heat of his body concerning me.

"You're still really hot," I sniffle, frowning at how abnormally warm he still feels.

"Why, thank you."

I pull away slightly to look up at him, rolling my eyes as a wolfish smile appears on his face.

"I mean your *temperature*." I reach up and place my palm across his scorching forehead.

"My immune system isn't great." He murmurs, eyes closing as he leans into my touch. "Especially in the cold."

Concern weighs itself heavily on my chest.

"Yet you chose to walk," I scold him before withdrawing my hand. "In the snow. During a blizzard."

"I told you," He whispers, voice rasping. "I needed to see you."

The all too familiar softness in his gaze overwhelms me and an odd prickling sensation spreads in my chest, realising how the outcome of his travel could have easily ended life-threateningly dangerous.

"You know snow blindness is a thing?" I say, exasperated. "*Photokeratitis*. They have an official medical term for it because it's a very serious, very real condition. And you– *impulsively* travel during one of the worst snowstorms recorded in Swiss history. The blizzard could have *blinded* you, August! Whilst you were out walking! What if you got lost? Or injured? Or worse! Did you not think about that?"

His gaze further softens, grey eyes warm with affection.

"How do you even know about that?"

"What?"

"Photokeratitis."

"*The internet*."

August pauses, the soft intensity in his gaze all too new and all too familiar at the same time.

"You blind me every day, Tinker-Talent." The corners of his mouth tug into a small smile. "Nature has nothing on you."

"Don't." I turn away, overwhelmed. "Don't do that."

Needing to distract myself from his heartfelt admissions and the haywire of my emotions, I begin to get up.

"Mahalia–"

"I'm going to make you food," I announce. "You've had rest, now you need to eat."

"*Mon cœur-*"

"If you want to shower, there's a bathroom on every floor," I say. "I'll get some clothes for you."

Chapter 50

Keeping my hands busy is the only way I can distract my mind from the torrent of thoughts and fustercluck of feelings I'm currently experiencing, which is how I found myself in the kitchen, preparing something for August to eat.

I've opted for the standard Filipino remedy of lugaw (rice porridge) and salabat (ginger tea). Both are a recipe of my grandma's, ones that she would make for me whenever I got sick when I was younger.

Having just finished cooking the rice porridge, I'm halfway through making the tea for August when my grandma enters the kitchen.

"How is he, hija?"

I look up from peeling the ginger.

"Well rested," I answer quietly. "He's currently taking a shower."

"Poor boy." She shakes her head, a worried expression on her face. "All that travelling must have exhausted him."

Grimly, I nod. "He gets sick when he's out for too long in the cold."

My grandma glances at my little prep station of ingredients before her eyes trail towards the stove.

"At least you know how to look after him." She says. "You're making him lugaw?"

"And salabat," I nod, feeling my smile falter under the weight of my emotions.

Nervously, I fuss around the kitchen, feeling my grandma's eyes on me as I finish chopping the ginger into slices and add it to the boiling water.

"You never mentioned a boyfriend," She ponders out loud.

I rack my brain to think of a plausible enough explanation as to why August would be here without outwardly lying. Deceiving my grandparents, especially my grandma, is impossible so there isn't even any point in trying. She's far too perceptive and she'll just see right through it.

"It's new." I blurt out.

My mouth is running before my brain can even catch up and comprehend the statements I'm saying.

"Kind of," I add, inwardly wincing. "We haven't put an official label on it or anything."

I bite my tongue to prevent myself from saying anything else. It wasn't exactly the most appropriate thing to say but it's as close to the truth as I can express without having to lie to my grandma, from my perspective of the situation anyway.

Everything *is* new to me.

From his confessions to my feelings, attempting to make sense of them is unfamiliar territory. In addition to that, whatever situationship August and I had then, there isn't an official label for it now.

"That's fine. You both take your time." She nods. "I'm just glad you finally found someone. Your Papa and I were getting worried about you."

"There's no need to worry, Ma."

"I'm always going to keep worrying, I'm your Mama." She fixes me a look. "But knowing that you have someone like August makes me a little less so. He was the one that accompanied you on that trip, wasn't he? And bought you all those sewing supplies?"

I blink.

"You don't think I pay attention when we talk on the phone?" My grandma shakes her head at me, affectionately.

I look back on all the shared experiences August and I had together. How much I want to keep making new memories with him.

"Does he take good care of you?" She asks me.

The question hangs in the air.

Since meeting August, he'd always had the best intentions for me. Always looking out for me and tending to me, whether I knew it or not. He's never

CHAPTER 50

been outwardly vocal about it, choosing instead to let his actions speak rather than his words. His way of showing he cares is quiet but it's there.

My heart blooms at the realisation.

I nod. "He does."

"Good," My grandma looks at me. "I'm very glad to hear that."

She gives me a warm smile before patting my cheek.

"I can't believe it!" My grandma exclaims, teasingly. "Lili's first boyfriend!"

From the living room, I hear the loud chatter from my cousins.

"They're together-together?"

"I knew it!"

"See, I told you he was her boyfriend."

My eyes widen and I can only watch as my grandma playfully winks at me before leaving the kitchen and joining in the conversations with my cousins.

I shake my head at their antics, letting out a long exhale.

Placing the mug of tea and the bowl of rice porridge on the wooden serving tray, I carefully lift it from the counter and exit the kitchen, ignoring the teasing comments and loud giggles from my cousins about me and August.

I'm walking down the corridor when I feel a tiny presence skipping over next to me.

"Hi, Ate Lili!" Dayna beams, big brown eyes twinkling. "Is Kuya Auggie feeling better?"

I shake my head. "Not yet, Dayn."

"Oh." She pouts.

"But he will be soon," I reassure her with a smile. "He just needs plenty of rest and plenty of food."

I gesture at the tray and she looks up at me expectantly.

"Are you looking after him?"

"Of course." I nod.

Sensing a silhouette by the stairs, I glance up to find August mid-ascent.

"You should be resting," I scold him.

"You've been gone a while."

He's freshly showered and looking more awake but I can tell he's still feeling lethargic as he steps down to meet me, hand splayed against the wall for support.

"Hi, Kuya Auggie." Dayna timidly pipes up from behind my legs. "I'm Dayna."

"Hello," August smiles, crouching down to her level as he reaches us by the bottom of the stairs. "Little Dayna."

His attempt to make light conversation with Dayna despite the exhaustion on his face tugs at my heart.

"I'm not little," She frowns. "I'm five."

"Ah, of course. I do apologise." August smiles gently at her before directing his gaze at me. "Do you need help?"

He gestures towards the tray I'm holding and I shake my head.

"I need you in my bed." I look at him sternly.

He blinks, giving me an impish smile before I realise my words.

"*To rest,*" I correct myself. "I need you in bed, *resting*, so you get better."

I try not to fluster as he slowly stands, looking at me with that softness again.

"Ate Lili is right." Dayna chimes in, less reluctant around him now. "If you're sick, you have to sleep and eat a lot. Like my Ate when she got sick last week and all her boyfriends came to the house and looked after her."

"*Boyfriends?*" August blinks before turning to me.

Dayna nods enthusiastically, holding up two peace signs with both hands.

"Ate has four," She giggles.

"She probably means her guy friends," I whisper to August before turning to Dayna. "Can you help take Kuya August to my room, please? Be careful, don't rush."

Dayna nods before she takes August's hand and bounces up the steps. Following closely behind them, I watch as she talks animatedly about a mythical winter spirit, August joining in and entertaining her the entire walk up the two flights of stairs.

I enter my room to find Dayna fussing over the blanket, as if to put

CHAPTER 50

August to bed, and I couldn't help but smile.

"All done." Dayna softly pats August's forehead. "Rest lots, Kuya Auggie."

"Thank you, little Daynie."

She gives August a toothless grin before hopping down from the bed and exiting the room with a small giggle.

"Were you also that adorable as a child?"

I shake my head. "I terrorised my grandparents with shears and thread clippers, unfortunately."

A small chuckle escapes August and my heart flutters at the sound. Putting the tray down on the bed, I reach towards his forehead to place the palm of my hand against it.

"You're still warm," I comment, hesitantly. "But you're not scalding to the touch."

August watches me, gaze molten silver, and I try not to fluster at the way his eyes glide over my lips as I speak.

"Eat," I gesture towards the bowl of lugaw and the mug of salabat. "It's rice porridge and ginger tea."

He eyes the boiled egg, chopped scallions and toasted garlic on top of the lugaw before digging in and I get up to draw the blinds shut in my room. August is hungrier than I initially thought because he's halfway through the bowl by the time I walk back to the bed.

"I overheard everyone downstairs." He clears his throat, taking a sip of the tea.

"Sorry," I grimace, sitting back down on the bed. "I've forgotten how chaotic my cousins can be."

"First boyfriend?" He asks. "That you've brought home to meet the family, right?"

I bite my lip nervously. "More like, ever."

"You've never had a boyfriend?"

"I mean, you were my first time, so."

A long, awkward pause settles between us and I shift uncomfortably, suddenly finding the lint on my duvet cover all too interesting.

August blinks at me. "What?"

"It's never really been a priority." I shrug. "I don't, um, date that much. It's not like I'm not interested, I've just never had the time. I'm too focused on other things."

"Wait, stop." He shakes his head. "What do you mean I was your first time?"

"Oh," I fidget slightly before clearing my throat. "In Toussaint."

Staring at the near-empty bowl of lugaw, I mentally prepare myself to answer the spate of questions he might have. It would be pointless to try and skirt around the issue.

"That was your first time?"

I look up to find August gawking at me, grey eyes wide like saucers.

"Yes." I nod.

"As in..." August trails off, almost as if he wants to be corrected.

"Losing my virginity?" I try not to fluster. "Yes."

August blinks.

Once, twice.

His eyes squint, assessing me, before shaking his head.

"No," He scoffs. "You're lying."

I frown, crossing my arms. "Why would I lie about something like that?"

His mouth opens before closing again, gaping like a fish, as he struggles to formulate a response and I don't think I've ever seen him look visibly disturbed in the time I've known him.

"How?" August stares at me, unblinking.

"How?" I wrinkle my nose, suddenly feeling self-conscious under his gaze. "How did I remain a virgin for twenty-two years, is that what you're asking? Umm, I don't know August, by not having sex?"

I feel a little stupid saying it out loud, August looking more and more uneasy as the realisation sinks in for him.

"But you..." He trails off. "You didn't say anything. You didn't even– There was no–"

He pauses, eyes glazing over as if remembering the events that happened that night.

"There was no indication on your end that it was your first time,

CHAPTER 50

Mahalia."

He narrows his eyes at me.

"You said you were on *birth control*."

I can feel the heat crawling up my neck at the suggestion behind his comment.

"I was!" I answer, embarrassed. "*I am*. For my *period*. It regulates my menstrual cycle. And it helps with cramps."

"I was your first time," August looks genuinely unsettled. "Mahalia, *what the hell?*"

Inwardly, I wince.

The thought of the experience not being as enjoyable to him as it was for me due to my inexperience didn't even cross my mind at the time. August has a reputation, for crying out loud. Maybe I should have told him it was my first time after all.

"I understand it might not have been the best experience for you but it's not as if I didn't try," I mutter, defensively. "There's no need to be insensitive about it."

It's not like I was expecting to offer up my virginity to the Peroxide Prince of Paris.

I try not to let my insecurities get the best of me but the thought still stings a little.

"Mahalia— no." He shakes his head, bewildered. "You were fine. Fuck, you were more than fine."

August pauses as he stares at me, his eyes glazing over again.

"Hell, you were *insatiable*." He comments shamelessly. "You certainly didn't perform like it was your first time so excuse me for being a little skeptical."

I flush hotly.

"Was I really your first time?" He queries.

I nod.

"You should have told me," He visibly winces. "I would have been gentle."

"You were," I blush, flashes of the night in Toussaint replaying in my mind.

August fidgets on the bed, leaning against the headboard.

"After like your *fourth orgasm*," He retorts disbelievingly.

I blush at the explicit nature of his comment as he brings an arm over his eyes, letting out a low, defeated groan.

"Why are *you* so upset about *my* virginity?" I question him.

"I'm not upset!" He replies, a little too quickly.

"Then how come you're freaking out so much?"

"I'm not freaking out!" He replies, somewhat hysterical.

August lets out a long, resigned sigh as he grabs one of my plushies, looking like he's having an existential crisis.

"I don't regret it," I confess timidly. "If that is what's troubling you. I know it was my first time but I'm glad it was with you."

Determined, I peer up at August, hoping to convey the wholehearted nature of my sentiment.

"Mahalia," He groans. "You really shouldn't *say* things like that, while *looking* at me like that."

"Like what?" I blink, puzzled.

August releases another long exhale before shuffling out of the duvet and rising from the bed.

"Where are you going?" I ask, watching as he grabs a towel from my clothes airer.

"I'm taking another shower," He mutters. "A cold one this time."

Chapter 51

It's an industry-recognised verifiable truth that the Peroxide Prince is hardhearted— reserved and standoffish with an ever-present scowl on his face. So witnessing him interact with my family members in an overly engaging manner, all mega-watt-smiles and tongue-in-cheek replies is more than a little baffling.

In fact, it's almost dangerous.

How ridiculously charming he can be, given the opportunity.

Sitting on the sofa in the living room, August is showing my cousins the pictures he's taken during our trip to Toussaint, print photographs now digitised on his phone. Perched next to him, Dayna is peering over the pictures as August scrolls through them one by one.

"She worked on the regalwear collection for the Royals of Touissant." He reveals, opting to leave out the fact that he's related to said monarchs of the Mediterranean country. "We went on a trip over the summer and it was gorgeous. Wasn't it, *mon cœur?*"

I can only nod as August talks animatedly.

"Ate Lili made clothes for a prince?" She gapes, wide-eyed.

"Working towards designing for the whole royal family," August elaborates, proudly. "The Royals of Toussaint have only worked with fashion *brands* in the past, not a specific designer so it's a very significant feat."

Just as I'm about to comment, the sound of the front door opening followed by a cold gust of wind draws our attention to the entrance hall.

"It's a nightmare out there!" A voice exclaims.

"We didn't think we would make it out of the high street." A deeper voice adds.

Aunt Luisa and Uncle Jeremiah step into the living room, casting a hush over the space. There's a sense of disquiet as everyone acknowledges their arrival before a chorus of greetings erupts from my aunts and uncles. My cousins scuttle over to greet them and I shift on the sofa, a sense of unease settling in my stomach as I stand.

"Lili, can you take the boxes from the study and store them in your room for the time being?" My grandpa's voice echoes from the kitchen.

"Sure," I reply, grateful for the distraction as I rise from the sofa.

"I'll help," August offers as he stands with me.

Shuffling out of the living room, I feel a set of eyes scrutinise August and I as we make our way to my grandpa's study.

"Nobody calls you Hallie." He comments as we step into my room after finally collecting the cardboard boxes from downstairs.

"Technically, none of my family do." I laugh lightly, scrunching my nose. "But everybody else back in London does."

"*Lili?*" August asks, teasingly. "It's cute."

"Reduplication," I explain with a shrug, making my way over to the window. "Filipinos like repetition, I guess?"

He sets the boxes down on my worktable, grey eyes catching the ones underneath with my name taped on them.

"It's going to take some time getting used to," He admits. "*Lia.*"

"Why does it sound so unnatural coming from you?" I snort, drawing the blinds close.

August strides over to the bed, plopping down casually. His arms stretch across the entire double and I'm glad to see him more active and less lethargic.

"You don't have to keep your room dim for my sake, you know." He insists, sitting up. "I like seeing you in the light."

"Charmer," I comment with a smile, bounding over to him.

"Only for you," He chuckles, tugging me to stand between his legs. "Lia. Lili."

CHAPTER 51

I wrinkle my nose playfully. "So unnatural."

My fingers twitch, a sudden urge to play with his hair but instead, I smooth out the shoulders of the jumper he's wearing. It's one of the two grey woollen knits I've been working on since arriving in Switzerland and it surprisingly fits him perfectly.

"Your grandma calls your grandpa your name," He states, looking up at me. "Is that another nickname system I should know about?"

I tilt my head to the side. "What?"

"Mahal," He pauses for a moment, attempting to remember the word as he re-pronounces it. "*Mahal*. I've heard her call him that a few times."

My heart stutters, not expecting the term of endearment in my native tongue to have such an effect on me.

"Love," I say.

August blinks for a moment. "Yes, *mon cœur?*"

"No," I giggle. "It means love. *Mahal* means 'love' in Tagalog. It can also mean 'expensive' but, um, in that context it means love."

"Ah," He nods in understanding.

August pauses, his eyes crinkling and the corner of his mouth quirking up, amused.

"What?" I blink at his expression, moving to sit next to him on the bed.

"So your name is…" He pauses, turning to me, the smile on his face widening. "*Love Heart?*"

His smile is impossibly dazzling as he gazes at me and my heart stutters, finding the expression on his face all too endearing.

"*How fitting,*" He comments.

"What?"

"Loveheart," He chuckles, the sound warm. "I'm surprised your middle name isn't 'Amour' instead of 'Aurora'."

I bite my lip. "I think I would have preferred that, really."

Hearing the different variations of *love* on August's lips pulls on my chest in a way that I can't quite describe and I feel it again.

An unravelling in my heart.

"The couple that came today," He inquires. "Who are they?"

Falling backwards on the bed, I try not to let my discomfort show. "Uncle Jeremiah and Aunt Luisa. He's the oldest out of my uncles."

"No children?"

I shake my head. "They've been trying for *decades* though."

The ceiling suddenly looks a lot more interesting as I stare at the whimsically painted clouds across the expanse of my room.

"Everyone seemed a little on edge when they arrived," August observes, lying down next to me.

"There's usually some sort of drama happening at family events every year," I shrug. "But I wouldn't know much about recent years. This is my first Christmas back in Switzerland in four years, so."

"That's a long time to spend away from family," August comments. "What happened?"

My fingers spasm, the phantom feeling of glass slicing through skin and the faraway sound of bones crunching all too present.

Hesitantly, I lift my left hand to show him the scar.

August blinks, eyebrows furrowing as he takes in the white roughened line of skin tissue that curved from the middle of my palm to the back of my hand.

I stretch my fingers as wide as the limited mobility on my left hand will let me and I watch his eyes trail along each misalignment and noticeable deformity.

Slowly, his mouth drops.

My pinky finger is crooked, index and middle finger deviating from the usually straight alignment, instead bending slightly towards each other. When resting naturally or curled up into fists, there's no indication of any issues with my hand. However, splayed out and under closer inspection? There's no denying the disfigured state of it.

"I'm naturally left-handed too," I huff playfully, attempting to ease the tension. "Just my luck."

"Mahalia," He swallows, voice quiet.

His hand tentatively reaches out to touch mine.

"It was an accident," I say, quietly. "For the most part."

CHAPTER 51

August looks troubled, almost scared to find out.

"Hands on the table."

I blink at Uncle Jeremiah, staring at me with a stony expression on his face as he enters the dining room.

Confused about his demand, I frown, looking down at the empty dishes between my hands.

With the majority of the plates cleared after Christmas dinner, everyone retreated to the living room to continue the festivities but I stayed behind to help tidy the table.

"I don't understand," *I comment, my fingers twitching as they grip the edge of the glass dinnerware I'm currently holding.*

The conversation I overheard between him and my grandparents earlier replay in my mind and something lurches in my stomach.

"If no one is going to discipline you, I will." He continues. "Hands on the table, Aurora."

I flinch at the sound of my middle name, slowly placing the plates back down on the table.

He doesn't give me time to fully rest my palms on the oak surface when he grabs a wooden ladle from one of the casserole dishes and strikes it down. The faint crunching of my fingers as he hits my left hand is masked by the loud noise of the utensil slamming against the table and I grimace at the impact.

"What are you doing?" I exclaim, my eyes watering at the twinging pain on my left hand.

"Disobedient children need to be punished."

"I'm not a child," I turn to him, biting my lip to stop it from quivering.

Most definitely not yours.

Only when his eyes flash angrily and he strikes my hand, more heavily this time, do I realise that I voiced the statement out loud.

"Uncle Jeremiah!"

He jerks his arm, swiping and smashing the dinnerware on the wooden surface, ceramic and crystal flying everywhere. The loud crashes of tableware pieces hitting the floor lock me in place, causing me to stay deathly still. I hear the commotion of people rushing frantically to the dining room and I'm almost afraid to breathe.

From the corner of my eye, I see my uncle swing the wooden ladle again and I forcefully jerk back, my hand catching on the cracked crystal on the table.

The jagged edge of the glass cuts through my skin almost effortlessly and it takes me a moment to react. Pain doesn't register until moments later, when the gash on my palm gapes open and streams of scarlet decorate my skin, ribboning from my wrist and all the way down to my elbow.

August stays silent.

Consciously, I tug the sleeve of my sweatshirt over my hand as my fingers tremble involuntarily at the memory.

"Mahalia…" He begins, staring at me in disbelief.

"I know," I exhale shakily.

"Why the fuck would he do that?" He asks, almost demanding. "He can't discipline his own children because *he doesn't and can't fucking have any* so he takes it out on you? How does that make any sense?"

He shifts closer to me, his grey eyes darting across my face as if he's trying to find the answers there.

"I don't know." I shrug.

August looks at me for a moment, a torn expression on his face, before shifting to lie on his back.

A long silence falls between us and I couldn't help but feel that I may have overshared.

Eyes closed, he takes a deep breath before releasing it slowly.

"Tinker-Talent?"

I turn to August, sitting up.

"Hold me down."

I blink. "What?"

"Hold me down," He repeats. "Because if you don't do anything to restrain me right now, I'm going to end up bolting down those stairs and beating the absolute shit out of your uncle."

Reaching my scarred hand over to him, I splay it out across his chest,

CHAPTER 51

the erratic thrumming of his heart betraying the nonchalant expression on his face.

Delicately, he envelops his hand around mine.

"I'm okay," I reassure him. "It doesn't even hurt anymore. Just tiny little singes and twitches. But, technically, I get them on *both* hands and I've had jittery fingers since I was young so I think it's a me problem."

August sits up but he doesn't let go of my hand.

Instead, he keeps it firm against his chest.

"I can still make clothes, August," I comment, trying to lighten the mood. "I mean, I did get a First in my Graduate Showcase. You know, the Disney Princes collection that kind of went viral last year? And, um, I'm not sure if you've heard but I assisted with the Regalwear Collection for the Royals of Toussaint."

He lets out a short, strained laugh.

"Assisted?" He shakes his head. "You practically led the entire project."

Another silence settles between us before he reaches over to take my other hand. He places both of them against his chest before lifting them up in front of me.

"These are hands of the greats, Mahalia Hartt." August announces, pressing his lips on both of my palms. *"Hands of the greats."*

Chapter 52

Christmas Eve at my grandparents' house is the busiest day during the holidays. It's a semi-traditional festive affair as we typically prepare for the Noche Buena feast.

The lavish spread of traditional Filipino dishes like pancit (Filipino noodles), lumpia (spring rolls) embutido (meatloaf) is already being set up by my aunts in the living room whilst my uncles prepare the huge lechon (roasted pig) and hamon (cured ham) in the wood-fired oven in the backyard.

The house is filled with Christmas music on different floors of the chalet and lively chatter resounding in every room. The medley of voices belonging to my cousins singing karaoke in the living room is the loudest as I make myself useful in the kitchen.

Since I'm not the best at making Filipino desserts, I've opted to bake Christmas-themed cupcakes and cookies instead. I'm humming along to a song playing in the background when I feel a presence sneak up behind me.

"Need help?"

I turn around to find August, wearing another one of the jumpers I knitted. He's also sporting a festive deer headband and I laugh at the bells dangling from the antlers.

"And which reindeer are you supposed to be?"

"Cupid, apparently." August answers, a hint of amusement in his tone. *"Besoin d'aide?"*

"Please," I nod, pursing my lips towards the cupboard. "Can you get the

CHAPTER 52

sprinkles and the decorations for the cupcakes? I need to make the icing."

August strolls over and opens the cupboard as I begin gathering the ingredients for the icing on the counter.

"You do that a lot." He looks at me, the corner of his mouth tugging upwards.

"Do what?"

"Point with your lips."

His eyes trail down to my mouth and a rush of warmth floods my cheeks at the attention.

"Oh," I clear my throat. "It's a Filipino thing."

"Ah," He nods, a playful glint in his eyes. "And here I thought it was your subtle way of asking for kisses from me."

His flirty remark catches me off guard, causing me to nearly drop the tub of butter and mason jar of icing sugar. August chuckles affectionately as I curse out loud.

"Ate Lili said a bad word!" Dayna yells out, popping up from behind the kitchen island.

"Dayna!" I exclaim, whirling around to find her giggling. "What are you doing under there?"

"Hiding," She says matter-of-factly.

"From who?"

"Kuya Auggie," She answers. "We're playing hide and seek."

"Of course," I mumble knowingly.

Hearing the timer, I quickly make my way to the oven to remove the cupcakes from the oven. A hiss escapes my lips as the kitchen towel slips and the hot tray grazes my fingers.

"Loveheart, be careful." August lectures me gently. "There are oven gloves for a reason."

He turns on the tap and gently takes my hand, pressing a kiss to it before running it under the cold water. He stands with me for a moment before swiftly grabbing a pair of kitchen mitts, removing the tray of cupcakes from the oven and setting it on the cooling rack atop the island counter.

"*Et voila.*"

Next to the island, Dayna is giggling up at us.

"You know what, go back to the living room," I shake my head but keep my hand under the water nonetheless. "You're no help."

"I'm helping," August's chuckle sounds louder this time as he traps me between him and the sink. "Any way you need me to, *mon cœur*."

My brain short-circuits, my heart stuttering at the close proximity

"Dayna, please take Kuya Auggie back to the living room." I turn towards Dayna who's watching us with a grin. "He's causing a disturbance in the kitchen."

"Okay!" Dayna giggles, bouncing over to August and tugging on his leg.

August places a hand over his heart. "You wound me with your acts of betrayal, Mahalia Hartt."

"You're so dramatic," I laugh before pretending to scowl at him. "Now go. Entertain my family, since you seem to be very good at that."

I send him playful daggers and he beams, a smile so dazzling it leaves me a little lightheaded.

"Alright," He sighs sportively. "But no frowning."

He moves towards me, swooping down to press a kiss between my furrowed brows. I blink in surprise and his eyes sweep across mine, clearing his throat as he pulls away.

"Kuya Auggie, let's go." Dayna tugs on his hand, trying to pull him away.

"Go." I nudge him, smiling.

"Don't drop the cupcakes, cupcake." He winks at me and I roll my eyes.

Resuming my task of making the icing, I plug the mixer into the wall and begin measuring the softened butter into a mixing bowl. Sensing a presence looming in the kitchen, I look up to find my Uncle Jeremiah standing by the archway with hard-set eyes.

"Make sure to clean up your mess after you're done in here," He comments. "Don't give your Lola grief by not tidying up after yourself."

I nod robotically. "Of course."

A tense silence falls in the room, my fingers twitching as I begin adding the powdered sugar to the butter, my body operating somewhat in auto-pilot mode as I continue my tasks in the kitchen.

CHAPTER 52

"Is that going to be a thing?" My uncle's voice is harsh as he speaks.

It didn't differ from four years ago, his tone still abrupt and demanding. I turn to him confused, then realise he's talking about August.

"It's recent," I reply.

"So it's not serious?"

From across the room, I can see the displeased look on his face.

"It is serious."

My voice is steady as I reply. To some extent, it *is* the truth because *I'm* serious about it. It might be different for August but to me, my relationship with him is as genuine as my dedication to it.

"Does he know that?"

I face my uncle directly.

"He wouldn't be here if he didn't."

A silence follows as the machine stops whirring.

My body is back on autopilot mode as I grab a spatula and begin to scoop the icing inside the piping bag. Slowly, I detach myself from my surroundings. My thoughts are a whirlpool in my head, sending it spiralling as it filters through memories I've repressed from years ago.

I squeeze and release my fist, hoping to alleviate the eerie sensation of glass slicing across my palm.

"Are you even listening to me?"

My uncle is standing next to me now, yanking firmly on my arm as his voice cuts through my thoughts.

"I'm talking to you." He punctuates each word with a forceful jerk.

I gasp, panicked. "Stop."

The aluminium mixing bowl falls with a loud clamour as I drop it, the metal spatula clanging across the kitchen counter. The piping bag I'm holding slips from my hand and it splatters on the floor, staining the hardwood with red icing.

Shakily, I reach out for the kitchen counter but my uncle harshly grabs my wrist and a sharp pain shoots up my elbow.

"Don't—" I draw in a sharp breath.

It's not uncommon for my uncle to get aggressive. But the strike is still unexpected. I attempt to tug my hand away, the sting bolting across my wrist and spreading across my fingers.

"I c-can't feel my hand," I stutter, winded.

Tears begin to blur my vision as I try to flex my hand free.

"Don't be so dramatic," He scoffs.

As if to prove a point, he tightens his grip on my wrist and twists. The sound of my bones cracking under his grasp makes my stomach lurch and I'm instantly reminded of Christmas from four years ago.

"Uncle Jeremiah!"

My voice feels oddly distant and distorted as I shout.

The experience is almost out-of-body as I watch him raise his other hand and I close my eyes tightly, bracing myself for the impact but it never comes.

Instead, clashes and crashes.

Everything happens so quickly that I barely have time to register the wild commotion unfolding before me.

Long limbs, fists flying and a flash of platinum locks.

"August!" I gasp.

The ringing in my ears is overwhelming, my heart hammering against my chest at the sight of August being aggressively pulled back by my cousins.

"Don't ever fucking touch her again." His voice is seething, grey eyes murderous.

"You little shit," My uncle spits, sharply turning in my direction.

August immediately breaks away from my cousins, shifting towards me within seconds as Gabe and Russ scramble to hold him back again. I stand, unmoving, as August tugs me behind him protectively.

"Pack your bags," My uncle fumes. "Neither of you are welcome here."

Tension escalates as he edges near me again and I flinch, August instantly squaring up. Another round of chaos erupts at August's subtle movements, the rest of my uncles shoving past to drag Uncle Jeremiah out of the kitchen whilst my aunts cry out in distress. There's more scuttling in the kitchen before everyone freezes at the sound of my grandma's booming voice.

"Enough!" Her voice echoes, silencing every person in the room.

CHAPTER 52

"Everyone in the living room."

In the silence of the kitchen, everyone scurries out.

"Mahalia, August." My grandpa addresses us, his voice taking on an authoritative tone. "My study. Now."

In the corridor, a dozen pairs of eyes trail after us as we shuffle out of the kitchen and into my grandpa's study. Side by side, August and I stand in front of his desk, like school children being scolded by their teacher.

"I don't like violence, young man." My grandpa begins, hazel eyes staring intently at both of us.

There's a lurching in my stomach, the ache I feel in my wrist shooting up my body and straight to my chest.

Immediately, I speak. "Papa, he's not—"

He raises a hand to quiet me, his expression turning dour, and I know better than to defy my grandpa when he's being as serious as he is now.

"I see it as a last resort," He says ominously. "I find it concerning you've resulted in that kind of behaviour, especially in my own home."

"Pa, it's my fault." I plead. "August didn't mean—"

"Mahalia." My grandpa interrupts me with a stern voice.

He looks at me sharply and I wither under his gaze. In the time I've been in my grandparents' care, neither of them have ever raised their voice at me. I've always been a well-behaved child in their presence since I never had a reason to act out. So to be on the receiving end of my grandpa's reprimand is a little disheartening.

"I apologise for the aggression on my end, sir." August begins to speak. "I can say with absolute certainty that I have never and will never lay a hand on Mahalia in that way. I don't ever wish to disrespect you in your home, please know that. But I care about your granddaughter very much and I won't ever stand for her being mistreated in any way, regardless of place or person."

A tense silence follows as August continues.

"I've fought for her then and I'll fight for her now," August says, voice steady. "Every battle, every single time."

My head turns towards August at his admission. His gaze is unwavering, stoic yet determined, as he meets my grandpa's eyes.

I see a flicker of recognition in my grandpa's face as he peers over August.

"Mahalia," He calls my name.

I turn to my grandpa. His facial expression doesn't betray his emotions, hazel eyes unreadable as he continues to assess August. There's barely a hint of the usual warmth in his eyes, just a steeliness that's almost unrecognisable to me.

"Yes, Pa." I swallow.

"See to your Mama about your wrist," He orders. "I need to speak with August alone."

"Papa," My eyes well up at the dismissive tone in his voice.

I take a step forward to reason with him but August gently reaches for my hand.

"*Mon cœur*," He whispers softly, tugging me to him.

I turn towards August looking at me with reassuring grey eyes.

"No catastrophising," He says quietly, pressing his lips to my forehead before placing quick, gentle kisses on both my palms. "Get your hand looked at, okay? I'll be out soon."

I nod, glancing over at my grandpa who watching us in quiet assessment. He must have noticed how hard I'm trying to hold my tears in as his hazel eyes soften.

"It won't be long, Lili."

My childhood bedroom suddenly feels far too small and I find myself on the floor by the foot of my bed as I wait for August. Pressing my legs to my chest, I lean my forehead against my knees as I rock back and forth. The stinging sensation of my wrist doesn't quite compare to the painful throbbing between my ribs.

I feel it.

All the blanket stitches I've spent looping through the fraying seams of my heart, being picked apart.

The sound of my door opening prompts me to lift my head and I watch as August steps into my room.

CHAPTER 52

I burst into tears almost instantly.

August doesn't say anything as he sits on the floor beside me and I bury my face into my hands, struggling to suppress the emotions that keep resurfacing.

"Mahalia."

I can sense his hesitation, thick and heavy and I bite my lip to contain the strangled sobs crawling up my throat.

August pauses before he sighs.

"Come here."

The warmth of his body surrounds me as he gathers me in his arms and another wave of wrangled cries takes over my body.

"Oh, *mon cœur.*"

Tucking my head under his chin, he positions me in between his legs and pulls me to his chest. I shut my eyes tightly to prevent the hot gush of tears from falling but I feel the wet splotches on his neck nonetheless.

"I'm so sorry, August."

I clutch at my chest, finding it more and more difficult to breathe, my ribcage feeling like needles puncturing through my lungs.

"What are you apologising for, hmm?" He asks gently, dropping a long and lingering kiss on my forehead.

The act of intimacy causes me to unravel and my body shakes uncontrollably, violent tremors with each wave of sobs pulling me under.

I ball my hands into fists in an attempt to ground myself, distinctly feeling my nails digging into my palms but I find myself numb to the pain.

"Tinker-Talent, none of that now." He says softly.

August's fingers smooth over my knuckles as he tries to pry my hands open.

"Don't do further damage to your hands."

I shake my head, attempting to blink away the tears gathering in my eyes.

"Open up, loveheart." His voice is gentle as he brings my hands to his lips. "You need to look after these. Hands of the greats, remember?"

He kisses my palms, eyes molten silver as they glide over my face.

"Papa's disappointed in me, isn't he?" I sob uncontrollably.

"Quite the opposite." August wipes away the tears on my face with his thumbs. "He's so proud of you, he told me so himself."

I whimper, voice strained as I blink up at August. "Are we—is he k-kicking us out?"

My breaths are heavy and uneven as I tearfully take in breathless gulps of air.

"Of course not," He shakes his head. "He just wanted to make sure that you and I were okay."

"A-and are we?" I ask, tearful. "Are we okay?"

"We're more than okay, loveheart."

The nickname tucks itself into my heart, slowly loosening the knots around my chest.

August's presence is a calming tide that washes over me, my cries eventually subsiding into small sniffles. Feeling my eyes droop, I curl into him reflexively, seeking comfort as he gently rubs soothing circles on my arms.

"Are you sleepy?" He asks me, voice gentle.

Sluggishly, I nod. "A little."

I tug absentmindedly on the heart-shaped patches of the jumper August is wearing, exhaustion enveloping me.

"Alright, up we get."

Sliding an arm under my knees, August picks me up bridal style and gently sets me down on the bed.

"Shuffle," He requests, tapping lightly on my waist.

Drowsily, I shift over the duvet covers to make room for him. Sidling over to me, August is delicate in his movements as he shifts to lie on his back and pulls me snugly into his arms.

"August?" I mumble tiredly.

"Mhm?" His voice is a soothing murmur as he draws me closer to him, softly rubbing my back.

Laying my palm on top of his chest, I incline my head and press my lips lightly against his jaw.

CHAPTER 52

"Thank you."

He reaches for my bandaged hand carefully, dropping a kiss on my wrist before adding one to my temple.

"Always, loveheart."

Chapter 53

I wake up slowly to the sound of buzzing.

There's a comforting weight around me, a warm presence pressed against my back and I hum in content before a sharp pain shoots up my wrist.

I wince, blinking languidly as I open my eyes. They take a moment to adjust to the subdued lighting of my room.

Disoriented, I turn to find August and realise that we've somehow shifted into a spooning position. I try to sit up, struggling to break free from his hold as I reach for my phone vibrating on my bedside table.

"August," I whisper loudly.

Tapping on his arms, they only proceed to get tighter around me.

"Five more minutes," He murmurs sleepily, shifting to bury his face on the curve between my neck and shoulder.

His lips trace against my bare skin and I feel my cheeks flush at the close contact. A warmth pools in my belly as my heartbeat picks up but August is none the wiser, in the state of half-asleep and half awakeness.

"Aug-ust." I squirm around in another attempt to break free but his hold on me is rock solid.

"Mhm," He lets out another noncommittal noise, arms loosening ever so slightly.

I quickly take this opportunity to reach my non-injured hand out to grab my phone, exhaling in celebration as I manage to grasp it between my fingers.

"Hello?" I answer, not bothering to check the Caller ID as I swipe the call.

CHAPTER 53

"Bitch, I am flying to Switzerland and castrating your scum of the Earth uncle, I swear to God Hallie I'm going to–"

"Merry Christmas to you too, Gigi."

"I cannot fucking believe the audacity of that man."

Her voice is pitched higher, frenzied as she speaks over the phone.

"I'm booking the next available flight to Geneva and dragging you out of there, after I punch the living daylights out of that pathetic excuse of a human being. Blood is thicker than water be damned, Hallie. He lays another finger on you and I will break and dismember every single–"

August groans noisily behind me, the sound of Gigi's frantic rant loud enough to wake him. I nudge him with my elbow in an attempt to silence his grumbling but it's too late.

"Christ, Winters, can you be any louder?" He grunts and I wince at his response. "As much as I'm all for detaching limbs of abhorrent family members, there's a time and a place for that."

There's a long pause on the other end of the line and I wait.

Maybe Gigi didn't hear–

"Wait–"

"I swear it's not what you think it is," I cut in.

The rustling of the bedsheets and the fact that August sounds like he just woke up probably isn't helping my case.

"Are you in bed with the Peroxide Prince of Paris?"

"It is exactly what you think it is," August chimes in playfully.

The glaring sound of a video call coming in follows his remark.

"Gigi!"

"Answer the call, Mahalia Hartt."

"We're not decent." Is the deadpan reply from August and I turn around to smack him in the chest.

"August," I stress.

"Oh my god!?" Gigi's shriek cuts through the conversation and I put the phone even further away from my ear.

"We are 100% decent." I roll my eyes as his arms eventually unwind from me. "He's just being an ass."

I deflate at the loss of contact but I do my best not to show it as I sit up, turning on the lamp on my bedside table.

"You wound me, loveheart, truly." He pouts, placing a hand on his chest as he sprawls himself out on my bed.

"*Loveheart?!*" Gigi exclaims as August grins at me sheepishly.

"It's a long story," I shake my head at his antics.

"*I... I have so many questions, wow.*"

August shifts to lie on his side, bringing an arm around my waist and pulling me close to him as he rests his head on my lap.

The action is so smoothly executed it catches me off guard at how natural it feels.

"You and me both," I mutter to myself.

Gigi pauses, her voice turning serious.

"*Are you okay, Hals?*" She asks, worry edged in her tone.

"I'm okay," I reply. "I should have seen it coming, really."

"*No one banked your psycho uncle pulling another one of his fucking stunts.*"

"I thought things would be different," I reason, disheartened.

August looks up at me steadily, his gaze flickering to my hands as they curl into fists.

I splay them back out, grimacing apologetically at the awful habit I can't seem to shake. August looks at me once more before taking my hands and interlacing them with his.

"*Are you staying there for New Year's too?*"

"No," I answer. "I'll head back. It doesn't make sense for me to be here if all I'm going to do is cause so much trouble."

"*Hallie, you're not the problem here.*"

August squeezes my hand in quiet encouragement.

"I know." I squeeze his hand back, slowly tracing my thumb over his knuckles. "But I don't want to entertain the idea of being here anymore. I'm better off elsewhere, you know? Somewhere I can be productive. I just... It's so difficult and I've been trying so hard and I..."

My voice trembles as my eyes begin to water.

"*Oh, honey.*" I can hear Gigi tearing up on the other side and I bite my

CHAPTER 53

lip.

"Sorry," I sniffle, sitting up. "No sorrow soirées."

My uncle's words echo in my head and I scratch against at my chest, feeling the thread that held my emotions in place unravelling again.

August sits up, shuffling to press his back against my headboard before tugging me to sit on his lap. He doesn't say anything, just listens intently as Gigi and I continue our conversation.

"Hallie. None of this is your fault."

"I know," I reply. "But I'm going back to London regardless."

"Do you need me to head up? I'm sure I can spare a couple of days."

"It's okay, Gigi. Thank you."

"Are you sure?"

August takes my hands and intertwines our fingers again, pulling me closer to him.

"Yes," I reassure her before clearing my throat. "August is with me."

His presence is like a warm blanket. I can feel the steady beating of his heart as he tucks me close to his chest.

"She's in good hands," August comments loud enough for Gigi to hear as he kisses my forehead. "I'll look after her, I promise."

His admissions tugs on my heartstrings, pulling the plug on my emotions and I feel the waterworks starting again as Gigi and I say our goodbyes.

I hang up the phone call, turning to face August, my vision blurring with unshed tears.

"I'm–"

"You better not say sorry," He interrupts me. "I will kiss that apology from your mouth so don't even try it."

I let out a shaky laugh.

"Are you threatening me with a kiss?"

He shakes his head. "I'm threatening you with multiple kisses. Plural."

"That's not very intimidating."

My chest feels lighter, August's attempt to soothe my anxiety as I tap on his lips playfully.

"You're pushing it, loveheart."

"I am so s–" I'm interrupted by the quickest, lightest touch of his lips against mine and I blink multiple times. "–cared."

It was barely a kiss, a short peck but the fluttering in my stomach intensifies as his eyes flicker down to my mouth.

"I…" He clears his throat. "Take that back. I thought you were going to apologise, my mistake."

"You can't take back a kiss." I shake my head, wrinkling my nose. "It's not allowed."

He scoffs playfully. "What are you going to do about it?"

Feeling brave, I look up at him before leaning up to give him a longer peck on the lips.

August looks at me, eyes glazing over before I pull away shyly, blinking up at him.

"Not the eyes," He groans. "Don't give me those eyes, Mahalia Hartt, please."

Chapter 54

It's 3 o'clock in the morning when I'm quietly tiptoeing down the stairs to go to the kitchen.

After yesterday's incident, the house has been so thick with tension that everyone is walking eggshells around each other. August and I locked ourselves in my room to avoid issues from further escalating. It's frustrating to know I'm the one that inadvertently caused it but I'm also aware I'm not the root problem in this situation.

From the landing, I see my cousins all sardined up between pillows and blankets in the living room, sound asleep. I tread lightly towards the kitchen, thankful my woollen socks mute the sound of my footsteps.

Grabbing a glass from the cupboard to pour myself a drink, I pick up a jug of water, wincing as I attempt to balance it between my injured hand.

"Lia, be careful."

I turn to find my grandma walking towards me, a shawl wrapped around her.

"Sorry, did I wake you?" I ask quietly.

She shakes her head, walking towards me as she takes the pitcher from my hands and begins pouring the water into the glass.

"I was still up in your Papa's study." She answers, voice quiet.

There's a sad and distant look in her eyes as she quietly assesses me. Her normally bright eyes are downcast and I feel her expression tug painfully on my heart.

"I'm sorry, Mama." I say.

My grandma blinks, a frown appearing on her face.

"What on earth are you saying sorry for?"

"Everything," I respond instantly. "For causing a disruption, for troubling you. I don't mean to be an inconvenience, Ma, especially after so many years of being away. I'm so sorry."

"Oh hija…" She begins. "You have nothing to apologise for."

My grandma sighs, long and heavy, and I feel the weight of dejection in her exhale. Shoulders drooping, she turns to me.

"I don't condone your uncle's behaviour." Her lips press together in disappointment, frustration in her eyes. "Your Papa and I do our very best to make him see sense but…"

Her sentence trails off quietly, a sad resignation in her gaze.

"I'm sorry, Lia." She turns to me, her dark eyes shining with unshed tears.

"You don't have to apologise, Ma." I shake my head. "You shouldn't apologise for his behaviour."

There's a long pause between us before she speaks again.

"August is good to you, anak." She says and I can only nod, offering a half-hearted smile. *"Mahal ka niya talaga."*

He really loves you.

My breath hitches, the sharp intake of air lodging itself in my chest. Hearing the remark in Tagalog sends a warmth throughout my entire body.

"We're not…" I trail off. "We're not at the 'L' word stage yet."

In reality, August and I aren't at any stage. Just endlessly floating around 'are we' or 'aren't we'. A 'sort-of situationship' with no official label. But I couldn't necessarily disclose that information to anyone here.

Especially my grandma.

She examines me, eyes inquisitive, as I try to think of exactly what to say.

"Tell that to your Papa," She says, a small smile appearing on her face. "He's convinced August is going to ask his permission to marry you soon."

My eyes balloon and I can almost feel them pop by the triggering nature of the sentiment. Trust my semi-traditional grandparents to make that

CHAPTER 54

leap.

"Your Papa gave him a stern talking to about your relationship earlier," She reveals. "The boy seemed very determined, even disclosed his five-year life plan. Your Papa was extremely impressed."

I purse my lips. "I don't think he'll be–"

The creak of the floorboard brings me back to attention and I turn my head towards the sound. August hovers by the archway, eyebrows furrowed and rubbing sleep from his eyes, like he's just woken up.

"Hello, *po*." He clears his throat, voice groggy.

My grandma acknowledges him with a small nod. "Hello, anak."

"Are you okay?" I ask, stepping towards him.

"You were gone when I woke up," He replies, reaching for me. "I missed you."

My heart stutters at the admission, warmth spreading in my chest. There's a brief moment where he just stands there looking at me, grey eyes soft and earnest in the pale glow of the kitchen.

"Are *you* okay?" He whispers, tucking a strand of hair behind my ear.

Despite the dimness, August is as visible as ever, and I nod wordlessly.

"Did you need anything, hijo?" My grandma asks, studying both of us curiously.

"Oh no, uhh, thank you Madame Hartt." August turns to my grandma, shaking his head politely. "Just… Maha-um, *Lia*."

He waves his arm awkwardly as he gestures towards me, body shifting sluggishly and I bite my lip at how endearing he looks— all dazed and confused.

"You don't need to be so formal around me," My grandma regards him. "Everyone calls me Lola. Mama is fine too."

A pause hangs between us all and I try not to let my nervousness show at her open display of acceptance.

"Thank you," August takes a breath before continuing. "I apologise for my behaviour earlier. It wasn't my intention to be hostile in your home, especially since you've been very hospitable to me. But I hope you understand that your granddaughter means the world to me, I only have the best interests at heart and I will always do right by her."

His words wrap around me, cocooning me in a blanket of warmth.

I fought for her then and I'll fight for her now.

"I know," My grandma nods.

She doesn't say anything else.

"We were thinking of spending New Year's back in London." I begin, clearing my throat. "I have a lot of work I need to do, Ma. I hope that's okay?"

Sadness flashes in her eyes but she nods nonetheless.

"I understand, hija." She says.

"I'll visit again soon, okay?" I tell her reassuringly, offering a faint smile. "It wouldn't be another four years."

Her lips twitch into a small smile, nodding at me.

"Can we talk?"

My voice trembles at my own request, already feeling the nerves before I've even started the conversation.

August stills, looking up.

He's sitting on the edge of my bed as he helps organise the clothes I'll be taking back to London.

His hands stop folding, surprised by the unexpected question.

"Should I be worried?" He asks.

"No," I shake my head.

Yes.

Maybe.

"I don't know." I let out a frustrated sigh.

My fingers twitch in anticipation. I've never been good at eloquently expressing my thoughts, let alone my feelings. Though I very much feel everything, it's difficult for me to communicate my emotions in a way that's straightforward.

I'm a patchwork of catastrophic thoughts, restless hands and inarticulable feelings.

August chuckles.

CHAPTER 54

"I don't think I'm ever going to get tired of your little soliloquies," He quips. *"Lia."*

I scrunch my nose, playfully. "Unnatural."

He grins at me affectionately before placing a kiss on the frown between my eyebrows. Taking my non-injured hand, he intertwines our fingers before pulling me to him.

"Alright, my little yarn of anxiousness," He begins. "Unravel."

He looks at me, patiently waiting for me to continue.

"What are we doing, August?"

I blink up at him, trying not to show the restlessness I feel.

"We're packing to go back to London?"

He glances towards the pile of clothes on the bed before turning to me quizzically.

"No," I shake my head. *"What are we doing?"*

He pauses, contemplating.

"What do you want us to do?"

"Jean-Luc," I stress.

He tilts his head to the side before smiling, "Aurora."

"I asked you first," I grumble, jutting my lip out.

He doesn't miss a beat this time.

"I'd like you to be my girlfriend."

I blink.

"That's where *I'm* at, if I didn't make it clear enough." He adds. "I like you, a lot. I've liked you for quite some time now and I would love for you to be my girlfriend."

The promptness of his reply catches me off guard, his sincerity even more so.

"Oh," I respond, dumbly.

My chest feels surprisingly light and I feel the threads of my emotions being pulled in all directions.

A smile quirks on his lips.

"Is this your way of subtly rejecting me?"

"What?" I gape. "I didn't say anything."

"Exactly," He muses. "You're not saying anything."

"Sorry, I'm…" I swallow quietly. "A-are you sure?"

"Am I sure?" He echoes, blinking. "If I like you?"

I nod, still hesitant.

August scans my face, grey eyes glinting with a shy softness.

"Well, *yes*." He replies, emphasising the word. "It's been impossible not to, the tinkering talent that you are. You've stitched your way into my heart with your glitter threads, non-internal dialogues and anatomically incorrect heart-shaped patches."

Bringing my bandaged hand to my chest, I press it to my sternum to alleviate the endless fluttering I'm feeling.

"They're *stylised* hearts."

"Yes, *mon cœur*." He grins, before asking teasingly, "Anything else you'd like to add?"

August looks at me expectantly, as if sensing my never-ending thoughts.

I voice the idea I've been thinking about since leaving London. It feels like a pipe dream of sorts. But I've thought about it a lot and I genuinely feel like it's the right choice for me.

"I want to start my own fashion label."

His eyebrows shoot up and I nervously play with the bandage around my wrist.

"I'm probably going to go back to working part-time at Tito Boy's in the meantime," I continue. "I know it seems like a step backwards instead of a step forward but it won't be a waste of my time. I think it'll be better because I can focus on the upcoming collaborations I have. I still have Mahalia Made. And I'll keep using it until I rebrand and officially launch the actual label. I know it sounds like a decision made on a whim but it's— it's not."

I'm babbling nervously now, my thoughts convoluted.

"I have enough sketches that could potentially turn into something, like a proper collection. And, um, I'm thinking of building up my clientele list on a more individual basis rather than commercial— like more prominent clients in the industry. Given the right funding and clientele and marketing,

CHAPTER 54

I think... I think I can do it."

"I know you can," He says with conviction. "You don't have to justify yourself, Tinker-Talent."

It's a little nerve-wracking to have August be the first to know but I'm glad to have shared it with him nonetheless.

"What are you thinking of calling it?" He asks.

I pause.

"MAHALIA," I answer. "I know it sounds conceited, naming it after myself but it makes sense."

It feels right.

"It's perfect," August states, then adds without hesitation, "I'll invest in you. I can get your collection in publications, take photos of your work, you can even collaborate with the atelier. They have a Designer Initiative programme in Paris and—"

My eyes widen at his suggestions.

"August," I cut him off, frowning. "That's not why I've told you this."

The last thing I want is for August to think I'm only interested in him because of his reputation. My stomach lurches at the thought and I immediately shake my head in disapproval.

"I have no intentions of exploiting your name to leverage my brand or–"

"You have it anyway," He interrupts, voice earnest. "Every name. Me as August, me as Jean-Luc, me as Vante."

He takes my hands gently, leaning down to press a kiss on my palms.

"I'm yours, loveheart." He affirms. "All of me."

Chapter 55

"Maybe we shouldn't mention anything to anyone yet," I say, a little nervously.

August and I are standing in a semi-empty carriage on the underground as I warily glance around.

"About us, I mean." I lower my voice into a whisper, even though I doubt anyone would be listening to our conversation. "Being together."

I haven't fully considered the implications of what being *with* August would be like. In Switzerland, we were in our own little bubble— our own little world. Being back in London, however, is *reality*. A reality that I'm not entirely too sure how to navigate.

August booked his usual apartment-hotel in Mayfair but he hasn't left my flat since we landed back in London a few days ago, choosing to spend every single day with me instead. It's oddly disconcerting how easy it is for me to be in his presence.

He fits perfectly.

But it's almost too good to be true.

The tube rumbles to a halt as it reaches another stop and August tugs me towards him, letting passers-by behind us walk past. There was still more than enough room in the tube but he pulls me close to him nonetheless.

"I can already sense you catastrophising, loveheart." He gives me a pointed look. "I'm not changing my mind about anything."

This relationship with August is still so fresh, it doesn't feel like a tangible reality. It's almost a hazy dream of sorts, like I would wake up in my childhood bedroom in Interlaken, only having dreamt about August

CHAPTER 55

travelling all the way to Switzerland to see me.

"I understand where you're coming from though," He continues. "There's a time and place for everything. You're there to speak to Rowan about work, not to talk about us."

He presses a kiss on my forehead in reassurance and I feel my anxiety ease

"Sorry— it sounds so stupid." I wince.

"There's no need to apologise, *Lili*." He reassures me.

I blink at the use of my childhood nickname.

August shrugs. "It's growing on me."

"You're nickname-obsessed." I laugh.

"And you aren't?" He gives me a pointed look. "Nepo Baby Germaphobe."

I roll my eyes, playfully. "Are you ever going to let that go?"

"Nope," He shakes his head. "It was damaging to Vante and my image."

I scrunch my nose before smiling appreciatively at August's attempt to relieve my anxiety. The tube stops at High Street Kensington and August takes my non-injured hand as we begin walking out of the station and head to the restaurant.

"Aren't you two a sight for sore eyes," Hero greets us by the door. "I knew you were both dropping by today but I didn't realise you'd be coming in together."

August and I stand awkwardly next to each other. Since it's New Year's Eve, the restaurant is closed but both Rowan and Hero are in to do preparations for the restaurant in the New Year.

August clears his throat. "I saw Lia on the way."

"*Lia?*" Hero blinks.

"Maha-lia," August corrects himself. "We, uh, got on the tube together."

"Right..." Hero eyes him suspiciously before turning to me. "Rowan's in the back office doing admin, your little furry friend's in there too."

I smile at Hero in thanks before nodding towards August. I'm about to make my way to the back of the restaurant when Rowan exits from the kitchen, a pet carrier in his arms.

"It's like your cat has a sixth sense," Rowan says in greeting. "He started meowing loudly when you came in."

Rowan places the cat carrier on the table before he slides himself over to sit on the chair.

"Thank you for catsitting Calix," I say, sitting down opposite him. "I know it was super last minute of Gigi and I to spring it on you but we really appreciate it."

"No problem," He replies. "It was nice to have some sort of company over Christmas."

"You didn't visit your family this year?"

"I went for *Noche Buena* and *Simbang Gabi* but I didn't stick around for Christmas Day," He divulges. "You know my aversion to family drama."

"Tell me about it," I mutter to myself, nervously tugging on the sleeve of my blouse to cover the wrist support I'm wearing.

Rowan glances down at the cuff but doesn't say anything.

"Gigi mentioned you visiting your grandparents over the holidays." He nods. "How was your Christmas?"

"Fine," I answer robotically.

A flash of concern crosses Rowan's face but he doesn't pry which I'm thankful for. Crying in the restaurant would not be ideal.

"I saw your message about doing part-time at Tito Boy's again." He turns to me quizzically. "I thought everything was going well at Holmes? Hero was bombarding me with all these articles written about you."

From the corner of my eye, I can see August and Hero talking quietly by the booth in the corner.

"I'm thinking of starting my own brand," I say quietly.

There's a pause as Rowan regards me with a small smile.

"About time," He nods. "I better get those front-row seats Hero keeps raving on about."

"Thank you," I reply with a faint smile. "I still have a lot of work to do before even reaching that stage. Building up a clientele and all of that."

"Is that why he's here?" Rowan tilts his head towards where August is currently sitting. "Hero mentioned he was coming in today. Is he one of

CHAPTER 55

your clients?"

I rack my brain for an excuse.

"Well, uh, yes— technically." I reply. "But not yet. We've, um, discussed it briefly but we still need to— uh, work out the logistics. It's still early stages yet."

In more ways than one, I think to myself.

"Ah," Rowan nods, eyes skimming over August and Hero before landing on me. "I'm assuming you're busy tonight?"

I shrug, still unsure. August and I hadn't discussed actual plans for New Year's Eve.

"Well, I'm throwing my annual taster party at the townhouse," He reveals, then calls the duo over.

"You throw a dozen taster parties in a year, Rowan." I blink.

Inside the carrier, Calix meows as August and Hero walk over to our table.

"I swear this cat has a personal vendetta against me," Hero comments. "It ignored me the whole time I was giving it attention earlier."

"*He*," August and I simultaneously correct him.

I clear my throat, glancing towards August.

"Well, you never did feed him," I mutter to myself. "So that's probably why."

Rowan chuckles as he turns towards me.

"Pop round for my New Year's Eve taster, Hals."

"Taster?" August asks, glancing at me.

"Rowan Ramos' celebratory feasts," Hero answers.

"It's lowkey," Rowan explains, rolling his eyes. "Just a tame evening in to celebrate the new year with friends."

With Rowan, there's no such thing as 'tame' when it comes to his cuisine celebrations. It's never just a handful of people and it's always a little too extravagant than most, especially with his reputation.

"I'm attending, as usual." Hero adds then turns to me. "You can bring Snaps as your plus one since I'm already bringing someone."

August fixes his gaze on me. "You're going?"

"That remains to be seen," Hero answers for me. "Hallie's been a no-show every year."

I huff quietly. "I was always busy with uni deadlines, you know that."

"What's your excuse this time then?"

I glance over at August.

We haven't discussed official plans for spending the New Year yet as part of me is still expecting him to up and leave for New York or Paris.

"You should come," Rowan turns his attention towards August. "Maybe it'll be an incentive to get this one to come too."

Rowan motions towards me and I pull a face at him as he chuckles.

"It's tonight," I clear my throat. "If you're interested."

August nods with a small smile. "I'd love to."

Chapter 56

The dinner party at Rowan's is in full swing by the time August and I drop by. Though I was the one initially anxious, it's August's nervousness that I feel more prominently. He hides it well but I see the tell-tale signs of said anxiety as we stand by the front door of Rowan's townhouse in Kensington.

"Well if it isn't Little Miss Designer," Rowan grins as he opens the door. "I honestly didn't think you'd show up."

"Why wouldn't I?" I blink as he pulls me into a hug.

"You've failed to make an appearance every single year." Rowan deadpans before turning to August. "Hey man, good to see you again."

From the entrance, I can hear the soft music of acoustic rock floating down the hallway.

"Thanks for inviting me," August says, handing him a bottle of Romaneé-Conti pinot noir.

"You Parisians and your expensive wine," Rowan chuckles. "Great job for dragging her out, by the way."

"Excuse me?" I jut my lip out in mock indignance. "He's my plus one."

"Technically I invited him too." Rowan looks at me before turning towards August. "You joining masterclass when it starts again next week or are you jetting off back to New York?"

"Oh, uh, yes." He answers, distracted. "I'll be in London for a little while longer."

We step into Rowan's entryway, the atmosphere warm as his flat buzzes with loud chatter and lively conversations. Despite knowing Rowan for nearly four years, I've been to his place a total number of three times. It's lavishly designed with elements of Filipino culture scattered around the space.

"You're still attending his cooking classes?" I ask.

August nods, lowering his voice just so I'm the only one who can hear.

"My girlfriend's very particular with food," He whispers. "It's Michelin star or nothing."

He winks at me as Rowan leads us down the corridor, tugging me close to him playfully.

"Snaps!"

Turning towards the voice, I see Hero approaching us.

"You made it!" He beams.

"What happened to a small get-together?" I remark, surveying the bustling room and glancing around the very busy, people-filled space.

"Word got around that I had fashion royalty in attendance," Rowan chuckles. "I have a couple of buddies from The Scullery who want to have a chat with you, by the way. They're interested in custom suits."

"Tell them to get in line," August interjects.

Rowan laughs as he turns to me. "Can I introduce them to you real quick?"

I nod, smiling as I exchange a look with August.

"Snaps, can you help in the kitchen?" Hero asks.

"Sure," August nods before clearing his throat and turning to me. "See you."

Walking to the living room, Rowan guides me to a group of his friends from The Scullery. They're all chefs in the industry, naturally, and I listen attentively as they chat amongst themselves and talk animatedly about food. I find myself glancing over towards the kitchen more than a handful of times to catch a glimpse of platinum blond hair.

Once I feel like I've done my share of socialising, I excuse myself from the conversation and eagerly bound for the kitchen to look for August.

With expansive marble countertops, state-of-the-art appliances and high-quality stainless steel cookware, Rowan's kitchen is most definitely

CHAPTER 56

fit for his reputation in the industry. It's a wide space with multiple cooking zones, all currently filled with culinary creations and decadent desserts he prepared for his taster party.

Platters of different canapés and hors d'oeuvres accompany his main menu as well as a huge charcuterie board with mini cheese platters, artisanal bread and exotic spreads. I blink at the expensive brands of fine wines and spirits, similar to the ones at The Duke & Dalton next to the imported chocolates and petit fours platter.

"So much for a 'tame taster'." I shake my head, nibbling on a pistachio macaron.

Keeping myself entertained in the kitchen, I hover near the platters of food on the central island, piling up a selection of different canapés on the plate until I have a little mountain of food.

"This mine?"

Familiar arms wrap around my waist from behind and I turn my head to see August.

"Ah, yes she is." He confirms, leaning down to kiss my cheek.

My heart flutters at the open display of affection, even more at how natural it feels to be in his arms.

"Have you tried any of the food yet?" I ask, lifting my plate.

He shakes his head before tilting it towards my plate and opening his mouth playfully.

Rolling my eyes, I bring an Oyster Rockefeller shell to his mouth. I watch as August chews experimentally before swallowing, eyebrows knotting slightly.

"Is it good?" I ask.

"Salty." He pulls a face. "I need something sweet to wash it down."

I reach for an eclair from the petit fours platter, offering it to August when his lips press softly on mine. A content hum escapes him as I return the kiss, my mouth lingering against his.

"Sorry," He whispers, pulling away. "I was having withdrawals."

I wrinkle my nose, giggling. "You taste like oyster."

He grabs a couple of chocolate truffles before popping them in his mouth and leaning down to give me another kiss.

"Better?"

"Better." I grin shyly.

The sound of Hero's voice before he enters the kitchen causes August and I to awkwardly shuffle away from each other.

"There are a few people who want pictures," Hero says.

Turning towards August, I give him an encouraging nod. I would probably have to get used to this sort of thing around him, sooner or later.

"Go ahead," I say. "I'll be here."

"Not with him," Hero shakes his head. "With you."

I blink.

"Me?"

"You *are* Mahalia Hartt, fashion's latest *Design Darling*, right?" Hero asks, jestful. "Yeah, I read the articles. That asshole kept telling me to click the links for traction."

August flusters but quickly collects himself. "You're such a little shit."

"Anyway," Hero continues. "They're a fan of your work. 'Sickeningly obsessed'— their words, not mine— with the royal suits. I think they want autographs too."

"Are you sure?" I respond, a little perplexed.

"They said they've been following you since your Disney Prince collection last year." Hero replies.

The corner of August's mouth curls upwards, a proud sparkle in his grey eyes as he regards me. I look up at him with a small smile, feeling the warmth of his gaze.

From the corner of my eye, I can see Hero eyeing us suspiciously.

"Don't keep your fans waiting," August smiles at me teasingly. "I'll be here."

"Fireworks in five, everyone!"

Rowan's voice drifts from the living room.

Loud, excited chatter continues as people begin shuffling into their coats

CHAPTER 56

and jackets. After speaking to the handful of fashion royal enthusiasts, who did in fact want a picture with me, I find myself back with August as we join others in bundling up into their woollen knits.

Reaching out into my coat pocket, I bring out the pair of sunglasses.

"Here," I hand it to him. "For the fireworks, just in case you need it. I brought mine too."

I placed my large, rounded sunglasses on top of my head and August chuckles, pulling me to him.

"Let's go."

Following the crowd, August and I make our way to Rowan's backyard. It's a large, manicured lawn with neatly trimmed hedges and topiaries, rockets and pyrotechnics of varying sizes scattered all over the garden, waiting to be set off for the New Year fireworks display. Around twenty or so people are already gathered in the garden, bundled up in scarves hats and gloves as August and I join them.

Walking down a paved pathway lined with elegant lanterns and flower beds, we ultimately settle for the space under a pergola with lush vines and roses.

"Cold?" August asks, a white puff of air billowing out of his mouth as he brings an arm around me.

I shake my head but I shuffle close to him nonetheless.

"Warm."

He slips his hand into my coat pocket, intertwining our fingers as the countdown begins.

"10... 9... 8..."

A chorus of voices all join the sequence as August pulls me closer towards him. He presses his lips on my temple as the sparklers around us begin lighting up and everyone reaches the end of the countdown.

"3... 2... 1..."

Loud cheers erupt in the landscape of Rowan's backyard, the whistling and crawling sound of flares and rockets shooting up the night sky.

"HAPPY NEW YEAR!"

A kaleidoscope of vibrant colours erupts as the fireworks display unfolds.

Fiery blossoms of red, gold and green burst into dazzling shapes of varying sizes and I look up in awe at the glittering shower of sparks that rain down from the explosion. The scent of gunpowder lingers in the air as the smoky trails eventually disappear, only to be replaced with new fireworks whittling in the sky.

I turn towards August, to find him already staring at me, his sunglasses no longer on his face but on top of his head. He regards me with a soft expression, the contours of his face illuminated by the multi-coloured spectacle. He lifts the sunglasses from my face and pushes it on top of my head.

"Happy New Year," I say, smiling up at him.

He mirrors my smile before lifting me up by the waist.

"August!" I giggle.

He spins me around the wooden platform of the pergola as I wrap my legs around his torso.

"Happy New Year, loveheart."

Angling my hands, I hover them over his eyes as a makeshift shield to ease his vision from the brightness of the fireworks.

"I believe you owe me a New Year's kiss," He smiles up at me.

Without hesitating, I tuck my hands under his jaw and I swoop down to press my lips on his. I feel him smile against the kiss, biting softly on my bottom lip. Slowly, I pull back to see a fond expression grace his face as he hums in content.

My heart swells, impossibly full of all my affections for August, and I wrap my arms around his neck before leaning down to shower his face with tender pecks.

August beams as I slowly pull away, grey eyes glittering brighter than the fireworks.

"I can't wait to see you take over the world, Mahalia Hartt," He says, gently. "And I get to be there with you, every step of the way."

IV

Epilogue

MAHALIA

Dreams.

That's the theme I ultimately decided on for my debut presentation at Women's Fashion Week in London.

It's fitting, especially with my initial experience of working in fashion.

After an intense eight months of creating the collection, it's finally being showcased to the public. It veered away from the chaotic affair of a fully-fledged catwalk since I wanted my debut to be intimate and intentional. It felt more aligned with the theme itself so I opted to do an evening presentation instead.

The designs came relatively easy. Soft outlines, wispy concepts.

A pastel colour palette reminiscent of soft clouds and sunsets, flowing fabrics like chiffon and silk, whimsical prints featuring stars, moons and celestial motifs in the style of *toile de jouy*. Silky slip dresses and nightgown-inspired pieces exude 'bedtime chic' aesthetic and I incorporated delicate lace and embroidery details to mimic intricate dreamscapes.

A lot of tulle and glitter too, much to the surprising encouragement of a certain platinum-haired photographer.

I smile at the thought of August, wishing he was here to join me but still grateful for him even though we're currently three and a half thousand miles away from each other.

"Hallie!" A sing-song voice interrupts my thoughts and I turn to find Gigi entering the venue. "Oh my god, this is such a dream!"

"Thank you." I exhale in relief, finally finding a familiar face. "That's the theme. Press release?"

The presentation is being showcased in a decently sized ballroom at Regent's Park with soft, diffused lighting as well as ethereal drapery and fabric installations cascading from the ceiling to create a dreamy atmosphere. The clothes are being showcased on both models and mannequins standing on miniature pedestals equivalent to Greek podiums, twinkling lights adorning each elevated platform.

"Is August here yet?" Gigi asks.

I shake my head. "He's still in New York. His schedule didn't match up so he won't be here until tomorrow afternoon."

Despite our demanding work schedules, long distance hasn't felt like a hindrance to our relationship. With messages throughout the day, flowers during weeks that he's away, and even ordering food at my flat so we can eat together (him at lunch and me during dinner), August is good at making his presence felt, even amidst our conflicting timetables.

"You're both booked and busy," Gigi comments before taking out her phone sheepishly. "Care for a little interview with yours truly?"

"What happened to the interview we did last month?"

"That's for print," Gigi replies with a wink. "Digital wants me to write a short article about the event itself. You always gain us traction on the website whenever we publish an article about your work."

"Alright." I nod, laughing. "Here or in the office outside? We can—"

I pause when someone reaches out for my arm.

"Delivery for Miss Mahalia Hartt?" A voice clears their throat and I spin around, blinking at the familiarity of it.

In front of me is a towering bouquet of what seems like every possible flower known to man. Pastel blooms of orchids, lily of the valleys, hydrangeas, tulips and peonies complimented with delicate foliage are meticulously and beautifully arranged.

I blink as I notice the head of platinum hair, just barely peeking out behind it.

"August?"

"*Bonsoir mademoiselle.*"

I gasp in surprise, the sight of his twinkling grey eyes and soft smile tugging at my chest, as he pops his head from behind the bouquet arrangement that dwarfed his already impossibly tall figure. Even after nine months of being together, his presence still has a way of making me feel flutters everywhere.

Standing next to August is a tall, gorgeous woman with light blonde hair and grey eyes peering over me.

"Mahalia," she addresses me warmly, a soothing quality to her voice. "It's lovely to finally meet you."

Beside her, a man in his early fifties dressed in an impeccably styled three-piece suit is appraising the dresses in front of us with an aloof, discerning eye.

A realisation hits me as I blink at the couple standing before me, finally registering the company with him.

"Mrs. Vante, Mr. Vante— hi." I manage to greet them, a mix of awe and apprehension in my voice.

"Darling please, call me Adeline," She says gently. "I cannot believe it's taken our son this long to introduce us to you."

Her smile reminded me of August's. On the rare, but surprisingly increasing, occasions that I would catch it. Though his stoic scrutiny is very reminiscent of his father's, his smile is a carbon copy of his mother's.

"*Maman*," August turns to her. "It's been a busy year for both of us."

Adeline sweeps her grey eyes over me in a perusing manner before nodding.

"Your collection is *heavenly*, I must get my hands on a few of the nightgowns."

"A wonderful collection, Miss Hartt," Cedric remarks.

My brain short-circuits before I reply, somewhat clumsily. "Thank you, sir."

"I'm surprised you've chosen to present to the general public," He adds. "Craftsmanship of this level would be quite difficult to scale prêt-à-porter. It would be wise to aim it to appointment-based clientele in the future."

"Cedric, stop being so overly analytical and appreciate the collection for what it is," Adeline chides, casting him a look before turning to me. "Don't mind my husband. It's the designer in him."

"I am merely providing constructive criticism, *ma cherie*." He replies. "Work of haute couture standards should receive such feedback."

I smile appreciatively at both of them.

"The production of the garments in the collection is made-to-order so it's still leaning towards the limited scale of high-end fashion," I reply. "I wanted the debut collection to be accessible to a larger audience since exposure is the main priority of the brand at the moment."

"I see," Cedric nods. "We'd like to discuss a possible collaboration with you regarding a bridal collection for Vante Atelier."

My eyes widen as Adeline turns to him, almost mischievously.

"What a splendid idea, darling! A *Mahalia x Vante* wedding collaboration!"

The mention of my name combined with the fashion house causes August to choke on his champagne and we glance at each other, his grey eyes shifting nervously.

"Now may not be the best time to be discussing that," He interjects, doing his best to stay composed.

"Nonsense," Cedric waves a hand dismissively, much like the way August often does. "This is an opportune time. We are in a fashion event, are we not?"

"*Papa*," August stresses, his French accent surfacing. "I'm sure we can organise a meeting at a more *convenient* time."

"D'accord," Cedric replies. "We'll do brunch tomorrow to discuss the wedding partnership as well as your move to the city."

August coughs, champagne once again going down the wrong pipe and my brows knot in confusion.

"Son, do be cautious of your suit," Cedric sighs. "Champagne may look invisible but it will still *stain*."

"*Mon ange*," Adeline gives her son a knowing look. "You haven't told Mahalia about London?"

"London?" I turn to August who's eyeing both his parents with a pointed expression.

"We should probably put this somewhere." He clears his throat, picking up the bouquet from the floor. "The office, loveheart?"

"Of course," I nod in understanding before turning towards his parents. "Thank you so much for attending the presentation, I really appreci–"

"*Allons-y, mon cœur.*"

August doesn't give me time to say goodbye properly as he excuses our presence from the conversation. Balancing the arrangement of flowers with one hand, he gently grabs my arm and hurriedly drags me to the small office located outside of the ballroom.

"I am so sorry about all of that," He shakes his head. "I explicitly told my father to avoid discussing work tonight but he just can't help himself sometimes."

"It's okay," I smile at August reassuringly. "I read up on Vante's recent venture into bridalwear. It seems like your dad's intentionally monopolising every fashion front possible."

He shakes his head.

"My *maman's* the mastermind behind it," He mutters. "They're trying to prove a point."

"Oh?" I turn to him inquisitively.

August doesn't say anything, as if contemplating something. His movements seem rigid, almost strained as he places the huge bouquet on the desk. If I hadn't become so attuned to his behaviour, it would have gone unnoticed.

"August?"

His eyes soften as he walks back over to me, enveloping me in a bone-crushing hug.

"Hi," He leans back to look at me, an endearingly dopey smile on his face.

I giggle, wrapping my arms around his torso.

"Hi yours–"

He interrupts me with a soft kiss, "God, I missed you."

August sighs in content as he pulls me closer to him, the familiar scent of his cologne washing over me. I nose the soft texture of his silk shirt, liking the way it feels on my cheek as I bury my face into his chest. He presses his lips on top of my head before tucking my head under his chin.

"Long distance is pure agony," He adds.

"I know," I reply, jutting my lip. "I missed you too."

It's been a little over a month since August and I last saw each other in person. Though we speak every single day, preparations for my debut presentation at London Fashion Week had taken up my entire schedule for the season so it had been almost impossible for me to free up any time for August. Similarly, August had been inundated with work in New York resulting in very limited opportunities for us to meet in person.

Over the past six months alone, we've seen each other a total of four times.

"I can't believe you're here," I gaze up at him. "I thought they were going to keep you longer at the studio."

"And miss my little tinkering talent's debut?" He tuts. "Now, that's ridiculous."

After handing over and stepping down from his role as Director of Communications at Holmes, August began work on opening up his own photography studio in New York. He's still a board member at Vante and loosely involved with projects in Grayson but he's fully focused on his photography work under Jean-Luc.

Over the past few months, he's started working on collaborative projects with indie publications in New York as well as the odd freelance work for magazines here in London.

"I know how important this is for you, loveheart." He adds. "I wouldn't have missed it for the world."

A surge of emotions courses through me.

The pressure of my 'dreams' debut presentation at Fashion Week has been a *nightmare* organising for the past month and I'm grateful for August who has been nothing but supportive. Staying up with me during sleepless nights, listening to my breakdown over calls.

"Thank you," I say. "For the flowers. For coming to London. For being here."

"*Pour toujours, mon cœur.*" He responds.

The three little words are on the tip of my tongue but I swallow them down, feeling them flutter around in my stomach.

"There's something I want to talk to you about." August leans back to look me in the eye, his expression shifting back to nervousness. "I'm considering moving to London."

I blink. "You are?"

"Temporarily," He adds. "Well, semi-permanently. MODUE reached out and they want me to do contractual work for the magazine. They like the fashion editorials and celebrity shoots I've been doing lately. I've also spoken to Chaewon about possibly doing some freelance work for the agency. LIFT also contacted me to do photography seminars at the university so I'm looking at being based in London for the next year or so."

The possibility of August relocating to London sets off a flurry of emotions inside me. No more long-haul flights, no more late-night conversations due to different timezones, no more attempting to dissuade August from using his private jet whenever I had separation anxiety.

"Nothing's set in stone yet," He continues. "But I wanted to know your thoughts."

The nervous tick of his jaw followed by the hesitant brush of his palm on the back of his neck betrays the nonchalant front he's masking.

My hand reaches up, fingers gently caressing the side of his face.

"You moving to London would be a dream come true," I say quietly, tracing the line of his jaw. "But I know how important New York is to you and how much you've fallen back in love with the city since dedicating yourself there. Your photography, your studio— all the work you've been doing for the past year, it's all in New York."

The last thing I would want is for August to give that up, not when he's invested so much of his time and energy to establish it independently from Vante.

"That's true." August kisses my palm before leaning into my touch. "My work is in New York. But my heart is in London."

His eyes scan my face, grey eyes brimming with a tenderness that tugs on my heartstrings.

"I want to be here, loveheart." He affirms. "With you."

His smile is gentle, his gaze soft.

God, I love him.

My vision blurs and my throat constricts at the overwhelming wave of emotions that pull me under. I struggle to articulate myself but I feel it. Those three little words rising back to the surface.

"Unless..." He interprets my silence as uncertainty, his own hesitation seeping into his voice. "If you think that's moving too fast, we can slow down. It's not as if we'll be *living together*. We'll just be in the same city. It'll be like how it was before– how they are currently– if that's what you want. I know you're busy with MAHALIA and I would never expect you to put anything on hold or to prioritise—"

I stop his ranting with a gentle kiss.

"I love you."

The words flow effortlessly from me, the warm gush of emotions that follow surging throughout my entire body.

August stares at me, wide-eyed, mouth opening and closing in surprise. He's frozen to the spot and I can almost see the gears in his mind turning, the cogs in his brain working overtime to make sense of my not-so-little proclamation of love.

"Yes," I look up at him, smiling.

He blinks at me owlishly and I lean up to give him another peck on the lips.

"Yes?" He questions.

I nod. "To everything. To London, to you, to us. To being together now and to living together in the future. Yes."

August looks at me, eyes flickering with different emotions before he picks me up and twirls me around. He showers my face with loud, hurried kisses, his face beaming as he grins up at me.

"I love–"

"Mahalia!"

Both August and I turn towards the door as we hear Gigi's voice and the familiar clacking of her heels against the floor.

"In the office!" I respond aloud as August gently sets me down. "I should probably go back out there. Gigi wants to do a quick interview for MODUE."

"Again?" He retorts with a playful huff. "What does a man have to do to be able to spend time with his girlfriend?"

I beam at him. "Move to London."

A loud knocking resounds against the door, August and I turning towards the noise.

"You both better be decent!" Gigi yells. "I do *not* want a repeat of last time."

August chuckles before interjecting loudly, "You might want to wait then! We're still–"

"Behave," I prod his chest, scolding him with a mock glare before giggling.

He leans down for another kiss, smiling as I wrap my arms around his neck. Pulling away, my heart flutters in my chest at the sight of August's smile.

"Mahalia Aurora Hartt," He whispers gently. "I love you."

His gaze holds mine as he utters those three little words, the sentiment stitching itself onto my heart.

I lean up to press a kiss on his lips.

"I love you too," I beam, exhaling a breath. "August Jean-Luc Vante."

About the Author

Yinnie Lin is a fashion fictionist, romance reader and lover of literature.

You can connect with me on:
- https://linktr.ee/yinnielin
- https://twitter.com/yinnielin
- https://www.tiktok.com/@yinnielin
- https://www.instagram.com/yinnielin

Subscribe to my newsletter:
- https://tr.ee/aRAyt5w42w

Printed in Great Britain
by Amazon